SWEET DELIGHTS

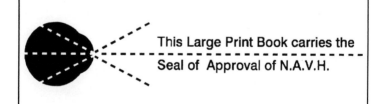

This Large Print Book carries the
Seal of Approval of N.A.V.H.

SWEET DELIGHTS

TERRI BLACKSTOCK, ELIZABETH WHITE, RANEE MCCOLLUM

THORNDIKE PRESS
A part of Gale, Cengage Learning

GALE
CENGAGE Learning

Detroit • New York • San Francisco • New Haven, Conn • Waterville, Maine • London

GALE
CENGAGE Learning

LIBRARY OF CONGRESS CATALOGING-IN-PUBLICATION DATA

Blackstock, Terri, 1957–
    Sweet delights / by Terri Blackstock, Elizabeth White, Ranee
McCollum.
      p. cm. — (Thorndike Press large print Christian romance)
    ISBN-13: 978-1-4104-1904-0 (alk. paper)
    ISBN-10: 1-4104-1904-5 (alk. paper)
    I. White, Elizabeth, 1957– II. McCollum, Ranee, 1968– III.
Title.
PS3552.L34285S94 2009
813'.54—dc22   2009018526

Published in 2009 by arrangement with Tyndale House Publishers, Inc.

CONTENTS

■ ■ ■ ■

FOR LOVE OF MONEY
TERRI BLACKSTOCK

■ ■ ■ ■

This book is lovingly dedicated to the Nazarene.

CHAPTER ONE

Blake Adcock couldn't eat the bowl of hot soup the waitress set before him, anymore than he could eat the filet mignon that he'd cut up into bite-size pieces so it would look as if he'd tried. He couldn't eat the baked potato that he'd poked at with a decided lack of gusto or the restaurant's famous chef salad that was wilting before his eyes. He'd sat there for three hours, ordering things he didn't want, because there was no place else to go. Home would mock him tonight: the congratulations banner his employees had hung across his living room; the ribbon tied across his home office doorway waiting to be cut to mark the first milestone of his lucrative new business; the models of his different car designs with sold signs waiting to be taped on. All the little luxuries his staff had arranged for his "celebration." No, he could not go home and face the consequences of his naive hope . . . not when his dreams had collapsed like the toothpick castle he'd built in third grade.

But that waitress — Julie was her name — didn't mock him. She smiled with full lips the color of raspberries, and her eyes, tired though they were, reflected that smile. "If you aren't hungry for that soup," she said in a soft alto voice with just a trace of amusement, "I could take it back and see if the chef will knock it off your ticket."

He smiled up at her and noted the wisp of blonde hair caught in her eyelashes. He had the urge to push it away. "No, it's fine. I'll eat it."

She tipped her head. "Like you ate all this other stuff? You know, where I come from, a meal like this would have fed a family of five for two days, and you haven't touched it. 'Waste not, want not,' my aunt Myrtle always says." She stepped closer and leaned toward him as he shot a guilty look down at the food. "What's really the matter? Is it the rain? You don't want to go out and get wet, so you feel like you have to keep ordering things so we'll let you stay?"

Blake leaned back in his booth and glanced past his reflection on the rain-spattered window. Traffic lights peppered the dark Detroit highway. An interstate leading everywhere . . . and nowhere. His gaze strayed to the reflection of the woman still smiling down at him. *Man, she's pretty,* he thought. He turned back to her and set his chin on his palm. "To tell you the truth," he said, "it's the company that's keeping me here."

"The company?" The thought amused her. "I hate to break this to you, but you're alone."

He laughed softly. "Not when you're standing here, I'm not. I figure the only way I can keep you coming back is to order things."

A blush crept up her cheekbones, and she glanced away, embarrassed.

"It's Valentine's Day, you know," he said. "It's a crime to be alone on Valentine's Day."

She gave him a crooked smile. "Yeah, I've thought that myself." She tipped her head and glanced down at his ringless left hand. "What's really the matter? Marital problems?"

He tried to look shocked and insulted. "If I were married, would I be sitting here flirting with you?"

"Stranger things have happened," she told him, that grin tugging at the corner of her lips again.

She knew he wasn't married, he thought.

She wasn't looking at him apprehensively. Only warmth shone in her green eyes, filtering through the chill of his failure and pointing him toward hope. Still, it seemed important to clear the notion from her mind. "No, I'm not married or otherwise attached. Matter of fact, I have no ties at all. Not to a woman . . . or a family . . . or a job . . ." His voice trailed off as he realized his levity was giving way to the disappointment with which he'd been wrestling all afternoon.

Julie's eyes instantly widened in understanding. "Oh, so that's it." She studied him for a moment, as if gauging his need or desire to talk. Finally, she slipped into the seat across from him and leaned toward him with her arms folded on the table. Her eyebrows arched in sympathy. "You lost your job."

This time his laugh held a cynical note. "No, I didn't lose it. Quit it months ago. A pretty good one too."

Her eyes narrowed. "Why?" she asked as if she cared, as if his problems had some impact on her. Was compassion a service of the restaurant, he wondered, or was it just her nature to care about people? Blake eyed his lukewarm, untouched coffee and brought it to his lips, stalling for time. How did one spill his guts without evoking pity?

That was the last thing he wanted from her. He set down the cup and gave a shrug.

"I was a design engineer at GM, but I quit so I could start my own business designing inexpensive vans and cars for handicapped people." He propped his jaw on his hand and looked out the window again. As if to add percussion to his story, the rain began to pound harder. "I had a big contract with a friend of mine who has a business called Access, Inc. He sells specialized equipment like that. He hired me to do twenty vans to start with. Paul said he'd pay me in advance as soon as I finished the prototype, and then I could pay my staff and part of my bank notes and start producing the vans."

His story came to a halt as the injustice of the day returned to him. He was not going to blame this on Paul, he told himself as he stared out into the night. It was not his fault.

"You couldn't finish it?" Julie prodded gently.

He shuffled his plates around a bit. "Oh yeah, I finished it. And I delivered it today. Only Paul couldn't pay, because he'd made some bad investments that left his business on the verge of bankruptcy. It wasn't a big surprise. He kind of warned me last month, but I was almost finished, and I kept hoping things would turn around." The words

15

were uttered matter-of-factly, as if the events were typical.

Julie whistled softly. "That's too bad."

He met her eyes. There was no pity there, and somehow that comforted him. "Yep. So now I'm broke, jobless, and don't have a clue what I'm going to do next."

Julie pulled his untouched soup to her side of the table, picked up his spoon, and took a sip. She tilted her head and looked at him with thoughtful eyes as he watched her. "Doing business with friends doesn't pay. You lose a lot more than you gain. Good friendships are hard to come by. You can find a business partner anywhere."

"Is that another of your aunt Myrtle's nuggets of wisdom?" he asked, smiling.

"No, that one came right from firsthand experience."

"Well," Blake said, "our friendship is still intact. Paul and I go way back. And as far as business partners go, there isn't anyone else who knows this stuff like he does. He's made some major strides in making life easier for disabled people, and he knows what they need because he's confined to a wheelchair himself. He just made some mistakes with his money."

Julie set down the spoon and leveled her gaze on him. "You're pretty forgiving."

He laced his fingers together and lifted his shoulders. "Forgiveness never even entered my mind. You forgive people for committing wrongs. Paul hasn't done wrong. He just made some mistakes. Besides, what good would it do to be bitter?"

"Well, at least there's a bright side," Julie said.

"A bright side?" He couldn't wait to hear what it was.

"Yes. You still have the prototype. The van. You could market it yourself, couldn't you?"

Blake's shoulders fell a few inches, and he let his focus drift outside the wet window again. "No. I left the van with him. If he could find a way to market it anyway, maybe we could both get our business back on —"

"You gave him the van?" Julie cut in. "Just *gave* it to him? Didn't he pay you anything at all?"

Blake loved her reactions, and he smiled. It was good to have someone to talk to, someone who seemed to care — even if she didn't understand the bonds of childhood friendship. "Yeah, he gave me something. Did the best he could. He gave me a hundred dollars . . . and this." He reached into the briefcase on the seat next to him and withdrew the heart-shaped box of chocolates.

17

"Valentine candy?" she asked. "You spent — what? — probably tens of thousands of dollars designing that van, and he gave you a hundred bucks and a box of chocolates?"

With a chuckle in his voice, he said, "Actually, there's a little more." He opened the box and withdrew a sweepstakes card. Grinning, he began to read: " 'You have won twenty million dollars —' "

"Yeah, right."

" '— if you are chosen the winner. To be announced on February 15 at 8 p.m., drawing held during *Wheel of Fortune.* Sweepstakes sponsored by Sweet Tooth Chocolates and ABC television.' "

"See, you scratch off this square to find the number underneath, and if they call it, you win. Guess he figured he was giving me a shot at twenty million dollars."

She ate another spoonful of soup. "And you still consider him a friend?"

He laughed then and met her gaze across the table. "He meant well. I told him that the sweepstakes ticket wasn't worth the cost of the chocolates. But ole Paul, dreamer that he is, said it could be worth twenty million. I took it to make him feel better."

Julie shook her head. "Some people would have thrown it at him. But you're worried about his feelings?"

18

He brought his napkin to his mouth, even though he didn't need it, then dropped it to the table. "Well, of course my bubble was popped. But so was his. And he had a lot more to lose."

A moment of quiet settled between them, scored only by the piano playing in the corner, the quiet voices of nearby late diners, and the patter of the rain against the window.

"You're a nice man," Julie said.

The words seemed to soften the rhythm of the rain as the tempo in Blake's heart sprinted. This was no bartender-type of concern. Julie was sincere, and it showed in her honest, sparkling eyes. His troubles began to seem far away, and the promise of a discovered treasure lifted his heart.

"I'm not so nice," he said. "I'm just doing what's been done for me."

"What's that?" she asked.

He shifted in his seat and leaned forward, locking into her gaze. "There's a story in the Bible about a servant who owed something like a million dollars to his master. No way he could ever pay it back, so when his master called him in to pay up, the servant begged for mercy."

Julie set the spoon down and sat straighter, listening.

Blake went on. "So his master had mercy on him and forgave his debt. But as soon as the guy was outside, he found someone who owed him a hundred bucks, and he demanded payment."

Julie nodded. "And when that person couldn't pay, he refused to have mercy and had him thrown into jail until he could pay his debt."

"You know the story?" Blake asked.

"Yes. Jesus told it," Julie said. He wasn't sure, but her eyes seemed to mist over as she went on. "The other servants went back and told their master what he had done, and the master called him back in. He asked him how he could refuse to forgive such a small debt when he'd been forgiven so great a debt."

"And the master threw *him* into prison," Blake added. "And, see, I'm that guy who owed a huge debt. And Jesus, my master, forgave me. Paid the debt for me. So how could I hold this little thing against my friend Paul?"

She seemed to be struggling with her own emotions. She stared down at the pattern on the tablecloth, then brought her misty eyes up to his. "You couldn't," she whispered. "I couldn't, either. My debt's been paid, too."

She's a believer, he thought. She was like him. His heart leaped, and he blinked back the mist in his own eyes. God had led him here tonight, he thought. Straight into this restaurant . . . to his own special Valentine's gift.

He picked up the heart-shaped box of chocolates, looked down at it for a moment, then handed it to her across the table. "Here," he said in a soft voice. "I want you to have this. No one like you ought to go without chocolates on Valentine's Day."

She took the box as more tears welled in her eyes. "That's so sweet . . . but it's yours. . . ."

"See, I think it was yours all along. God had Paul give it to me so I'd have something to give to you."

She smiled and smeared a tear under her eye. "Thank you," she whispered. "I wish I had something for you."

"Are you kidding?" he asked. "You've given me something, all right. You've taken my mind off my troubles. That's priceless."

She breathed a soft laugh. Opening the box, she took out the sweepstakes card. "Here, at least keep this."

He grinned and left it lying on the table. "Yeah, can't do without my twenty million. I'm holding my breath until *Wheel of For-*

tune tomorrow."

She sighed. "Boy, what I would do with that kind of money."

"Tell me," he said, enjoying the dreamy look in her eyes.

"Well, I'd quit this job because I'd be able to finance the fashion show I've been working on to show my designs, and I'd go to New York, to the garment district, and hire designers to work for me, and I could buy all the supplies I need. . . ."

"You're a fashion designer?"

"Yes. I'm working on a line of clothes for women who are tired of the sleazy choices we have in stores today. Modest, pretty dresses for women with integrity and self-respect. But, as you can see, I'm just getting started."

As he watched the smile work on her glistening eyes, he wondered if he should ask her what time she got off. Should he take her somewhere? bask in her warmth a little longer? And what if she said no? The disappointment over his failing business he could take. But rejection from her? He wasn't sure.

"More coffee?" she asked finally.

"No thanks. I've bothered you enough tonight. I hope sitting here won't get you into trouble."

"It won't," she assured him. "My shift ended about thirty minutes ago."

"Thirty minutes? And you've stayed because I —"

A coy smile skittered across her lips. "You needed a friend."

He found himself struggling for some quick comeback that would make him seem less affected by her. "I appreciate it," he said finally.

She stalled for a moment, as if waiting for him to make a move.

Should he ask her out for coffee? Oh, that would be smooth, he thought, considering that he had just refused her offer for more coffee. Maybe they could go dancing. It was only eleven, and Valentine's Day, after all . . .

His thoughts trailed off as he realized he would need every penny he had just to eat for the next week. He could invite her to come watch a movie at his house — but she might find that a little too intimate when she hardly knew him. She didn't strike him as the type who would go home with a virtual stranger.

"Well . . ." She stood up reluctantly, reached in the pocket of her uniform for his tab, and laid it on the table. "I hope things work out for you. I know they will."

Her voice alone soothed him. It had a

deep honey sweetness, with a directness that lent it a unique credibility. He took the bill, looked down at the amount, and felt his lungs constrict. A hundred and fourteen dollars! How was he going to pay this? The thought of being thrown with the ruthless servant into debtors' prison crossed his mind, and he wished he'd never reminded her of that parable.

While he sat staring at the bill, Julie wandered away toward the kitchen. Blake rubbed his temples. Had he gone insane? Sitting here ordering a meal fit for an Arab prince, all because he was attracted to a waitress who made him feel less alone?

He left a fifteen-dollar tip — fifteen dollars more than he could afford — and took the ticket to the cash register. His forehead beaded in a cold sweat as he pulled out his credit card and handed it to the cashier. He held his breath as she made the phone call to check his credit limit. And when she looked apologetically at him as she set the phone in its cradle, he realized his problems were rapidly multiplying.

"I'm sorry," the young woman said. "But you've already reached your limit on that card. Do you have another one?"

"No," he admitted with a groan. Until a few weeks ago he hadn't needed more than one. On the brink of panic, he pulled out his wallet and found the hundred-dollar bill Paul had given him. "How much did you say it was?"

The cashier checked the bill again. "One fourteen eighty-three."

Blake rubbed his eyes. He had only the hundred-dollar bill and . . . and the tip he'd left for the woman who'd been the only bright spot in his night. If he took it back, the possibility of seeing her again would be ruined, for she'd see him as an ungrateful no-account. But if he didn't . . .

Heaving a sigh, he went back to the table and grabbed the fifteen dollars. The first woman he had related to in months, he fumed, and he had to stiff her! She had probably anticipated a big tip, and she deserved it. He looked in his billfold again, as if by some miracle he'd find a ten or twenty hidden in the folds. But all he had left was the lone hundred-dollar bill. Now he almost knew how helpless Paul had felt today.

Well, he'd always been good with IOUs. If he at least left that, it would show her that he wasn't a complete deadbeat. And maybe — when he stopped beating himself up for being an extravagant jerk — it would provide him with an excuse to see her again.

He searched his wallet for a piece of paper but found nothing. He looked around on the table and saw the sweepstakes ticket he had left lying there. Hurriedly, he ripped it in half and pulled a pencil out of his pocket. On the back of the ticket, he wrote: "IOU $15. Blake Adcock."

He set it on the table where she'd be sure to see it and shoved the other half into his pocket. As an afterthought, he added a P.S. "If this is a winning ticket, I'll take you to New York."

Gulping back his humiliation, he straightened and glanced toward the kitchen, hoping he could leave before Julie saw what he'd done. Jerking the money out of his wallet, he hurried to the cash register and dropped it on the counter. "I'm kind of in a hurry," he said. The cashier gave him a peculiar look that told him one didn't sit for three hours if one was in a hurry.

"Need a receipt?" she asked.

"Why not?" he said, reaching for it. He could at least add it to his loss when he filed his pathetic income-tax return.

He dropped the few cents in change into his pocket. He stuffed the receipt into his wallet and started for the door. But Julie stopped him as she came out of the kitchen. She had put on a fresh pair of jeans and wore a bright red sweater; her coat was thrown over her arm. Her eyes looked even more alive against the bright color, and he suddenly wanted to ask if there was an oven available into which he could stick his head.

"If you're up to staying out a little longer," she said, the words tumbling out as if she'd spent all the time in the back summoning her courage and was afraid it would flee, "I know a quiet little café near here where we could go and talk."

With his heart falling to somewhere in the vicinity of his ankles, Blake turned to the glass door and watched the slanted needles of rain cutting down on the pavement. "I-I can't, Julie. I really need to go."

Julie's face reddened, and Blake wanted to do himself bodily harm. With an exaggerated shrug she said, "Okay, no problem. I should get home, anyway. I've been on my feet for hours, and I have a million things to do."

She turned back toward the table, and he hovered at the door, wishing there were some way to keep her from seeing her tip. "Julie?"

She turned back to him with eyes that hadn't completely given up.

"Thanks for . . . for listening."

Her smile faded, and he saw her swallow.

Her eyes lost their luster as she realized that was all he was going to say. "Sure," she said quietly.

He looked down at the floor and called himself every degrading name he'd ever heard, plus a few he invented for the occasion. Then, as she started back to his table, he stepped out into the storm.

The piercing strength of the icy rain as it hit him felt like the only justice he had experienced that day.

Julie Sheffield watched through the window as Blake disappeared into the night, his broad shoulders slumped against the rain and his silky hair absorbing the water. She'd read him all wrong, she decided. She had been sure he was attracted to her, yet . . .

Blowing out a heavy sigh, she told herself that she really did have to get home, anyway. She had a full night of work to do on her dress designs if she was going to stay on schedule. Working with stitches would be good therapy tonight, she thought dismally. It would help her forget the fluttering feeling she'd had when she thought she had finally met someone she might like to spend some time with. Not like the others who came into the restaurant late at night.

"Oh, well," she said, trying to find the

bright side. Maybe he'd at least left her a good tip. Heaven knew, she needed every penny she could scrape together these days. Juggling two jobs — or one job and one difficult dream — wasn't easy, and a good tip could pay for the pearl buttons she needed for her latest creation. She looked down at the cluttered table and shifted the plates, looking for the money usually tucked under a saucer or an ashtray when a customer left. When she saw the IOU propped against a glass, her stomach plummeted.

"You've got to be kidding," she mumbled. She picked up the ripped half of the sweepstakes ticket. The note on the ticket sent her blood pressure up. An IOU for a tip? An *IOU?* And the note about New York was like a punch line in a predictable joke. She glanced around her, humiliated for having spent so much time on a man who probably wouldn't give her another thought. New York, indeed. She hated herself for liking him.

But he wasn't just like all the rest, was he? He had seemed like a genuinely nice guy. Knew the Bible and everything. He seemed to be a real Christian, and that had moved her to tears. She had prayed so many times that God would send her one of his own, someone who shared her beliefs and her values. For a while tonight, she had believed God was answering that prayer. Was her judgment so warped that she hadn't seen Blake for what he really was? He'd paid over a hundred dollars for food he hadn't even touched, and he didn't even bother to leave her a 10 percent tip! *Ten* percent? *Five* percent would have been better than nothing.

She looked down at the ticket again, and a ribbon of shame curled through her. What was the matter with her? The guy probably didn't have anything else. Hadn't he confided in her about his misfortune? And he *had* mentioned that all he'd been paid for his work was a hundred dollars and a sweepstakes ticket. Maybe he figured that box of candy was her tip. Maybe he'd given her all he had.

Except his time. He hadn't been willing to give her that, when she'd had to psych herself up to ask if he'd like to go somewhere. She grabbed her purse from behind the counter, her mind weighed down with regrets. *I should leave the candy,* she told herself. Yet she tucked the box under her arm all the same.

As she stood in the rain beneath the dim streetlight waiting for her bus, she looked back down at the ticket. Did the IOU mean she'd see him again?

She honestly didn't know whether to hope for that or not.

Julie had overcome her disappointment by the following night and decided that God had intervened to protect her from someone who wasn't what he seemed. She told herself that she hardly remembered the dark-haired Blake Adcock or the blue eyes that had drawn her in from the moment she'd taken his order.

There were more important things preying on her mind. She sat sprawled on her living room floor with an elegant gown draped over her lap as she did the delicate beadwork on it. She had her first show to think of — the show that she had been working on for more than a year. It would be her debut as a solo fashion designer, even if it was in the city's smallest mall with amateur models and was taking every last penny she'd saved.

No, she had hardly thought of him at all, she told herself with congratulations. So what if they'd shared a moment of communion, a moment of reaching out and understanding? So what if he'd given her a box of candy, which she'd tossed into a drawer when she got home? So what if she'd believed his line about enjoying her company? So what if she'd known he was attracted to her, just as she was to him? So what if he'd seemed like a direct answer to prayer?

Maybe the emotion stirring in her because of another lonely Valentine's Day had caused her to imagine things that weren't real. Or maybe they were real, but he had some rule against going out with waitresses or blondes or Christians. Or maybe she had been too assertive. How was he to know that it had taken every ounce of courage within her to invite him out?

The doorbell rang. Placing her needle between her lips, she stood up and laid the gown carefully over her sofa, next to some of her other designs that were almost ready. "Coming!" she mumbled around the needle. Jerking it out of her mouth and jabbing it in the arm of the sofa, she fluffed her shoulder-length hair and brushed back her bangs. It was probably one of the waitresses who'd agreed to model her clothes in the show coming for a fitting, she thought as she rushed to the door. She swung the door open.

"So we meet again," Blake Adcock said in a lazy drawl that belied the dancing delight in his eyes. He thrust a handful of fake poinsettias at her, and she wondered if he'd just plucked them from her next-door neighbor's pots. Despite the cool grin on his face and the suave way his shoulder leaned against the jamb, there was a definite glaze to the same blue eyes her heart had stumbled over the previous night. His breathing was heavy, as if he'd run six miles to her door, and one side of his shirttail hung out of his jeans, as though he hadn't taken the time to tuck it in completely.

"Well, well," she said, unable to suppress her smile. She cocked her head and crossed her arms as she surveyed the man who had kept her from sleeping last night. "I didn't expect to see you again."

"It took some doing," he admitted. She hadn't noticed the dimples in his cheeks the night before, but the sly smile tugging at his lips enhanced them now. "You *would* choose tonight to take off work. And your boss acted like your address was a matter of national security. I had to bribe the red-haired waitress."

"Bribe her? What did you have to bribe her with, Blake?"

"I'm real good with IOUs," he admitted.

"So I noticed. Did you promise her New York, too?"

Blake laughed and threw a delighted glance toward the eaves over her door. "Oh, boy, are you going to be surprised when I tell you why I'm here."

"I doubt that," Julie said. Somehow the laughter in his eyes was contagious, and she couldn't help matching it. "You're here to give me these stolen flowers and pay off your IOU, right?"

"Wrong," he said, laughter rippling in his voice. "I came because of that half sweepstakes ticket I left you. You know — the one that probably ticked you off because you thought it was worthless?"

Julie narrowed her eyes and bit her lip, trying to hold back her grin. She had to admit he was cute when he was mysterious. "I vaguely remember something like that," she said.

Blake took a deep breath and pulled his half out of his pocket. In a voice vibrating with controlled excitement, he said, "Well, Julie, you might want to go get it. I was just watching *Wheel of Fortune,* and they drew the winning number. If my eyes aren't playing tricks on me, we're about to be rich."

Julie sucked in a breath. "The winning number? How much?"

Blake's grin trembled. "Twenty million dollars," he whispered. "Ten for me and ten for you."

CHAPTER TWO

"Ten million dollars?" Julie threw a hand over her heart and stumbled back from the door. *"Ten million dollars?"*

"You got it," he said with a shaky note of euphoria. He took her hand and started to dance. "We're rich. Millionaires!"

Julie pulled away. "Wait. This can't be. You can't become a millionaire with a little piece of paper."

"I'll prove it to you," he said. "Go get your half. They said we have to head to our nearest ABC affiliate by midnight to claim our money."

Julie's face went slack as she racked her brain. Where had she put the ticket? Her hands fell helplessly to her sides as her eyes darted from place to place around the room.

"Julie, the ticket," he pressed.

She nodded quickly, holding up a hand to quiet him as she tried to think. "Just give me a second," she said. "I need a minute."

Alarm narrowed his eyes. "A minute for what?" he asked slowly.

"To think about . . . where I put the ticket. I don't think I threw it away."

Blake gasped. "You don't think . . ." Carefully, he stepped inside the door. "Are you telling me that you lost a ticket worth twenty million dollars?"

"No," she said quickly. "I didn't lose it. I just can't remember what I did with it."

"Well, think!" he blurted. The cords in his neck began to swell. *Think!*

"I'm trying to!" she shouted back. "But you're making me nervous!"

"*I'm* making *you* nervous?" He closed the door — too hard. "Julie, if you don't come up with your half, my half isn't worth a nickel."

"You think I don't know that?" She darted down the hallway into her bedroom, not caring that Blake was on her heels and that he'd see the cluttered state of her house. "I didn't know it was worth anything! Neither did you. If you had, you wouldn't have left it!" She began digging through her dirty clothes hamper for the jeans she'd worn the night before.

"Hey, I left that ticket out of the goodness of my heart."

She found the jeans and yanked them out,

then dug into the pockets, which were distressingly empty. "The goodness of your heart?" she scoffed. "You left that ticket to insult me." She threw down the jeans and dug out her sweater. "To put me in my place."

"What place?" Blake asked as his eyes followed her every movement.

"My place as just another waitress. Because you think I'm beneath you."

Blake snatched the sweater from her hands and frisked the pockets. "Beneath me? You think I'd spend three hours flirting with someone if I thought she was beneath me?"

"Depends on how bad the weather is!" she threw back. She knocked over the clothes hamper and scanned the inside, in case the ticket had fallen out of a pocket.

"You thought I sat there because of the rain? Did you really interpret my note and that ticket to mean I was too good for you?"

Julie marched out of her room and grabbed her purse off the couch. "How did you want me to interpret it?" She dumped the contents of the purse onto the coffee table and began sorting through the folded receipts, empty gum wrappers, and loose change with trembling fingers. Blake joined her.

"The same way I interpreted it when Paul

gave it to me." He picked up a sticky, unwrapped cough drop and cringed. "Don't you ever clean this purse out?"

"I've been busy!" she snapped.

He unwrapped some folded papers and shook them out. "When Paul gave the ticket to me, I saw it as a gesture of goodwill. He was doing the best he could at the time. I almost left you the whole thing! I didn't have anything else."

Julie glanced up at him, reluctant to admit he could be telling the truth. But it hadn't been his failure to leave a tip that had hurt, she thought. It had been the rejection, the indifferent way he'd shrugged her off and walked out.

"You ought to be thanking me instead of making me feel like pond scum. I had enough of that last night." He opened the last receipt, found nothing, and threw it down. "It's not here, Julie. Where is it?"

She panned the room again. "I don't know," she whispered.

Blake got up and scanned the small house. Her designs were draped over the sofa and hanging from hooks on the wall. Bolts of expensive, elegant material lay on a table with the sewing machine, and notions and accessories were scattered in various stacks without order. "I don't know how you find anything in this place. It looks like a rummage sale." He went to the couch and began snatching up the dresses to look under them. "What *is* all this junk, anyway?"

Julie's cheeks stung as she rushed forward to rescue the dresses from his rough handling. Draping them over her arm, she caressed them as if they were small children who had been abused. "This *junk*," she said through clenched teeth, "is why I'm working nights as a waitress. They're my designs. I've been working on them for months, and they're good."

"Right now they're in the way," he said. He began throwing the cushions off the couch and running his hands along the edges.

"*They* belong here. *You* don't! Now get your hands off my furniture!"

He reeled around to face her. "Your car! Maybe you left it in your car!"

Julie clutched the dresses to her chest and backed away. His eyes were getting too wild, and she didn't trust him. "I don't have a car. I had to sell it."

Blake's jaw dropped. "What kind of person lives in Detroit without a car?" he asked in a cracked, high-pitched voice.

"The kind who has to spend her money on more important things!" she shouted with indignation. "I'm not above riding the bus!" She started back down the hall to hang up her designs, but he was behind her in an instant.

"Julie, don't you understand? If you find that ticket, you can *buy* the bus! Please! Help me look for it!"

"I *was* helping, until you started mauling my dresses," she said. "I don't like people insulting my work!"

"We're talking about *twenty million dollars!*" he shouted. "Who *cares* about your work!"

"*I* care!" she yelled back.

"Okay, I'm sorry!" he said, as if to appease her. "I didn't mean to insult your work. I'm just anxious to find —"

"You called it junk!" she reminded him. "If you had any taste in clothes, you'd know that these are masterpieces. They'll give women options! They can look elegant without looking trashy. Beautiful, without exposing themselves. They're going to be worth a lot of money!"

Blake folded his hands in a dramatic praying gesture and moaned. "Julie, you'll *have* a lot of money if you'll just find that ticket. Please! Where do you keep your garbage?"

She crossed her arms militantly. "Where do you think?"

"I don't know. Judging by the rest of this place, it could be anywhere!"

Julie marched toward the kitchen and found the garbage can tucked in a corner. "I'll go through it myself! I don't need any glassy-eyed man rifling through my trash!"

"I'm not glassy-eyed!" he said as he watched her dump the garbage on her counter.

She pulled out a wet paper towel, a soup can, a potato chip bag. "You could be a murderer for all I know," she muttered as she continued sorting through the trash. "How do I know there is a winning number? How do I even know the sweepstakes entry is authentic? You could have made this whole thing up."

He caught his breath, incredulous. "For what reason? To get close to you? You're beneath me, remember? At least that was your enlightened impression!"

Her hands began working faster, in jerkier motions, as she realized she wasn't going to find what she was looking for. "Last night my enlightened impression was that you were a nice man who needed a friend. I liked you. But you know what they say. You never know a person until you've shared a sweepstakes ticket with him."

His mouth fell open. "Who says that? I've

never heard anyone say that."

"I just said it," she snapped.

He snatched the trash can from her hand and violently began shoving the trash back in. "Last night you seemed like a nice woman I might like to know better. I never would have guessed that under all that beauty and compassion was someone who valued an unhemmed dress more than a twenty-million-dollar sweepstakes ticket. Priorities a little mixed up? I think so!"

"I'll be just as well off if I don't find that ticket as I will if I do, because that un-hemmed dress is worth a mint if I sell it. I can live without ten million dollars if I have to. Can you?"

"No!" he shouted. "Especially if I lost it all because of you! What kind of airhead loses a twenty-million-dollar ticket?"

"What kind of airhead gives one away in the first place?" she bellowed.

"Then we're both airheads!" he admitted. "We'd make a great pair. We probably deserve each other."

"We probably do!" she volleyed.

He pivoted toward her and brought his angry face intimidatingly close to hers. "Close your eyes!" he said.

"Why?"

"So you can concentrate!"

She closed her eyes reluctantly, furiously.

"Where did you leave the ticket?" he asked.

Her eyes snapped open. "Oh, this is great. Yelling at me is really going to help me concentrate."

"I don't know how else to get through to you!"

"And I don't know how to get through to you! What do you want? Blood?"

"The ticket!" he shouted. "I just want the other half of my ticket!"

"*Your* ticket?" she asked.

"*Our* ticket. The ticket."

"If I find that stupid ticket," she muttered through her teeth, "it isn't going to be *our* ticket. It's going to be *your* ticket. I didn't ask for it, I didn't want it, and I sure don't have to subject myself to this kind of abuse for it!"

"Just *find* it," he ordered, "and we'll talk about what to do with it then."

Julie squeezed her eyes shut and tried to concentrate.

"Think," he said, lowering his voice. "What was the first thing you did when you got home last night?"

"I took off my shoes," she said. "You see, I'd been running myself ragged waiting on one customer who kept ordering —"

"Then what did you do?" he cut in, more calmly now.

"I turned on the stereo. Then I came in here and got something to drink."

"Did you have the ticket then?"

Her eyes opened, and she focused on the wall, seeing the blurry events unfold. "I think so. I remember looking at it and thinking you were just like all the rest."

A slight grin softened his features, but his voice remained sharp. "Then what did you do?"

"I went to —" She stopped suddenly and snapped her fingers in the air. "My sewing basket! I put it in my sewing basket when I got out what I needed!"

Blake threw his hands together and glanced at the ceiling. "Thank you, Lord," he mumbled aloud, "for giving her a temporary lapse in her insanity."

Julie caught the barb and jutted her chin. Stalking to the sewing basket, she reached into her tray and grabbed the ticket half. She threw it at him. "It's all yours."

Blake caught it and matched it to his half of the ticket. Relief swept visibly over him, and he collapsed onto the couch. "I can't believe it," he said. "You found it. We're rich."

"Not *we*," she said, planting stubborn fists

on her hips. "*You.* I don't want anything to do with your money or your insults or your wild greed. Just get out before you start hyperventilating, and take the ticket with you."

"Julie, it's yours, too."

"Go ahead. I won't take it. I may not have money, and I may not have a car, and I may not even have a glamorous think-tank job, but I do have pride. I don't want to have anything to do with a man who calls me an insane airhead. Not even for ten million dollars."

Blake threw back his head and gave a genuine laugh — a laugh that was pulled from deep inside, where tense fear had just been harbored. "That's good. You're almost convincing. But nobody in her right mind would pass up ten million dollars."

"Well, according to you, I'm not in my right mind, am I?"

Blake stood up and faced her, undaunted. "Julie, come on. This is no time for making some noble statement."

"I'm not trying to make a statement," she said. "I don't need your ten million dollars, and I don't want it."

"*Everybody* needs it," he said. "*Everybody* wants it."

"Not me."

His smile began to fade as he realized just

how stubborn this lady was. "Julie, we were under a lot of pressure. Both of us. I don't do well under pressure."

"I won't take the ticket," she said again.

"And I won't leave until you do," he told her with an equally obstinate shrug. "The winner has to report to the nearest ABC affiliate by midnight. It's nine thirty right now. I'm not going alone."

"Fine," she said. "Then you'll miss it and lose your fortune."

"Fine," he returned. "So will you."

They stood staring at each other for what seemed an eternity, each certain the other would back down. Finally, Blake reached for the phone and began dialing.

"Calling ABC?" Julie asked.

"Nope," he said. "I'm ordering a pizza. It looks like we're going to be here for a while."

CHAPTER THREE

The clock said 11:18. Julie and Blake sat staring at each other across the single remaining slice of cold pizza, as if it represented the torn sweepstakes ticket that neither would touch. She sat with her lips pursed, trying to ignore the two ticket halves lying on the coffee table like a future fading in and out of grasp. Blake had to admit he admired her. How many women could actually carry a bluff so far?

Anyone else would have taken the money and run. But it was the principle of the thing that motivated him. Besides, he liked her little game. He had always found that the most difficult things in life were the most rewarding.

"So . . . how about those Lions?" he asked to break the silence tingling between them.

"I don't have much time for sports," she admitted. "I wouldn't know." She unfolded her legs, dusted crumbs off her jeans, and started to stretch.

"What *do* you have time for?" he asked. He gave a sweeping glance around the cluttered room. "I mean, besides housework."

Julie shot him an insulted look. "I clean my house," she returned. "Things are just . . . a little out of place right now."

He rubbed his hand over his stubbly jaw and laughed again. "You didn't answer my question, Julie. What does a woman like you do in her spare time?"

"A woman like me doesn't have spare time," she said. "I work too hard."

"If you had money, you could have all the time you wanted."

"Money can't buy time." She stood up. "Speaking of time, I don't have any to waste. I hope you don't mind my working while you waste yours." She picked up a container of tiny beads.

Blake gave a soft chuckle and stretched out his arms dramatically before clasping them behind his head. "You know us millionaires. We love wasting time." Offering a lazy yawn, he propped his feet on the coffee table. "You know, if you had money, you could buy a dress like that. You wouldn't have to make it yourself."

Her eyes flashed at him. "I am a fashion designer," she bit out. "This is an original

— *my* original. Why would I want to buy one?"

"Well, it's just so much work. If you had money, you could hire someone to sew those little thingamajiggies on."

"If I sell this dress, I *will* have money, and I'll be able to hire help."

"But you still won't have time."

"I'll have self-respect and a sense of accomplishment," she said. "And you can get your big feet off my table."

He grinned wider, but he didn't budge. "I'll buy you a new table."

"If you don't go claim your money, you won't be able to."

"And you'll be responsible for my poverty for the rest of my life," he returned.

Julie grabbed the needle out of the sofa arm and took aim at him. "If you don't get your feet off my table, I'll be responsible for something much worse than poverty."

Blake dropped his feet and gazed up at her. "You're dangerous," he said, a mischievous lilt to his voice.

Julie gave him a victorious smile and plopped back down in her chair, making a grand ceremony of propping her own feet on the table.

Blake stroked his index finger over his lips and tried to suppress his laughter. This one

49

was a rascal. She'd probably wait until the clock said it was ten minutes to twelve to give in . . . and that was only thirty minutes away. Well, he thought, it only made things more exciting.

He could almost believe she meant to give up the money. But he knew better. Any minute now she'd start to sweat and fidget. . . .

Any minute now, Julie thought with an inner chuckle. Any minute now he'd start to look at his watch and pounce on that ticket. And he would expect her to pounce on it, too. Apparently he wasn't used to women who had the strength of their convictions. She'd show him how stubborn she could be.

"So what are you going to do with your half?" he asked with his disarming grin.

She glanced up from her work. "Flushing it down the toilet comes to mind," she said. "That is, if you don't intend to take it."

His deep, tumbling laughter made her smile. "I'd dare you," he said, "but I won't."

"You're catching on," she returned with a wink.

He dropped his elbows to his knees and leaned forward. "You know, this may be hard for you to admit, but we're a lot alike."

"Us?" she asked with a laugh. "How?"

"We're both cool," he observed. "We just won ten million dollars each, and we're both pretending we couldn't care less."

"*You're* pretending," she said.

"And we're both pretty confident. You think I'm going to give in, and I know you are."

"Then one of us must be wrong," she pointed out.

"And we're both stubborn."

"One out of three isn't bad," she said.

He looked at his watch, compared it to the clock ticking away on her wall. She glanced at the clock. "What's the matter, Blake?" she asked. "Getting a little nervous?"

"Nope," he said calmly. "We still have twenty-eight minutes. And I'm not going without you."

Julie threw down her dress and raked her hand through her hair. She couldn't concentrate on her work when there was a man staring at her, waiting for her to crack, and when time was flying by as though disaster were on its heel. "What difference does it make to you? It was your ticket to start with. Why can't you just take it back?"

"Because I gave it to you. I wanted you to have it. You were nice to me."

"Well, I don't charge for being nice to

people. I didn't expect to be paid for it."

"You expected a tip."

"For doing my job, not for being nice to you," she said.

"Well, whatever we expected or got out of it, the fact remains that we both won, and we'll both claim our money. Otherwise —" he rubbed his hands over his face and arched his brows firmly — "we both go on as we have been. Struggling, dreaming, failing, reaching . . ."

Her eyes met his, and for a moment she wondered if he knew more about her than he was telling.

"It would be fun," he said. "I can't think of anyone else I'd rather become a millionaire with."

Julie stood up and began to pace slowly. "Let's face it, Blake. You aren't going to believe me until it's too late. And I'm not going to believe you, either. You need that money, and I know you're not going to pass it up."

"You need it too. If you had it, you wouldn't have to keep working nights as a waitress."

That was true, she thought. But it was his money. His. And he had said such vicious things to her when he thought she'd lost her half of the ticket. She sat back down and pulled her feet onto the chair with her, dropped her head onto her bent knees, and tried to think clearly. He was bluffing, she thought. He'd run out in the next five minutes with both halves of the ticket. He wouldn't really risk losing it all just because she refused to take half.

His patient bullheadedness intrigued her. How many men would care whether or not she wanted it? How many men would have waited the space of a heartbeat once she'd given the ticket back?

She shook her head and looked up at him as he waited for her to change her mind. Despite the things he'd said to her, she couldn't help seeing the gentle vulnerability peeking through his expression at odd times, as if some sense of honor lurked behind his mask of indifference. Last night she had really liked him, but would she have ever seen him again if God hadn't drawn them back together with a torn sweepstakes ticket?

Had God really been behind this? she wondered. Was this how he planned to answer her prayers after she'd cried out in her loneliness? Was he giving her a miracle now, after she'd suffered through heartbreak and injustice? Jack — the man she had been in love with, the fashion designer she had worked for — had put his ego above their relationship. He had fired her when he realized that the customers placed higher value on her designs than on his, even though the designs bore his name, not hers. Crushed but not defeated, she had tried to start over alone. She had decided to put her own name on her creations, but jealousy had made him claim that she had stolen his designs, discrediting her.

Nothing had been easy since then. Not only had she been thrown back to the drawing board professionally, but she'd faced the added problem of rising above Jack's miserable allegations. Plus she had to make a living while she got started. A waitressing job in an upscale restaurant had been the perfect answer. It netted her not only enough to survive but a little something to put into her dresses.

That was why she had related so well to Blake. They'd each had dreams, and each knew failure. Each had clung to a down-but-not-out demeanor through it all, and remained devoid of bitterness or blame. So what would happen when he collected his winnings and went on with his life, fulfilling his dreams? Would he remember the little blonde waitress he'd butted heads with, the one who gave up her winnings for some

hazy principle she didn't even fully understand? Or would she be filed under "history" and never thought of again?

The thought depressed her. But if she accepted the ticket, they would be somehow
yoked together. She would owe him, and
that couldn't be good.

Her eyes strayed to the clock again. Eleven
thirty-eight. It seemed like no time at all
since it had been nine thirty. Where had the
time gone? And still Blake made no move
to leave. He wasn't even showing the typical
signs of anxiety, as she was. He seemed
relaxed, calm, even a little amused.

"Is it hot in here?" she asked.

He shrugged. "I'm comfortable."

He watched as she lifted the hair off her
neck and glanced at the clock again. "Blake,
it's 11:38. You'd better go."

"Not unless you come with me."

"Twenty million dollars, Blake! Just go
claim it!"

"Uh-uh."

Julie wiped the perspiration from her
forehead and watched as the second hand
traveled around the numbers. She snatched
up the tickets and handed both halves to
him. "Blake, please."

He waved her away. "I'm a man of honor,"
he said seriously and without any particular

55

urgency. "When I give something to some-one, I can't take it back. Even if it means I lose in the process. You should have learned that about me last night, when I told you about giving the prototype to Paul. I keep my word."

"But, Blake . . ." Her plea trailed off as she realized it was futile. Setting the half tickets back on the coffee table, she listened as the clock ticked off agonizing seconds that dragged into minutes.

At eighteen before twelve, their eyes met. *I can't wait to see him grab those tickets and dart out,* she thought.

But that moment never came. Blake's eyes were amused, placating, but never anxious.

Hers, on the other hand, must have been glossy, frustrated, borderline frantic. If he lost twenty million dollars because she refused to take half . . . she clutched the roots of her hair and swallowed hard. Ten million dollars could have gotten her father out from under the debts he had worked at the steel mill to pay off until the day he died. It could have given her mother a new start instead of a grieving end. It could still help her two sisters in a way that she'd never been able to help them before, and it could get her church out of debt, feed the poor, support several missionaries. . . . The things she could do with that money would roll over into the next sweepstakes, and they'd never have the chance again. The next winner might gamble it all away. He or she might spend it on drugs or waste every penny.

The clock's ticking sounds punctuated Blake's slow, relaxed breathing. How could he be so calm? If he didn't run out in the next thirty seconds, she'd have to do something. The second hand descended to the two, the three, the four, and still Blake didn't move. But his smile grew more pronounced in his eyes as he noted the changes in her expression.

Twenty million dollars! What kind of person would sit there and let twenty million dollars go down the tubes because of a misplaced sense of honor? she wondered. What kind of *airhead* would sit calmly on her couch while — she caught the direction of her thoughts and hauled them back. She was acting the way he had acted earlier. Calling him names when she was just as foolish as he!

Suddenly she sprang to her feet. "My shoes!" she shouted in a rush. "I'll get my shoes and you start the car!"

Blake was out the door in seconds, leaping over the untended shrubs in her yard

57

and fairly skidding on his feet as he reached his car. In ten seconds flat they were on their way, each clutching half of the propitious ticket as his car threaded through shortcuts and wove its way toward the television station.

"We must be crazy!" she mumbled. "Wasting all that time! We'll never make it!"

Blake only smiled.

A car ahead of them insisted on driving the speed limit, and Julie sat forward in her seat. "What's wrong with these people? Don't they have anything better to do than ruin the lives of innocent people?"

Blake laughed.

He passed the car impeding their progress and made a turn onto a street that would get them to the highway. But half a mile from the on-ramp they heard a loud whistle and a roaring engine. Julie sought the source of the light shining over them. "A train!" she shouted. "Can't you beat it?"

"No," he said. "Just take it easy. It's all right."

"All right?" she bellowed. "How can it be all right? We have eight minutes to get downtown! *Eight minutes!*"

"Sixty-eight minutes," he corrected with a smile. "I turned your clocks ahead when you were paying the pizza man."

The emotional bubble in Julie's chest bobbed between fury and ecstasy, then crashed like a lead ball. "You *what?*"

"Hey," he said with an infuriating shrug, "I may be honorable and all that, but I wasn't about to take the chance of losing twenty million dollars. Not even for you!"

CHAPTER FOUR

"Of all the underhanded, conniving, manipulative —"

Her reaction seemed not to surprise
Blake, though his annoyance was clear in
his voice. "So I tricked you into accepting
ten million dollars, Julie. Sue me."

Julie set her eyes on the train rumbling
by. It was a cool night, and the smell of rain
dominated the air, a sign that another storm
was not far away. The sound of the heavy
train roaring over the tracks seemed to
under score her irritation, though she wasn't
sure why his deception had the power to
douse her excitement. "I should have known
that you wouldn't have that kind of honor,"
she muttered, "sitting in my living room like
you cared whether I took it or not."

Blake's splayed hand raked quickly
through his dark hair, then settled back over
the steering wheel. "I did care, Julie. I do
care. That's why we're sitting here arguing.

If I didn't care, I'd have left your house at nine thirty with both halves of the ticket and never looked back!"

"Why didn't you?"

"Because I'm a man of my word. I don't intend to apologize for that."

Silence settled between them as the rusty boxcars rattled past, and Julie focused on a spot on the windshield. He seemed much too close in the tiny sports car, and his expression clearly illustrated his bruised feelings. What was it about this man that his surprises, his unpredictability, constantly left her disappointed?

"Tell me something," she said after a moment. "What if I had been stubborn right up to the last minute? Would you have left me and claimed the money then?"

"No." There was no hesitation in his answer, no doubt in his blue eyes as he regarded her across the darkness. She felt her heart rate speed up, and she wished she hadn't been so lonely for so long.

Blake made a big deal of stretching and lowered his arm across the back of her seat, reminding her of the "smooth" ploys of a sixteen-year-old in his dad's car. He leaned toward her, his lips entirely too close to her ear as he said, "At that point I probably would have picked you up, thrown you over my shoulder, and taken you with me."

A tiny smile broke through Julie's scowl, for his admission restored a bit of her faith. Yes, that was exactly what he would have done, she thought. Finally she allowed herself to look at him, and her heart halted in midbeat. "Why?" she whispered hoarsely. "Why didn't you just take the money and run?"

"Why did you have to test me?" he parried. "What made you so sure I was a scumbag who wouldn't have given you a thought if you weren't the key to my fortune?"

She gave the idea a moment's thought. "Because men are usually after something. There's almost always a motive."

Blake cleared his throat, as if he couldn't accept being cleared completely. "Well, I never said I was completely without a motive." The confession left his eyes smiling. "When I saw you last night, I did sort of hope we could see each other again."

"Last night you didn't even want to have a cup of coffee with me," she reminded him.

Blake dropped his left wrist over the steering wheel and leaned even closer, the arm at her back closing in. The breath of his words whispered against her lips, and this time it was not her imagination. "Last night I wanted very much to spend more time with you," he said. "I wanted to find out everything about you. How many sisters and brothers you have, if you like old movies, where you're from, whether your parents are still living, what you do during the day, what you would like to do, whether or not you're seeing anyone . . ."

"Then why didn't you just ask?" she whispered, paying careful attention to his lips.

"Because I felt like a loser," he said, "and you aren't the type of woman who deserves a loser."

It was too pat, she thought. Too easy. But somehow he seemed sincere. "I'm from a town called Wry Springs," she said. "It's about an hour from here. I'm an only child, and my parents aren't living. Dad worked in the steel mill until the day he died, and we struggled all our lives. I don't have much faith in money or people who have money, because I never had any, and I was happy anyway. My family always found happiness in our relationship with each other. I guess that's why the ticket didn't mean that much to me. I don't need money to be happy. So now all your questions are answered," she said, glancing down the tracks where the end of the train was still not in sight.

"Not all of them," he whispered. "You

didn't answer the ones about old movies and boyfriends."

She struggled not to smile. "Yes and no."

He moved even closer. "And which question does the yes answer? Yes, you like old movies, or yes, you're seeing someone?"

Julie felt a hot, sweet heat scalding her cheeks. "You'll have to figure that one out for yourself, Adcock," she whispered.

He smiled. "Would you really trust me to form my own conclusions?"

"I can't trust you with the time of day."

She caught his grin, in spite of her efforts not to. His hand moved to cup her chin. The gentle touch sent a charge through her nerves. "Julie, last night I had a hundred and fifteen dollars and a credit card charged to the limit. My bill was $114.83. I was humiliated that I didn't have a tip, so I got out of there. I spent the rest of the night more frustrated about the woman I would never get to know than the fact that weeks of my work were down the drain and I was broke."

She wet her lips. "You . . . you really thought about me last night?"

He was watching her lips, as if giving serious consideration to kissing her. "Did you think about me?"

"Yes," she admitted.

"And what did you think?"

Her words came out in a mesmerized whisper. "I thought you were a cheap creep and that I was better off if I never saw you again."

His eyes danced, as if she'd just given him wild praise. "What else?"

"That you were a white-collar snob who wouldn't stoop to dating a waitress."

He blew a low whistle and stroked her cheek with his thumb. "And?"

She struggled not to smile. "That you were a pretty good-looking, cheap, creepy snob."

"Pretty good-looking, huh?" he rumbled. "Now we're getting somewhere."

"I know I'll hate myself for admitting it."

"Then I'll admit something too," he whispered. "I thought you were worth groveling for. I almost went back after I left, knowing I would humiliate myself even more."

"Almost? Is that supposed to comfort me?"

He moistened his lips. "It'll have to do for now. You should know that I sold my coffee table this morning to raise money so I could pay your IOU tonight."

"Your coffee table?"

"Yes. It's a marble-topped antique. Belonged to my grandmother."

"And you sold it to pay my tip?"

"No. I sold it so I'd have a pretense for seeing you again."

Julie swallowed. He swallowed. As they looked into each other's eyes, gone for a moment were thoughts of the sweepstakes, and the money waiting for them, and the time that sneaked by much too quickly.

Gone, also, was the train.

A horn behind them blared, and several more in the line of traffic behind them sounded. Someone rolled down his window and cursed.

"The train's gone," Blake and Julie said together.

Shifting back into Drive, Blake jerked the car forward.

He reached across the seat and took her hand. And as they drove, Julie thought more about the feel of his hand on hers than she did about the money waiting for them.

But as soon as they reached the downtown area, the excitement seemed to strike them both. "Ten million dollars," Julie whispered in awe. "I'm going to have ten million dollars."

"I'm gonna buy my neighbor, Mrs. Davis, a big-screen TV," he said. "She's home-bound and half blind. And I'll buy Paul a

Jacuzzi to help with his circulation."

"I'll be able to quit my job and work full-time on my designs," she said in a dreamy voice.

"And I'm getting my mom one of those doorbells that plays some long tune when you ring it. And a new car with a phone in it."

"I can hire an assistant to help me," she went on.

"I want a compact disc player for every one of my nieces and nephews."

"I could rent one of those good PA systems for my show," Julie said.

"A yacht," Blake added. "I'll buy a yacht for my church, for Sunday school parties and retreats."

"Ten million dollars," Julie whispered again.

"Ten million dollars," he echoed.

They reached the street on which the ABC affiliate was located, and a coil of panic rose within her. What if it was a mistake? What if the number wasn't the winning number? What if there were two million other winners? What if the ticket was a fake? "Are we going to be brave when they tell us it was all a big mistake, or are we going to break down and cry like babies, then trash the place?"

67

"I vote for trashing the place," he said, "but since it isn't a mistake, it won't come to that." He took her hand again and squeezed it as he came to a stop in front of the building. "Well, are you ready for this?"

She massaged her stomach. "I think I'm going to be sick. Maybe you'd better go in and make sure it's real. I don't take disappointment very well."

"We'll both go, and we won't be disappointed. Trust me."

"Trust you?" she asked. "The man who turned my clocks ahead?"

"It was for a good cause," he said. "Now come on."

Stark terror changed her breathing rate. "I can't. My legs won't move."

"If your legs don't move, they won't be able to walk in there and claim all that money."

"They'll figure out a way," she muttered. "Just give me a second."

She gazed through the window into the lit offices. No one in there knew the winner was here in Detroit. She wondered if anyone of authority was here. Had they been briefed on what to do if the winner appeared?

"You know, our lives are never going to be the same after tonight," he said.

"Probably not," she agreed. "We'll always

look back and remember the night we thought we'd won ten million dollars and were mistaken."

His deep, melodic laughter relaxed her a little. "We're not mistaken. We're rich."

Numbly, Julie forced herself to open the car door. Her feet touched the ground, and she managed to make her legs move. Blake was beside her in a moment, with his arm around her shoulders. But his own trembling told her he needed support nearly as much as she did. "You know," he said with a wry grin as they started up the steps and into the building, "ten million is a lot, but twenty is more. We ought to give some serious consideration to getting married and pooling our winnings."

Julie gaped up at him. From the laughing look on his face it was obvious that the idea had been facetious. But she didn't find it amusing. "Don't press your luck, Adcock. I haven't given them my half of the ticket yet."

"Well, come on, Julie," he teased. "How can you not see that this relationship is blessed?"

Before she could answer, he had swept her into the office and announced their presence.

"The tickets are bogus," Julie said a little

while later as they sat in the station manager's office, watching through the glass window as the evening news anchor spoke into the telephone.

"No, they aren't," Blake said. "They're just checking for authenticity. They can't just give twenty million dollars to anybody off the street. And then they've got to set up the satellite feed showing them giving us the money. This whole thing is for promotion, you know. They aren't going to do it in secret."

Julie glanced at him, and her heart fell when she saw the doubt in his face. "Wouldn't it be something if we went through all this and weren't winners, after all?"

"That is not even a possibility, Julie. Just be patient."

He took her hand, laced his fingers through hers. That callused touch felt like security, optimism, but its slight tremor kept her from completely abandoning her doubts.

"But what if we don't win? I'm just trying to prepare myself."

"If we don't win, we're no worse off than we were before," he said, as if he were already beginning to accept the disappointment. "In fact, we're better off because we met each other. Pretty good deal, if you ask me."

She looked up at him and saw that he meant it. He considered that a plus, and that knowledge made the situation seem less urgent to him.

"Not much better off," he added with a grin. "But a little."

Playfully, she swung at him. The door to the outside opened suddenly, and Brett Bodinger, Detroit's award-winning meteorologist, came in followed by perky Susan Stevens, Detroit's award-winning news anchor. A camera crew filed in behind them with tape rolling. Susan Stevens puffed her perfectly coiffed hair and smacked her recently painted lips. "Are you ready?" she asked the cameramen as they flicked on their lights and positioned them over Blake and Julie.

"Anytime you are," one of them said.

The woman turned back to the baffled couple and grinned from ear to ear, making certain that she never put her back to the camera. "Congratulations, Mr. Adcock and Miss Sheffield. You're going to be millionaires!"

It took a moment for the words to sink in.

In that moment, Julie realized she had

known all along that the tickets were authentic.

Blake realized that he had never really believed it.

Their stunned eyes met as they both rose to their feet, and finally Julie threw her arms around Blake and squealed with delight. Blake lifted her off the floor and swung her around. She laughed like a little girl on a carnival ride. "We won!" she said over and over. "We're rich!"

The cameras recorded the whole scene without interruption, and then the reporters zeroed in on the way they had gotten the ticket. After the initial feed to New York, the news anchors set them up at their news desk, from which they did satellite interviews with a dozen stations across the country.

"What do you think this win will do to your relationship?" one of the reporters asked.

"Well, I wouldn't say there really is a relationship," Julie said. "I mean, we just met last night."

Blake tried to look wounded. "I'm crushed. We were just talking marriage not twenty minutes ago."

"Blake!" Julie's face blushed to crimson. "*He* was talking marriage," she corrected.

"Something about pooling our winnings or some such nonsense. We hardly know each other."

"Do you regret giving her the ticket?" the man continued. "You could have had the whole jackpot for yourself."

"No, I don't regret it," Blake said. "I like having women deeply indebted to me."

Julie caught her breath as the reporters laughed, but the next question left her little time to work her indignation into anger.

"What are you going to do with the money?"

A lyrical note of laughter undulated on Blake's voice. "It depends on when they plan to give it to us. If we get it tonight, I might go out and buy a restaurant in Greek Town or something." The reporters laughed with a shared exuberance that no one in the room could help feeling.

"And you, Miss Sheffield, what do you plan to do with the winnings?"

"I'm a fashion designer," she said, "and I plan to invest most of it in my business."

"But aren't you going to splurge with any of it?" someone asked.

"Sure," she said. "Maybe I'll buy a new pair of shoes."

Toward the wee hours of the morning, Julie felt as if she and Blake were two aliens in a room full of spectators. She was too distracted to find it odd or awkward when he held her around her waist, and her nerves prompted her arm around him as well. And neither had the slightest suspicion just how far those tiny gestures or their flirtatious teasing would be carried when news of their winnings hit the morning media.

It wasn't yet dawn when the two weary winners were walked back to Blake's car, followed by a throng of cameramen. They filmed as the couple waved victoriously and began to drive away, like a bride and groom on their way to the honeymoon.

"So what do you think?" Blake asked when they were back on the freeway. "Are you glad you met me?"

"Yes, but you may not be so glad you met me. The reporters were right, you know. It could all be yours."

He chuckled. "I'm glad I met you, Julie. And I'm glad we won together. It wouldn't have been as much fun without you." He suppressed a yawn. "So what do you want to do to celebrate? We could go get breakfast. Any restaurants you'd like to buy?"

"I want to get some sleep," she said. "We have a big day ahead of us."

Blake snapped his fingers as if to acknowledge defeat. His grin was incorrigible, but he let the teasing drop. "How long before we have to be at the television station?"

She checked the digital clock on the radio. "Five hours. That'll give me three hours to sleep and two hours to get ready."

He yawned and stretched. "This'll be fun. Telling everybody how it feels to be stinking rich."

"Should be easy enough."

"Yeah."

He took her hand and held it. It felt more natural than it should have, and no alarms went off in her head. They were quiet, both lost in dreamy smiles and contented memories of the night as they drove to Julie's house. Once there, Blake pulled into her driveway and cut off his headlights. "So you're sure you don't want to spend any of that tonight, huh?"

"Definitely," she whispered. He made no move to get out of the car.

"Well," he whispered, leaning toward her, "I had a really good time tonight. You're fun to be around. Even when there's no sweepstakes ticket involved."

He moved closer, and she didn't move away. Their lips met in a sweet union that made her heart race. Gratitude welled up inside her, and she wondered if it was really possible for her loneliness to end at the same time as her financial problems. Maybe God really had brought them together. Maybe there was a chance . . .

A light flashed and they jumped apart. Two photographers stood at the window, aiming and flashing, recording their kiss. Just as Blake opened the door to confront them, two cars screeched to a halt at the curb, and more photographers jumped out. "We've got to go inside," he said quickly. "It's about to get crazy. Come on!"

"No!" Julie said, stopping him before he got out of the car. "You can't come in. They'll blow it all out of proportion. Especially after that picture they just took. I have to go in alone."

"But I can't leave you here with a throng of madmen outside your door!"

"I'll be fine," she said. "They want a story, that's all. They're harmless enough. Besides, Aunt Myrtle is just across the street. She'll probably have the police here in fifteen minutes."

He surveyed the crowd growing around the car, bulbs flashing. "All right," he said with a sigh. "I have to go home and change sooner or later. Are you sure you'll be all right?"

"I'll be fine," she said, shading her eyes

from the blinding flash of the bulbs. "I'll see you at the television station."

"Yeah. And Julie?"

She turned back to him.

"They're sending a limousine, so don't take the bus, okay?"

She giggled. "A limousine. Thanks, I would have forgotten. Bye."

"Bye."

She climbed out of the car and pushed through the shouting reporters and photographers and ran to her house. It wasn't until she was safely inside that she heard Blake's car starting up.

And she had to admit that he had been right. The best thing so far about winning the sweepstakes was that she'd met Blake Adcock.

CHAPTER FIVE

"Sweepstakes Sweethearts Win $20 Million!"

The headline on the front page of the Detroit newspaper was like cold water flung into a sleepy, groggy face.

"Sweepstakes sweethearts?" Julie cried aloud.

"Pardon?" asked the chauffeur in the front seat.

"Nothing," Julie said absently as her eyes dropped to the picture of Blake and her in an ecstatic clench as he swung her around. "I . . . I was just . . . never mind." Suddenly feeling queasy, she leaned forward in the spacious limo to the stack of morning papers. Her banker had given them to her when he had opened the bank early to take care of the wire transfer from New York. Moving the first offensive one off the stack, she glanced at the second.

"Lovers Split Ticket and $20 Million!"

was the next headline. The photo below it was of Blake and her with arms clamped around each other's waist as they laughed together and answered questions.

"Oh no," she said with a moan.

Reluctantly, she looked at the paper beneath it. "Sweepstakes Winners Talk Marriage." Beneath the headline was a photo of the two of them in his car, engaged in the kiss that never should have happened.

She brought her hands to her face and covered it, as if that could protect her from the wrath of her aunt who lived across the street from her. "Sweethearts?" Myrtle Mahogan would ask in an accusing, hurt voice. Then she would tell Julie how humiliated she was to see her "little Julie" being mauled by a man Myrtle hadn't even met. It wouldn't matter that Julie had won a fortune. To Myrtle, the imagined shame and disgrace would be much more tangible than the concept of lifelong wealth.

The car that was almost as big as Julie's bedroom pulled in front of the television station, where in moments Julie would be hooked up to an earplug and broadcast via satellite to a network morning show in New York. The added coverage would force Blake and her into some sort of artificial relationship that would either ruin the delicate feelings they had begun to feel for each other, or propel them into something much faster than either of them could handle.

There was only one thing to do, she thought as the chauffeur opened her door for her. She would have to dispel the myth of the Sweepstakes Sweethearts as soon as possible. She decided national television was as good a place to start as any.

Dressed in a blue suit, Blake sat in the television station, where the employees skittered around him like trained penguins, bringing him coffee, doughnuts, and croissants. Chuckling within, he fought the urge to demand a shoeshine and a snack of grapes, hand-fed to him by some awestruck beauties. He didn't think he had quit smiling since the night before, and the way he figured it, he was probably going to be smiling for the next twenty years — or at least until his money ran out.

He checked the diamond cuff links he hadn't been able to afford when he bought them and, finding they were still shining like the pleasure in his eyes, reached to the makeup table in front of him, to the newspapers that had been brought in while he was being made up for the lights. Glancing over the headlines, he began to laugh. Well, there were worse images a millionaire could have, he thought. If he was going to be labeled "sweetheart" to anyone, he could do far worse than Julie Sheffield.

He grinned as he looked over the pictures, recalling the ecstasy when he'd swung her around and the euphoria as they'd answered questions. But when he came to the picture of them kissing in his car, his smile faded.

Wait a minute, he thought. This was taking things a little far. He had known the press had taken those pictures of them in a clench, but he'd credited them with a little more taste than to splash them all over the papers. How would this look for Julie? She would be humiliated and embarrassed. And he didn't blame her.

A commotion arose across the studio as the subject of his thoughts entered and was engulfed in a crowd of well-wishers. Quickly, he dropped the papers in the trash can and searched for something to cover them with. A sign beside the mirror that read Keep Smiling was all he found, so he tore it down and stuffed it in the wastebasket to hide the papers, in the remote chance that Julie hadn't seen them yet. Then he stood up to wait for her.

Fashion photographers would have killed to get her for their magazine covers if they saw her today, he thought as he watched her smiling and talking with the camera crew. She was attired in a loose-fitting dress, belted at the waist, and it had an original and untrendy style. It was probably one of her own designs, he thought. The purple background of the printed cloth was a nice foil for the blended swirls of yellow, green, red, and black. The silky fringe of her blonde hair teased close to her long eyelashes as she dipped her head shyly and answered questions.

Their eyes met across the room, but hers darted away. Her face flushed the color of young rose petals, and he knew that she had seen the papers. Now she would be uncomfortable just talking to him, he thought with a surge of anger.

His dazed excitement over the money temporarily assuaged, he ambled toward her, hands in his pockets. Was it just the way she looked that was making his heart do an aerobic workout, he wondered, or was it the lady herself?

The crowd seemed to hush as he approached, as if everyone waited to hear the first exchange between the now-famous "sweethearts."

"Hi," he said.

She swallowed and glanced away. "Hi."

"Did you get any sleep?"

"No," she said. "Too many reporters outside. You?"

"Too excited."

"Yeah," she whispered.

Feeling as clumsy as a nerd with the class beauty, Blake sought out the news director in the crowd. "When will we be on?"

"Not for thirty minutes or more," the man said.

"Then could I have a moment alone with Julie?"

"Certainly," the director obliged, and everyone smiled with approval. "Right this way to the greenroom."

The porcelain tightness that passed over Julie's face told Blake that he'd made a mistake. She didn't want to be alone with him, and she especially didn't appreciate his asking for privacy in front of the entire staff of the television station.

The greenroom wasn't green at all but a bright blue that did nothing to calm the nerves of those waiting to be televised. Soft, overstuffed couches filled the room, and there was a wet bar in the corner and a monitor on the wall so they could watch what was going on in the studio. Julie went in and stood awkwardly in the room. Blake knew that for every step forward he had made with her, the morning papers had pushed him ten steps back.

The news director reached for the door to close it, but Blake stopped him. "Leave it open," he said. "We don't need that much privacy."

"Sure?" the man asked.

"Absolutely."

When the man had left them alone, Blake turned to Julie. "What's the matter?" he asked.

"I'm tired," she said. "I'm not used to getting a lot of sleep, but I usually get some."

"Yeah, me too."

There was more on Julie's face than fatigue, Blake thought as he watched her drop her clutch purse on the couch and flop down. She slipped her finger through one of her gold earrings. "Do you know what they're saying about us?"

He lowered to the arm of the couch across from her. "Yeah. Afraid I do."

"Well, it isn't true!"

Blake chuckled. "I know it isn't."

"Well, *they* don't know it." She took a deep breath and rubbed her hand over her forehead. "And my aunt doesn't know it."

"Julie, I'm sorry. I shouldn't have kissed you last night. I should have known —"

Julie nodded, as if she agreed with him.

84

"And you shouldn't have teased about marriage, Blake. That was like throwing a bone to a pack of starving dogs, and now they want even more. But I was as much at fault as you for the kiss. I didn't exactly fight you off."

He was silent for a moment as he recalled the kiss that had gotten them into so much trouble. A sly grin crept across his face at the memory, and he turned to a soda machine in the corner, as if studying the selection of beverages.

"What's so funny?" she asked.

He gave a shrug. "Nothing."

"No, tell me. I want to know."

He turned back to her and leaned against the machine. "I was just thinking that no matter how much it was blown out of proportion, I think if I had it to do all over —" he rubbed the smile on his face — "I'd still kiss you."

"Blake . . ."

He shrugged helplessly. "Sorry, but you asked."

Julie dipped her face and studied the paisley pattern of the carpet, fighting the flattery that nevertheless seemed to calm her. "Well, we have to fix this. We have to make sure that the reporters have nothing else to go on. In fact, we should probably go out of our way to make it clear that we're not involved."

Blake slid his hands into his pockets and paced to the window, glanced out, then turned back to her. "What if we did the opposite? What if we gave them what they wanted until it was old news and they left us alone?"

"Absolutely not," she said adamantly. "I don't want another failed romance to wind up in the Detroit gossip columns."

"Another?" he asked. "Has this happened before?"

Julie closed her eyes. "Forget I said that. I just meant that I don't like to play games."

"I'm not asking you to. We don't have to do anything. All we have to do is smile at each other now and then — be ourselves — and they'll have a field day with it."

"That's why we have to go as far to the opposite as we can. We can't smile at each other, Blake, and we can't touch each other, and we can't be in the same car together or the same house. We've got to tell these people that we didn't even meet until the night before last and that there is absolutely nothing between us!"

"Julie, it'll just make us more mysterious. They'll hound us until they have something. This is the kind of story people love."

Julie got up. "I don't care! It's my life we're talking about! My reputation!" She took a breath, as if trying to calm herself. "Maybe I should invent a boyfriend. Or you could tell them you're engaged."

Blake leaned back against the windowsill, playing along. "You mean lie?"

"Well, you didn't mind lying last night about the clocks. Just a little lie."

"Yeah, that could work. I could bring Lola on TV with me. She's had me pegged as husband material for a while now."

"Lola?" Julie asked, a surprised sparkle of jealousy in her eyes that was not lost on Blake.

"Yes. She's a little brassy, of course, but I like her free spirit. Maybe you could lend her one of your classy dresses to wear, since most of her wardrobe is suitable only for the stage."

"The stage? What is she? A singer?"

"No, Lola's a little tone-deaf." He chuckled, then shrugged. "I guess I could get her on the news with me later today. It would certainly dispel the rumor that you and I are involved. That is, if you're sure that's what you want."

Julie stared at him for a moment, but slowly her gaping mouth closed. A soft grin pulled at her lips as she regarded him. "You aren't dating anybody named Lola."

"Sure I am," he said.

"You don't even know anyone named Lola," she challenged. She studied him, as if uncertain. A smile broke across his face.

He flung out his arms dramatically. "All right, you caught me. But I'll be glad to go out and find someone for this afternoon's broadcast if it'll make you feel better."

In spite of herself, Julie seemed relieved. "I don't think that will be necessary. As long as we don't flirt, I think we can manage."

Blake closed the distance between them. "But see, that's the hard part," he said in a low voice. "By the way, have I told you what a knockout you are this morning?"

A rosy blush painted her cheeks. "Thanks."

"That one of your designs?"

"Yes."

"Nice," he whispered.

She studied her purse for a moment, tracing the pattern with a finger as she searched for a change of subject. "So, did they wire your money all right?"

"Yeah. Four hundred thousand, to start. The bank opened early for me. Funny how accommodating they can be when you have money. They even gave me a digital camera for making a deposit over two thousand dollars. The way I see it, they owed me about two hundred cameras. What did you get?"

"A deposit slip," she said. "I would have liked a camera."

"I'll give you mine," he said.

She laughed softly. "I couldn't believe it. It felt strange getting a deposit slip for almost four hundred thousand dollars!"

"Cheapskates," Blake teased. "I thought they'd give it to us all at once."

"I'm glad they didn't. Just imagine getting a check for four hundred thousand dollars every year for twenty-five years."

"Yeah, well, the IRS is getting a pretty big check every year for twenty-five years too."

"Render unto Caesar what is Caesar's. You won't hear me complaining."

Blake laughed. "Me, either. I can scrape by on four hundred thou a year, even minus the taxes. If they'd just set me loose so I could spend it."

Julie went to the window and looked out. Her eyes lost their dreaminess and took on a practical glint. "I guess I should postpone my fashion show. If I had more time, I could do it up really nice. I'm going to quit my job today so I have more time to work on it."

"You're going to quit?" he asked.

"Yeah," she said. "I was only working as a

89

waitress to support myself until I could get my designer business off the ground. I don't have to do that now. I just hope the mall will work with me on another date for the show. I had to do some pretty fast tap dancing to make them agree to it in the first place."

Blake was behind her before she knew it. His hands closed over her shoulders, and he looked over her head, out the window, seeing worlds farther than the brick building in their view. "Julie, sweetheart, do you hear yourself? You put a mint in the bank this morning and you're worried about whether the mall will let you do your fashion show. You can afford to buy the mall. You can have that show anywhere, anytime you want."

Julie looked over her shoulder at him, and the truth of his words seemed to dawn in her eyes. "You're right."

"Then forget about it and just have fun for a while. You'll never win ten million again."

She turned around to face him, her big, innocent eyes meeting his; she smiled in a way that only he, a fellow winner, could understand. It held the suppression and the ecstasy of disbelief . . . and the beginnings of belief.

And it made his heart do drumrolls.

"How am I going to make it through live television if I don't have you to prop me up?" he whispered.

"No touching," she maintained, though the mesmerized look on her face told him she didn't mean it.

"We can't even hold hands?"

"We *especially* can't hold hands."

He brushed the hair out of her eyes. "But what if we really did want to get involved? What if we really wanted to make all those headlines come true?"

"*If* that were the case," she whispered noncommittally, her eyes sparkling like morning sun, "we'd just have to do our hand-holding in secret."

His face brightened. "In secret, huh? I like it."

"I said *if*."

A grin captured one side of his mouth. "I heard what you said," he whispered.

A knock sounded, and they leapt apart, as if they'd been caught doing something more than just smiling at each other.

"We're about to go on," the news director said. "We need to get a sound check."

Blake's hands plunged into his pockets. Julie's wrapped around her purse. Together they walked to the set, staying a few feet apart. But the director had other plans. The tiny bench they were seated on was meant for only one, but he insisted that they sit there together. "So we can get you both on the screen at once," he explained. "Just cozy up together."

So they made the most of it, sitting awkwardly, shoulder to shoulder, until the director insisted that Julie lean more into Blake. She did as she was told, but Blake felt her stiffness and knew that if she hadn't been so nervous she would have been protesting loudly.

They inserted their earplugs and clipped on their mikes. Near the camera was a monitor, where they could see the host of the show talking with an actor. "We're following *him?*" she whispered.

Blake sensed a note of awe in her voice. "I'll bet *he* never made ten million in one night," he mumbled into her ear.

The actor's interview ended, and a soup commercial followed. "Stand by," the director said. "New York wants to do a sound check. Say something."

Blake took the gauntlet. "That wasn't her in the car with me, Aunt Myrtle. It was Lola. The photographers just superimposed Julie's head over the body."

Julie slapped at his chest, incredulous, though a smile did battle with her glower.

"Blake, stop it. If you say anything like that on the air, I promise I'll get up and leave."

Blake grabbed her hand, wrestling her still. "Yes, Aunt Myrtle, they forced us into that kiss. The photographers cut out the terrorists holding guns to our heads."

"Blake, I'll kill you!" Julie hissed.

"Perfect," some laughing, New York voice said in their earpieces. "That's exactly how we want you to play it."

Julie's smile faded. "Play it?" She looked at Blake. "I mean it," she whispered, as if to keep them from hearing. "I don't want to feed this fire. Please . . ."

He held his fingers up in a Boy Scout salute. "I promise. I won't embarrass you."

"Stand by," the director said again, this time chuckling.

Julie tried to find some stock in Blake's promise. But the memory of his cheating with her clocks and playing into the press's hands with talk of marrying their fortunes reeled back through her mind.

They waited, tense, as the theme music played and the host mentioned that it was half past the hour. And then, before they could catch their breath or wipe their palms, they were on the air.

"Sweepstakes sweethearts" were the first

words out of the host's mouth, and Julie thought she was going to be sick. When he'd finished telling the viewing audience the unique reason for their splitting the ticket, he turned to the camera. "Julie, Blake, how do you feel today?"

"Like ten million bucks," Blake said.

Julie threw him a look, wondering if he'd spent his three hours alone that morning figuring out that line.

The man laughed. "Julie?"

"I feel great," she said.

Blake threw her a look that asked if that was really the best she could do.

"Any further thoughts of pooling the winnings and making it legal?"

Julie wondered if her face was searing in living color. "Uh, I think we should clear something up," she cut in before Blake could answer. "This 'sweepstakes sweetheart' business is a little too much hype. The fact is that we met only two nights ago, the night he gave me half of his ticket."

"But there must have been something there if he gave you half of a twenty-million-dollar sweepstakes ticket."

"It was a tip," she explained.

"You must be some waitress!"

"It was the uniform," Blake interjected. "I

have a weakness for women in uniform."

Julie gasped and glared at him.

Blake winced, waiting for her to strike him. The crew erupted with raucous laughter.

"Tell me," the host said, thankfully changing the subject, "what do you plan to do with the money, Julie?"

Julie cleared her throat and tried to regroup, telling herself it would all be over soon. "I'm a fashion designer, and I plan to invest in my business, but I haven't had time to think of specifics yet."

"She designed what she's wearing," Blake added. "Isn't that a knockout?"

Julie ground her heel into his foot, out of the camera's view. Blake flinched and set his teeth.

"Fantastic," the man said. "Ten million ought to get you well on your way. What about you, Blake?"

"I don't know," he said in a strained voice. Julie lifted her heel, and he breathed with relief and glanced at her with an expression that one would wear in the presence of a lunatic. Then, bringing his eyes back to the camera, he added, "Maybe I'll buy a castle or something. A couple of pinball machines. Who knows?"

"Who knows, indeed," the host said, as if

those three words held the wisdom of a whole council of wise men. "Are you planning any grand celebration together? Besides the one we've already read about?"

"I promised to take her to New York," Blake blurted, and Julie's eyes flashed again. Fearing another dig into his foot, he quickly covered himself. "Really, Julie meant what she said. We aren't involved. We actually just met night before last, and we know very little about each other. As a matter of fact, I've been seeing someone else."

"And he's not my type at all," Julie threw in.

"And I don't generally like blondes," he added.

On that ridiculous note the host thanked them and broke for the weather, and Julie and Blake remained motionless on their seat.

"If I had a gun," she mumbled through compressed lips, "I'd shoot you right here on national television."

"Julie, I'm sorry. Those things just slipped out."

Julie stood up, jerking the earplug and mike off, and raged down at him. "Just slipped out? The bit about New York? How could you?"

"I just told the truth. I get all stammery

96

when I lie. You didn't want me to get all stammery on national television, did you?"

Julie groaned viciously and started off the set, and Blake limped after her. "And why'd you have to crush my foot that way? I probably have a fracture in the shape of your heel."

"That isn't my heel print, Blake. It's teeth marks from ramming your foot into your mouth every time you opened it!"

"Julie, it's no big deal," he said, hobbling faster. "I'll do better next time."

"Yeah." She swung back to face him. "I just bet you will. You'll just stiffen your spine and stand up for my honor and reputation, won't you, even though you don't generally like blondes!"

Blake nodded innocently. "I'll make Aunt Myrtle proud of you. And just for the record, I made up the bit about not liking blondes."

Biting her lip, Julie crashed her heel into his other foot. He yelped and grabbed it, hopping as she stalked away. "Are you crazy?" he shouted after her.

She turned at the door and wagged a finger at him. "Yes! The next time you decide to let some innuendo about me 'slip,'" she said, "remember that I have other shoes at home. Sharper ones!"

She was thankful Blake had the good sense to stay quiet as she hurried out the door.

CHAPTER SIX

Julie slept hard that night and most of the next day. It was dark when she finally emerged from her bedroom. She peeked out the window and saw that some reporters still lurked out in front of her yard. She had unplugged her phone so it wouldn't wake her; now she plugged it in so she could call her aunt Myrtle. The phone began ringing instantly. Too tired to talk to another reporter, she unplugged it again to stop the ringing. Her machine blinked urgently, and when she rewound the tape, she saw that it was full.

She listened through ten messages; then a familiar voice startled her. It was Jack, the designer she'd once been in love with, the one who had betrayed her. He had heard of her win and wanted to congratulate her. He thought they might have dinner, if she would call him back.

Julie sighed and stared down at the phone.

She supposed she was more attractive to him now that she was rich. The thought brought back sad memories of rejection and pain. He had shaken her life after their last meeting a year ago, when he'd fired her from his design studio. No, she wouldn't call him now, she thought. His business had suffered when she'd left and taken her talent with her, even after he'd spread word that every design Julie had created had been stolen from him. When she heard of his lag in profits, Julie determined that God had taken vengeance. But the scars on her heart hadn't healed, and she was not about to expose them to Jack again.

Wrenching her thoughts away, she went to the kitchen, looked in the refrigerator, and sighed when she saw how empty it was. *I'm a multimillionaire,* she thought, *and I don't even own a carton of milk.* Right now she would have given a whole year's payment for a pint of yogurt. She was afraid to go to the grocery store for fear she'd never get out alive when the press and well-wishers surrounded her. But she'd bet it wasn't that way for Blake. He was probably ordering everything in.

She laughed lightly. They were so different, yet she couldn't stop thinking about him. She would have to stop, though, because the last thing in the world she needed now was to fall head over heels in love with him, only to find later that it couldn't work. Then the whole world would know about the split. It would be worse than last time, when everyone had watched and waited for her reaction to Jack's callous behavior and his contention that she was washed up as a designer. But *everyone* in the fashion circles had been only fractional compared to *everyone* who was following her alleged affair with Blake through the media.

The doorbell rang. Julie cringed and refused to answer it. A hard knock followed.

Was Blake having these problems, too? she wondered. Or was he enjoying all the attention?

If only the press would get tired and leave, she could concentrate on her work. She wondered if she'd see Blake again, now that they had nothing throwing them together. The thought of not seeing him again disturbed her, and she leaned back in her old, lopsided recliner and closed her eyes. She felt herself relax as she realized the worst part was over. There were no more interviews, at least for a while.

A purposeful knock sounded at the window on the side of her living room, and she sprang up and sucked in a breath. *A photographer,* she thought. He had found a way to get past her fence!

The knock sounded again, louder this time, and she rushed out of her recliner and looked around the room for a weapon. Her eyes fell on a seam ripper on the coffee table, and she grabbed it. It was the first time a photographer had actually knocked on her window. He must be pretty desperate — and a little crazed — if he was willing to do that.

Holding her seam ripper out in front of her as if it were the weapon that could save her, she slowly stepped toward the window. This was it, she thought. It had gone too far, and she was going to put a stop to it!

Gritting her teeth, she stepped beside the window and took a few deep breaths for courage. She didn't care what the papers said about her after this. She'd had enough, and she was going to make sure that this reporter didn't get away without a few of his seams ripped!

Slowly she reached her hand under the curtain and threw back the lock. Then, as quickly as she could manage, she flung open the window and closed her eyes as she thrust forward the measly weapon.

"Julie, no!" came a strangled voice. A hand

reached out to grab her arm as a body came through the window and thudded to the floor.

Wrestling free as she realized her seam ripper wouldn't do the trick, she reached for a lamp and swung it high in the air.

"Don't kill me. I give!" the man said in a high-pitched whisper. "It's me, Julie!"

Julie stepped back from the window and flicked on the lamp she clutched in her hand. The face of Blake Adcock winced up at her.

CHAPTER SEVEN

"Blake, what are you doing here?"

Blake gave her a haggard look, but that familiar grin broke through his scowl. "I can't talk right now," he said with a groan. "I'm wounded. Are you going to help me up, or do you plan to take a few more stabs?"

Julie set the lamp down and kicked a pile of laundry out of the way. "Did I hurt you?"

"Almost." He stood up and checked the contents of a loaded pillowcase he carried. "Luckily those clothes on your floor broke my fall. And the ice pick — or whatever it is — only caused a minor flesh wound."

"It's a seam ripper," Julie informed him.

"A seam ripper," Blake repeated. "Terrific." He showed her the scratch on his hand. She hadn't even broken the skin.

Julie grabbed a sock off the floor and used it to pat the scratch.

Blake jerked back. "Julie, I don't mean to

insult you, but I'd rather not have my wounds attended to with a dirty sock."

"It isn't dirty," she said. "That pile is clean laundry. I haven't had time to fold it yet. Now give me your hand." Reluctantly, Blake extended it. "So how did you get over my new fence without getting hurt?"

Blake glanced down at his torn jeans and the scratch on his leg. "I didn't. Take it from me, that fence is effective."

Julie assessed the damage and gave him an exasperated look. "Are you crazy?"

"Hey, I had a security fence put in today. I thought I had it figured out after I climbed over mine. No one even saw me leave. I walked to a pay phone and called a cab, and he dropped me off on the street behind here."

"Why did you do all that?"

"Because I wanted to see you."

He looked at her through the dim, flickering circle of light cast by the lamp. She felt suddenly self-conscious about her hair inching out of its binding. His voice dropped in pitch. "You said that we'd have to do our hand-holding in secret. If we hadn't won gazillions together, we'd be on a dinner date with my coffee table money. Right out in the open. You know it's true."

"I don't know any such thing."

"Face it. You're a snob. If I weren't a zil-lionaire, you'd go out with me."

"No, never," she whispered. His lips were much too close, and he smelled of winter-green.

He grinned, not believing a word. "Sure?" he asked. "You liked me that first night. I know you did."

"I was trying to get a tip."

"Yeah, that's you. Miss Mercenary. But even if you were after a tip, I liked you. I would have had you head over heels for me by now if it weren't for the money."

He was too close, and her heart was pounding too hard. She couldn't help the grin tugging at her lips. He made her laugh when she didn't want to. She feared she had already fallen for him.

"So what do we do now?" she asked.

He cocked his brows. "I brought food," he said. "From the looks of your refrigerator the other night, I gathered you don't have food in the house, and I figured you wouldn't go out to shop. So I decided to feed you. I brought a picnic."

He reached into the pillowcase and pulled out a tablecloth and spread it on the living room floor. She fell to her knees, giggling. "You brought everything?"

He shrugged. "I would have brought it in

something more romantic than a pillowcase, but I didn't think I could sneak in effectively with a basket." He reached in and pulled out an elaborate brass candleholder. *"Voila!"* He pulled out a candle and set it in the holder. "And now, to set the mood . . ." He reached into his pocket and withdrew a match, then lit the candle. "Ah," he said when the flame caught and lit her face with a faint golden hue. "I knew you'd be beautiful in candlelight."

She swallowed. "Blake . . ."

He set the candle on the tablecloth and pulled out the food, grinning at the unsettled look on her face. "Peanut butter and jelly," he said. "It was all I had."

"It's my favorite," she said, sitting down. She took half a sandwich and bit into it. "Crunchy," she said with a smile.

He sat also and regarded her for a moment. "You're very easy to please," he said. "You know, my mother said I should snap you up before some fortune hunter does."

Her eyes laced with amusement. "Your mother said that? I never thought of you as having a mother."

"Did you think I was born in a test tube?"

"Guess I just never considered it."

"Maybe you thought such a *manly* man didn't need a mom."

"No, everybody needs a mom. I miss mine. She died five years ago."

"I'm sorry." Blake's eyes took on a sudden grief, as if he'd known her mother.

Julie looked at her bare feet. "No, it's okay. She was suffering. Cancer. But I have a lot of peace because Mom found Christ just before she died. She was in a Christian hospice, and the dear woman who ran it won her to Christ, so she had a happy ending. I owe a lot to the Spring Street Hospice Center. I'm looking forward to giving them a fat donation."

"Maybe I will too," he said. Julie watched as he pulled a can of Sprite and two plastic cups out of the pillowcase. He divided the pop into both cups and handed her one. "To our money," he whispered. "May it bring great happiness."

She watched him drink. "How is the money going to bring you happiness?" she asked.

He ran his finger around the rim of his cup. "It's going to get my business going, for one thing."

Their knees touched as they sat cross-legged, and they leaned toward each other as if some magnetic force drew them together. "How? I thought your business depended on your friend Paul. If his business is floundering, how will your money help?"

"I'm going to help him," he said. "I'm going to give him the money he needs to get back on his feet."

"Bad idea," Julie said. "He didn't manage his own money well. How do you know he can manage yours?"

"He will," Blake said.

"I know you mean well," she said, "but it might just ruin your friendship. Believe me. I've been in business with someone I cared about before."

"The designer you mentioned? The one in the gossip columns?"

"Yeah."

Blake reached over and his hand tightened over hers. "What happened?"

Julie ran the fingers of her free hand through her ponytail. "He got jealous of my designs, fired me and humiliated me, slandered me publicly, then hired a new young designer with less talent. It was a much safer relationship for him."

"Oh." Blake studied her hand with a scowl. "I'm sorry."

"It's okay," she whispered. She took a deep breath and reached for her sandwich, trying to seem unaffected. "He's suddenly interested again, now that I have money.

Thinks I'm a fool. Anyway, my point is that when it comes to business, you should stay as far away from people you care about as you can. I learned that the hard way."

Blake's face was solemn, and his eyes glistened. "Then you and I won't do business together. We'll keep it strictly personal."

Once again, she fought the grin on her face. "But we have to think. Why are we attracted to each other? Because of the money? Because we treat each other like human beings when everyone else treats us like we cured cancer?"

"We liked each other before all that, Julie. God brought us together. Let's just remember that." He kissed her hand, making her heart jolt. "But I don't intend to get to know you by scaling your fence every night. I've decided it's time for me to keep my promise to you."

"What promise?"

"To take you to New York."

Julie caught her breath. "No, Blake. That's a bad idea."

"Couldn't be," he said, combing his fingers through her hair. "I'm just suggesting we go for the day. Manhattan is a great place to spend time together and find out what we really feel for each other — without the media to draw conclusions for us. I mean, think about it. With all the celebrities and hotshots there, we're two of the littlest fish in the sea. Nobody will even notice us."

"I'm not going to New York with you," she argued. "I can't."

"Yes, you can."

"What will people say?"

"They'll say, 'Where'd they go?' We'll leave secretly."

She sat paralyzed for a moment, considering it. No phones, no photographers, no interviews. If they could, indeed, get away without anyone knowing, she might have some peace. And some time with Blake.

"When would we leave?" she asked.

"In just a few hours — before dawn. If we leave that early, the press won't see us," he said, his eyes sparkling as if she'd already consented.

"But what about airline tickets?"

"Leave that to me. You just start digging for your walking shoes, and I'll use your phone to line everything up."

Julie didn't move just yet. "*If* I go, I'd pay my own way. And we have to behave appropriately. I don't want to give Christ a black eye by making it look like I'm some high-rolling 'sweepstakes sweetheart' who's too intimate too fast with some guy I met in a restaurant just two nights ago."

"Too intimate too fast?" he asked, amused. "How do you figure that?"

"We kissed on page one, okay?" she reminded him.

"But I didn't mean to kiss you on page one. I thought I was kissing you on page three."

She tried to bite back her laughter and shoved him. "I'm serious!"

"So am I! I'll be a perfect gentleman, Julie," he promised. "I want to honor Christ, too. And I always keep my word."

Reluctantly, Julie agreed to go.

It was well after midnight when Blake called Paul and reminded him of every favor he'd ever done for him.

"I think mine tops all of yours, Adcock," his friend said in a groggy voice. "I gave you the twenty-million-dollar ticket, remember?"

"Oh yeah, there's that," Blake agreed. "But I need one more little bitty favor, buddy."

"What little bitty favor would that be?" Paul asked.

"I want you to pull some of those strings of yours and hire a luxurious private plane to take Julie and me to New York."

"Now? Do you know what time it is?"

"Yes, but the lady wants to go before dawn. You wouldn't let a little thing like sleep stand in the way of a favor for a pal, would you?"

"A private plane," Paul said with resignation. "And someone to fly it, I presume?"

"Yeah, that would be nice," Blake said. "But I want it to be so discreet that even the pilot doesn't know about it."

"The pilot has to know about it," Paul said. "Unless you intend to fly the plane."

"Oh yeah. Well, just tell him to keep quiet. I have a little lady here whose reputation is already in dire straits. We seem to be a volatile combination, at least in the papers, and I don't want any more explosions."

"Got it," Paul said. "I know just the plane. But it'll cost you. Think you can come up with the bread?"

"I think I can manage to find a few extra bills lying around," Blake said. "How long will it take you?"

"Two hours," Paul said. "Meet me at the express gate at the airport, and we'll have you on your way."

"We'll be there," Blake said.

"So I finally get to meet her, huh?"

"Yeah. But don't get your hopes up. The lady only dates new money these days."

"As opposed to borrowed money?" Paul

laughed.

"Hey, I am not giving you a loan," Blake said. "It's a gift. As you just pointed out, you gave me the ticket."

"I'd rather consider it an investment," Paul corrected. "One that you won't regret. And if God had intended for me to keep that ticket, I would have. So pack your bags and meet me in two hours. If I see any reporters lurking around —"

"Create a diversion," Blake finished. "Take an employee hostage or something."

"You got it, buddy."

It didn't take long for Julie to change into a versatile dress that would work for the nicest of places as well as the most relaxed. When it was time, they called a cab to meet them two blocks away and made their way quietly out her back gate. Julie didn't remember when she had ever had more fun as they stole through the night to the waiting cab.

Paul was waiting for them at the express gate at the small private airport. Julie observed the blond hunk whose disability was only apparent by the wheelchair in which he sat. The man reached for Julie's hand when Blake introduced them and pressed a kiss on it that told her his charm more than compensated for his problems.

"You look even lovelier in person than you do on television," he said.

She gave him a skeptical grin. At this late hour, she knew she probably had dark circles under her eyes. She turned to Blake. "Your friend just lost all his credibility. I'll never believe another word he says."

"I'm wounded," Paul said, a hand over his heart. "She doesn't believe me."

"Take it from me," Blake said, "her verbal wounds are much better than the ones she inflicts with her seam ripper and the heels of her shoes. So where's the plane?"

"Over there," Paul said, pointing out the large window to a plane warming its engines on the dark runway. "That jet over there."

Blake's grin was instant. "Perfect."

"Perfect?" Julie asked, astounded. "That's just for us? It'll cost a fortune!"

"We *have* a fortune. Two of them."

"Not for long if we spend it this recklessly." She turned back to Paul, who watched her with laughing eyes. "Couldn't we take a Cessna or something?"

He shrugged. "I could've gotten a crop duster, but the man said he wanted luxury."

"But . . . a jet? I don't know."

"I'm paying for this part," Blake said, taking her by the arm and leading her to the door. "And it's already arranged, so please try to grin and bear it." He turned back to Paul, who rolled behind them. "Poor thing. She just has to endure so much."

"Be kind to her, Adcock. Every now and then dress her in a burlap sack and feed her cold cereal so she'll feel a little more secure."

"You two are impossible," she said. "I'm not a cheapskate. It's just that I don't like to spend money."

"I see the difference," Blake said. "Don't you, Paul?"

Paul nodded adamantly. "It's very clear to me."

"Oh, let's just go. I'll try to enjoy it without thinking about how many bolts of silk I could buy with this money."

"I'll buy you all the silk you want when we get back," Blake said as he pulled her out onto the tarmac. He bit his lip like a little boy trying to suppress his delight. "Oh, this is gonna be great!"

CHAPTER EIGHT

"This isn't an airplane; it's a hotel with wings!" Julie exclaimed when they had boarded the luxurious jet.

"Oh, don't exaggerate, Julie," Blake said. "It doesn't even have a swimming pool."

Julie gaped at him as he stepped inside as if he'd been raised there, dropped his duffel bag on the floor, and plopped down on a couch. "Blake, what has gotten into you? This isn't necessary. We could have taken a plane a tenth this size and it would have been fine."

With a flourish, he propped his feet on the coffee table and clasped his hands behind his head. "But I wanted to impress you."

Julie laughed and laid her big purse on the floor, kicked off her shoes, and stepped over them. "Impress *me?* I was impressed a few days ago when you couldn't even afford a tip!"

The exclamation struck Blake as funny. As if he couldn't contain the silly giddiness that was so apparent on his face, he began to laugh.

"Blake, what's so funny?" she asked, trying not to catch the laughter herself.

"I was just thinking," he chortled, "about how I couldn't even afford to put gas in my car a few days ago. . . ."

"And now you've rented *Air Force One*."

"Yeah. And if it flies well, I might even buy it."

Julie's face flushed, and she peered out the window to remind herself that they were still on the ground. "And if it doesn't fly well?"

Blake lifted a rugged brow. "You can swim, can't you?"

The plane began to roll down the runway, and Julie tumbled to the sofa as her hand slapped over her stomach. "I just hope the designer put as much attention into this thing's engine as he did into its carpeting."

"I don't know," Blake teased, examining the deep pile. "This is pretty nice carpeting."

It wasn't until they were in the air that Julie managed to loosen up. If the engine wasn't strong enough to support a bar and enough couches to fill a hotel lobby, they would have crashed by now, she reasoned. Besides, there was something to be said for the boyish enthusiasm Blake exuded.

"Why don't you go to sleep?" Blake asked when her spirits mellowed enough to make her pull up her feet onto the sofa.

"Can't," Julie said. "It isn't everyday I fly off to New York on a jet with a man I hardly know." She watched, smiling, as Blake sifted through a stack of brochures about New York. "I like Paul," she said. "Tell me about him. How did he become a paraplegic? Was he born that way?"

"Nope. In college he was our first-string tight end." He glanced up from the brochure. "I, of course, was the quarterback."

"Of course."

"Paul and I used to get into some real messes." Blake chuckled, as if the old days were spelled out on the pages of the flyer he was holding.

"So what happened to him?"

Blake's face sobered. "We were driving home for spring break our senior year, and an eighteen-wheeler ran us off the road." His voice dropped to an almost inaudible level as the memories flashed through his mind. "The car rolled a couple times. To make a long story short, Paul had a lot of injuries. I walked away, but he never walked again."

Julie straightened. "Oh, Blake. I'm so sorry."

He nodded and met her sympathetic eyes. "I felt guilty for years. I'd been driving, and I kept thinking that if he'd been driving, maybe his reflexes would have been sharper, or maybe I would have been hurt instead of him. But Paul is a Christian, and he trusts God's sovereignty. He really believes that it would have happened the same way no matter who had been driving. He never blamed me for a minute."

"No wonder he's been so good at helping disabled people."

"Yeah. He turned his handicap into an advantage and built his business out of his own frustrations. How many people do you know who could take something like that and make it into something positive?"

"So you wanted to be a part of it?" she observed softly.

"Sure. There are people who need those cars and vans I've designed and Paul wants to sell. It wouldn't be fair if he had to let it all go."

"And that's why you loaned him money."

"Just a little," Blake said defensively. "Just

enough to get him going again. I can afford it."

Those four words were becoming all too familiar. Julie stood up and felt the plane jerk as it hit an air pocket. She quickly dropped back down and hooked her seat belt. "Blake, I know you mean well when you say that, but even ten million dollars has to run out sooner or later. If you aren't careful, you're going to I-can-afford-it right back to where you started. We're only getting four hundred thousand a year, before taxes."

"Julie, you haven't got any idea how much money that is, do you?"

"Well, it isn't like I've had experience. I know it's more than my father ever saw in his entire lifetime. I know that if it's spent right, it can make life easier, more secure."

"It can make life fun!" he exclaimed. "And I'm going to show you as soon as we reach New York."

"Spending money has never been fun for me," she said.

"That's because you never had any before. You just wait. This'll be a ball."

"If I shop," she argued, "it will be for my business. For cloth and accessories and retailing ideas . . ."

"You need to resolve to spend it only on

things you don't need."

Julie breathed out a heavy sigh. "I could never do that." She set her hand on the window, as if she could reach through and grab a handful of cloud. "You know, my family was lucky to have food on the table. I always did all my shopping at Goodwill when I was growing up. But I tried to put things together with style, and pretty soon I started to like finding old clothes and setting trends with them. By the time I was in high school, I lost my image of the poor mill worker's daughter and became the dare-to-be-different queen. Just as one of my ideas would catch on, I'd try something else. I realized then that I could set trends, and I didn't need a fortune to do it. I can make women look good without looking cheap. They can be stylish and trendy, and still dress modestly. Even when Jack stole my designs, he didn't get the concept. He didn't understand about glorifying God with what you wear. All he knew was that the designs sold well."

"Did they keep selling well for him?"

"Not after he made his own changes to them. They bombed."

"Then God fought that battle for you. He's honoring what you do. Even the sweepstakes money may be God's way of telling you that he wants you to succeed."

"You think so?" she asked. "Because sometimes I wonder if it's not just a test. And if it is, I wonder if I'll pass."

"Test or reward," Blake said, "whatever it is, I intend to have fun with it."

The cab driver who took them to Times Square chattered incessantly in a language they couldn't understand, but when he pulled to the curb and let them out, Blake tipped him a hundred-dollar bill.

Julie gasped. "Blake! You accidentally gave that man a hundred dollars!"

"It wasn't an accident," he said against her ear, keeping his voice discreetly low.

"You can't go around tipping hundred-dollar bills!" she whispered.

"Want to bet?" he asked with a grin. He ushered her into a restaurant with white tablecloths and a maitre d' who looked as if he didn't approve of them. Blake gave him a hundred-dollar bill for a table.

"Why did you do that?" she asked. "It's not very crowded here!"

Blake grinned. "I just wanted to. It's fun."

Julie moaned and scanned the menu on the wall as the maitre d' checked for a table. "Look at these prices! And this is breakfast?" she whispered. "I can't eat here!"

"Why not?"

"Because I don't want to pay for this!"

"Then I'll pay for it."

"*You'll* be out of money by the time he gives us a bill!" she said.

"Julie, don't be ridiculous. We deserve a little —"

"You want to know what I deserve?" she asked, raising her voice. "I deserve an Egg McMuffin. That's all I need."

"Julie, you're acting like a pauper. You said you were going to loosen up and try to spend a little."

"Blake, I have very specific plans for my money. I don't need you making plans for me, thank you. I agreed to this trip because I needed to relax. How can I do that eating fifty-dollar eggs? You can stay here if you want," she said, "but I'm going to find a more practical place to have breakfast."

Like a teenage boy who had been dragged away from a wild day at the fair, Blake woefully followed her back to the busy sidewalk. "So much for that tip."

"Well, maybe next time you won't be so quick to do that. We could have eaten two really nice meals on that hundred dollars."

They reached a diner just across from the big television screen at the center of Times Square, and she threw up her hands. "See now? This is more like it."

"This is a mom-and-pop diner. Don't you want to try something more fun?"

"No, I don't. I'd just like to eat a normal-priced breakfast in peace, if you don't mind."

He followed her in and surreptitiously tipped the hostess a hundred dollars before she led them to a table by the window.

"That's much better," Julie said when they had been seated. "Now isn't this nice?"

"I should probably thank you," Blake said with a resigned sigh as he perused his menu. "Without you I'd probably be spending like there was no tomorrow."

"Would you be tipping thousand-dollar bills instead of hundreds? Come on, Blake. You're already spending like crazy, with or without me."

"I'm just having fun. And besides, it gives pleasure to others. What's wrong with that?" he said.

She drew in a deep breath and let it out in a rush. "I'm sorry," she said. "I'm just very tired. All this excitement and no sleep."

"Maybe coffee will perk you up."

As the waiter poured her coffee, Julie felt the energy seeping back into her already.

Blake couldn't get enough of observing

Julie's face as she finished her breakfast and watched the rush-hour activity on the sidewalk. Her eyes were huge as she seemed to take it all in. People flew past with purpose and direction in their strides, but their faces were strained and tense. Still, she took great joy in the famous area she had seen so often on television.

He sat watching her, remembering her sweet smile the night he'd met her in the restaurant. She only got more beautiful the longer he knew her. And that was unusual. Before, it had always seemed that women lost their appeal when the mystique wore off. There was always some fatal flaw in them.

It wasn't that Blake was a perfectionist when it came to women. He wasn't, really. It was just that he liked spontaneity, and it seemed his whole relationship with Julie had been based on just that. So far, she had none of the major flaws that had made him flee other women. There was no pretense with Julie. If anyone could keep his millionaire's feet on the ground from here on out, Julie could.

"So what are our plans for the day?" Julie asked after Blake had tipped the waiter a hundred dollars. She had started to protest again but then realized that the waiter probably needed the tip. A hundred-dollar tipper in her restaurant would have made her week.

He grinned. "I was just thinking of a cruise around New York Bay. It's only a few hours, and then we can come back and we can go to the garment district."

"A cruise around New York Bay!" she said. "That sounds wonderful." She waited at the table as he made a phone call. As he led her out, she felt that thrilling twitter of anticipation. A cruise around Manhattan Island with Blake Adcock was about the most romantic thing she could think of.

That twitter of anticipation, however, turned to a jolt of disbelief an hour later when Blake led her to the dock where the boat awaited them. The staff were lined up as if they were greeting royalty, and Julie was baffled to see that they were the only passengers. "I thought this was a regularly scheduled cruise boat," she said.

"It is," Blake said.

"Then why are we alone?"

"Because I rented the whole thing just for us."

As the boat's engine began to roll, Julie realized she should have known.

CHAPTER NINE

As they cruised around the bay, Julie drank in the sights of Manhattan and the sight of the Statue of Liberty and the droves of people lined up to get in. Blake drank in the sight of Julie taking in the sight of Manhattan. Watching her enjoy it was already one of the highlights of his day.

"It's a beautiful day," Julie acknowledged as they returned to the dock. "I'll never forget it."

Blake pulled her head against his shoulder and stroked her hair, watching the way it glided through his fingers. "Beautiful," he agreed.

"Thank you," she whispered.

He dropped a kiss on her temple. "My pleasure. Let's go find a nice place to eat lunch," he said.

She wondered what "nice" meant to him. Another class-conscious maitre d', or was he going to buy out an entire restaurant?

"I'm not that hungry," she said. "I think I'd just like to get a salad somewhere."

"Julie, I know you're hungry. You just don't want to spend any money. But loosen up," he urged gently. "This is fun. It's as bad to hoard money as it is to blow it."

"Blake, watching money go down the tube is not fun for me. It upsets me terribly. That 'fun' could support the Spring Street Hospice Center for years."

"The money isn't going down the tubes. Think of it as a contribution to the New York economy."

"New York's economy is just fine."

He tugged her into another restaurant with white tablecloths and a snobbish maitre d', tipped him as he had the others, and got them a table. She had that look on her face when they sat down.

"Okay, if it makes you feel better, from now on I'll be as frugal as a monk."

"Sure you will," she said skeptically. His charm seemed to be working, sapping the irritation right out of her. "Are you telling me you've abandoned your wish for a Jacuzzi for Paul and a CD player for every niece and nephew?"

He chuckled lightly. "Not really," he rumbled.

"And the fancy doorbell for your mother?"

"I was thinking of getting one that plays Handel's *Messiah*."

"The whole thing?"

"Well, no. Maybe just the 'Hallelujah Chorus.' "

"And the yacht?"

"My church doesn't want one," he said. "I'll get them a bus instead."

"Oh, Blake . . ."

"Oh, Blake . . ." he mimicked. "You know, this whole thing is just unreal. Who in the world would have guessed that I could spend almost a million dollars in just two days?"

"A million dollars!" Julie shrieked. "Are you serious? You only *had* a little less than four hundred thousand!"

He doubled over, laughing. "Funny how being rich gets you deeper into debt!"

Julie looked queasy. "Tell me you're kidding," she whispered. "Tell me you haven't really spent every penny you had."

"Don't worry, I still have a fortune. I still owe a fortune. It's not what you have but what you owe. Right?"

Julie's face turned pale.

"I'll be good from now on," he said. "I promise not to throw any more money away. But if I run out of money, I'll always —"

"Have mine to fall back on?" Julie muttered.

"Well, yeah. I was thinking this morning, and I have this great idea about our teaming up. We pool our money and open a building with Sheffield Fashions on one side and Adcock, Inc., on the other. We borrow the whole ten million of mine against our future payments, so we can have it now, and then we aggressively invest yours. We live off earnings from our companies and our stock dividends. So I've spent a little much. . . . But with yours added to mine it could work. The money would grow along with our businesses, and we'd have even more coming in each year."

She gaped at him, her disappointment clear. "You've given this a lot of thought, haven't you?"

"Well, yeah. I mean, doesn't it sound like a wise idea? We make a good team, Julie."

"I thought you said we wouldn't do business together. That we'd keep this strictly personal."

"Well, we would. I wouldn't interfere with your business, and you wouldn't interfere with mine. We'd just pool the money. What do you think?"

She stared down at the lantern on their table, as if the light had suddenly illuminated something she didn't want to see. "If you'd wanted my half, Blake, you shouldn't have given me the ticket."

"I don't want your half, Julie. I'm not regretting that. I'm just saying —"

"That you've already blown yours and now you want mine."

He closed his eyes and sighed heavily, then leaned in and took her hand. Locking into her gaze, he said, "Julie, you've got me all wrong. I'm not after your money. It was a bad idea, okay? Stupid. Don't let this ruin our time together."

"All right," she said. "I'll try."

But he could see that it would require great effort because his idea had already been planted in her mind.

CHAPTER TEN

Julie couldn't shake the feeling that the money was the driving force in her burgeoning relationship with Blake. It changed how she looked at every effort he made for the rest of the day, and it made her spirits lag like a four-day-old helium balloon.

That afternoon Blake wanted to shop, but Julie couldn't stand the thought of watching him throw more of his money away. She suggested that they split up and do their shopping separately, then meet back at the Russian Tearoom at six. Blake seemed surprisingly happy to oblige.

For the first time since she had won her ten million dollars, Julie learned just how much freedom it gave her. She strolled in and out of retail dress and accessory shops from West 42nd Street to West 34th; she felt anticipation and excitement growing inside her at the new career opportunities her money afforded her. She would open a retail shop, she decided at some point during the afternoon, an outlet in which to display and sell her designs, a place to offer women the opportunity to have dresses custom-designed for them. She could hire specialists in leather and cashmere, and junior designers to execute her creations.

It was midafternoon when she began to miss Blake. She wondered what he was buying. She wondered how many hundred-dollar bills he'd doled out today. She had to admit — though never to him — that it *was* fun watching his face as he passed out those bills. The thought made her wish she'd stayed with him today, just to see his brilliant eyes and the looks on the faces of those with whom he shared his wealth. He was right, after all, she decided. It was fun to have money. She didn't intend to be without it again.

Strolling down Broadway with a wrapped bolt of silk under one arm and a bolt of hand-printed fabric under the other, she saw a man's watch displayed in the window of a store. It reminded her of something Blake would wear, for it was both down-to-earth and elegant. It was practical enough to work in, but with its white-and-gold contrasts it was suitable for the swankiest dinner club patronized by the world's most eligible bachelors.

Eligible bachelor, she thought, her heart tumbling on the words. They would go home soon. In a few days, the press would grow tired of them, and they would become caught up in their own endeavors. Blake Adcock would have the coveted reputation of the town's most eligible bachelor, and women would line up for him. Men would line up for her, too, but it would be for no other reason than the money. How would she handle that? How would he?

The thought that she would have to carefully guard against those after her money depressed her. But the thought that Blake would, too, depressed her even more. What if they both wound up in relationships with barracudas and gold diggers? What if they lived lives of misery because of the people this money would attract?

She went into the store and checked the price, gasped at the cost, then decided that she wouldn't spend it on him. She thought of putting the money into the bank instead, drawing interest on that amount, and watching it grow.

But then she wouldn't see Blake's surprise and joy that she had spent some of her money on him.

She considered the watch again and

thought that buying it would mean playing into his hands. Hadn't he already devised ways of getting her money for himself? Wasn't he really one of those gold diggers circling her as his prey?

Of course not, she told herself. Not Blake. Not the man who had no bitterness when his business failed. Not the man who put his best friend's feelings over his own disappointment. Not the man who had shared Christ with her in their first meeting.

But was he still the man she'd met in the restaurant that night? Was she the same woman?

Ashamed that spending money on Blake was such a battle, she decided to step off the cliff and buy the watch. When it was wrapped and ready, she hurried to the Russian Tearoom, anxious to see Blake's face when he opened it.

Julie felt her heart leap with joy when she saw Blake waiting for her with several big bags under his arm.

"Hi," she said, biting her lip as if she held every secret in the world just under the surface of her smile.

"Hi," he said, as if he, too, had a secret. He got the maitre d's attention, and the man led them to their table. They took their seats, the corner of the table between them.

"Did you clean out the city?" she asked as they leaned close together.

"Just about. You?"

"I bought some cloth," she said, still grinning. She set down her bolts in one of the empty chairs but held the watch behind her back.

"Cloth?" he asked, his eyebrows arching in frustration. "Julie, didn't you buy anything for yourself?"

"The cloth is for me," she said on a thread of laughter.

"I mean, something irrational. Ridiculous. Even just that new pair of shoes you told the press you would buy."

"I decided I could live with what I had," she teased.

"Julie . . ." The look on his face was despairing, as if he had tried and failed to show her good sense. "You're a millionaire. You need to act like one."

"Okay, okay," she said, giggling. "If it'll make you feel better, I did buy something kind of ridiculous. In fact, it is so ridiculous, I'm embarrassed to show you."

Blake's expression relaxed. "Good," he said. "I was beginning to wonder about you. What did you get? Don't tell me — let me guess. That crystal pineapple in the window of Tiffany's."

"No," she said, still holding the box behind her back.

"What, then? Show me."

That familiar heat crept up Julie's cheeks as she held out the small wrapped box. "You open it," she said. "It's for you."

"For me?" The curious, amused look in his eyes faded to poignant surprise. "You bought something for me and nothing for yourself?"

"I told you," she said softly, "I bought the cloth."

Stricken, his eyes held hers for a moment, as if her gesture meant worlds to him. "Thank you," he whispered.

The gratitude in his voice made her laugh, more from nerves than amusement. "Blake, you haven't even opened it!"

"It doesn't matter," he said. "It's the fact that you thought of me that counts. It means a lot to me."

"Oh, boy." Julie covered her face. "Am I glad I didn't buy you that roll of toilet paper made of fake hundred-dollar bills. I almost did, you know."

"It wouldn't matter if it was a gag gift," he said. "It's just so important that you —"

"Blake, just open it, for heaven's sake! I'm breaking out in a cold sweat!"

"Okay," he said. "I'll open it."

His hands trembled as he tore into the wrapping. If he was really that moved that she had bought him something, she thought, she'd have to make a habit of it.

He looked up at her as he pulled the top off the box. And when his misty blue eyes fell to the watch, he tipped his head and lifted his brows as if he'd never been so moved in his life. Then he pulled it from the box the way one would handle the crown jewels.

"I'll never take it off," he said softly.

"Well, you'd better. It isn't waterproof."

He swallowed and held his hand out to her. "Come here."

Obediently, Julie leaned into him, and he slid his arms around her. He buried his face in her hair and held her desperately tight. "I missed you today. So much."

"Me, too," she whispered. Then, pulling back, she tried to lighten the intensity of the moment. "Well, aren't you going to show me your toys?"

He let her go, and his hands went into his pockets. "Sure," he said. "Only, I didn't exactly shop for myself, either."

"What?" She looked at the boxes he'd dropped into the chair next to him. "Nothing for yourself?"

He shook his head slowly.

"Not even cloth?"

A grin tore at his lips.

"Not even a pool table or a pinball machine?"

Breathing a heavy sigh, as if the moment of truth were approaching, he reached for one of the large boxes and handed it to her. "Open it," he said softly.

She knew her eyes were shining as she took the box. Biting her lip, she tore open the paper.

A rich ebony mink coat lay waiting to be stroked, and she jerked her hands back. She saw people at other tables looking, and she wanted to hide under the table. "Oh, Blake! I can't accept this. It cost a fortune!"

"You're worth a fortune," he said, smiling as he pulled the coat from the box and held it up for her to slip into. "And I insist."

"But I'm not the mink type. Blake, please. I can't wear a coat that cost more than my house!"

"Yes, you can," he insisted. "I want you to. You wouldn't deprive me of the pleasure of seeing you in this, would you?" He slipped it over her shoulders. It caught on her chair, and she pulled it down, straightening it. Her hand lingered on the soft fur. Grabbing the lapels, he pulled her close.

"Oh, Blake," she murmured. "You shouldn't have."

"But I did," he said. His kiss pushed through all her barriers and all her reservations, but somehow the fear was still there.

The feeling that he would not — could not — be hers, the feeling that tomorrow would come and she would find herself alone and aching and humiliated just as she had a year ago with Jack, kept rushing her heart. Instead of seeing the gift as his offering to her, she saw it as her own money draining right before her eyes. He'd probably already borrowed on his. Spent next year's and the next year's . . . now he would want hers.

But she wondered if it was a trade-off — her money for his love. Maybe it was worth it.

He tipped her face up to his and gazed into her eyes. "I think I fell in love with you while you were eating my soup that first night," he whispered. "I had prayed for help that night, and God led me right to that restaurant. I had never been there before. And there you were, Julie. It was the worst time in the world to fall in love, but I had no control over it."

A lone tear rolled from Julie's eye, and she reached up to frame Blake's face with shaking hands. He kissed her again and she felt she'd been released, but she wasn't sure to where. Was it a paradise? or another heartbreak? It seemed impossible that she — a woman who had been hurt more than her share, a woman who couldn't imagine anyone loving her without motive — could really love a man like Blake without getting her heart broken.

Blake didn't demand a reply from her. Instead, he wiped the tear under her eye. "I didn't get the chance to give you your most important gift," he said, his voice growing hoarse.

"Blake, the mink is too much already. You shouldn't have —"

"Just open it," he said quietly, handing her a small velvet box.

Holding her breath, Julie gazed at him for a moment, then looked down at the box. Carefully, she opened the top. The three-karat diamond ring startled her, and she caught her breath.

"I love you, Julie," he whispered, tipping her face back up to his. "And I think we make a good team. Forget my idea for joining forces in business. What I really want is for you to be my wife."

In the seconds it took for Julie's heart to begin beating again, a million thoughts raged through her mind. He had suggested marriage the night they'd won the money and told her more than once that if he ran out, they would always have hers to fall back on. Was that what all this was about? Was it all a ploy so he could correct the mistake he'd made by forcing her to keep her half of the ticket? Had he so enjoyed having money that he couldn't stop thinking what twice as much would do for him?

Could greed really drive someone into feigning love and asking for a lifetime commitment? How would she ever know if it was real?

Tears sprang to her eyes. "I . . . I can't take this," she said. "I'm sorry." She thrust the ring into his hands, trying to keep her tears at bay.

"Julie, why?"

"Because."

"But I love you," he said. "Maybe it's too soon. Maybe I jumped the gun. But I missed you this afternoon, and I realized that I don't want to go home and resume our separate lives. I want you with me —"

"Don't! Don't push it," Julie bit out. "Please."

She could hear the surprise in his voice. "Why? You owe me an explanation, Julie," Blake said. "Tell me why!"

She swung around, her face burning. Suddenly it all seemed clear to her. All the tenderness and romance, all the attention . . . "Why do I owe you, Blake? Because of the ticket? Because of the money?"

"What?" Blake asked. He seemed completely baffled. "What has the ticket got to do with —"

"I have to go," Julie choked, cutting him off. "I'm sorry, Blake. I'm not going to marry you. You gave me the ticket and made me keep the money, even though I would have been fine to just give it to you. But now I'm in this too deep, and I have plans and hopes and dreams. And it's not fair for you to spend all of your money and come after mine. I can see through all this, Blake. The mink and the ring, the trip and everything . . . they're all investments. You're hoping for a huge return, and you can get it by marrying me."

Blake's face drained of color as he sat frozen before her. "That's what you think?" he whispered, as if she'd knocked the wind out of him. "You think I wanted to marry you because my money is running out? Is that the kind of man you really think I am? Greedy and selfish and conniving?"

"Money changes people!" she shouted. "Maybe you were that way all along — I don't know. But you're not the man I hoped you'd be."

"You got part of that right, anyway," he said sadly. "Money does change people. It changed you. You couldn't have cared less about money the night we won. Now you're hoarding it, scared to death somebody's going to take some from you. Well, I don't want your money, Julie! And forget the proposal, because you're not the woman I hoped you would be."

Swiping at her raging tears, Julie thrust the mink at him, grabbed her bolts of fabric, and ran out of the restaurant.

Blake threw down enough money to cover the bill, grabbed his things, and raced out behind her. He caught her standing on the street trying to hail a cab.

"Where are you going?"

"Home," she said. "I'll take the next commercial flight out." When a cab passed her, she put both bolts under one arm, then roughly dug into her purse with her other hand. "Here. My half of dinner tonight." She threw some bills at him. "I guess I owe you that much."

"You don't owe me anything," he muttered, trying to give the money back.

She tried to stop another cab, but it sped

past. She couldn't stop her tears. "I didn't want it to end like this."

His eyes flashed to hers. "Then what did you want, Julie?"

She stopped and stared down at the sidewalk, trying desperately to hold herself together until she was away from him.

"Answer me, Julie," he said more firmly. "What is it you want?"

"Nothing!" The word seemed to rob her of every ounce of strength she possessed.

"Exactly!" he returned with equal desperation. "You don't want anything because you feel so unworthy. You can't let yourself love me because you can't believe that I could actually love you for yourself. There has to be some reason, doesn't there? some motive?"

"Yes!" she cried. "Yes, there has to be a reason. There always is. You want what I have."

"But I have what you have, Julie! I don't need your money!"

"You'll owe everything you won in six months, Blake!" She touched her forehead with her fingertips. "It's not that I don't want to share. I just don't want to be wanted for the money."

"Is it so hard to believe that I love you because of you?"

"Yes!" she shouted. "Yes, it is. We hardly know each other. We met four days ago! The money complicates everything!" A cab stopped, and the driver got out and loaded her bolts of fabric into the trunk. She wiped her eyes and turned back to Blake. "I have a plane to catch. I have to go."

"Then go! Run away and see where it gets you!"

And she did. Julie got into the cab. When she arrived at the airport, she ran to the ticket counter. Fortunately, she was able to purchase a ticket for a plane leaving within the hour. She ran to her terminal and down the jet bridge and into the coach class of the commercial jet. When she was seated, waiting for it to take her back to Detroit, she realized she was still running.

When she finally made it home, Julie crawled onto her bed and lay in a ball for ten minutes, allowing herself only that amount of time to cry out her heart. Misery was inevitable for her, she thought, for she always fell for the wrong men. Great sobs racked her body, and she wished with all her heart that Blake had been different. She could have convinced herself of that if she'd tried, she thought. But she would always know, in the deepest corridors of her soul, that he did not love her for herself any more than Jack had.

There was only one thing to do, she thought. She would launch headfirst into her business, hire a staff, finish her designs. Maybe that full-speed-ahead work would make her forget Blake Adcock. And maybe it would soothe the wish gnawing in her heart that he would come storming through that door at any moment and shake her fears and accusations right out of her.

Weeks passed as Julie worked ceaselessly, drawing out the new ideas she had had since returning from New York. Her new formal creations were sadder, with flowing, romantic lines and softer fabrics. They each reminded her of her days with Blake — of the wind rustling through his hair on the cruise around New York Bay, the sunlight bathing their faces, the laughter in his eyes — but she didn't want to be reminded, so she worked harder.

She found a building in which to sell her line, with studios upstairs where several junior designers worked executing her designs, and several expert seamstresses put them together. Already she was taking orders from people who had seen her on television in her own design, and so her custom business was getting under way. She capitalized on the dramatic, everyday styles that her customers seemed most interested in. Her fashion show was back in the planning stages, and her waitress friends had been assured that they could still model her clothes.

To anyone looking in from the outside, it would have seemed that Julie Sheffield was on top of the world. No one would have guessed that every night Julie cried herself to sleep, because no amount of work could smother the love for Blake that still smoldered in her heart.

It was raining one night when she got home. As she rummaged in her drawer for a sweater to change into, she ran across the box of chocolates Blake had given her that first night, the chocolates that had held the sweepstakes ticket. She remembered how moved she had been when he'd given her the candy. She had almost cried.

It had been raining that night, too.

She looked out the window that Blake had climbed through. The steady drizzle left her tiny house feeling even smaller and lonelier. She gazed out through the rivulets of water tracing designs on the panes, recalling the night he had brought her a picnic. Peanut butter and jelly sandwiches, and candlelight in a pillowcase.

He had talked her into running off with him in the night.

What was it her mother used to say when Julie was in high school? "There's no point in starting something you can't finish. You can't learn from it or lay it to rest until you've seen it through."

Her mother had been referring to the dozens of dresses Julie had started with bits and pieces of secondhand dresses, then abandoned from frustration and fear of failure. Now, in the loneliest days of her life, she wondered if her mother might have used the same advice about love. Julie had left things hanging with Blake, had run away as fast as her plane would carry her, and she couldn't put him behind her until their relationship was laid to rest once and for all.

New tears rolled down her face, and she leaned her forehead against the window-pane, remembering his words that had seemed so true. *"I had prayed for help that night, and God led me right to that restaurant. I had never been there before. And there you were, Julie. It was the worst time in the world to fall in love, but I had no control over it."*

Was it all a lie, or had she ruined the truth in it?

She went to the telephone beside her bed

and pressed a fist to her mouth. If only he had called her when he'd gotten back to Detroit, she thought, maybe he could have convinced her that she was wrong about him. More than anything else in her life, she wanted to be wrong.

But he hadn't called. And he hadn't come over.

Had any of it actually been real?

A persistent, gnawing need to know took hold of her. If it was real, she had to hear him say it. And if it wasn't, well, perhaps she could go on with her life without thinking of him three hundred times a day.

Controlled by an irrational need to hear his voice, she bit her lip as tears rolled faster down her cheeks. With a trembling hand she picked up the telephone and dialed Blake's number. He answered on the second ring.

"Hello?" It was quiet behind him, and his voice seemed much too close to her ear. Much too familiar. Much too sweet against the bitter silence she'd suffered since she'd seen him last.

"Blake?" she choked out. "It's Julie."

He caught his breath, then said softly, "Julie." His tone teetered between relief and apprehension.

Julie grabbed a tissue out of the box on

her bed table and wadded it over her eyes. "I . . . I just wanted to ask you one thing, Blake," she said.

"What?" he whispered.

She swallowed, steadied her voice, and went on. "What we had in New York. That morning on the boat . . . and in the restaurant, when you said you loved me. Was it real? I have to know the truth."

She held her breath and waited an eternity before Blake's broken voice reached across the line. "It was real, Julie. It was real."

Closing her eyes, she hung up the telephone and lay back on the bed, staring at the ceiling. *Why? Why didn't he say it was an illusion?* she asked herself miserably. *Why couldn't he just have taken that opportunity to lay it to rest once and for all?*

The phone rang almost immediately, and Julie only looked at it. She knew it was Blake. But she was too confused to talk to him, and she needed time to think.

So she lay staring at the ceiling as the phone rang incessantly, her painful tears soaking into her pillow.

"Answer, Julie," Blake whispered. "I know you're there." He held the phone in one hand, the receiver in the other, as he paced across his bedroom. Finally it had come, the call he'd been praying for, the sign that said she still cared. He had been too hurt and too proud and too stubborn to make a move before, after the things she had accused him of, but her whispered question had changed everything. Now it was time to get her back.

But the phone continued to ring. An anxious, broken mist welled in his eyes. "Answer!" he cried aloud. Was she just lying there beside it, listening and refusing to pick it up? Was she that determined to lay their feelings to rest?

He counted out three more rings and told himself that he would get dressed, hightail it to her house, and break in again if he had to, if she didn't answer in the next thirty seconds. . . .

Suddenly the ringing stopped, and he heard her presence on the other end, though she didn't speak.

"Julie," he said, bending over suddenly, as if she would hang up if he stood erect. "Julie, don't hang up. Please."

She didn't hang up, but she said nothing, and he found himself groping for the right words. It was several moments before he came up with anything. Rubbing his moist eyes, he sat on the edge of his bed and closed them. "Julie, I wish I'd never seen that sweepstakes ticket. I wish I could just turn back time to the night in the restaurant when you ate my soup and brightened my night. The best thing about winning that money was that I got to know you in the bargain. And now that's the only important thing."

The sound of her muffled sob broke his heart, and he tried to steady his voice. "Julie, you've got to trust me. You've got to trust yourself."

"But I can't do that," she rasped, "because my judgment always stinks."

Blake opened his mouth to speak, but before the argument could leave his tight throat, Julie had hung up again.

Defeated, he threw down the phone and slumped over it, shoving a splayed hand through his wet hair. There must be something he could do, he thought miserably. There must be some way to prove his love for her.

Tell me what to do, Lord. Show me how to fix this.

But nothing came to mind. He paced his house — back and forth, back and forth — running scenarios through his mind, alternately begging God for help, then concocting schemes of his own. But he couldn't see any good outcome from any of them.

■ ■ ■ ■

I need closure, Julie thought as she held the box of chocolates in her lap and navigated her way to his house. She needed to undo the tender memories that seemed to hold her captive.

She reached his house in the secondhand car she had recently bought and pulled quietly up to the curb. She got out in the rain, clutching the box to her heart, and opened the gate on his fence. Then she stole up to his front porch and laid the box of chocolates down in front of the door.

She straightened up and looked at the door, knowing he was in there, just on the other side. All she had to do was knock, and this misery could end. But she would never know if it was her or the money. She would always wonder.

She turned and hurried down the steps and back out across his wet lawn. As she got into her car to drive away, she wished she'd never won the sweepstakes. How different might things be if they'd had a losing number? Would he have sold that coffee table, come to pay off his IOU, and start a relationship without the complications of millions of dollars?

With all of her heart, she suddenly began to hate the millions of dollars she had won. None of it was worth the loss of a relationship that could have been so good, she thought. The money had become a master over her, even though she would have vowed she was above that.

No one can serve two masters.

She began to weep as she drove home, realizing that in hoarding her money and protecting it from Blake, she had forgotten about her relationship with God. The money had even ruined that.

"Forgive me, Lord," she said aloud. "Please forgive me, and show me what I need to do."

After an hour or so of pacing and thinking, Blake knew there was only one thing to do. He had to go to Julie's house, see her face-to-face again, declare his love for her, and not leave until she believed him.

He grabbed his keys and rushed to the front door, threw it open . . . and almost stepped on the box of chocolates. Frowning, he stooped down and picked it up. He looked around for some sign of Julie, but she was gone.

Was this really the end? he wondered. Was it her way of saying that she wished she'd never met him?

Suddenly sapped of his energy, he went back in and sat at his table. He opened the box, remembering the sweepstakes card that had been inside it. The card that had changed his life.

Things had been so simple just before that. He had given her the box, and she had gotten tears in her eyes. He had realized that God was in this. He hadn't gone there by chance, hadn't stumbled on this special woman by accident.

And if God had led him to her, wouldn't God help him find a way to get past the money and win her back?

An idea came to mind, perking him up instantly. He tore through his drawer for a business card he'd kept, then dialed the number of the public relations director at ABC in New York. He asked for her extension, then waited for her to answer.

"Jeanine Stegall."

"Mrs. Stegall," he said in a rush, "this is Blake Adcock. The one who won ten million dollars a few weeks ago?"

"Yes, Mr. Adcock. How are you?"

"Well, not so good," he said, heart pounding as if the end of his dark tunnel was in sight . . . but still just out of reach. "But I think you can help me. You see, I'd like to give the money back. At least, the part I haven't already been paid. Is there some way I can just cancel the rest of those payments and throw my money back into the jackpot for next year's Valentine's drawing?"

Mrs. Stegall was apparently stunned. "Mr. Adcock, have you been drinking?"

"No. I'm stone-cold sober. Scout's honor."

Mrs. Stegall cleared her throat. "Well, this is highly irregular."

"But can it be done?"

"Absolutely not. We gave you that money. The amount of paperwork was astronomical. The IRS is involved, and several banks and governmental agencies. We can't undo it!"

"But I don't want it!" He messed up his hair, trying to find the words to explain it to her. "See, it's kind of a God thing. I mean, I don't think I'm the guy God meant to have all this. Maybe he just gave it to me to hold for a while, maybe to teach me something. I've learned, okay? I can't deal with this money."

"Then I suggest you give it to a charity of some sort, Mr. Adcock."

"I'd do that, Mrs. Stegall, except how do you know which ones are legitimate? I mean, maybe God actually had me holding it for somebody else, you know? Like, somebody who really needs it, somebody who can do something with it that would help Christ's kingdom and meet people at the point of their need. . . ." Even as he spoke, it became clearer to him.

"I wouldn't know about that, Mr. Adcock."

"Well, I just mean that there's got to be a person or group or foundation or something that could do a lot more with this money than I could. If I could figure out who that is . . ."

"That's your responsibility, Mr. Adcock. I just dispense the winnings. I can't tell you how to spend them."

He groaned with frustration. "Well, thank you very much for your help! You're all friendly and gushing when you're giving me money, but the minute I try to give it back, it's all business!"

"Mr. Adcock, do you hear yourself? This really isn't making a lot of sense."

"Oh, just forget it." With that, he slammed the phone down. The ring of impact had hardly died away before he snatched the phone back up and dialed Paul's number.

"Hello?"

"Paul?" Blake's voice cracked as turmoil wobbled in his voice. "I need somebody to talk to, buddy. Can you spare a couple of hours?"

"Sure, Blake," his friend said. "I'll be right over."

CHAPTER ELEVEN

Julie never went to sleep that night, so when she rose the next morning, she looked in the mirror and moaned at what stared back at her. She looked like a phantom, was nauseated from crying, and her head ached as if she'd been banging it into a wall. For a while, she blamed Blake. But it wasn't his fault, she realized finally. It was the money.

The stupid money that she'd never even wanted in the first place. The money that had brought the two of them together and had ultimately torn them apart.

Two masters.

"I don't want to serve money," she told the Lord. "I want to serve you. I trust your will so much more than my own. If I didn't have to keep wondering if the money was the motive . . ."

If she could just get rid of this money, things would be clearer, she thought. It wasn't making her happy. Maybe it could make someone else happy, instead.

The Spring Street Hospice Center.

Not so long ago, she'd told Blake that she was going to donate a big chunk of money to them. They needed it. Their work was crucial. They could share the good news of Christ and give peace and even joy to terminal patients. If she gave them the money, they'd never have to raise funds again, never have to wonder if they'd still exist from month to month.

Joy like Julie hadn't felt in weeks sprang up inside her, and she knew this was God's idea, not hers. Hope grew within her as the day rolled on, and she called her lawyer to draw up the necessary documents to have her money donated to the hospice. All she kept for herself was the seed money she needed to keep her business going.

And as the finality of what she was doing became clear to her, she felt as if the weight of ten million dollars had just been lifted from her shoulders.

Paul did everything in his power to talk Blake out of what he was about to do. "Aw, don't do it, buddy," he pleaded as they found the building with the sign that said Spring Street Hospice Center.

"Give me one good reason why I

shouldn't," Blake said with more verve in his voice than he'd had in weeks.

"Give me one good reason why you should," Paul returned.

"Because," Blake said, "you wouldn't take it all."

"I let you give me only what I needed, but I think this is crazy. Give me another reason."

"Okay. Because they need it. They led Julie's mom to Christ before she died. Think of all the people they could help. They meet people's physical needs so people will trust them with their spiritual ones. Isn't that what we've always said we'd be about in our own work?"

"Blake, for heaven's sake, there are other ways to help them."

"For heaven's sake is precisely why I'm doing this."

They parked the car, then sat and let it idle for a moment.

"You're doing this for Julie," Paul accused. "But what if you make this grand, sacrificial gesture and you still don't get her back?"

Blake set his teeth and swallowed at the blunt question. He'd given that a lot of thought. "Paul, I'm doing this because the money has made me lose the only things that matter to me. Julie was right. I don't know how to handle it, any more than I knew how to handle her. It caused me too much pain."

Paul set his elbow on the window and rubbed his face with his hand. "But, Blake, if you give it away, you won't ever be able to get it back."

"I don't ever want it back," Blake said. "All this money has taken away my pioneer spirit. That grit that made me shuck my job and try designing those cars. When I had the money, all I wanted to do was sit back and let somebody else do the thinking for me. And that's not the way I want my life to be. Struggling is part of the challenge. It's also part of the reward."

Paul moaned and looked fully at his best friend. "Are you sure, man?"

"I'm sure," Blake said. "Are you with me or not? You can wait in the car, you know."

Paul opened the door and wrestled his chair out of the backseat. "How often does a guy get to watch his best friend give away a fortune?"

Blake only laughed as he got out of the car to set his life back on the right track.

Julie wore her biggest smile since she'd won the sweepstakes as she signed the last of the documents that turned over her winnings to the Spring Street Hospice Center. It had taken a full day to take care of the tedious business. She drove back to her house, and as she turned into the driveway, she saw a familiar car waiting. She looked up to her porch, and there was Blake sitting on her porch steps.

Her heart began to hammer. What would he think when he learned what she had done? Would she regret doing it if he reacted badly?

She got out of her car and slowly walked toward him. When he got to his feet, she saw that he held the box of chocolates in his hands.

They faltered for a moment, absorbing the sight of each other with remorseful eyes.

"Blake, what are you doing here?"

"I have to talk to you," he said carefully. "Can we go inside?"

She nodded and unlocked her door, and he followed her in.

Just get it over with, Julie thought. Either he wanted her, or he didn't. "I need to talk to you, too," she said.

Blake's defense barriers sprang up at her cool voice, and that vulnerability in his eyes seemed to vanish. Instead, he looked guarded. She sat down and gestured for him to follow, but he remained standing. One hand slid into his pocket, and the other clutched the heart-shaped box.

"You first," he said.

Julie gulped back her tension. "You were right," she said, her raspy words tumbling out too quickly. "About my changing because of the money. So I figured there was only one thing to do."

He waited, his body tense as a bowstring, as she struggled for the words.

"I can't help wondering if you want me for my money. So I got rid of it. I'm a little better off than broke right now, but I have no hope of getting my ten million back. It's gone. Take me or leave me." Tears filled her eyes as she mumbled the words, for the astonished look on Blake's face told her that he would leave her.

But instead of watching him walk away, she watched the guarded expression fall from his eyes as a smile slowly stole across his face. Before Julie knew what was happening, he had covered his face with both hands and was laughing hysterically.

"What's so funny?" she bit out.

Blake stopped laughing and reached for her hand. He pulled her up and stepped close to her, still laughing. "I'm sorry . . . I didn't mean . . . it's just that . . . so funny."

Julie jerked her arm free. "It is not funny!"

"Yes, it is. Don't you see?"

Julie planted her fists on her hips. "No, I don't see! Why don't you tell me?"

"You gave up the money so you could have a fighting chance with me!"

Fury pumped through her veins. "I did not. I gave it up because I couldn't serve two masters. Because the Lord showed me that I had changed. That the money was making me miserable. Other people needed it more than I did. . . ."

"That's priceless!" Blake shouted, doubling over again. He banged his fist on the table as he shouted with laughter. "I can't stand it!"

Julie took a deep breath and wondered if she should call someone, if the pressure of the money had finally made him snap.

He wiped his moist eyes and tried to speak. "See . . . mine's gone too."

"Of course it is, Blake. That's why I thought you wanted *my* money."

"No!" His gales of laughter almost blew her over. "You don't understand. I didn't spend it all. I invested some in Paul's business and some in mine." He sniffed and leaned back against the table, as if the laughter had taken too much from him. "And the rest . . ."

A deep frown wrinkled her forehead. "The

rest is gone, isn't it? You spent it all. Even what they haven't paid out yet."

"Well, it's all gone. I'll say that. But it's not where you think." He took both of her hands in his and brought one to his lips. He kissed it, then touched her face, so gently that it brought tears to her eyes.

She gulped back her emotion. "Then we're both broke."

"Right," he said and started laughing again. "And if you thought I'd turn and run because I couldn't get yours, you're wrong. I've never been so happy to hear anything in my life. Now I can prove to you that I wasn't after your fortune. Now I have a chance. . . ."

Her face changed. "Then you still want me? You still . . ."

"I still love you," he whispered, the mirth still dancing in his eyes. "But you may not want me."

"Of course I want you! I've always wanted you. I've been miserable thinking about all the trouble you were getting into with all that money."

Blake began to laugh again. "Well, you were right. See, I gave mine away too. Even what I haven't gotten yet."

"What?" She pictured him handing thousand-dollar bills to everyone he saw, until there were no more left. "Blake! Who on earth did you give it to?"

"The Spring Street Hospice Center," he said. "Your story about your mother coming to Christ there kept harping on my mind. I thought it was the best use of my money."

Julie stepped back, awestruck. "The hospice center? You gave it to the hospice center?"

"Have you seen their building lately?" he asked. "They desperately need a bigger place, and they need all kinds of equipment. They need more staff members, more beds —"

Julie flung her arms around Blake's neck, and he stopped midsentence and lifted her from the floor, holding her as if he couldn't bear to let her go again. "Oh, Blake," she whispered against his ear. "You *are* the man I hoped you would be. I love you. I think I loved you from the beginning, that first night when you talked about Christ with me, and I knew that you were the kind of man I'd prayed for, but the money muddied the water and I was so afraid. . . ."

He breathed out a long sigh of relief, and she felt a tear run between their faces. She wasn't sure if it was his or hers.

He set her carefully down, then wiped her

face and gazed down at her with wet eyes of his own. Then he handed her the heart-shaped box, the one that had started all this trouble. "I wanted you to have this," he said. "Open it."

She pulled the top off, as she had done just weeks ago, and saw all the uneaten pieces of chocolate in their little brown cups. But pressed down into the center one was something that hadn't been there before. It was the sweepstakes ticket that he had left her that first night, the one the television station had laminated and allowed them to keep as a souvenir, with the fifteen-dollar IOU and the note that had made her so angry.

"I was going to tell you that I was dead broke, that I wouldn't have given all my money away if I was so greedy that I'd connive to get yours. I was hoping you'd see that I didn't care about the money and let us just start over, from that first night. Give me one more chance."

"I'm the one who needs another chance."

He took fifteen dollars out of his wallet and handed it to her. She took it. "We've already been to New York," he whispered, "so now that I've paid my IOU, we can start fresh. How about just a dinner date here in town? Or . . . a lot of dinner dates . . . that might lead to . . . something even more important?"

She smiled. "Starting slow is good. I like that. And yes, I'd love to have dinner with you."

"No doubts? No fears?"

"Just about your using your credit card to pay for it." He laughed, and a smile glowed in her green eyes. "It won't matter that we aren't rich anymore, Blake. Because we *are* rich, whether we have money or not. Being broke might be our greatest asset."

He crushed her against him, then began to laugh in a deep rumble against her ear. "Well, you know when I said I was broke? I didn't mean, *totally* broke."

She stepped back and looked up at him. "What do you mean?"

He shrugged with that boyish charm that had never failed to enchant her. "I still have a little something."

"Like what?"

"Like . . . I kept a tiny bit to pay back some debts and get my business off the ground . . . and a tiny bit to live on while I struggle."

"Blake!" she said, grinning. "How much, exactly?"

"Just a million," he said. "Split over twenty years. That's not so much. I've prayed a lot about what a healthy balance is. I think it's having enough to live on, enough to spend a little on people I love, enough to give away some. And I wanted a little nest egg just to get a family started . . . if and when it leads to that, and I mean absolutely no pressure by saying that. . . ."

She smiled at the thought. She had hoped that he had something permanent in mind, even if it was too soon to plan for it yet.

"You think we'll ever regret it?" she asked as they walked out to his car. "Giving up all that money?"

"No," he said. "Because that ticket won us a lot more than money, and we won't ever have to give that away." He leaned down to kiss her, and as he did, her heart sent a prayer of gratitude to heaven.

"Besides," he said against her lips, "there's always next year's sweepstakes."

RECIPE

Death by Chocolate

Thanks to Jeanie Young for her help with this recipe. I don't cook at all! But I do eat, and this is my favorite recipe that I enjoy when someone else cooks it.

4 eggs
2 cups sugar
1 cup oil
1/3 cup cocoa
1 1/2 cups self-rising flour
1/2 tsp. vanilla
4 Heath bars (or your favorite chocolate candy bar), crushed
1 5-oz pkg. Cook and Serve chocolate-flavored Jell-O pudding mix
Large tub of Cool Whip

Prepare brownie layer by stirring together eggs, sugar, and oil. Then add cocoa, flour, and vanilla. Mix well. Spread in an un-

173

greased 9 × 13 cake pan. Bake at 350° for approximately 20 minutes. Check for firmness. Set aside until cool. Cut into small squares.

Meanwhile, prepare pudding as directed on package. Set aside until cool.

To assemble, layer the ingredients in a deep container in the following order:

(1) Brownie chunks
(2) Cooled chocolate pudding
(3) Crushed candy bars
(4) Cool Whip

Repeat until dish is full, ending with Cool Whip. If any candy is left over, sprinkle on top. Then brace yourself, because it's going to be good!

ABOUT THE AUTHOR

Terri Blackstock hasn't always written for the Lord. Just over a decade ago she was an award-winning secular novelist writing for publishers such as HarperCollins, Harlequin, and Silhouette. With thirty-two titles published and 3.5 million books in print, she found that she was miserable. The compromises she had made in her career had taken their toll on her spiritual life, and she yearned to renew her relationship with Christ.

After much soul-searching and wrestling with God, she finally told the Lord that she would never write another thing that didn't glorify Him. Thinking she might never be published again, she began planning ways to supplement her income, while she worked on her first idea for a Christian novel.

Because she enjoyed reading suspense novels, she tried weaving a faith message into a fast-paced page-turner with ordinary people in jeopardy. When Christian publishers expressed great interest, she realized that a secondary job would not be necessary. God was paving the way for her to enter the Christian publishing world.

Since that time, she's sold 2 million Christian novels. She has over thirty Christian titles, many of which have been number one best sellers. Her latest book, *True Light,* reached number one on the Top 50 of all Christian books the first full month it was in stores. *Night Light* was the winner of the 2007 Retailer's Choice Award for General Fiction. Both books are part of her popular Restoration series which began with *Last Light.* Other reader favorites include the Cape Refuge series, the Newpointe 911 series, the Sun Coast Chronicles series and the "Seasons" books written with coauthor Beverly LaHaye.

Terri has appeared on national television programs, such as *The 700 Club* and *Home Life,* and has been a guest on numerous radio programs across the country. The story of her personal journey appears in books such as *Touched by the Savior* by Mike Yorkey, *True Stories of Answered Prayer* by Mike Nappa, *Faces of Faith* by Jon Hanna, and *I Saw Him in Your Eyes* by Ace Collins.

■ ■ ■ ■

THE TROUBLE WITH TOMMY

ELIZABETH WHITE

■ ■ ■ ■

ACKNOWLEDGMENTS

Many thanks to my brothers-in-law, Timmy and Chris, shade-tree mechanics extraordinaire, who provided much of the inspiration for "Tommy" — not to mention most of the crazy car episodes. You are both choice warriors. Thanks to Uncle JP for teaching me how a coon dog is supposed to behave!

*In loving memory of
my maternal grandparents:
Thomas Pinkney and Maude Pierce Evans*

CHAPTER ONE

"Now, hon, if you need anything, just give me a holler! You've got my number, don't you?"

Standing on the deep front porch of her newly leased cottage, Carrie Ann Gonzales Pierce waved the business card in her hand as LaDean Cumbest, the lone real estate agent in town, climbed into her orange Pinto and backed out in a cloud of red dust. The little car jounced over the potholes in the yard that passed for a parking lot. LaDean rolled down the window, stuck her arm out in lieu of a signal, and turned left onto Old River Road.

Carrie felt like she'd just lost her last contact with civilization. Except for the one-horse garage next door, her closest neighbor was the bait shop a mile away in Vancleave. Calling that dumpy garage over there a business was a stretch, too. She could smell gasoline and oil fumes all the way across the yard.

"Lord, what have I gotten myself into?" she muttered, hugging herself and shivering miserably in her thin red cotton sweater and wornout Levi's. The Mississippi Gulf Coast, famous for its mild winters, had undergone a rare cold snap that hadn't let up since Christmas two weeks ago.

New Year's Eve. Carrie was thirty years old today, and she had just emerged triumphant from one of the hardest years of her life. She'd buried her husband, Brad, without once breaking down. She'd faced the humiliation of his affairs before she moved back home to Granny's house. And now she was the proud new owner of her own business, Carrie Ann's Chocolate Confections and Catering.

She ought to be ecstatic. But part of her wanted to run down to Granny's house and climb up in the tree house with a doll to cuddle.

She wandered over to sit on the porch rail. Paint flaked off under her hand, and she added a note to her mental list of things to do to get her new business up and running. There was nobody to rejoice with her in her new independence. Her family was all down at Granny's house, getting ready for to-night's barbecue and fireworks.

There was nothing to look at but the garage, which was obviously closed for the holiday. Both bays were shut like giant sleeping eyelids, and a hand-painted Closed sign hung tip-tilted inside the sloping front window. However, she could see signs of life at the rear of the building. Through a curtainless open window, bluegrass music poured in obnoxious waves into the quiet afternoon.

Who'd be hanging out in a garage on New Year's Eve? Maybe she should walk over and introduce herself.

After checking to make sure the front door was locked, she crunched across the mixture of gravel, oyster shells, and Bahia grass that made up her side yard. It occurred to her that some landscaping would be in order, after she set up the inside of the shop.

The garage faced Wade-Vancleave Highway, sloping down to her own tiny lot, which gave onto Old River Road. Carrie stopped at the edge of her neighbor's gravel parking lot and put her hands on her hips.

On the side of the cinder-block building bold, crooked, crimson letters advertised TUNE-UPS, OIL CHANGES, BRAKES, TRANSMISSIONS. SATISFACTION GUARANTEED OR YOUR MONEY BACK! The cars lined up three deep in front of the closed bays might be Volvos, Bimmers, and Audis, but to Carrie's mind, a broken-down car was a broken-down car.

The grease monkey who owned this place could use a little business advice. Aesthetic improvement would undoubtedly increase revenues — for both her and him. Maybe she could talk him into at least repainting the side of the building and parking the broken cars behind the building, where she could see the end of a bass boat on a rusty trailer sticking out.

Shaking her head, she squeezed between a black Jaguar and a silver gray Celica and peered into the office window. Since it was pitch-black inside, all she could see was her own reflection.

She backed off quickly. *Lord, do I really look that tired?* She poked her fingers through her short cap of blonde hair and blinked. *Maybe I need a facial.*

Suddenly the glass door to her left opened with a jerk and the loud clank of a cowbell.

Carrie jumped in surprise.

"Sorry, I'm closed today," the young man said politely in the deep, thick Mississippi drawl she'd never quite eliminated from her own voice. He leaned against the doorjamb, his gaze sweeping her quickly, then gave her a lazy half grin. "Unless it's an emergency."

Carrie felt her breath riding high in her throat. What was he doing up here in the front of the building? In the dark? "I-I don't need a mechanic," she stammered, doing some looking of her own. He appeared to be in his mid-twenties, dressed in faded-to-white Levi's with the knees ripped out, and a Saints sweatshirt whose sleeves had been hacked off with less than tailored precision. Her gaze stopped at his bare feet, propped casually one on top of the other. "How did you know I was — ?"

"I watched you walk over here."

At that, her gaze snapped up to his olive-skinned face. Gold. His eyes were a gold-shot light brown, rimmed with black around the irises and sooty lashes that matched his hair.

"In fact, I sorta watched you all afternoon."

Carrie took another step back. "Well, I guess I'd better go."

The young man chuckled and pushed the door open a little farther. "Oh, man, I didn't mean to sound like a psycho. I thought you knew who I was." He stuck out a big brown hand. "I'm Tommy Lucas."

Carrie frowned, dredging her memory. She'd been away from Vancleave for ten years, but she thought she would have remembered that infectious grin. "I'm sorry, I don't —"

"Phew!" He grinned. "Guess I've finally outrun my reputation."

Reputation? She reluctantly let his hand swallow hers. She noticed it was clean, except for a thin rim of black around the fingernails.

"You're Miranda Gonzales's sister, right? I graduated with her," he added.

"Yes. Carrie Pierce." She jerked her hand back from the intimacy of his firm grasp.

"Oh, that's right, you got married while you were in college." Tommy shook his head, clicking his tongue with disappointment. He began to rattle a tattoo on the door frame with both hands, holding the door open with his shoulder. "So what are you doing back down here in the sticks?"

Carrie wondered if this Welcome Wagon foray of hers had been a serious mistake. She briefly wondered if she could get out of her contract and find another place to set up shop. "Uh, my husband died," she blurted distractedly, "and I came home to live. Well, I'm not living at home, exactly; I'm staying with my grandmother until I can afford —"

Now why was she pouring out her life story to this total stranger? This young *male* stranger? She supposed it was his open, inquiring expression, as if she were the sum and total of his interest at that moment. A real listener — a rarity these days.

"Hey, I'm sorry for your loss." His expression softened in sympathy. "Can you come in for a minute? I was gonna go fishin' this afternoon, but —"

"Oh no!" Carrie retreated another step. "I've really got to get back to Granny's for our family's New Year's shindig. I just wanted to come say hello." *And ask you to paint your building.*

"I understand," he said with a wistful tilt to his wide mouth. "I'm at loose ends, so I'd keep you here all day if I could." He winked. "Tell Roxanne I said 'Hey and stay out of trouble.' "

"You know my granny?"

"Everybody knows your granny," he said with a chuckle.

"Okay, I'll tell her." She studied him as she backed away. Maybe she should invite Tommy to the house. He looked a bit lonely, standing there beating "Wipe-Out" against the door frame. But to invite a stranger into a family gathering would be a little . . . weird. She turned and smiled over her shoulder. "See you later."

He gave her a thumbs-up. "Happy New Year."

"Same to you."

And happy birthday to me.

That evening, Carrie clutched the receiver of Granny's '60s-era black kitchen wall phone. Without thinking, she interrupted her younger sister's monologue, blurting, "Miranda, honey, I'm so glad for you, but Mom wants to hear it straight from the horse's mouth. Congratulations again — love you, bye!"

Fortunately, her mother burst into the kitchen just then. "Grant said Miranda's on the phone!" exclaimed Linda Gonzales, her sweet, round face alight. She took the phone and promptly burst into tears. "Oh, baby!"

Feeling restless and unreasonably out of sorts, Carrie gave her mother a strained smile and wandered outside into Granny's backyard. Under the huge, spreading pecan tree that shaded the barbecue pit, she found her brother Grant wrestling with the hand crank of the old ice cream freezer. Their grandmother, dressed in stretchy, black denim pants, a hot pink sweatshirt, and a Braves baseball jacket, was dumping table salt around the ice.

Granny looked up, her wizened pixie face

split in a big grin. "I hear I'm about to be a great-grandma. Again!"

Putting her hand on her own flat stomach, Carrie didn't immediately respond. The subject of babies always made her sad. Brad had never been "ready" to start their family. He wanted first to amass all the stuff he thought he needed to establish a successful medical practice. An expensive car. A big house. A country club membership. A well-dressed wife. Having babies of their own had taken a dismal backseat in their marriage.

"Don't you think Miranda's kind of young to be having a baby?" Carrie asked, sitting down at the picnic table.

Granny gave her a sideways smirk. "I had four by the time I was Miranda's age."

"Oh, right, back in horse-and-buggy days!" Laughing, Grant ducked as Granny reached to swat him with a newspaper lying on the table. "I quit with this thing. Ice cream's got to be hard as a rock by now."

"Why are we having ice cream in this weather anyway?" Carrie asked, shivering. "It must be forty degrees out here."

"Come on, sourpuss, it's birthday tradition." Grant took the newspaper and wrapped it around the top of the freezer. "What's the matter with you? You've been mean as a snake ever since you got home this afternoon."

Carrie shrugged, then yelped when Granny put a freezing-cold hand to her forehead. "Granny!" she sputtered.

"Are you comin' down with something, child?"

"No, I'm fine!"

"Grant —" Granny gave her grandson a minatory look — "would you go get the burgers out of the fridge? And see if you can find the barbecue tools — I think they're in one of the kitchen drawers."

"Well, *that'll* keep me occupied all night," he grumbled good-naturedly but obediently ambled toward the back porch.

Granny patted Carrie's knee as she plopped herself onto the picnic bench beside her. "You feelin' kinda left out tonight?"

"Left out? Why would I feel left out?" Carrie squirmed because she felt more than left out. She felt envious of Miranda and ashamed of her envy. She also wished she had acted on her impulse to invite Tommy Lucas over for dinner. Maybe if she had, she wouldn't have time to think about her own nasty feelings.

Come on, Carrie Ann, you're a grown-up, she told herself. *Get over it.*

Granny was uncharacteristically quiet for nearly a full minute. Finally she heaved a sigh. "Honey, the older I get, the more I long for you children to have what Jesus called 'abundant life.' I'm so sorry your Brad took off for heaven before you had a chance to really be a family."

Carrie wasn't so sure Brad was in heaven, but she forbore to mention that to Granny. She knew what her grandmother was getting at. "I really am excited about Miranda and the baby." She linked her ringless fingers together. "Granny, can I tell you something?"

"Of course, darlin'." Deep afternoon shadows fell across Granny's wise, compassionate face, dulling the fiery red of her hair. Carrie's heart constricted with love for her.

"If Brad and I had had children, it would have been a disaster."

Granny frowned. "Well, it's true you'd have had to raise them by yourself —"

"No, that's not what I mean." Carrie struggled to articulate the weight she'd carried for more than five years. "Granny, Brad didn't *want* children. All he was interested in was pleasing himself. For the last few years of our marriage, he did everything he could to humiliate and hurt me. Sometimes I think I almost hated him. I would never have divorced him, but now I feel guilty because he died!" Carrie slumped, hiding her face. What a horrible relief to have finally blurted out the truth.

"Oh, darlin'." As her grandmother's skinny arm went around her back, Carrie smelled the concoction of raspberry and coconut that was uniquely Granny. "I wondered why you never came home from Atlanta. We all thought you were just happy and busy."

"Busy, yes. Happy . . . ?" Carrie sat up a little, her fingers pressed against her eyes. "Brad always made fun of my countrified family. I had to drag him here the few times we came back after the wedding." She looked at her precious grandmother's horrified face and swallowed back tears. "Granny, I missed y'all so much, but I'd chosen my husband, and I knew I had to try to make it work."

"Darlin', every married couple has things to work through. Didn't you have friends? A pastor or a counselor you could have gone to?"

Carrie shuddered with cold and nervous emotion. "Our 'friends' were Brad's coworkers. Everybody seemed so much more sophisticated than I was. I never did learn to fit in, and after a while, I didn't even know who I was. Brad didn't want to go to church, and I didn't push him. I guess I should have gone by myself . . ." Her voice petered out miserably.

"Carrie, listen to me." Carrie felt Granny's tiny, fragile hand rest on her head. "I can't fix your heartache and guilt in five minutes. In fact, nobody but the Lord Jesus can, and sometimes even he takes awhile. But what I do know is that he sees and understands every bad decision you've ever made, every hurtful thing that's happened to you. It's never too late to start clean with him."

"Oh, Granny, I'm so tired of feeling this way. . . ."

Granny laughed softly. " 'Come to me, all of you who are weary and carry heavy burdens, and I will give you rest.' Trust the Lord, Carrie. You gave your heart to him when you were a little girl, and he wants your whole life."

Carrie turned her face, which streamed with tears, toward Granny. "How do you always turn a conversation into something spiritual?"

"It's a gift." Granny winked. "Why don't I pray for you now and promise to bring your name to the Lord every mornin' first thing?"

"I thought you always did that anyway — for all your grandchildren." Carrie smiled through her tears.

"I do, but sometimes my little chicks need a reminder." Granny closed her eyes and lifted her face. The hand not resting on Carrie's head turned palm up as if offering a gift. "Dear Father, my Carrie needs a fresh filling right now. I pray for you to speak to her heart, comfort her, and show her how to release her fears and doubts and guilt to you. I pray that in your timing you'll bring her a man who will cherish her and be the spiritual leader of a godly home. I give her to you in the name of Jesus. Amen."

"Amen," Carrie whispered. She dabbed underneath her eyes with her sleeve, then gave her grandmother a determined look. "You might as well know, though, that last part ain't gonna happen. I don't want another man."

Granny's severely plucked eyebrows lifted in patent skepticism. "And why not?"

"Granny, I was a total bomb at marriage. I'm not risking that again."

"Oh —" Granny blew an inelegant raspberry. Carrie had to laugh. "The right man comes along, and you'll change your tune."

Carrie sighed. "I'm not sure I'd even recognize the right man." An image of intense amber-colored eyes in a lively, dark, masculine face popped into her brain, but she erased it instantly. No way!

"Hmmm." Granny's eyes sparkled with dreadful matchmaking fervor. "There's this cute young fella I met at the auto parts store. When he found out I'd been changing my own oil, he offered to do it for me free. . . ."

Carrie knew with sudden clarity that she had been royally set up. She groaned. "His name wouldn't happen to be Tommy Lucas, would it?"

Granny beamed. "So you've met him already?"

"You're the one who talked me into leasing that cottage for my shop. You knew I'd eventually meet him. He said — and I quote — 'Tell Roxanne I said hey and stay out of trouble.' "

Granny laughed. "He's such a tease."

Carrie shook her finger under Granny's button nose. "What were you thinking? He's at least five years younger than I am, and he's a — a grease monkey!" Hastily she added, "Not that I'm interested in dating again anyway!"

"You don't have to date him," Granny said reasonably. "But it won't hurt to have a nice neighbor — you know, to watch your place when you're not there, maybe work on your car every now and then."

"How's he going to watch out for me when I'm not there?"

"Well, he lives in the back of the garage —"

"Granny!" Carrie huffed. "And this is the guy you picked out for my 'right man'?" She took Granny's hands and bent to look her in the eyes, so there would be no mistaking her earnestness. "Listen, thank you so much for your prayers. And thank you for wanting to watch out for me. But I just can't go through the pain of another relationship like the last one. I'm finally free to start over after five years, and there's no way I'm jeopardizing that freedom." She gently shook Granny's fingers. "Okay?"

But Granny tipped her head in her bird-like way and merely said, "We'll see." She looked around at the back door, which Grant had typically left wide open. "Wonder what happened to those barbecue tools." She smiled at Carrie and bounced to her feet. "Let's get the fire started."

"These are the times that try men's souls," Tommy informed his Bluetick coon dog. Skywalker reclined with sultanlike abandon on a piece of mustard-yellow shag carpet donated by some past customer. Normally a hunting dog would be either tied to a stake outside or penned in a dog run. But Tommy had adopted Sky three months ago from the animal shelter in Mobile, and Sky still had identity issues.

Skywalker rolled one eye upward with supreme indifference to this recent bit of wisdom from Thomas Paine, blew out a heavy, snorting breath, and went back to sleep.

"Somebody invents doggy antihistamine, they're gonna make a million bucks," Tommy said. He rolled out from under the 1957 Ferrari 250 Testa Rossa he'd been working on and looked up at the ceiling of the garage. It was black with mildew — probably the source of the offensive smell he couldn't quite eliminate from the garage.

He rubbed his eyes and yawned. He hadn't slept much last night. And not because he'd been out prowling the bars, as he might have been doing on New Year's Eve even two years ago. Nope, those days were dead and gone.

And good riddance.

It was the fireworks that kept him up last night. Seemed like every soul in Vancleave had been popping firecrackers and bottle rockets and Roman candles until nearly dawn. He'd sat for hours in his boat out on the river, without catching the first bite, but letting the sparkles and bangs and explosions entertain him. It had been cold as frog lips, but he didn't mind, because it kept him from noticing how alone he was.

Well, there is the Lord, he reminded himself, glad all over again. *No, I sure wouldn't go back.*

He rolled off the dolly and walked to the open door of the bay. He was tinkering on the car today because it gave him something to do. And an excuse to keep an eye on the cottage next door. He leaned around and surveyed its empty yard. Suppose that dark-eyed babe came knocking on his door again?

"She is something, isn't she, Lord? Carrie Ann Pierce." He rolled her name around his tongue like a piece of candy. She might need something. Not that he had anything to impress her with. But maybe he could help out with her car. He always noticed people's cars. She drove a black Nissan 300ZX, cute as a bug and not much bigger. There was some money in that car. He hoped she kept it serviced regularly.

His heart suddenly took a jog into his throat when, as if he'd conjured it from his thoughts, the ZX came around the curve spitting gravel, passed the cottage, and pulled up in his own parking lot. "Look alive, Sky," he said over his shoulder. "Company's coming!" The dog groaned without moving.

Tommy looked down at himself. "Oh, ma-a-a-an!" Same jeans and sweatshirt he'd had on yesterday. He didn't even have time to clean his hands, so he crammed them in his pockets and sauntered outside into the cold January morning.

Carrie Ann was getting out of the low-slung car, using her fingers to brush at her short blonde hair. He noticed she had the daintiest little ears he'd ever seen on a woman, accentuated by a spray of thin filigreed hearts dangling from each lobe.

Oh, man, he had a soft spot for short hair and pretty ears.

Today she wore a long wool coat buttoned tight around her neck and heavy hiking boots. When he got close enough, he could see that her expression was even more vulnerable than yesterday. Standing beside her car with the door open, she looked ready to take off at any moment.

He smiled at her, wondering why a beautiful woman like her would look so uncertain. Well, her husband dying recently might make her sad, but she didn't look sad, exactly, just . . . wary.

He took the initiative. "Mornin'!" He walked toward her, but not close enough to scare her away. *At least I've got my shoes on today.*

"Hi." She cleared her throat and looked over his shoulder. "Are you open today?"

He couldn't tell if she was surprised or just curious. "Not exactly. Piddling with my hobby. Unless you need me." *Way to go, Lucas,* he mentally kicked himself. *That really made sense.*

She frowned, puzzling out his words, then smiled. He didn't think she'd smiled yesterday. He would have remembered that dimple beside her mouth. "You work in a garage, and you play with cars on your day off?"

He supposed that did sound pretty lame. "Yeah, but I like to read, too."

Carrie Ann gave him a skeptical look and apparently decided not to pursue the subject. "Well, my granny sent me over here. If you're not too busy, would you like to have New Year's dinner with Granny and me today?"

A weird combination of elation and disappointment rushed through his chest. Elation that God had heard his prayer, and disappointment that the invitation had come from the old lady instead of the young one.

But the prospect of a home-cooked meal overrode any lingering chagrin. "Is she making black-eyed peas and pork?" He made the mistake of pulling his grimy hands out of his pockets and doing the *snap-snap-pop* thing with his fingers that was Skywalker's signal to come. Suddenly a blur of black-gray-and-white fur came streaking out of the garage and pinned Carrie against her car.

She screamed.

"Skywalker! Down!" Tommy lunged for the dog, who was more excited than upset. Tommy patted anxiously at Carrie's shoulder as he struggled to contain his panting pet with the other hand in his collar. "He's not mad at you; he's just glad to see you."

He wasn't prepared for the peal of laughter that exploded into the morning air. "I'd hate to see him when he's after a coon."

Tommy managed to convince Skywalker to lie down and gave Carrie a sheepish grin. "I haven't had him for long. I've been trying to retrain him. How'd you know he's a coon dog?"

"My brother hunts with Tree Walkers." Carrie crouched at eye level but at a respectful distance from the dog. A smile quirked her lips. "Grant doesn't think much of Blueticks, but this one's beautiful." She extended her hand to Skywalker, knuckles up, for him to sniff.

201

The dog gave Carrie's slim fingers an obsequious slurp. Thinking *beautiful* wasn't a word he'd ever heard before in reference to Skywalker, Tommy watched Carrie give Skywalker a good scratch behind his long, floppy black ears. Her nails were elegantly manicured, with clear polish and blunt white tips.

Then his gaze traveled up her arm to the greasy black smear on the shoulder of her light-colored coat. He looked at his hands again. "Oh, good grief! I got your coat — I'm — !"

She craned to see what he was talking about, and the smile disappeared. "It's okay," she sighed, rising and dusting dog hair off her front. "I was taking it to the cleaners tomorrow anyway."

That's the sweetest lie I ever heard, Tommy said to himself. "I've got some grease remover in the shop, if you'll —"

"No, thanks," she said hastily. "This is cashmere, so I'd better take it to the pros." Her big eyes widened even more as she spotted the Ferrari in the garage. "My goodness, that's a pretty car. It looks like a red Batmobile."

Tommy felt pride swell his chest. "It doesn't run yet, but I'm getting there."

"Is it yours?" She looked incredulous. He

could hardly blame her.

"Well, yeah. I bought the body for practically nothing from a guy I ran into at Talladega, then some of the guts —" He stopped when he saw her eyes glaze over. "I've been putting it together one part at a time for a couple of years."

"That's . . . fascinating." She backed toward her car. "Listen, Granny said she'll have lunch ready about noon, so why don't you . . . um . . . clean up and come on over. You know where we live?"

"Yeah, like I said, everybody knows Roxanne. Thanks again for the invitation, and I'm so sorry about your coat —"

"Never mind, Tommy." Her smile was genuinely forgiving, and Tommy found himself on the edge of a yawning precipice. "Just bring your appetite."

He could hardly believe it. A woman who could take grease and dog slobber without batting an eye. And who looked like a princess on top of that. Right next door! She had come to personally offer to feed him, when she could have just called him on the phone. Maybe she was a little bit . . . interested in him?

"Will do." He grinned and grabbed Sky's collar to keep him from jumping into the car with Carrie.

Lord, he thought as he watched her drive off, *it's not even my birthday. I don't know what I did to deserve this.* He snapped his fingers at Skywalker. "Come on, you troublemaker, you. Let's go scrape off some dirt."

CHAPTER TWO

Carrie shoved the grease-smeared, camel-colored coat into the back of Granny's guest room closet. "There!" she muttered. "Good excuse to never see it again." Brad had bought it for her with money they didn't have because he said he was tired of seeing her in her old navy pea coat. Her clothes and the car were two things she'd managed to salvage out of the financial aftermath of his death. And barely enough money to start the business.

Then it occurred to her that she ought to at least donate the coat to the Salvation Army so somebody could get some use out of it. What was she going to need with a full-length cashmere coat down here on the Gulf Coast anyway?

She pulled it out again and picked at several stiff black-and-gray dog hairs still clinging to the front. She smiled. Tommy's dog really was beautiful, if one appreciated hunting dogs. Grant's hounds were working dogs and wouldn't have anything to do with anybody but him. Skywalker, however, had a sweet, almost melancholy, expression in his dark eyes.

Skywalker's master was an interesting case, too. Carrie stood in front of the closet. What did one wear to have lunch with a coon-hunting, bass-fishing grease monkey? A cute one, though. Probably the chinos and rugby shirt she had on would be fine. She brushed her hair, decided against lipstick, and wandered into the kitchen.

Granny, wrapped in a pink-flowered apron over a black suede zipper-front dress with a leopard-print collar and cuffs, was removing an enormous pork roast from the Crock-Pot.

"Granny, did you invite the entire Seventh Fleet without telling me?"

Granny laughed. "We can always have leftovers. I imagine young Tommy can pack away some food, too."

"Ummm." Carrie opened the oven to check the sweet potato pie she'd made earlier that morning. "He seemed awfully glad for the invitation."

"I bet." Granny gave Carrie a sly look. "How 'bout those brown eyes?"

"I'd say they're more amber," she said,

then blushed. "Not that I really noticed. Oh, I hear somebody at the door. That must be him."

Carrie scooted into the den, ignoring Granny's grin.

When she opened the door, Tommy stood there with both hands extended, palms up. "All clean, teacher. No grease, no grime."

"Hmmm." She pretended to examine them, noting the scars grooving his tough skin and the Spiderman Band-Aid on his left thumb. "Okay, I guess I can let you in." She looked up to find he'd combed his wet hair back, revealing the clean triangular lines of his face. The morning's stubble was gone, and he smelled of something faintly spicy. He was dressed in jeans and a gray flannel shirt. Carrie put her hand against a sudden attack of butterflies in her stomach. *My goodness, he cleans up well.* Something about his openly pleased expression put a smile on her face.

"Come on in," she said. "Granny's about to put the food on the table. How are you at slicing a roast?"

"If it's anything like carving a deer, I imagine I can handle it."

Carrie shuddered. "How can you eat Bambi?"

"Oh, now don't start that," he admonished

her. "It's not any different than eating Wilbur."

"Wilbur?"

"Didn't you read *Charlotte's Web*?"

"Sure, but —"

"Or Elsie."

"Elsie?" Carrie giggled in spite of herself. "You mean the Borden's cow?"

"Right. And Foghorn Leghorn."

"Oh, I say, yeah, I say — would you cut that out, son?"

They'd reached the kitchen by then, where Granny was filling jelly jars with ice. At the sound of their laughter, she asked, "What's so funny?"

"Nothing." Carrie wiped the smile from her face.

Tommy walked over to Granny, threw an arm around her shoulders, and bussed her on the cheek. "Hey, gorgeous!"

Granny playfully punched him in the stomach. "Flattery will get you a huge meal around here!"

"That's what I was counting on." He took a deep breath of the heavenly kitchen smells, gave a sigh of contentment, and picked up the tea pitcher. "Can I help?"

Carrie took the pie out of the oven and set it on the counter to cool, surreptitiously watching Tommy, who was making himself at home with the glasses and silverware. Brad would have plunked himself in front of the TV and waited to be served.

When everything was finally on the table — Granny seated at the end, with Tommy and Carrie on either side of her — Granny held out both hands. "Tommy, would you say the blessing?"

"Sure," he said agreeably and bowed his head. "Dear God, thanks for the food, thanks for these two beautiful ladies, and thanks for a new year. Amen."

Carrie blinked. *Well, that was short and sweet.* But he hadn't seemed at all uncomfortable praying. His mother must have brought him up right.

During the meal, Carrie found it a culinary experience in itself to watch Tommy eat with the gusto of a man on death row. He praised the roast. He marveled over the black-eyed peas, dumping canned tomatoes over them until his entire plate swam with juice. He ate enough turnip greens to choke Wilbur himself. He saved his corn bread for last, as if it were dessert.

Chin in her palm, Carrie observed him, ignoring her own meagerly filled plate. He sank strong white teeth into the bread and closed his eyes blissfully.

"There is a God," he said indistinctly.

Carrie met Granny's twinkling eyes. Granny said, "Carrie made the corn bread. You know she studied cooking in college."

"No kidding?" Tommy turned those astonishing eyes on her and popped the crust into his mouth.

"Well, yes, but I learned to make corn bread from Granny. The secret's in the seasoning of the skillet."

"You'll have to show me sometime. I bet I could learn to do it."

Carrie couldn't help smiling, picturing Tommy's long, lanky body swathed in an apron.

"She made the sweet potato pie, too," Granny said helpfully.

Carrie gave her grandmother an annoyed look. She felt like a young maiden being touted to a new beau.

"Sweet potato pie?" Tommy yelped. "That's my *favorite!*"

"Well, isn't that a coincidence!" said Granny.

Since Granny had decided on the dessert that morning after Carrie tentatively offered to drive down to invite Tommy for lunch, it was clear that some ulterior motive was jumping around beneath Granny's hennaed curls. Carrie shoved her chair back. "I'll start the coffeemaker and cut the pie."

Ten minutes later they were seated in the den, Carrie with a mug of black coffee in her hand. Tommy and Granny each juggled a tall glass of milk and a big piece of pie covered in mountains of Cool Whip. Tommy settled in the brown cowboy-print recliner that still smelled faintly of Grandpa Hugh's pipe tobacco. He looked absurdly at home, balancing his saucer on one knee and winking at Granny as he clinked glasses with her.

He's so sweet, Carrie thought, *but no matter what Granny thinks, I'm not ready to get back into the dating scene. Especially with a kid five years younger than I am who works in a garage for a living.* Her conscience jabbed her. *I'm not a snob, Lord; I just don't have time for this.*

But she did have to be polite until he decided to take off and go back to poking around under the Batmobile. "So, Tommy, I understand you graduated with my sister Miranda. How 'bout filling in the years in between. Where did you go to college?"

Some of the delight faded from his face, but he said matter-of-factly, "I barely made it out of high school. Never went to college."

"Oh." Carrie could have bitten her tongue. She was sensitive about some of her own less-than-stellar career choices. Like getting a business degree, then spending six years making minimum wage as a bank teller.

Tommy slugged down half the glass of milk and licked off the white mustache. "I made some stupid mistakes in my time. But finally, about five years ago, I went to work for a guy who saw my interest in motors and taught me how to fix things instead of steal 'em and tear 'em apart."

Carrie's mouth dropped open. He'd just admitted he was a thief!

"Carl introduced me to the Lord, too." Unbelievably, tears welled in Tommy's eyes, and he blinked them away rapidly. "He moved away to go to seminary, let me buy the shop for what I could afford, and — here I am!"

"Carl Henry is going to make a wonderful pastor." Granny leaned over to put her hand on Tommy's corded forearm. "You remember him, Carrie?"

"Yes, of course I do." Carl had been one of the worst geeks in her senior class, forever messing around with computers and cars. Forever going on about "Jesus this" and "Jesus that." It made sense that he'd wind up in the ministry. "He used to lead a Bible study before school that I went to sometimes," she said.

When I wasn't too busy flirting with baseball

players. Maybe if I'd paid more attention to the Bible, I wouldn't have gotten snowed by a shallow jerk like Brad.

"What about you?" Tommy asked. "How come you went all the way up to Ole Miss to go to college?"

"I wanted to be as far away from home as I could get and still avoid out-of-state tuition," she admitted ruefully. "Grant chose Mississippi State, and Miranda went to Southern. We're one mixed-up family!"

He laughed. "Yeah, you are. Must make football season interesting around here. So you majored in home ec?"

Carrie shook her head. "Restaurant management. I fancied myself a business-woman."

He put down his plate and glass, leaned over to give her an intent look. "You'll do great."

Carrie glanced away, embarrassed by his admiring stare. "Maybe you could give me some tips on advertising. While I'm waiting on my equipment to be delivered soon, I thought I'd put up some flyers, maybe run an ad in the paper."

"Well, I mostly depend on word of mouth. I've got all the business my buddy Matthew and I can handle by ourselves."

"You do all the paperwork and every-thing?"

"Yeah, such as it is." He chuckled. "Taxes give me a hard time come April, but so far I've kept myself out of bankruptcy."

"I'm worried about that, too. Maybe I should find a good CPA."

"I know a guy in my church I could recommend."

"Oh, thanks, I —" Carrie stopped, re-alizing she'd been leaning toward Tommy, drawn by the sparkle in his eyes, hanging on his every word. She glanced at Granny, whose smirk was clearly visible behind her milk glass.

Carrie took refuge in her coffee mug.

"Looks to me like you'd better get some business before you figure on ways to spend your money," commented Granny, swiping the last crumbs of piecrust off her saucer with a finger and popping them into her mouth.

"How long before you can actually cater a job?" Tommy wanted to know. He seemed oblivious to Carrie's confusion and to Granny's Machiavellian streak.

"I guess I could cook right now out of Granny's kitchen," Carrie said, "but it will be a lot easier when I get my own place set up with a commercial stove and refrigera-

214

tor. I have to be inspected by the health department, too."

"I think I know somebody who might want a caterer pretty soon," Tommy said, and Carrie could practically see the wheels turning in his head. *Uh-oh.* She was afraid to ask what he had in mind.

Then he stuck his hand in the pocket of his jeans, pulled out a rubber band, and twisted it around his pinkie.

"What are you doing?" Carrie asked.

"That's to remind me to call my aunt Janelle when I get home. Want some more coffee?" When Carrie shook her head in bemusement, Tommy picked up Granny's plate, stacked it with his own, and carried all the dirty dishes into the kitchen. Momentarily Carrie heard the dishwasher rattling.

She stared at the doorway through which Tommy had disappeared. She had never before had her first impressions of a person so thoroughly turned upside down. What *was* Tommy Lucas? Reformed crook? Backwoods Bubba? Undereducated mechanic? Rising young businessman? Denim-clad saint?

Granny let out a low whistle. "That," said Granny, "is a gentleman."

That, Tommy told himself the next Sunday

215

as he stood behind Carrie, waiting to greet the pastor after the service, *is a lady.*

He enjoyed how the gold clasp of her necklace rested gracefully under the curve of her hair and the faint scent of something — apples? — drifting from her hair. She was dressed modestly but elegantly in a slim-fitting dress with a fluffy white sweater pulled across her shoulders. Her heels put the top of her head just about the level of his lips.

He was trying not to appear to be following her around, but ever since the lunch at Roxanne's last week, he found himself thinking about Carrie and hoping for another invitation. This past week, as he'd helped her move supplies and lighter equipment into her shop, he'd observed a woman he was coming to admire and wanted to know more about.

During this morning's worship service, he'd sat two rows behind her family with his employee and friend, Matthew Lamont, and kept an eye on the back of her head. During the "welcome" she'd turned around and caught his eye, smiling. Content, he'd directed his attention to the music and the sermon.

Brother David, the pastor, took Carrie's hand and gave her a sympathetic, welcoming smile. "Carrie . . . I heard you were back home after your husband's passing. I'm so sorry for your loss."

Her response was, Tommy thought, oddly unemotional. "I'm glad to be home," she said quietly.

"If there's anything you need — counseling or prayer — please call on me." The pastor patted Carrie awkwardly on her arm and turned to Tommy as she slipped out the door. "Tommy! Glad to see you."

"Uh, yeah, same here." Tommy shook hands quickly and squirmed his way past the people blocking the doorway. By the time he made it down the broad concrete steps leading to the gravel parking lot, Carrie had disappeared. He quickly scanned the remaining cars, hoping to see her ZX. No, but there was Roxanne's big white Buick parked under the only pecan tree in the lot.

Bingo!

He crunched across the gravel, rehearsing how he was going to invite himself over for lunch again. Then he saw Roxanne get out of the driver's seat and move to the front of the car and pop the hood.

"What's the matter?" Tommy called as he approached.

Roxanne was leaning so far under the car's

domed hood that her feet dangled off the ground. Her orange pantsuit stuck out from under the hood like a goldfish being swallowed by an albino whale.

Tommy neared and gave Carrie a friendly wave.

Through the open window she returned a worried smile. "I don't know. Granny said Daddy put some oil in her car last week; then he got beeped and had to leave for the hospital. Just now when Granny tried to start the engine, it made this horrible noise and . . . uh . . . just shut down."

"What kind of noise?" Tommy asked, prepared to operate.

"Like this." Carrie put her hands around her throat and pretended to choke. *"Awrck!"*

Tommy laughed. "Okay, let me take a look." He rolled up the sleeves of his only dress shirt and quickly skinned off his tie, cramming it into the back pocket of his jeans. "Roxanne!" he said loudly.

She wriggled backward until her feet touched the ground again. "Tommy!" she panted. "Am I glad to see you!"

"What kind of oil did Dr. G put in? Maybe it's the wrong kind."

"Well, it should be the same kind I always use, like you told me to. I've been carrying some around in my trunk since my car started that slow leak —"

"You need to bring it in and let me fix that," he said mildly, reaching for the dipstick. When he realized he didn't have a rag in his pocket like he usually did, he shrugged and used his tie to wipe the oil off the stick.

Except it wasn't motor oil. It was thin, translucent, and had a chemical odor wholly unlike petroleum.

He sniffed the soiled tie. "Roxanne, let me see the bottle this came out of."

*Tsk*ing and muttering about her pot roast burning, Roxanne trotted around to the trunk and returned with a brown motor oil bottle. "Here it is."

Carrie got out of the car and joined her grandmother. Both women stood watching Tommy anxiously.

Tommy looked at the front of the bottle and nearly exploded. "Roxanne! Did you look at this masking-tape label? It says ROUNDUP, bigger'n Dallas!"

Roxanne snatched the bottle. "I wondered what happened to that! I was going to poison the weeds in my flower beds yesterday —"

"You mean Daddy poured weed killer into Granny's car?" Horrified, Carrie looked up at Tommy.

"Well," said Roxanne philosophically, "the

stuff's guaranteed to kill anything green. Guess it works on white, too."

Tommy was not inclined to laugh. He felt like a good friend had just been done in. He loved this big old Buick. Ran like a sewing machine — or used to. "Roxanne, this stuff will destroy your engine." He unclipped his cell phone from his belt and dialed the number of the closest tow company. "We'll have it towed to my shop."

While he made towing arrangements, he kept an eye on Carrie. Roxanne didn't seem too concerned, but Carrie was shivering in the stiff gulf breeze. He wished he had a jacket to give her.

When he hung up, he looked around. The parking lot was now empty, the front doors of the church closed and locked for the afternoon.

Roxanne, who had been arguing with Carrie in a heated undertone, suddenly grabbed Tommy's sleeve. "Tell her she needs to go home and get out of this wind," she said, jerking her head at Carrie. "You won't mind giving her a ride, will you?"

Oh, to be a knight on a white horse right about then! Unfortunately, all Tommy had at the moment was his black Kawasaki motorcycle.

"Uh, no! Of course not. I mean, I'll be

glad to!"

"Granny, I'm f-fine!" Carrie insisted. "I'm not leaving you here by yourself!" She gave Tommy a nervous look, and he wondered if he'd inadvertently done something to put her off. She'd been friendly enough when he'd helped her move.

In the end, they all waited until the tow truck arrived; both women rode with the driver, and Tommy followed on his bike. It was nearly two o'clock by the time they reached the shop. Tommy had the driver back the Buick into the right-hand bay. Roxanne would be first priority Monday morning.

Tommy, Roxanne, and Carrie stood inside the garage, staring at the Buick in silence. Finally, Tommy said, "Friends and family, we have gathered here today to mourn the passing of our beloved —"

Carrie gave a shout of laughter. As Tommy grinned back at her, their eyes met, and a jolt of pure chemistry nearly pinned him to the wall. He even forgot that his stomach was turning itself inside out with hunger.

"Daddy's never going to live this down!" Carrie gasped, holding her stomach, tears streaming down her face.

"What if he treated his patients like he did my poor car?" snorted Roxanne.

"Man, that's not even funny!" But Tommy found himself exploding with laughter. "Come on, we'll borrow a truck I've been working on, and I'll take you ladies home."

"And you'll stay and eat pot roast with us," Roxanne declared. "Might be a little overdone, but we'll put lots of gravy on it."

"With mashed potatoes?" Tommy ventured hopefully.

"And Carrie's homemade yeast rolls." Roxanne waggled her absurd eyebrows.

"I have just gone to glory!" Tommy sighed and ducked into the office to retrieve the keys.

Monday morning Carrie slammed the door of her shop's mailbox, tucking a boxful of new business checks under her arm and shuffling through what looked like bills. Depressed, she stood in her empty parking lot, looking across at Lucas Import Service, where Granny's car was now parked outside the open bay. Inside, she could see the motor hung from a pulley attached to the ceiling. It looked like the carcass of a huge mechanical animal.

Tommy and his sidekick, Matthew, whom she had met briefly at choir practice last Wednesday night, walked around the motor, poking it and discussing it, for all the world like two butchers regarding cuts of meat. Tommy laughed at something Matthew said and slung an arm around the boy's hulking shoulders. Matthew probably wasn't much younger than Tommy, but he seemed juvenile in comparison to Tommy's . . .

What could she call it? He wasn't self-absorbed. Or cocky. Just absolutely centered in who he was, without pretense or worry whether anyone liked him or not. She knew, because she had watched him at church and at her grandmother's house. And this past week when he'd helped her move into the shop, carting in box after box of kitchen supplies.

She'd been on the verge of walking over to visit with Tommy and Matthew, but then she thought of Brad, and as usual, that sucked away any impulse to make male friends. Especially young, single, male friends.

Carrie wheeled around and headed for the cottage to finish painting the latticework, which she planned to decorate with silk greenery for the lobby.

Better safe than sorry.

CHAPTER THREE

"Hey, Sky, you in the mood for a praline?" Tommy jerked his head in the direction of Carrie Ann's Chocolate Confections and Catering, where lights were coming on behind the gauzy white curtains, and the professionally painted Closed sign flipped to read Open.

Since Skywalker seemed more interested in chasing coons in his sleep than either candy or women, Tommy sighed and went back to work. Now that he'd gotten Roxanne's car back in commission and returned to her, he worked outside as much as possible, because the garage didn't have windows facing the cottage next door.

I'll be glad when spring gets here, he thought, blowing on his red, chapped fingers. He selected a wrench from the rolling cart he'd pulled into the driveway and bent over the exposed innards of a '92 Toyota minivan left yesterday by his pastor's wife.

He'd hated to tell her it wouldn't be ready in time for her trip to a women's Bible conference, so he'd been working since five this morning.

Skywalker whined and wriggled more firmly against Tommy's leg. The dog apparently objected to the cold, too. "Sorry, boy." Tommy gave the hound an absent pat. But he wasn't sorry enough to move the car into the garage.

Ever since the Roundup episode two weeks ago, he'd been working up the nerve to ask Carrie out. The more he saw of her, the more she intrigued him. Classy girl. No, not really a girl. She wasn't inwardly focused like most of the women his age he knew. She displayed a passionate love for her family. She was a hard worker and showed good sense and a woman's determination to get her business off the ground.

Last Monday her kitchen equipment had arrived in an eighteen-wheeler so big it blocked the entire intersection for half the day. His own customers had complained at the inconvenience, but he'd apologized and suggested they come back tomorrow. That shut them up. Then a few days later, the health department visited. Apparently Carrie passed with flying colors, because the GRAND OPENING banner went up the next day.

He'd wandered over during her open house on Saturday. He couldn't believe how quickly she'd cleaned and organized her new establishment. Inside, she'd turned flea-market wicker furniture into an elegant white-painted haven with pouffy cushions and flowery upholstery and green plants everywhere. At least he assumed they were green. Because of his color blindness, Tommy never could get red and green straight, which was why his wardrobe consisted of a fine collection of jeans and sweatshirts. Even Carrie's cash register was a classy antique with a bell that dinged every time the cash drawer opened.

He could hear the wind chimes tinkling above the swing her father had hung on the porch. Dr. Gonzales and Carrie's brother, Grant, had been there a lot the first week, helping her paint the porch rail and clean up the scraggly yard. Roxanne and Linda Gonzales had worked inside on the furniture and curtains, the two of them singing loud enough to wake every soul in the cemetery across the highway.

Tommy wondered what it would be like to have such a tight family.

Suddenly, the cordless phone rang, startling him so that he whacked his head on the Toyota's hood. Rubbing the rising bump, he picked the phone up. "Lucas Import Service." He listened, sighed, and said as patiently as he could, "No, ma'am, I don't sell rugs. It's okay. Thank you and have a nice day."

When was Aunt Janelle going to call him back? He'd left a message nearly two weeks ago. He knew she was busy. She ran a florist shop in Mobile, but she and Uncle Ronny were his only relatives who even acknowledged his existence. Janelle was the ideal person to give Carrie's business a boost.

He glanced at the empty parking lot next door. Carrie had had maybe ten customers since her grand opening. She needed help. Granted, Vancleave wasn't a metropolis by any stretch of the imagination, but there ought to be enough business to keep her busy if she could get word of mouth rolling.

Tommy sat down on a bucket, absently running his hand down the bony ridge of Skywalker's back. *Lord, I know it wasn't any accident you brought Carrie to work next door to me. How do you want me to help her?*

Snatches of Scripture from last night's single's Bible study ran through his mind, but because he couldn't remember it all, he went to get his Bible off the tool bench in the garage. Here it was, Philippians 2: "Is there any encouragement from belonging to Christ? Any comfort from his love? Any fellowship together in the Spirit? Are your hearts tender and sympathetic?"

Tommy stopped and smiled to himself. *Tenderness* and *sympathy* summed up pretty well his new feelings for Carrie Pierce. Yes, and a strong dose of attraction.

He kept reading: "Then make me truly happy by agreeing wholeheartedly with each other, loving one another, and working together with one heart and purpose. Don't be selfish; don't live to make a good impression on others. Be humble, thinking of others as better than yourself. Don't think only about your own affairs, but be interested in others, too, and what they are doing."

He closed the Bible on his finger and bowed his head. *Lord, I don't know her well enough to know if she's a believer, but does that matter at this point? Can't I just be kind to her and let you work out the details?*

"Are you feeling okay, Tommy?"

He looked up. *Wow, Lord, that was fast.*

Carrie leaned around the minivan, her heart-shaped face framed by the upturned collar of a short navy coat.

He jumped to his feet, dumping Skywalker's rear onto the gravel. "Oh, sure, I was just reading my Bible and praying."

"Out *here?*"

"Why not here?"

"Well, it's just . . . never mind. I saw you working one minute, and the next you were hunched over with your head down . . ." She floundered.

She'd been watching him, too! Rejoicing, he took pity on her. "So how's business going, now that you've got your kitchen set up?"

Carrie inched toward him around the front of the minivan. The trace of anxiety in her dark eyes belied her bright smile. "I'm having a great time making candy. I've always wanted to experiment with some recipes I learned in college."

"If you ever need a taste tester, I volunteer," he said, pulling up another bucket. "Have a seat."

"No, thanks, I — well, all right. Maybe for just a minute." She sat down and folded her arms. They looked at one another, and finally Carrie blurted, "Tommy, I'm scared to death this business is going to bomb. I don't want to ask my dad for money, but I don't know what else to do. I've done all the advertising I can afford."

Tommy drew a breath and blew it out slowly. *Okay, Lord, I need help here.* He leaned toward her, forearms on his knees.

229

"Carrie, you know what I do when I'm stumped about something?" She shook her head. "I pray."

"You sound just like Granny." She rolled her eyes. "I already prayed."

He hesitated. "I've got to ask you something, and I don't want you to take it the wrong way."

"Well?" She tilted her head, frowning.

"Do you know the Lord personally?"

"You mean, did I walk down an aisle and get baptized? Sure, when I was about ten."

"Well, yeah, but when you did that, did you repent of your sins and trust your heart to Jesus?"

Carrie looked puzzled at his question. "Of course I did. Isn't that what everybody does?"

"I wish," Tommy sighed, relieved that she seemed to have a relationship with Christ. "If God's not answering your prayers, Carrie, there could be a lot of reasons. Sometimes it's because we're asking with wrong motives. Sometimes he's simply got a better plan for us."

"I don't see how he could object to the motive of feeding myself. And if God's got a better plan," she muttered, "I wish he'd let me in on it." Carrie bit her lip and snapped her fingers at Skywalker, who sat on her foot and blissfully allowed his chin to be scratched. "I refuse to be a failure anymore."

She waited, gently rocking her plastic bucket, avoiding Tommy's eyes. Eyes that were filled with a peace that was in direct contrast to the barely contained energy of his body. Eyes that had seen, in less than five minutes, what people who'd known her all her life couldn't drag out of her.

I'm afraid to fail. Career. Marriage. Pleasing God. She had made a mess of it all. But there was something about Tommy Lucas that had broken through her fear and made her seek him out this morning. She hoped this wasn't the biggest mistake of her life.

"Would you be comfortable praying with me?" Tommy turned his hands palms up, the fingers gently curled. A fresh Band-Aid adorned a different finger, and the rubber band was gone from his pinkie.

"Did you call your aunt Janelle?" she asked to avoid his question.

"Uh-huh." He reached for her hands.

Not wanting to hurt his feelings, she gave them to him and felt immediately comforted by his strength and gentleness. She closed her eyes, washed by regrets that she and Brad had never prayed together.

"Father," he began, "I want to thank you

for my new friend Carrie and to ask you on her behalf to give her direction and strength and inspiration. Sorry we have to get to the end of the road before we turn to you. But thank you that you welcome us back when we do. I pray not just for her business, but for her *life,* that you'd pour your Spirit on her and bring her joy and new desire to follow you. In Jesus' name." He waited, as if to give her the opportunity to pray, but since her throat was clogged with most unwelcome tears, Tommy quietly said, "Amen" and squeezed her fingers gently.

"How did you get like this?" she asked, once she trusted herself to speak.

Sliding his fingers from hers, Tommy blinked. "What do you mean?"

"So . . . so content. I mean, look at this place."

He did and evidently saw something different than she did. He shrugged and grinned. " 'I have learned how to get along happily whether I have much or little. I know how to live on almost nothing or with everything. I have learned the secret of living in every situation, whether it is with a full stomach or empty, with plenty or little. For I can do everything with the help of Christ who gives me the strength I need.' " He paused sheepishly. "Our Sunday night

Bible study has been in Philippians for a while."

"I know, but —" Carrie recalled the disparaging remarks her father and brother had made concerning Tommy Lucas's background, education, and prospects while they'd helped her get Confections ready for business. She suspected they didn't really know him. Tommy could have chosen to humiliate her father about the Roundup in Granny's car. But he'd chosen, instead, to treat pouring weed killer into a motor as a natural mistake anyone could have made. A spark of anger kindled on Tommy's behalf. "Listen, it's cold out here," she said. "Why don't you come get a cup of hot cocoa, and I'll let you try one of my chocolate-covered apples."

Tommy bounced up off his bucket, looking as if he'd just been summoned for the Rapture, when the phone rang. He found it under a greasy towel near a pile of used tires. "Lucas Import," he said abruptly, rolling his eyes at Carrie and mouthing, "Don't leave." Suddenly his eyes widened. "Aunt Janelle!"

As he listened, Carrie watched his expression change from surprise to respect to delight, all in the space of one minute. "Yes, ma'am!" he exclaimed, grinning and giving

Carrie a thumbs-up. "We'll be there in ten minutes." He pressed the Cancel button and tossed the phone onto the front seat of the minivan. "Come on, we've got to get over there while she's in town. Wanna take my bike or your car?"

"Get over where? Tommy, wait a minute!"

She and Skywalker trotted after him into the garage, where he went over to a liter-size pump bottle labeled Fast Orange and slathered his hands with citrus-smelling orange goop that magically began to dissolve the grease. He wiped his hands on a marginally less greasy rag, then picked up a motorcycle helmet adorning an air pump. "Here, you take this one. I've got another one on the bike."

"Tommy Lucas, I'm not getting on the back of a motorcycle in the middle of January!"

"Okay, no problem; we'll take your Z."

Carrie dug in her heels. "Not until you tell me where we're going!"

He pressed a button that closed the open door of the garage, leaving Skywalker inside sulking on his carpet. "Churl's Cut 'n Curl."

"Excuse me?"

He laughed. "My cousin's beauty shop. Churl's Cut 'n Curl."

"What kind of name is Churl?"

Tommy shrugged. "I don't know; it's just a name. Listen, we've got to hurry. Aunt Janelle's over there getting her hair done, but she's got to be back in Mobile by noon."

"That's fine, but why do I have to go?"

"Shoot, I forgot to tell you. My aunt owns a florist shop in Mobile. She's got all kinds of contacts in the wedding business, and she can be a big help to you if she likes you."

"Tommy!" Carrie felt like hugging him. "You are truly a prince!"

"I know. You can kiss me later." He grabbed her hand. "Let's go."

In less than five minutes, Carrie was seated in the passenger seat of her own car, headed down Old River Road. Tommy had walked around the car, practically drooling, until she'd given in and offered him the keys. "I'll be careful, I promise," he'd said, reverently cranking the engine and then sitting there listening to it purr sweetly for nearly a minute.

"It still smells new," he sighed as he navigated a sharp turn in the narrow road.

Carrie, who'd been enjoying the competent way he handled the wheel and the unsettling feeling of masculinity he brought into the small space of her car, grimaced. "It's transportation."

"Carrie, this is not just transportation; it's

man's best friend."

"You sound just like Brad," she muttered.

"Who's Brad?"

"My husband."

Tommy clicked his tongue and gave her a cautious glance. "Was this his car?"

"No. If it was it would have been wrapped around a telephone pole." When Tommy winced, Carrie sighed. "I'm sorry, but it still makes me angry."

"I guess I'd be angry, too, if my spouse was killed in a wreck," he said sympathetically.

"Well, yeah, there's that. But I'm angry with myself that I let him run over me from the first day we met. I'm angry that I didn't insist we go to counseling when things started getting hairy between us. I'm angry that he gave me *things* instead of himself. I'm angry that he was with another woman when they pulled him out of that wreck." Carrie heard her voice getting higher and higher with every word, until it disappeared completely, and, humiliated, she put her hands to her face and leaned against the window.

She vaguely realized that Tommy pulled the car off the road near a bridge and stopped on a dirt road. He got out of the car and came around to open her door, where he crouched, his face level with hers. "Turn around," he said gently, putting one big hand on her knees and the other against the back of her head. She let him pull her head against his shoulder, where she lay shuddering and listening to the comforting thump of his heart. "It's okay," he said, and she suddenly felt like it was.

Lord, I wish I'd found one just like this guy the first time around — except a few years older, with a respectable job. Gentle, tender-hearted, and utterly reliable.

She sighed and relaxed. "I'm sorry, Tommy."

"Hey, you've had a rough time lately."

"I can't believe I told you all that stuff."

"Sometimes you know people by their heart."

Thoroughly rattled by her own candor, Carrie thought, *He's either the corniest or the most profound man I've ever met.*

"Yeah, well, I'm not usually such a whiny-baby." She sat up and wiped her face with her fingertips. "We're gonna miss your aunt Janelle."

"I bet she'll wait on us. She likes me for some reason."

Carrie found a tissue and blew her nose, while Tommy got back into the car. "I wonder why," she murmured.

■ ■ ■ ■

Tommy was relieved to see Aunt Janelle's Fleetwood parked in front of the beauty shop, which was in a red brick building that used to be a convenience store in the eighties. There were still a couple of old-fashioned gas tanks in front and a sign advertising Marlboros for sixty cents a pack. He pulled the Z up beside the Caddie and started to get out, but he stopped with one foot on the ground when Carrie burst into laughter.

He looked at her sharply. Was she making fun of his cousin's digs?

"Cheryl," she chuckled. "C-H-E-R-Y-L. *Cheryl*'s Cut 'n Curl."

"What's so funny?"

"Tommy, you're mispronouncing her name. It's *Sherr-ill*. Not *Churl*."

"Everybody in my family says it that way." He wanted to be offended, but the laughter on Carrie's face was such a welcome replacement for her tears, he simply shrugged. "You call her *Sherr-ill* if you want to, but she won't know who you're talking to."

Carrie giggled again but said okay and got out of the car.

Tommy held the door of the shop open

for Carrie. As he entered behind her, the chemical smells of perms and conditioners and hair spray nearly knocked him down. And people always said fish camps smelled. He shook his head, feeling immediately too big, too male, and too dirty for this place. Despite his color blindness, the virulent shades of the women's plastic capes and even the paint on the walls screamed, "Notice me!" There were mirrors everywhere, casting his lanky reflection all over the long narrow room. He'd never been inside Cheryl's shop in the six months she'd been in business, and he hoped this would be the last time.

Only for Carrie.

He stuck his hands under his armpits and stood by the reception desk, fielding the curious stares of stylists and customers. He hoped his cousin was out to lunch, or this was going to be a bumpy ride.

"Can I help you?" asked a big-haired, big-bosomed woman behind the desk. Her name badge said Pearl.

"Uh, no thanks, I'm looking for —" He spotted his aunt at the other end of the room with her head under the upside-down plastic bowl of a hair dryer. He jerked his head at Carrie, who followed him, looking around with interest. She outclassed this place by a country mile.

Aunt Janelle came out from under the bowl, and Tommy felt himself blanch. Her head was covered by a clear plastic cap, through which sprigs of green-painted hair sprouted like monkey grass. "Tom-Tom!" she exclaimed, hooking a soft pudgy arm around his neck and smacking him on the cheek. "I'm so glad you came over. I haven't seen you in a coon's age!"

Attempting to keep his gaze off the top of his aunt's head and trying not to breathe, Tommy hugged her. "Thanks for calling me back. I wanted you to meet Carrie." He tugged Carrie to his side, giving her a pleading look. "I'm going back outside. I noticed one of your tires is a little —"

"Delighted to meet you, Carrie," said Janelle, squeezing Carrie's hand, then grabbing Tommy by the elbow. "Now, Tommy, you've got to speak to Cheryl before you go. She's back there working on the books. Cheryl!" Janelle hollered toward the doorway behind her. "Come out here and say hi to your cousin Tommy!"

There was no way out. Carrie was looking at him curiously, so he briefly closed his eyes and prayed for strength. When he opened them, Cheryl was leaning against the door frame, staring at him with a mocking curve to her dark-painted mouth. She stuck her hands in the pockets of a black smock that covered up her tight jeans and T-shirt. He wondered if anybody else saw the hatred in those deep-set eyes.

"Well, Tommy," she drawled, shaking back a mop of curly bleached-blonde hair. "What a surprise. Where's your sidekick today? Standing on a street corner, I bet, threatening to send somebody to hell."

Tommy kept his temper with an effort. "I didn't come to argue with you, Cheryl. I brought my friend Carrie to meet your mom."

Cheryl's dead-bright eyes quickly scanned Carrie. "You're movin' up in the world, I see."

"Now, Cheryl," tsked Janelle. "Quit being so silly. Tommy's friend is a businesswoman like me and you. She's got a new candy shop and catering business, and I thought she might be interested in taking on some jobs in Mobile. All those Valentine weddings coming up, plus Mardi Gras, and everybody I know is swamped."

Cheryl's appraisal grew calculating. "You're not thinking about investing, are you, Mama?"

"I might," Janelle said offhandedly. Tommy saw Carrie's pretty mouth fall open. Cheryl

241

straightened abruptly.

Before fireworks could explode in front of all these innocent bystanders, Tommy jumped in. "Cheryl, Matthew says you went to Bible study with him last Sunday."

"Yes, I did, thanks to you," his cousin said with a smile as false as the color of her hair. "He pestered me about it until I gave in."

"That Matthew's a different boy since he went to work for you, Tommy," said Janelle, beaming.

"Yeah, a prude," muttered Cheryl.

Her mother ignored her. "I think he's going to make something of himself after all."

Tommy knew Carrie must think the whole bunch of them were crazy. Maybe it had been a mistake to come here, after all. Emotional undercurrents whirled like a riptide through the little salon.

But Cheryl apparently decided to be good. She released Tommy's gaze with a shrug. "You're looking kinda shaggy, Cuz. Want a haircut while you're here?"

He looked in the mirror, noticed his hair was beginning to kick up in curls over his ears. He brushed back the hank that had flopped in his eyes. He liked to keep it neat. Especially since he was hoping Carrie . . .

He glanced at her.

"I've got to get back to the store," she said

apologetically.

"Aw, come on, it won't take ten minutes," Cheryl said, whipping a plastic cape out of a nearby cabinet and whirling a chair around. "Have a seat, Tommy-boy; I'll fix you right up." She looked at her mother. "Mama, get back under that dryer or you're gonna have a mess."

Janelle sat back down and picked up her magazine. "You'd better catch her while she's in a good mood, Tommy," she advised. "This girl's been crankier than a sore-tailed cat lately."

Tommy met Carrie's eyes in the mirror as he reluctantly sat down. She smiled good-naturedly and took a seat at the empty station next to Cheryl's, while his cousin fastened the cape around his neck.

"I don't know what I'd have to be cranky about," Cheryl muttered behind a smile as she pulled a comb, scissors, and an electric razor out of a drawer. "Just because I had to move back in with the Grand Inquisitor and his wife. Daddy pesters me to death every time I leave the house. Bend your head down."

Tommy obeyed. He felt the buzz of the razor zip up the back of his head. "Cheryl . . . your dad just wants to make sure you're safe. I'm sorry things didn't turn out like you planned, but once you and Matthew get your act together, you'll be fine."

"I *was* fine until you stuck your nose in my business and turned Matthew into Saint Francis of a Sissy!"

To his horror, Tommy felt the razor burn a path all the way across the top of his head. Cheryl hadn't put a guard on the end of it, and there was now a two-inch bald strip right down the center, where his cowlick used to be.

"Oops," said Cheryl.

"Cheryl!" he roared, jumping to his feet.

Aunt Janelle came out from under the dryer and yanked Cheryl's arm up in the air as if she held a smoking gun. Pearl and a couple of other stylists grabbed Tommy by the arms, like referees in a wrestling match. Carrie sat in her chair with her hands over her mouth, eyes wide with disbelief.

All the filthy words Tommy had ever learned in the trailer park he grew up in swarmed into his mind like ugly, vicious wasps. Recognizing the source, he began to pray. He prayed like crazy. He shut his eyes, swallowed, and deliberately unclenched his fists. He took a deep breath, then a couple more, and finally relaxed enough that the women let go of him and backed away.

"You okay, Son?" he heard Aunt Janelle say. He opened his eyes. She was holding Cheryl, patting her back, looking sympathetically at Tommy.

"I'm fine." It came out through his teeth, but he said it. "I look like I got in a fight with a weed-whacker, but — I'm fine." He heard a snort of laughter from Carrie. He looked at her, and the mirth in her eyes brought a grin to his own mouth. "Wadda *you* lookin' at?" he growled facetiously.

"Oh, Tommy, your beautiful hair," she giggled.

"What beautiful hair?" He self-consciously plopped both hands on his head. "What am I gonna do about this?"

"Just shave it all off," Carrie suggested. "You'll look very —" she snickered — "very masculine."

"Oh, really?" He folded his arms and surveyed himself in the mirror. "You know what? I think that's a pretty good idea. Pearl, come over here."

"Me?" Pearl squeaked, placing a hand on her pillowlike bosom.

"Yes, you. You're the only person in this room I trust not to sever my head from my shoulders."

"But I haven't cut hair in —"

"There's a very big tip in it for you if you

don't nick my head."

Pearl looked at Cheryl, who shrugged sulkily, without the least repentance. "Go ahead; finish him off," Cheryl said.

Tommy clamped his lips together and sat down in the chair again. "Come on, Pearl. Carrie and I are on a schedule."

While Pearl bravely wielded the razor, Aunt Janelle patted her daughter's shoulder. "Now, Cheryl, you owe Tommy an apology." Without waiting for her to produce one, Janelle's eyes brightened. "I have an idea! To make it up to you, I'll have your friend cater a Mardi Gras party I just booked for next month. How does that sound?"

"But you don't even know me," said Carrie, looking uncomfortable.

Tommy saw Carrie glance at Cheryl, who gave a contemptuous snort. "If I were you, I'd go for it. The party's in Spring Hill, and those people got more money than sense." Cheryl stalked toward the front of the salon and said over her shoulder, "That is, if you think you can handle it." She opened the cash register with a loud *ding* and began to count money.

Aunt Janelle shook her head. "I don't know what I'm going to do with that girl." She smiled apologetically at Carrie. "Never mind her. Do you want the job or not? It'll be your chance to prove yourself."

As the last of his hair floated to the already hairy floor, Tommy met Carrie's troubled eyes in the mirror. He sighed. "Well, at least *something* good's gonna come out of this fiasco."

CHAPTER FOUR

Carrie pulled her ZX into the Quick-Stop and looked over at Tommy, who slumped in the passenger seat with his slick head laid back against the headrest. His eyes were closed, veiling his expression, but his mouth was still set in a grim line. The starkness of his profile, relieved only by straight black brows and heavy lashes, gave him the exotic look of an Eastern prince. She supposed she ought to feel sorry for him, but instead she found herself proud of his forbearance with his cousin's outrageous behavior.

When she cut the engine and said, "Are you okay?" Tommy rolled his head sideways to look at her.

"I feel kinda like Samson after Delilah got ahold of him." He smiled faintly, then noticed where they were. "You've got more than a quarter tank of gas. Most women wait till they're on Empty."

"Daddy trained me well." Carrie

shrugged. "Besides, you look like you could use a soda."

"You're an angel. I'll pump your gas."

"Deal." But when he started to get out, she put a hand on his wrist. "Just a minute, Tommy." She hesitated, struggling with herself. There had been more to that scene in the beauty shop than an "accident" with an electric razor. But Carrie had enough to worry about on her own, without the complications of caring about Tommy Lucas and his spoiled, selfish young cousin.

"What is it?" Tommy asked, his expression guarded.

"I know it's none of my business —"

"Carrie, you can ask me anything." He sighed and looked out the window. "I just hated to involve you in our family spat more than you wanted to be."

Carrie hesitated. "Okay, then I want to know what that was all about with Cheryl."

He scrubbed his hands up and down his face. "It's not a pretty story."

For the first time in a long time, Carrie felt the Holy Spirit breathing in her ear. *Lord, Tommy listened and held me when I needed him. Help me understand. Use me.* "Just tell me what's going on. If I'm going to work with your aunt, it might help if I . . ." She stopped, because that wasn't all the truth. The truth was, she wanted to understand what made Tommy Lucas the kind of man who would forgive and laugh at a malicious prank at his expense. The kind of man who would go out of his way to help a stranger next door.

Oh, Lord, don't let me get in too deep, she begged.

"Okay. Remember you asked for it. I grew up in a trailer park off Magnolia Road and was out of school more than I was in it. Your people would probably call mine trailer trash. I never knew my dad. But Aunt Janelle managed to go to business college, went to work for that florist, and worked her way up until she bought the shop. She's a good woman, Carrie. She always made sure I had shoes and clothes and even took me home with her sometimes when she thought Mama's boyfriends were getting too rough with me."

The stark truth in Tommy's golden eyes caught Carrie by the throat. *Oh, Lord, why didn't you protect him?*

He gave a half smile. "I was pretty much bad to the bone. Aunt Janelle tried hard, even took me to church sometimes, but I got in all kinds of trouble." Carrie tilted her head, listening, so Tommy went on. "Well, I did manage to graduate from high school, but I started running around with this motorcycle crowd, partying all the time, until I ran head-on into Carl Henry and the Lord. I already told you that story." Carrie nodded. "So when I found out my cousin Cheryl was hanging out with Matthew, one of my old buddies, I interfered. Now she's mad at me. End of story."

Carrie stared at him, perplexed. "That's it?"

He looked uneasy. "You'd probably better get her to tell you about it. It's not really my place."

Carrie thoughtfully tapped her nails on the console between them. She knew she could probably talk him into telling her more. *Lord, how much do I push him?*

Telling herself it really *wasn't* any of her business, she touched Tommy's hand. "Okay. If the subject ever comes up. Now what do you want to drink?"

Carrie went into the store, where Elvin Goff sat reading a newspaper behind the counter, his half-glasses perched precariously on the end of his long, narrow nose. "Hi, Mr. Elvin. Remember me?" She perused the soft-drink cooler and selected a Mountain Dew for Tommy and a cream soda for herself.

The proprietor removed his glasses and

squinted. "Well, bless my soul if it ain't Carrie Ann Gonzales. Sugar Baby queen of the South! You home from college for the weekend?"

Carrie plunked her drinks and two bags of her favorite candy on the counter and nodded toward the window, where Tommy could be seen lounging against the car, one hand on the gas pump. "Add this to the gas, please. No, actually, I'm home for good now." She smiled. The old man had apparently lost track of time, and there was no point explaining her more recent past to him. "I've got a new candy store, right next to Tommy Lucas's garage."

Mr. Elvin looked out the window and shook his buzzardlike head, muttering, "These kids and their weird hairdos." He bagged Carrie's purchases and took her credit card. "Gonna put me out of business, huh?"

"Nope, my candy is the expensive homemade stuff," she laughed. "You'll still have kids in here by the droves this summer, I'm sure."

"Guess that's true." Mr. Elvin winked. "You keep young Tommy straight now, you hear?"

Carrie blushed. "I will," she replied.

She fanned her hot face with her hand as

she walked back outside. She was going to have to watch how often she was seen running around with Tommy. People were going to get the wrong idea.

"I think you should lose the baseball cap, man," said Matthew as he handed Tommy a socket wrench. "The skinhead look's kinda cool."

Since Cheryl's twenty-two-year-old boyfriend sported a nose ring and a T-shirt that read "Gorillas have big nostrils because they have big fingers," Tommy wasn't noticeably comforted. "Yeah, well, a buzz cut in February's not my idea of a smart fashion statement."

"You just got it bad for that chick next door," observed Matthew. "Why don't you go ahead and ask her out? All she can do is say no."

"I've been trying to for the last two weeks, but she treats me like her little brother. Every time I go over there, she hands me a spoon to stir something."

"Well, look at the bright side. At least you come home with some kickin' candy. Want me to go open up one of those bags of green stuff?"

Tommy glanced through the doorway into his office/reception area. It looked like the set of *Willy Wonka and the Chocolate Factory*. Gallon ziplock bags of heart-shaped candy teetered in lumpy stacks on the metal desk and filled the seats of both Naugahyde-and-metal office chairs. "I'll be a hundred years old before I can eat all that," he said ruefully.

Matthew picked up a rag and a can of wax to start working on the Ferrari's passenger door. "It was really nice of her to give it to you."

"She said she couldn't use it. Who's gonna want green Valentine candy?" Tommy sighed. "I messed it up, so I, uh, bought it."

"You paid for all that? What are you, nuts?"

"It didn't cost that much." Tommy bent over the car again, twisting off the radiator cap. "I was helping. The food-coloring label got covered by a price sticker, and I thought it was red."

"Why didn't you just tell her you're color-blind?"

Tommy hunched his shoulders. "She already thinks I'm a redneck."

"You know what your problem is, man? You got a big fat load of pride, that's what."

Tommy looked at Matthew, whose square face was set in concentration as he almost worshipfully applied the wax to the candy-apple red paint. The words were profound, painful, and no less true for the fact that they came out of the mouth of a guy who less than two months ago had been destined for jail time. Tommy decided it was time to change the subject. "Did you read the passage in Ephesians I told you to read over the weekend?"

"Yeah, I did." Matthew sighed. "This Christian stuff is no joke. I thought once I prayed for salvation, that was pretty much it."

"No, it's just the beginning. You and Cheryl are starting off with a couple of strikes against you as it is. You better take advantage of this time to get to know the Lord, before you even think about getting married."

Matthew suddenly sat back against the cinder-block wall, the rag hanging limp in his hand. "Sometimes I think I'd give a million dollars to go back and change the last five years of my life."

Looking at him, Tommy saw himself and blessed God that nothing worse than a slap on the wrist from a juvenile court judge had ever happened to him. "I know, man." Compassion urged Tommy to sympathize, but reality was reality. "But a real man will hang tough. And I know that's what you are. I've seen you grow a lot in the last few weeks."

"I gotta tell you —" Matthew shook his head — "the idea of gettin' married scares me outta my mind." He grimaced. "If nothin' else, Cheryl's mother would drive me to homicide."

Tommy laughed. "Yeah, Aunt Janelle's a piece of work." He hesitated, sobering. "Look, Matt, I know you want to do the right thing and marry Cheryl. But I've told you what the Bible says about being un-equally yoked. Right now Cheryl's about as far from the Lord as she can get. I think you ought to wait and pray. She'll try to pull you off the path, and then you'll both be miserable."

"I guess." Matthew didn't look convinced, but before he could say more, the phone rang. He found it behind a bunch of air filters on the work bench and answered, "Hello? Lucas Import." He listened, then handed the phone to Tommy. "For you. Some hysterical female."

It was Joy Chapman, the pastor's wife, calling from her car phone. "Tommy, the brakes keep going out on me," she said, obviously in distress. "I've got all four kids with me, and I just left the grocery store —"

"Okay, I get the picture," he soothed. "Just drive here as carefully as you can. Since the garage is on a slope, that should slow you enough that you can cut the engine without tearing something up."

"I'm almost there. Bye."

As the connection cut, Tommy peered out the window and saw the malfunctioning minivan approach over a rise in the road. "Matthew, put the garage door up. Joy Chapman's on her way in."

Carrie was happily restocking a glass display case with chocolate-covered apples, pecan pralines, divinity, and fantasy fudge, when her father pushed open the front door and stuck his head in.

"You must be collecting kickbacks from every dentist on the Gulf Coast," he said, taking a deep, appreciative sniff of the sugary smells.

Carrie laughed and went to kiss his cheek. "Business has picked up a lot lately. Granny's been helping me put together gift baskets, and they're selling well to gift shops in Ocean Springs and Mobile."

Huey Gonzales stuck his hands in his pants pockets and wandered idly around the room. "I'm proud of you, sweetheart. I have to admit, I wasn't sure you could handle this on your own, but you've picked up the pieces and landed on your feet."

Carrie busied herself rearranging the cash drawer, not sure how to take that backhanded compliment. "Uh, thanks, Daddy."

She watched her father look out the side window — the one with the view of Tommy's hand-painted wall. She'd gotten used to its mismatched lettering and in-your-face advertising.

During their four weeks' acquaintance, she'd discovered that there was nothing subtle about Tommy. He would wander down the slope between their buildings at least once a day and stand around hopefully until she gave him something to eat. She'd finally convinced him that he couldn't stick his fingers into her candy syrup; she had even allowed him to help until he turned that enormous batch of Valentine candy greener than the hills of Killarney. His chagrin over his mistake had been endearing and funny.

More endearing than she wanted to admit.

Tommy wanted to ask her out. Carrie knew it, and she knew he knew she knew it. It was there in his eyes every time he looked at her. But . . . she couldn't imagine deliberately changing the texture of their budding friendship. Instinctively she knew that

Tommy, despite his cheerful, humorous outlook, would be serious about any romantic relationship in his life.

Serious and *romantic* in the same thought Carrie did not need.

So lately she'd avoided being alone with him as much as possible, tried to keep things light, and diffused his ardor with humor whenever she saw that expression in his eyes. She wouldn't even let herself ask any more questions about that disastrous encounter with his cousin Cheryl.

Apparently her father had been cogitating upon the problem of Tommy Lucas as well. "There's just something not quite right about that boy over there," he murmured, jingling the change in his pockets.

"What do you mean?" Carrie paused in the act of stuffing credit card receipts into a bank bag. "He's one of the nicest people I've met since I came back to Vancleave."

Dad walked to the front window and twitched the curtain. "Oh, I didn't say he wasn't a nice kid. He's calmed down a lot since the boys played baseball together. He used to be the one you could count on to get into a fight after the game."

"Daddy, what is your point?"

"He just seems to have no goals, no ambition. I mean, look at that place over there."

Since her father's words echoed what she'd said to Tommy's face a couple of weeks ago, she couldn't argue. However, she found herself feeling defensive on Tommy's behalf. "He's making a good living."

"If that's true, then why doesn't he do something about cleaning up the yard or at least putting up a decent sign?"

"Have you looked at 90 percent of the property in this county? Tommy has all the business he can handle. Why would he want to spend money to bring in more?"

"For one thing it brings down your property value. I'm thinking about *your* business, Care-Bear."

"Daddy, look at me." Carrie put her hands flat on the counter and leveled her gaze at him. "I am a big girl. I can take care of my own business."

Huey's tone took on a long-familiar fatherly edge. "Why don't you at least ask him to repaint the side of the building —"

"Because," she almost shouted, goaded beyond patience, "I don't want to hurt Tommy's feelings!"

Huey blinked. "So it's true."

"*What's* true?"

"People have driven by here late at night and seen you and the boy through the window. I asked your granny, and she

260

wouldn't talk, but Elvin Goff said he's seen you running around together. Carrie, you're very vulnerable right now —"

"People? What people?" Carrie felt like screaming in aggravation. She might have known she'd be the subject of gossip.

Her dad had the grace to look uncomfortable. "Seems like every patient I've seen in the last couple of weeks has commented about Carrie Pierce and Tommy Lucas keeping company."

" 'Keeping company'? How Victorian!" Carrie laughed. "So that's what this is about? You're afraid I'm going to take up with an auto mechanic? Daddy, I never took you for a snob."

Huey yanked at his tie as if it choked him. "You know better than that. I just don't want you getting hurt again."

Carrie stared at her father and remembered to breathe a prayer. *Lord, please help me be patient. Help me honor my father and still do what's right.*

She came around the counter and stood close to him at the window, taking his hands. "Oh, Daddy, I know you mean well. But I'm thirty years old." He swallowed and looked away as she continued. "I've learned from the mistakes I made with Brad. One thing I learned is that an education and a profession can be good things, but they're not the most important things in life. And since I've been home, I'm beginning to see what is important — things like loyalty and generosity and love for Christ." She squeezed his hands. "But I want you to know I have no intention of falling in love with Tommy Lucas, much less marrying him. He's been a good friend to me, that's all. Do you know he sends his customers over here for coffee or goodies? Not to mention reviving Granny's car after you poisoned it!"

Huey did not smile. "Carrie, he's a good bit younger than you. Have you considered *his* feelings? Elvin said the boy's pumped gas for you three times over the last two weeks and never takes his eyes off you."

Carrie's stomach dove. Her father might be interfering, but he was also right.

On the other hand, she didn't have to tell him so.

"Okay, Daddy, your point is taken," she said to satisfy him. "I'll be more careful of appearances. Remember, too, that Tommy's attention is likely to wander to somebody else at any time. We've only known each other for a month." She grinned. "He'll eventually get tired of eating green candy and filling my gas tank."

"I certainly hope so." Huey's eyes suddenly narrowed as he looked over Carrie's shoulder out the window. "That looks like Joy Chapman's van over there."

"Joy? Pastor David's wife?" Carrie turned to follow her father's gaze.

"Looks like she's having a hard time making it up the hill."

"Bless her heart. Tommy says she's got that van in the shop every other week." Carrie smiled and met her father's eyes. "And he fixes it for practically nothing. That's what I mean about Tom —"

"Carrie."

"What?"

Huey's eyes had widened. "Joy's gone inside the shop."

"Well, she probably had to use the phone —"

"Carrie, the van's rolling back down the hill! In this direction!"

Tommy heard a bloodcurdling scream and tore outside to find Joy Chapman chasing her van, which was rolling backward across the parking lot, right toward Carrie's Confections.

Frozen in horror, he saw that the van had gained just enough momentum from the slight slope that there was no way he or anybody else was going to stop its progress. Carrie's ZX, parked in front of the cottage, was right in its path.

"My children!" Joy sobbed. "My kids are in the van!" She tore across the parking lot, her hands flailing wildly above her head.

Like a slow-motion scene in a movie, the van connected with the sports car, a hideous-sounding crunch of metal shoving its elegant rear into the middle with accordionlike precision. The front of the ZX butted against the brickwork below the porch of the cottage, completing the massacre.

Tommy thought he just might throw up right then and there.

But almost immediately he came to his senses. Galvanized, he sprinted across the parking lot, passing Joy, who was running as fast as her short legs would carry her. He reached the van and yanked open the driver's door. The motor was still running, so he cut it, then sprinted around to jerk open the sliding passenger door. He'd worry about Carrie's destroyed vehicle later.

Three of the children were screaming, the baby in his car seat red-faced with hysteria. Only seven-year-old Benjy was remotely calm. "Hey!" he shouted, bouncing with excitement. "Let's do that again, Mr.

Tommy!"

Shaking with relief that none of them seemed to be injured, Tommy started unbuckling the closest seat belt, which held sobbing three-year-old Lindsey. She latched onto his neck like a spider monkey, nearly strangling him as he reached for baby Nathan's buckle.

He felt Joy clawing at the back of his shirt. "Let me have my babies!" He allowed her to peel Lindsey off his chest; then he worked to free the other three. By the time Benjy climbed out past him, Tommy was vaguely aware that Matthew had arrived, as well as Carrie and her father.

He turned around to find Joy huddled on the porch steps with all four children in her lap. "Oh, thank God," she sobbed over and over.

Feeling like his knees might not hold him up, Tommy sat down on the floor inside the open door of the van. Carrie sat beside Joy, with her arms around her and the sniffling children. Dr. Gonzales and Matthew, shaking their heads, were examining the damage to the Nissan and the van.

"Everybody's all right now," Carrie said soothingly. "Come on, Joy, it's okay."

Joy took a hiccuping breath, her round face still pinched with lingering panic.

"Tommy, haul that van off to the junkyard. I'm not getting in it again — ever!"

"Oh, now, I'll get it running again, good as new," he said. *If you'll leave it with me next time long enough to really fix it,* he mentally added.

"I don't know why it started rolling," Joy said tearfully. "I put it in Park. Isn't that supposed to hold it?"

"Well, yeah." Tommy got to his feet. "I'll have to look at it to figure out what went wrong. I promise I won't let you back in it 'til it's safe."

"Okay," said Joy doubtfully, hugging the baby closer.

"Who wants to come inside for hot chocolate and a stick of peppermint?" asked Carrie. "Joy, you can use the phone to call your husband to come get you."

"I don't like peppermint," whined Benjy, who was promptly shushed by his harried mother. She herded her brood into the cottage behind Carrie.

Tommy stood there looking after Carrie until the door closed behind her. She hadn't uttered one word of concern about her totaled car. She'd hardly even looked at it, instead focusing all her attention on the frightened children and their mother.

Since becoming a Christian, Tommy had

kept his heart open to finding the woman God had for him. Whenever he met someone new, the Holy Spirit would whisper, "Not yet. Wait." But Carrie Pierce had awakened some slumbering need in him that he could neither explain nor discount.

Lord, if anybody but you could see inside my brain right now, they'd lock me up and throw away the key. How can I be falling in love with a woman who won't stand still long enough for me to ask her out?

There was something, he knew, that kept a wall between them. After the day she'd fallen apart telling him about her husband, he'd turned it over in his mind many times, waiting for her to bring it up again, but she hadn't. He'd never again seen Carrie get flapped about anything.

Her marriage. He leaned against Joy's van, thinking, popping his hand against his fist. It was hard to imagine Carrie married to somebody else. But it had happened, and he couldn't do anything about the scars that scored her heart.

But God sure could.

Please, God, he added silently. *I want your will, but please let this be the one.*

With a sigh he leaned inside the van. He had to check one thing. Just as he'd suspected — the gearshift sat right next to the

N. Neutral, not Park. No wonder the van had rolled down the hill. But there was no way he was going to tell Joy Chapman she'd endangered her kids' lives with her own carelessness.

"If that dog digs in my trash one more time, I'm going to borrow Tommy's gun and shoot him myself!" Carrie muttered as she gathered empty bags of sugar, broken egg cartons, and other miscellaneous flotsam of the catering business off her back porch.

This was the third day in one week she'd arrived to find her garbage cans tipped over and the contents scattered from here to Sunday. Yesterday she'd actually caught Skywalker racing like a maniac out of the yard into the woods, as if fleeing from justice.

She let out an angry huff and slammed the lid on the last can. "What am I going to do with you?" she fumed, not sure if she was referring to Skywalker or his master.

Carrie sat down on the edge of the wooden porch and dangled her legs off the side. She picked up her *Daily Study Bible for Women,* which she'd laid on a plant stand upon discovering the spilled garbage. This spot had recently become her "quiet time closet."

She opened to the third chapter of Philippians, where she'd left off. Tommy had talked her into joining his Bible study, and she wanted to catch up on what she'd already missed. She began to read but found herself aware of her surroundings as much as the Scripture. The weather had warmed, and the woods between the cottage and the river were beginning to show signs of greening.

Carrie closed the Bible, her finger marking the place, and slumped with an elbow on her knee and chin in her palm. If she was honest, she'd have to admit that her irritation with Tommy — and with his dog — had more to do with the fact that he'd hardly come over at all this week, since the wreck of the minivan and her ZX. How could she tell him to leave her alone if he never showed up?

Is that really what you want? she asked herself. *For him to leave you alone?*

"No," she said aloud, so firmly that she startled a cardinal flirting his tail in her birdbath. She'd startled herself, too. She sat up straighter. "Oh, Lord, what am I thinking? I thought I knew myself. I thought I knew what I wanted. To be independent, run a successful business. What is it you want with me?"

Her gaze fell upon the page that had flipped open with her agitated movements and she read: "Yes, everything else is worthless when compared with the priceless gain of knowing Christ Jesus my Lord. I have discarded everything else, counting it all as garbage, so that I may have Christ and become one with him."

Thanks to Skywalker, she had handled a lot of garbage this week. It stunk. It added nothing to the landscape. Were there things in her life that she carried around like garbage, keeping her from being one with Christ?

As she kept reading, the apostle Paul's words scorched her like flaming brands: "No, dear brothers and sisters, I am still not all I should be, but I am focusing all my energies on this one thing: Forgetting the past and looking forward to what lies ahead, I strain to reach the end of the race and receive the prize for which God, through Christ Jesus, is calling us up to heaven."

Shaken, Carrie bowed her head and spent a long time praying about exactly what prize she ultimately longed for. Was it independence and business success? Or was it the prize of knowing Jesus Christ?

And how, exactly, did Tommy Lucas figure into her particular race?

CHAPTER FIVE

Carrie had just put a bag of freshly chopped onions in the freezer and started to clean the food processor when she heard a distinctive knock on the back door.

Tommy. *At last.* She was going to give him a piece of her mind about his dog and her garbage. He couldn't keep letting Skywalker run loose. She pulled the door open with an irritated jerk.

There was absolutely no reason why a man dressed in contemporary army-navy surplus clearance should make her brain disintegrate and her heart start pounding. Except for the fact that he had a full-blown red camellia blossom in one big, dark fist.

"You got a vase for this?" he asked. Then his nose wrinkled. "What's that smell?"

Carrie shook her head. "Onions." She took the camellia and opened a cabinet, from which she took a ceramic bud vase shaped like Elvis's head. Granny had brought it back for her from vacation a couple of years ago.

"Do you like onions?" Tommy followed her, looking anxious at this blip on the screen of his romance radar. He frowned at the food processor, the source of the offensive odor.

"Onions are a very useful vegetable," Carrie told him, amused.

"If you say so."

Carrie filled Elvis with water, but then set him down and turned to lean against the counter, holding the dense petals of the flower against her cheek. Her frustration dissolved in the immense pleasure of its velvety texture and exquisite color. She smiled warily at Tommy. "Thank you. What are you doing out this early in the morning? It's barely seven."

"Matt and I've been coon hunting."

It was Carrie's turn to wrinkle her nose. "Tommy —"

"Now don't start with the 'cute little raccoon' business. You don't know what pests those critters are."

It was on the tip of her tongue to tell him what a pest his dog was, but he changed the subject. "Matt says he loaned you his truck yesterday to make a delivery."

"Yes. Tommy, he's such a sweetheart." She

gave him a sideways look as she poked the camellia into the vase and arranged the leaves. "He and your cousin Cheryl seem like such an odd match."

"Maybe so. But she'll come around if we keep praying for her."

"Matthew says he's thinking about asking her to marry him."

"Mmmm. I know." He turned around to open the refrigerator. "Anything to eat around here besides onions?"

"He said you told him to wait until she becomes a Christian. And he asked me to try to make friends with her, maybe lead her to the Lord." She paused. "Was that your idea?"

Tommy came out from behind the refrigerator door with an apple under his chin, a tub of cream cheese in one hand, and a bunch of celery in the other. "Uh, I might have mentioned it. Where's the peanut butter?"

"But I've never . . ." Carrie rooted through the open pantry shelves lining one end of the kitchen, conveniently hiding her face. The thought of talking about her faith with a hostile party gave her the willies, but she couldn't admit that to Tommy. She found a better excuse. "Cheryl doesn't even like me!"

"She will once she gets to know you." Tommy found a knife, a spoon, and a plate and began to fix himself a snack. "Look, the rest of us have talked ourselves blue in the face. I just thought maybe if another woman close to her own age, a strong Christian, showed some interest in her — she might listen."

The fact that Tommy thought of her, Carrie, as a strong Christian was unexpectedly gratifying. Still . . . "I don't know, Tommy . . ."

He suddenly pointed a peanut butter-laden spoon at Carrie. "I almost forgot what I came over here for."

"What *did* you come over here for? Besides raiding my fridge and bringing me a flower." Wise or unwise, flowers made her insides melt.

Tommy shoved the peanut butter in his mouth and tossed the spoon into the sink. "Come outside. I've got a surprise for you."

"A surprise? What is it?"

But he just grinned over his shoulder and bounded down the back step, disappearing around the corner of the cottage. She followed him to the front of the shop, where she stopped short. Parked in her newly gravelled lot was a pink milk truck. No, too small for that. It had the boxy shape of a mail truck. A flamingo pink toaster on wheels.

"Wh— what is it?" she repeated. Tommy often had strange-looking vehicles in his own shop, but why would he park one of them over here?

A surprise.

"Oh, Tommy," she said inadequately. "Is this for me?"

He nodded, his eyes sparkling like smoky topaz. "If you're desperate enough to borrow Matthew's pile of junk, then you *really* need a vehicle. I spent all week fixing it up for your catering. Come look."

Carrie followed him around the truck. It was certainly big enough to deliver food. She lifted the rear rolling door and poked her head in to inspect the cooler and the warming oven installed along the side walls. "So this is what you've been up to all week," she said, sincerely impressed.

Tommy eagerly showed her the other amenities: cabinets for dishes, racks for storing small sundries, and hooks on which hung bungee cords of various lengths. Carrie inspected it all with delight, then went around to the front and got in the driver's seat.

"Boy, it feels weird to sit behind the wheel on this side," she said to Tommy, who leaned inside the opening beside her, his hands braced above his head. She gave the wheel an experimental twist.

"Just be careful not to drive on the wrong side of the road," he cautioned with a grin.

She shut her eyes, her elation fading. "Tommy, I can't afford this right now."

"Don't worry about it. You can pay me back when you get on your feet."

"That might not happen for a long time. I'm still barely making enough profit to keep the lights on in the shop." She turned to get out, but he was blocking the doorway. Her heart skidded around in her chest.

"Carrie —" He swallowed. Fascinated, she watched his biceps jump with the clenching of his hands. "You really don't have to pay me back ever. I make a lot more money than people think I do. I could sell the Ferrari and retire today if I wanted to." He held her gaze, and the expression she both dreaded and coveted settled softly around his mouth. "It's a gift from a friend to a friend."

Frightened by the sudden tension sizzling between them, Carrie prayed for wisdom and direction. "You are my friend, Tommy, but you know what? It has nothing to do with you giving me stuff." She pleaded with her eyes for him to accept her rejection gracefully. "I feel like I need to depend on nobody but the Lord to rescue me this time. The truck is wonderful, but it's — too much. . . ."

She felt like bursting into tears for no good reason.

There was a thick silence while Tommy, lips clamped and jaw ticcing, stared down at the gravel he was pushing around with the toe of his boot. Carrie listened to the soft *shooshing* sound of it and wondered if he would answer her at all.

Finally he sighed and said carefully, "I see why you'd be cautious, but I'm not your husband." What, she wondered, made him draw that connection? But he smiled faintly and popped the top of the truck with his hand. "Listen, this thing cost me hardly anything because it was abandoned in my lot by somebody who bought it at an auction, then brought it in to be fixed and couldn't pay for it. But if it'll make you feel any better, I'll let you make dinner for me and a guest."

"You and a guest?" Broadsided, Carrie blinked. *A guest?*

"Yeah. Plus Matt and Cheryl. For Valentine's Day."

"That's Saturday."

"Right."

"W-where do you want to have it, and

what do you want me to fix?"

"We can have it . . . here!" Tommy improvised, his expression warming. "After you close the shop. I don't care what you fix. Just dinner for four. Real romantic."

"Romantic," Carried echoed, feeling like a parrot. A big, stupid, featherbrained parrot without an original thought in her head. What had made her think Tommy giving her a catering truck was anything special? He was kind to *everybody,* even psychotic coonhounds and people who shaved his head for meanness.

Tommy's got a girlfriend.

She said it to herself again so there would be no forgetting it. *Tommy's got a girlfriend.*

"I've seen those real-life TV shows where they catch crooked mechanics on hidden video," said Mrs. Harris, a five-foot-two deacon's wife wearing a yellow silk wind suit and an intimidating pair of bifocals on a chain around her neck.

Tommy had never before noticed the woman's leanings toward the Dark Side.

She slapped the bill he'd mailed to her last week onto the counter and jabbed it with the long red nail of her index finger. "They say you come in with a minor problem, and while your car's in the shop, the

278

mechanic deliberately breaks something else, so he'll have an excuse to jack up the bill."

Lord, help me! Tommy kept his tone polite — just barely. "Now, Mrs. Harris, why would I want to do that? In this business my reputation's all I've got. Your transmission was going out, and your husband said to fix it."

"Larry's a pushover. There wasn't anything wrong with that transmission, and you know it." The woman's face reddened. "Joy Chapman said it took her four trips in the last three months to get her van right, and the last time her whole family nearly got killed."

Tommy closed his eyes. This had been a "day" since he'd gotten up that morning. He'd wasted nearly an hour looking for Skywalker, who had chewed through his lead. He finally found him snoozing across the back step of Carrie's candy shop. Carrie herself had yelled at him again about the dog getting into her garbage. Well, technically, Carrie never raised her voice, but he could tell by the little furrow between her eyes that she was upset.

Joy Chapman's betraying him with half-truths was the icing on the cake. "All right," he said, "if it'll make you happy I'll charge you for parts only. And you can go to somebody else next time." He reached for the bill.

"I'm not driving all the way to Ocean Springs to get my car serviced. Besides, you're the only mechanic in the area who understands German cars." Mrs. Harris whipped the bill out from under Tommy's hand. "I'll pay you this time. I just want you to know I'm watching you." She paid her bill, stuffed the receipt into her suitcase-size purse, and marched out of the office. Lifting her glasses, she gave Matthew a scathing look as she passed the door to the garage. "You ought to put your employees in a uniform," she sniffed just before she disappeared into the bright afternoon sunshine.

"Who died and made her queen of England?" Matthew demanded when Mrs. Harris was barely out of earshot. He pulled his head out from under the hood of the truck he was working on and ambled to the office doorway, watching Tommy slam the cash drawer and file Mrs. Harris's paperwork in a cardboard Fritos box under the counter.

"Aw, don't pay her any attention; she's just having a bad day," Tommy said as he looked up at his bizarrely dressed employee.

Matthew had on a pair of black jeans that were three sizes too big and a camouflage sweatshirt with the sleeves ripped out worn over a blue plaid flannel shirt. A dog chain laced with a leather thong circled his neck. At least he'd ditched the nose ring.

Matthew rubbed his nose, as if still getting used to the naked feel of it. "How can you be nice to people like that? I'd have told her to take her transmission and —"

"Matthew!" Tommy said sharply. "It's in our best interests all the way round to be kind to everybody."

"Yeah, but you don't have to let people run over you."

"Look, she's gonna think what she's gonna think, and arguing won't do a bit of good."

Matthew stared at him, obviously puzzled. "Why didn't you tell her it wasn't your fault Mrs. Chapman crashed her van?"

Tommy bent to flip through the files in the Fritos box. "It wasn't any of her business," he mumbled. He looked up to find Matthew's earnest face peering over the counter.

"Tommy, you're too good for your own good sometimes, you know that?"

"Aw, shut up," Tommy said, embarrassed. "Get back to work. We need to get that pickup out by five this afternoon, and I've got to study for a test tonight. I want to check the oil in Carrie's truck, too."

Matthew didn't move. "That's another thing. Giving her a vehicle in return for *dinner?* Reminds me of Jacob and Esau."

Tommy couldn't help grinning at Matthew's smug expression. "What do *you* know about Jacob and Esau?"

"I read it last night," said Matthew. "Dude sold his birthright for a pot full of venison stew."

"Where's Regis Philbin when you need him?" Tommy said, whacking Matthew on the arm. "You win a million. And I happen to think I'm getting a lot more than that by making Carrie happy."

"Man." Matthew mercifully backed off, whistling in sympathy. "You are one lovesick puppy."

Carrie walked up to the reception desk inside Cheryl's Cut 'n Curl with the same feeling floating around in her stomach that she got while waiting to get her teeth cleaned. She cleared her throat, and Pearl looked up from her rather slack-jawed perusal of *GQ* magazine.

"Is Cheryl here?" Carrie couldn't quite bring herself to say "Churl," so she compromised by pronouncing the hard *ch* at the beginning of the name. *Chair-rull.*

Pearl didn't seem to notice anything amiss. She popped her gum and grinned. "I remember you. You're Tommy's girlfriend."

It was a measure of Carrie's apprehension that she neglected to contradict the woman's assumption. "His hair's growing out again," she said with what she hoped was a friendly smile.

Pearl shook her large head and looked around, then leaned forward to whisper, "Girl needed a spankin' for doin' that, you ask me."

Carrie silently agreed. "Is she working today?"

"Well . . . she's back there doin' her nails. Ain't too much business today." Pearl hopped out of her chair with amazing agility. "I'll get her."

Carrie barely had time to look around the empty salon before Cheryl sauntered from the back room behind Pearl. Blowing on Sweetheart Pink nails, she gave Carrie a caustic smile. "Well, if it isn't Martha Stewart herself." When Carrie returned a puzzled look, Cheryl waved a hand. "Matthew never shuts up about how good you cook and how pretty your store is. What can I do for you today?"

Carrie steeled herself. "I need a haircut."

Cheryl absolutely goggled. "Is that some kind of sick joke?"

"No, I — I need a haircut," Carrie persisted; she was a woman on a mission. God had spoken to her clearly this morning out of the book of James: "Those who are peacemakers will plant seeds of peace and reap a harvest of goodness." That was all she meant to do. Plant a seed of peace.

And it was obvious that Tommy's cousin was dry ground. "Don't you remember what I did to Tommy?"

Carrie nodded. "I imagine you had a good reason, if you want to tell me about it."

Cheryl ran her tongue across her top lip, then suddenly reached to pull a towel and plastic cape out of a cabinet. "Sit down at the shampoo bowl and I'll give you an earful."

Ten minutes later, Carrie watched in the mirror as Cheryl skillfully snipped at the ends of her hair. So far, no major chunks had been cut out. Still, Carrie plowed with caution. "You mean you zapped Tommy's hair because he convinced Matthew to boot you out of his apartment?"

"It wasn't just that. It's that all-fired holier-than-thou attitude of his." Cheryl threw down the scissors and propped her hands on the back of the chair. "Not to mention that I had to move back in with my parents. I couldn't afford a place of my own."

Carrie met the hard green eyes in the mirror. "But Tommy's the least — I don't know — arrogant person I've ever met. Are you sure — ?"

"It's not what he *said*. It's that sweet, sad-eyed look he gives you, like he pities you. I can't stand it. And he used to be the prince of darkness himself. The hypocrite! He gets to have his fun, then spoils it for everybody else. And Matt's getting to be just like him!"

"But, Cheryl," Carrie fumbled for the right words, praying madly for wisdom, "aren't you still dating Matthew? He talks about you all the time."

"He does?" A flash of pleasure crossed Cheryl's face, quickly replaced by her characteristic sarcastic smile. "Well, he's got a funny way of showing it. He won't hardly even kiss me anymore."

"I take it you were . . . intimate?"

Cheryl snorted. "What do you think?"

"Well, now that Matthew's a Christian, I'm sure he wants to please God in every area of his life."

"That's fine, but he doesn't have any right to force his beliefs on me! Him *or* Tommy!"

Carrie felt her hands begin to shake. She had heard almost the exact words from her husband a month after their marriage. Cowed by his anger, she had bottled her frustration and learned to shut up, beginning her own slow slide away from her Savior. Oh, that she had had the courage to refuse to enter a marriage without Christ at its center.

Tears blurred Cheryl's eyes, but Carrie could still see the hurt and loneliness behind the bitter set of Cheryl's dark red mouth. "Cheryl, do you have any idea how much Matthew loves you? He doesn't want to hurt you — he wants to protect you and treat you with the utmost honor and respect. He even wanted me to introduce you to the One who loves you with a higher love than you could ever imagine."

"Oh, puh-lease. Why should I listen to you?" Cheryl turned her head. Carrie couldn't see her expression, except for a trembling chin.

"Cheryl, this is not about me or Matthew or even Tommy. It's not about you fighting with your parents. It's about the only way to real and lasting peace: yielding yourself to the Lord Jesus."

Cheryl suddenly grabbed a handful of Carrie's hair and snatched the scissors off the counter. Tears running down her cheeks, she glared at Carrie in the mirror. "I can't do that." She forked the scissors against Carrie's hair.

Carrie's stomach plummeted. She heard a loud, gasping noise from the reception desk. She'd forgotten all about Pearl. Praying that the receptionist wouldn't intervene, she sat still and held Cheryl's gaze. "That won't change the fact that he loves you." She meant Jesus and Matthew both. "And I love you, too," she added softly.

Just as suddenly as she'd picked up the scissors, Cheryl flung them back onto the counter and, wiping her eyes, rushed off into the back room.

Carrie sighed and took off the cape. She looked at Pearl, who appeared to be on the verge of vaulting the reception desk. "I guess that's all the hair I'm going to get cut today."

On Saturday evening, Valentine's Day, Tommy stood on Carrie's front porch, waiting for her to answer the doorbell. The sun had just gone down, and the cicadas were tuning up for an evening concert in the woods. Tommy figured he'd be a lot more comfortable out there with his gun and dog. He hadn't been this nervous since the day he took his high school exit exam. "Where is she?" he muttered to himself. "The lights are on, so she's got to be here." He stuck his hands in the pockets of his new chinos and turned to peer down the darkening highway.

Matt had gone to pick up Cheryl over an hour ago, and they were supposed to meet him here. By then he would have told Carrie that she was his date. He hadn't meant to deceive her. But the way this whole thing had happened had been totally dopey. The expression on her face when she had realized the delivery truck was for her had been so proud and stubborn. When was she going to learn to take from him without insisting on paying him back? He'd let her cook, thinking it was for some other girl, when the only woman he ever wanted to look at was Carrie Pierce.

Now he was going to have to tell her —

"Tommy!" He turned with a jerk at Carrie's breathless voice. "I'm sorry. I was back in the kitchen with my hands full of . . ." Her words trailed off as they stared at one another. She had on a pair of slim black pants and a simple white silk blouse that he supposed would look waitressy on anyone else. On her it looked fresh and classy and —

"Did you get your hair cut?" he blurted.

She brushed at the short wisps framing her face. "Do you like it?"

Unable to articulate his feelings, he smiled at her. Finally Carrie jerked her gaze away and looked over his shoulder. "Where's your date?"

"Uh, she . . ." How was he going to say this? Unadulterated truth. "Carrie, I don't have a date."

"She stood you up?"

"No, she never — I mean, there wasn't ever anybody else. Just you." *Smooth, Lucas.* He wanted to crawl under the porch where Skywalker often skulked.

Until that little smile curled the corners of Carrie's mouth. "Just me?" She started to giggle. "You had me cook dinner for myself?"

"Well, yeah. And Matt and Cheryl."

"Oh, Tommy, you are priceless. Come in." She backed up, and he passed her, feeling like the prize doofus of Jackson County. What did she mean by *priceless?*

He walked around picking up porcelain knickknacks and breathing in the faint scent of rose-petal potpourri that filled a cystal bowl on a side table, while Carrie lit the tall vanilla candles on the white cloth–draped table in the center of the room. The table was set for four, with heavy silverware and plates so fine he just knew his would break if he looked at it hard enough. The napkins were folded to look like swans. He'd never seen anything so pretty and so terrifying in his life.

When she turned off the lights, he noticed a small lamp burning beside the potpourri bowl. And the candles. Other than that it was dark.

"Carrie?" he said uncertainly.

"You said . . ."

Romantic.

"Matthew and Cheryl were coming," she finished.

She'd made it romantic for Matt and Cheryl. Not for him. He was relieved. He was disappointed.

He hadn't brought flowers. No wonder she didn't take him seriously. What yahoo came to a Valentine dinner without flowers? "Even Aunt Janelle couldn't find me a rosebud," he said out of left field.

"What?"

"I mean, they're on their way. Any minute now." To his everlasting relief, the doorbell rang. "There they are! I'll get it!"

The young couple came in holding hands, Matt beaming like he'd just won the lottery. Tommy glanced at Cheryl. He had to look again to make sure his cousin hadn't traded bodies with some other blonde. Maybe it was the low light.

Tommy flipped on the light, nearly blinding himself. "Did you two elope?" he demanded, and Matthew laughed.

Cheryl blushed, her smile a work of art. "Better than that. I accepted Christ."

Carrie started to cry, and Tommy looked from her to his friend to his cousin. He pulled out a chair and sat down hard. "Wow. I'm glad. I'm confused. What happened?"

"She did it all by herself this morning and called to tell me," Matt said proudly, kissing Cheryl's hand. "Just her and God, gettin' it all together."

"But I might not have, if Carrie hadn't come to talk to me yesterday," Cheryl said.

"B-but I thought you were mad at me," Carrie blubbered, wiping her nose on a "swan" she'd plucked off the table.

"I was. But you made me think. I'm tired of being angry and selfish. I realized Matthew *does* love me, and my parents love me, and God loves me, and I don't deserve it —"

Another swan bit the dust.

Tommy shook his head to clear it. "Carrie talked to you?"

Carrie put her hand to her hair again, and

he got the picture.

"Wow," he said again. He lifted his hands, said it louder, and jumped up to boogie around the table, grabbing Carrie's hands on his way by. Matt and Cheryl joined in, and the four of them enjoyed a joyful dance while the candles flickered and the other two swans became banners of joy.

Eventually they settled down long enough to eat the dinner Carrie had worked on all day: seafood gumbo, Caribbean salad, and a crab-meat casserole that Tommy didn't even want to try to identify. All he knew was that if he died tonight he'd go to heaven a happy man.

Then Carrie brought in The Cake. His eyes widened. "Your granny made me one of those one time when I serviced her car."

"She, uh, mentioned you liked it," Carrie said, slicing through the three tall layers of butter cake covered in thick fudgy icing. She put an enormous hunk on one of the fragile saucers and handed him a dessert fork. Then she served Matthew, Cheryl, and herself.

"Will you marry me?" he asked, only half facetiously. "Seeing as Roxanne won't give me the time of day?"

The dimple told him Carrie knew he was teasing.

"That reminds me," Matthew said, snapping his fingers. He dug in the pocket of his jeans and came up with a little black velvet box. Clearing his throat, he took Cheryl's hand and curled her fingers around the box. "I'm asking in front of witnesses who love us, babe. I want you to be my wife."

Tommy thought he might drown in female tears because both women promptly tuned up again. *Lord,* he prayed, *is Carrie going to do this when I ask her to marry me for real? When? When can I?*

Feeling like a kid looking in the candy-store window, drooling over lollipops, Tommy watched the smile playing around Carrie's lips as she observed Matthew and Cheryl.

CHAPTER SIX

Matthew and Cheryl left early, with profound thanks for the dinner and orange blossoms all but visibly blooming around their heads. They wanted to tell her parents about the engagement.

Carrie began stacking up dessert plates to take them into the kitchen. Tommy took the tray of dishes from her. "I'll do that. You sit down and enjoy your coffee."

"No, let's do it together. Then we can both sit down."

He was very quiet for the half hour or so it took to clean up the mess she always made cooking. For a man with less than orthodox organizational skills, he was remarkably thorough about cleaning things.

As she carefully put her wedding silverware in its velvet-lined box, it struck Carrie that just when she thought she had Tommy figured out, he would say or do something that turned her heart upside down. Giving her a catering van. Asking her to make a romantic candlelight dinner so she could be his —

She mentally squelched the word *date* because she had only been there to fill out the foursome with Matt and Cheryl. She squirmed at her own jealousy — there was no other word for it — over the last few days. What a pitiful female she was, to resent sharing Tommy's friendship with another woman. One day he would get married and move out of the garage. What was she going to do then? Go into mourning?

"What are you smiling at?" Tommy asked, handing her the soup tureen to dry.

"Nothing." She took the bowl, unthinkingly reaching to tuck in the tag that was sticking out of the back of his shirt. His skin was warm, but his shoulders moved restlessly as if he were cold. "What do you really think about Matthew proposing to Cheryl tonight?"

He opened his mouth to answer, but earsplitting barking suddenly broke out right outside the back door.

"That's Sky," Tommy said with perfect obviousness. "What's he up to?" He peered out the window into the dark backyard.

"I don't know, but I don't think you should open the —"

Skywalker charged into the kitchen, blue-black hackles at full attention, and heavy nails scrabbling on the linoleum.

"— dooooor!" Carrie wailed.

"Oh, for pete's sake," groaned Tommy, grabbing for the dog's collar and missing. Skywalker crouched, baying like the Beast of Borneo, in front of the broom closet. Carrie clapped her hands over her ears while Tommy shouted, "Skywalker! Down!"

Skywalker immediately dropped, but lay there whining, never taking his eyes off the closet.

"You think he's rabid?" Carrie asked nervously.

Tommy gave her an amused look. "There's somethin' in that closet," he said matter-of-factly.

"Yeah, a broom and a dustpan." Carrie gave Skywalker a disgusted look. "You want a mop head for supper?"

"A coonhound acts like this only when he's treeing." Tommy reached for the handle of the closet door.

"Wait!" shrieked Carrie. Tommy stopped and looked at her. "What if it's a snake or a skunk or something?"

"If it was a skunk we'd've known it by now. I don't think Sky would come in here after a snake. Back up, now." Tommy slowly opened the door.

Carrie let out a bubble of startled laughter. A skinny young raccoon sat on the floor of her broom closet, nibbling unconcernedly on a coconut macaroon, looking like the bandit he was. Skywalker snarled but held when Tommy placed a hand on his head.

The coon froze when the light hit him, but he held on to the cookie. Carrie was torn between amusement and anger. "How did he get in there?" she said.

"Dunno. Wish I had my gun," Tommy muttered.

"Tommy! You can't shoot a raccoon in my broom closet!"

Tommy sighed. "I was just joking."

Fortunately, Tommy had a live trap and managed to get the coon out of the closet and into the cage without getting bitten or clawed. Skywalker, not so easily subdued, allowed himself to be shut up in Carrie's laundry room only when she bribed him with a large ham bone.

With both coon and dog vanquished, Tommy and Carrie walked into the dark woods together, the coon-laden cage bumping against Tommy's leg and Skywalker howling in the distance. Tommy's flashlight gave them just enough light to find the narrow path and avoid roots and briars waiting to trip the unwary. The night sounds of leaves rustling underfoot and small animals moving in the trees around them comforted Tommy, as did the scent of wild dewberries and decomposed foliage spicing the cool air. He could look up and see stars etched like God's filigree above. Part of Psalm 8 came to his mind: *"When I look at the night sky and see the work of your fingers — the moon and the stars you have set in place — what are mortals that you should think of us, mere humans that you should care for us?"*

The miracle was that the Creator did indeed care for mortals, specifically, one Tommy Lucas. For once it didn't matter that he couldn't tell red from green, or that catalytic converters made more sense to him than stocks and spreadsheets.

His world put right again, Tommy set the cage down and crouched to put his hand on the latch. "You sure you want me to let him go?" he asked Carrie. "You know he'll just get right back in and steal your cookies again."

"You're not going to kill that animal in my presence." Her soft voice was as stubborn as he'd ever heard it. "I'll figure out where he got in and board it up."

"Probably under the house. Won't you

have fun crawlin' around down there with the spiders?" He could feel her shudder, and he let up on the teasing. "I'll do it tomorrow morning."

She knelt beside him, and by the dim light of the flashlight he saw her smile. "I'd appreciate it if you would."

He'd brave a whole army of arachnids for that smile. The coon, however, was noticeably short on gratitude. When Tommy opened the cage door, it snarled and bolted, lumbering off into the darkness, presumably to complain to the management.

"I guess I owe poor Skywalker an apology," Carrie said, sitting back on her heels. "He must have been trying to chase that coon out of my trash all this time, while I blamed him for making the messes."

"Don't waste any sympathy on that mutt. I don't know if he's ever gonna make a good hunting dog. He thinks he's your personal mooch."

"I've never seen a dog who likes candy as much as —"

"Candy! Please don't tell me you've been feeding him candy."

"I don't *feed* it to him," Carrie said patiently. "He smells the sugar on my hands and tries to lick it off when I pet him."

"Oh, good grief." Tommy put his head in

his hands. Training that dog was a hopeless cause.

"I'm sorry," said Carrie in a small voice. "I didn't know it would hurt him."

"As far as I know, chocolate is the only thing he's allergic to. Don't worry about it. If he dies, at least he'll die happy."

"Tommy!"

"I'm just —"

"Joking," she finished with him.

"Yeah."

They sat a few feet apart enjoying the stillness all around them for a moment, Tommy's flashlight squirting a narrow beam of light into the underbrush.

"What's that noise?" Carrie said and scooted closer to him.

"Probably just a squirrel." But he moved toward her and flashed the light around to reassure her. "You want to go back to the house?"

"No, it's nice." She breathed deeply and relaxed, her arm touching his. "I see why you like to come out here so much."

Another coin dropped into Tommy's love bank. "Are you warm enough?"

"Sure." She paused. "Tommy, can I ask you something?"

"Of course."

"Matthew said you made arrangements to

sell your Ferrari. Are you in financial trouble? Because if you are, I can give you my truck back, and I don't mind asking my dad —"

"Matthew talks entirely too much," Tommy said, exasperated. "No, I'm not in financial trouble, and I don't need a loan."

"I know it's none of my business —"

"It's not that. You can talk to me about anything. I just wanted it to be a surprise. I've been taking some night courses over at Perk," he said, referring to nearby Perkinston Community College.

"Well, that's wonderful! What are you taking?"

"Accounting. Business management. English lit."

"English lit?"

"I told you I like to read."

"Yes, you did."

The subdued tone of her voice made him shift the flashlight beam so he could see her expression. It was troubled. "What's the matter?"

Carrie squirmed, and Tommy could sense her discomfort. She said, "Tommy, has . . . anything I've said to you made you feel like you needed . . . well . . . improvement?"

"Of course not, but there comes a time when you get tired of the same old rut and need to make some changes."

"Really."

"Yeah, really." Honesty. *Okay, Lord.* "Well, your dad came in to get his air conditioner looked at a few weeks ago."

"The air conditioner? In January?"

"That's what I thought. Though, for the record, January is actually a pretty good time to get air-conditioner service —"

"Tommy —"

"All right, back to the subject. He was wandering around the shop while I worked, and we were talking about being in business for ourselves, and he suggested I needed a computer. One thing led to another, and I got the message that he thinks my garage is a pretty bad eyesore, and I need to make some, uh, home improvements. You know, to make a good reflection on your shop next door."

"I told him not to — What gives him the right —" Carrie let out a feminine little growl that made Tommy chuckle.

"He was just trying to help. And he was right. My system is no system at all."

"Listen to me, Tommy." She laid a hand on his wrist and got his undivided attention. "If you feel the need to make self-improvements *for yourself,* that's one thing. But don't ever change on my account. If

302

you had a Ph.D. it wouldn't matter to me."

It wouldn't matter? Did that mean what he hoped it meant, or was she saying, "Forget it, buster; you don't have a chance"?

He sighed and stirred the leaves with his feet. He might as well give it to her with both barrels. There was no point in pretending he was something he wasn't.

"Carrie, I have a lot of admiration for your dad, so I'm gonna listen to what he says. Did you know he's treated my mother and me for free since I can remember? I didn't find out about it until recently. And it wasn't him who told me." Carrie was silent, so he continued. "I might as well tell you my mama's never been able to hold on to money. She's had a regular parade of live-in boyfriends since I was a baby. These days she spends half her time and all her money at the casinos. I've prayed myself sick about her, but nothing changes."

She stared at him, as if arrested by some insight into the quagmire that was Tommy Lucas. He just wished he knew what she saw. "What you need is a prayer partner." She took his hand. "You prayed with me about my problem. Let me pray with you about this. And we need to pray for Cheryl and Matthew, too."

He looked into her eyes and found stillness and peace that hadn't been there six weeks ago. "You've changed, you know that?"

She dropped his hand. "Not really, I —"

"Yes, you have. You're full of the Holy Spirit now. . . ." The lonely place in Tommy that had been filled only by the Lord was now making room for Carrie. He reached over and almost reverently touched her cheek. "I always thought you were a beautiful woman, but now it's on the inside, too."

In her eyes he could see the old walls of fear going up. That jerk she had been married to had done a number on her. An irrational flare of jealousy tore through him. *Lord, am I going to have to deal with this the rest of my life?*

When she took an agitated breath, he withdrew his hand. "Okay," he sighed, "we'll pray." He bowed his head, longing to hold her hands but not daring to after her withdrawal. He listened, eyes closed, to Carrie's prayer, getting the sense of her words but mostly becoming aware of the simple presence of the Holy Spirit breathing comfort into his heart.

TRUST ME. I WANT THE BEST FOR YOU.

Lord, Carrie's the best.

DELIGHT YOURSELF IN ME, AND I

WILL GIVE YOU THE DESIRES OF
YOUR HEART.

Reluctantly, slowly, he let go of his longing and began to worship God, who had
been so good to him. Gradually he began to
sense his surroundings and the gentle scent
of Carrie's perfume mixed with pine. He
didn't know there were tears running down
his face until he felt Carrie's fingers wipe
them away.

He opened his eyes to find her leaning up
toward him, a strange expression on her
face. "Shoot," he said, embarrassed, swiping
his knuckles across his face.

But she whispered his name and laid her
beautiful, soft, slim hand against his jaw and
made him look at her. They stared at one
another until Tommy finally said in a hoarse
croak, "Carrie, do you want to kiss me?"

She shook her head slowly, but her mouth
came closer until he felt her nose bump his.
He smiled and tilted his head, waiting, his
heart a wild drum in his chest.

"I'm scared," she whispered.

"It's okay," he said and let her decide.

He saw her eyes drift shut and felt her lips
on his. He responded but bottled up his
exultation. There was plenty of time to tell
her how much he loved her.

But the minute he cupped his hand

around the back of her head to deepen the kiss, she was shoving at his shoulders, scrambling to her feet, panting. "Tommy, no! I've got to go home — Granny will be worried about me —"

"Hey, hey. No problem." He slowly rose, keeping his distance, but feeling slightly cross-eyed with lingering passion. "I'll walk you —"

But she was already taking off in the dark, luckily in the right direction. He followed and grabbed her arm. "Slow down! You're gonna trip on something."

She jerked her arm away. "I'm sorry. I knew I shouldn't have done that."

Hurt beyond description, Tommy stopped at the edge of the thinning woods as she hurried on. There was now enough moonlight that she could find her way back to her car.

Carrie seemed to realize, though, that she was alone. She slowed and halted with her back to him, her slim shoulders slumped. She turned around, walked straight back to him, and butted her head into his chest. He put his arms around her and stroked her hair.

"I'm a mess, Tommy," she said, her voice muffled in his shirt pocket.

"What did I do wrong?" he asked.

"It's not you; it's me. I told myself I wouldn't get so dependent again that I'd disappear. And here I am letting you do everything for me."

Lord, am I really doing that? I just want to love her. I want her to need me. God, help me; is that manipulation?

He had no answers.

So he squeezed her briefly, kissed the top of her head, and walked her to the cottage to lock up. After rescuing Skywalker from the laundry room, he went home to lie awake far into the night.

Monday morning — Tommy and Carrie had spent most of Sunday in church, avoiding each other's eyes — Tommy crawled out from under Carrie's cottage, trailing cobwebs and dragging a toolbox. "I found it. It was a spot close to the refrigerator, where some standing water must've rotted the wood awhile back."

"Thank you so much, Tommy, you didn't have to —"

"No problem." He took off his Braves baseball cap to pass his forearm across his dirty face and looked at her sideways. "Uh, for Skywalker's sake I hate to suggest this, but you might want to think about getting a cat."

Carrie squeaked. "You're kidding!"

"Nope. You gotta remember you're pretty close to the woods and the water."

"Raccoons, mice —" Carrie brushed a long gossamer strand off Tommy's shoulder — "spiders. Maybe I should start a wildlife shelter instead of a candy store."

Tommy took a step back. "Well, that's done, so I gotta get back to the garage. The lettering should be done on your truck this afternoon. You need it tomorrow, don't you?"

She shouldn't have been surprised at his distant manner after the crazy way she'd acted Saturday night. But she kept looking at his firm mouth, replaying the way it had felt exploring hers.

She nodded. "I've got a Mardi Gras party to cater."

"Okay. Holler when you get ready for Matt to take you over to the paint shop. See ya." He winked and swung off across the yard and up the slope toward the garage.

Carrie watched him walk away, hurt by his un-Tommylike lack of warmth. *Lord, I'm confused. One day he turns my heart to mush, and the next he treats me like his sister.*

She'd *thought* that was what she wanted. A little distance. But this was not fun at all.

Sighing, she headed into the cottage.

■ ■ ■ ■

Tommy walked into the office and found his employee drowning his sorrows in a two-liter bottle of Mountain Dew. Matthew sat on the desk, kicking his heels with a rhythmic metallic thump, the bottle dangling from one greasy fist.

Matthew gave Tommy a doleful look. "Man, I can't believe you actually did it."

"Is it gone?"

"It was just picked up ten minutes ago."

"Good." Tommy opened the mini refrigerator and yanked out a root beer. "I didn't want to be here when he took it."

"I just can't believe it," Matthew repeated. "First you get rid of the candy, now this. If you don't marry that girl soon, this whole place is going to the dogs. No offense, Skywalker," he assured the hound, who looked up from his pallet in the corner. Matthew tossed Tommy an envelope, which had been lying on the desk beside him. "Here's the moolah. I hope it makes you happy."

Tommy stuffed it in his jeans pocket without looking at it, then walked into the garage and stared at the empty bay where the Testa Rossa had been coming together for the past two years. His stomach felt like lead, so he chugged the root beer. *Carrie's worth it,* he told himself.

Matthew followed him. "I still think you're crazy. You had a car most men would sell their souls for, and you chucked it to go to *college.* You should've at least made sure Carrie —"

"I'm not going to college just for Carrie." Tommy spread his hands, a gesture encompassing the whole of his surroundings, in all their tacky glory. "It's time to grow up and quit spinning my wheels — pardon the pun. I can't marry and raise a family in the back room of a garage!"

Matthew pounced. "So you *do* want to marry her!"

"Well, of course I do." It felt good to admit it. Out loud. "But she's scared of something. I almost got her to tell me what it is the other night when we went out into the woods to release that crazy raccoon."

"Take it from me." Matthew shook his head. "You never know what's going on in a woman's mind. Since Carrie started discipling her, Cheryl's been changing every day. Asks me all the time what I'm reading in the Bible, wants to go to church every time the door's open."

Tommy felt his own anxieties fade. "Really? That's great, man."

"Yeah, well, my point is that I think you should make Carrie talk about whatever's bugging her."

Tommy hunched a shoulder. "I tried. Now I think it's time to back off and let God work on her." He dragged out the Fritos box and pretended to flip through the files. "Call Carrie and see when she needs a ride over to the paint shop to pick up her truck."

"I don't mind, buddy, but why don't you take her yourself?" At Tommy's look, Matt clunked the Mountain Dew bottle down on the counter. "Never mind. Where's the phone?"

After Mardi Gras, Carrie's phone rang off the hook. She was so busy that she had to hire a kitchen assistant and a high school girl to answer the phone while she cooked in the afternoons. She had a regular cadre of young waitresses on call to help her at large functions. She hardly noticed when spring rolled in with an explosion of floral beauty with which to decorate her tables, beginning with elegant tulip trees, the last of the camellias, lacy dogwood and bridal wreath, and the inimitable flamboyant azaleas.

It figured that on Granny's birthday, which she celebrated along with St. Patrick, the heavens would open with a downpour of diluvian proportions. Her entire family, including twenty-five adults and teens, fifteen kids under the age of twelve, and one incipient bambino in Miranda's tummy, were cooped up in Granny's tiny house. No barbecue, no picnic tables, no spreading out to the swing and glider in the front yard, no rides on Grandpa Hugh's ancient golf cart. At least the homemade ice cream tradition had been rescued. Two freezers nested in the double sink, effectively thwarting any attempt to run the water.

Carrie had wanted to entertain with organization and flair. After all, she *was* the caterer in her family. But it was like organizing a colony of fleas. Carrie thought she might put her head in the oven and end it all.

Nobody but Carrie seemed to mind the noise and chaos. The older kids were on the screen porch playing chicken-scratch dominoes; the men were in front of the television watching the NCAA basketball playoffs; and most of the women clustered in the kitchen, talking and laughing and wiping the runny nose of any toddler foolish enough to pass too close.

Carrie leaned against the doorway between the kitchen and the screen porch, listening to the hoots and giggles behind her, while trying to keep up with the conversation at the kitchen table and watch the progress of her enchiladas in the oven. No easy task.

She realized that her sister was trying to catch her eye. Carrie didn't particularly want to talk to Miranda. She was feeling cranky and discontented again, and that stupid bubble of jealousy kept floating to the top. Why she should feel that way she couldn't explain even to herself. Her business was going well, and she was totally independent for the first time in her life.

Miranda said quite loudly, "Do we have enough ice for this whole crew?"

Everybody stopped talking and looked at Carrie, so she was forced to answer. "I've refilled the trays at least four times today."

"I'm going to see if there's some more in the freezer out in the shed," Miranda said. "Come with me and make sure the lid doesn't fall on my head." She wiggled her eyebrows at Carrie, who sighed. Subtlety was not Miranda's long suit.

She and Miranda found a blue-and-red umbrella with so many broken spokes that it barely covered their heads. They made it to Grandpa Hugh's woodworking shed, wet to the knees and breathless from laughter.

Miranda tossed the umbrella into a corner and examined one of her soggy tennis shoes. Carrie reached for the handle of the freezer.

"Wait. We'll do that in a minute," Miranda said, dragging over a couple of stools that had been left near the wood-burning stove in the center of the shed. "You didn't think I got you out here just for ice, did you?"

"I'd hoped," Carrie said, reluctantly sitting down. "Why didn't you just say, 'Carrie, I need to talk to you'?"

"I wanted you all to myself for a minute."

"Well, you better make it fast, 'cause my enchiladas will be ready in about ten minutes."

"Okay, okay. I just want to know what gives with you and Tommy Lucas." Miranda's small face was alight with curiosity. She looked remarkably like their grandmother.

Carrie sighed. "I suppose it was too much to ask that Granny keep that to herself."

"No less than five people have cornered me separately since I've been home to ask me to talk to you." Miranda ticked them off on her fingers. "Granny. Mama. Daddy. Grant. Mr. Elvin at the Quick-Stop."

Carrie groaned. With an elbow on her knee, she laid her forehead in her palm. "Okay, Dr. Laura. Let's have it."

"They say you had this Valentine dinner."

"So? That was mainly for our friend Matthew to ask his girlfriend to marry him."

"*Our?* As in you and Tommy?"

"Well, Matthew works for Tommy. But yes, he's my friend now too. I'm going to cater their wedding in May." Carrie looked up, arrested. "What does Mr. Elvin know about the dinner?"

"Nothing. He was worried because you've been pumping your own gas for the last three weeks. He wanted to know if you'd broken up with Tommy."

"Oh, my soul," said Carrie. "What else?"

"Well, Daddy thinks you've lost your mind, driving around in a pink converted mail truck when he was willing to buy you a perfectly good used van he found over in Mobile."

"I'm paying for the mail truck myself," Carrie said grimly. *In spades,* she thought, in light of the Valentine's Day dinner and its resulting damage to her relationship with Tommy.

"And both Granny and Mom are worried about you not eating."

"I'm fasting and praying. What about Grant?"

"He says if you've decided to take up coon hunting, the least you can do is get a decent dog out of his new litter, instead of feeding that Bluetick hound of Tommy's."

"I *don't* feed him. Skywalker just sort of helps himself."

"Hmmm." Miranda leaned back against the freezer, a hand going instinctively to her slightly rounded tummy. "You are in love with him."

"Skywalker? I can barely tolerate him."

"Don't be coy with me, Carrie. This is the person who read your diary when you were fourteen years old. You know who I mean."

Carrie stared at her younger sister. Miranda could have wormed information out of O. J. Simpson. Carrie folded her arms and squirmed on her stool. "Tommy is generous and patient and the most practical Christian I've ever met. But he's too young, and he thinks organization is a rubber band around his finger, and he lets people take advantage of him . . . and . . . and it scares me how much I like him!" Carrie covered her face with her hands.

"Oh, gee, let's put him in jail," Miranda said, rolling her eyes.

Carrie peeked through her fingers and said in a small voice, "I hurt his feelings really bad a few weeks ago, and he hardly talks to me anymore."

"Are you sure you aren't just so busy he

can't get *to* you to talk? You need to talk to him."

"Oh, I don't know!" Carrie wailed. "Maybe. I don't think so." Carrie sat silent. She missed Tommy unbearably. Sometimes she even sneaked extra-meaty bones to Skywalker just to make sure he visited often. Tommy always came to get him.

"Come on, Carrie, I thought you were ready to take charge of your life. Give it the old Gonzales stiff upper lip." Miranda demonstrated.

Carrie mimicked her sister, then shook her head and reached into the freezer for a couple of milk cartons full of ice. "Hey, what's this?" She pulled out a gallon ziplock bag full of green heart-shaped candy. There were four more just like it in the bottom of the freezer.

"Looks kind of like that white chocolate candy Granny used to make for Valentine's Day." Miranda poked her head over Carrie's shoulder to see. "But it's *green.*"

"I know *what* it is. I just don't know why it's in Granny's freezer."

"Ooh! Ooh!" Miranda clapped her hands. "I love a mystery."

"Well, it's a long story," Carrie said. "Grab that pathetic excuse for an umbrella and I'll tell you on the way back to the house."

Later, when Granny opened her last present, everyone in the room groaned: Elvis painted in oil on black velvet.

"Geraldine's probably rolling in her grave," Granny cackled in delight. Granny's dearest friend had died nearly two years ago, and the two of them had argued amicably up to the end over the merits of opera versus rock 'n' roll.

"Where did that come from?" demanded Grant. Everybody in the family knew Granny had always coveted one of those paintings, but so far they had managed to talk her out of buying one at the gas station. The Gonzales dignity was on the line, after all.

Granny plucked out a business card that was stuck in the heavy, ornate gold frame. " 'Free oil, lube, and filter from Lucas Import Service,' " she announced. " 'Happy birthday. Love, Tommy.' "

Carrie felt the full brunt of forty pairs of eyes zeroing in on her like laser beams.

"Who's ready for cake and ice cream?" she said brightly.

CHAPTER SEVEN

Tommy was startled out of a sound sleep by his own voice on the answering machine. He rolled off the edge of his futon and fumbled for the phone. Light streamed through the sheet nailed over the window, so it must be morning. He found the receiver behind the milk-crate lamp table, after knocking off a stack of library books. " 'Lo," he croaked into the phone. "Ow!" Rubbing his shoulder, which he'd stabbed with the antler of a deer head propped against the wall, he struggled to come awake.

He heard Carrie say, "What's the matter?"

He straightened up. "Nothing," he said. Staring at the smear of blood on his hand, he tried to remember if he'd ever heard of getting tetanus from a deer antler. "What's up?"

"Do you know where your dog is?"

Uh-oh. He could hear clenched teeth on

the other end of the line. Cautiously he said, "Last time I saw him he was sacked out in the garage. I assume you're gonna tell me where he is now."

"He's in the back of my truck having an insulin attack after eating half my white chocolate mints!"

Suddenly wide awake, Tommy hooked the phone between his shoulder and his ear and started jerking on his jeans. "Oh, man, Carrie, I'm sorry! Where are you?"

"I'm at the Quick-Stop. In case you'd forgotten, today is Matthew and Cheryl's wedding day. I picked up the cake, then had to get gas, and —" She stopped on a frustrated groan. "Never mind, I'll explain later. Just come — get — this — DOG!"

"I'll be there in five minutes."

Tommy had to borrow a truck out of his lot, because he obviously couldn't haul Skywalker home on the Kawasaki. He could totally understand the dog's fascination with Carrie, but he was going to have to do something about the sneaking-off thing. An undisciplined hunting dog was worse than useless; he was dangerous.

Knowing, too, that the Lord would not use an undisciplined Christian, Tommy had tried for the past month and a half to concentrate on writing his final paper for his lit class. Learning to use his new computer. Holding Matthew accountable in his premarital studies with the pastor. Sitting for hours out on the river with a fishing pole in his hand, praying.

Tommy snapped off the country radio station with an irritable twist. Living and working so close to Carrie's shop without the luxury of running next door whenever he felt like talking had stripped his patience to the bare bones. When they happened to run into each other — usually at church or when the dog got loose — she wouldn't even meet his eyes. For the life of him, he couldn't tell what she was thinking.

Lord, you said you wouldn't give me more than I can stand. Surely she's going to crack soon. Father, I need you to intervene here. If you want Carrie and me to be together, please show me what to do.

He pulled up in the Quick-Stop parking lot, where he saw Skywalker tied to the icebox outside the store. Carrie's catering truck was still parked at the pump, but she was nowhere in sight.

"Bad dog, Skywalker," he said with a freezing glare as he walked by. The dog's ears twitched, and he flopped onto the sidewalk in shame. Tommy found Carrie inside, perched on the counter sharing a bag of Sugar Babies with Elvin Goff.

Carrie looked like a movie star stuck in an episode of *Green Acres.* She was wearing an elegant, cap-sleeved silk dress of some dark chocolaty color that matched her eyes and made her hair look like a fairy cap. Her slim legs were crossed, the top one kicking nervously. He looked at her face. *Make that angrily.*

"Well," drawled Elvin, "if it ain't the knight in shining armor come to slay the dragon-dog."

"Do you know how long I worked on that candy?" Carrie said with exaggerated civility. *Kick, kick* went the foot. "Two days. And now I've got to drive to Mobile to find some sort of substitute. The wedding is at two o'clock, and it is now —" she elaborately checked her watch — "ten."

Keeping a nervous eye on that foot, Tommy approached. She looked so beautiful, he wished he'd done more than drag on the nearest clothes and brush his teeth. He rubbed his bristly jaw. "How did he get in the truck?"

"He must have slipped in while I was loading this morning and hid somewhere until I took off. I didn't know he was back there eating the candy until I heard him burp!" She hopped off the counter and walked up to poke Tommy in the chest. "That is one very subversive dog."

Tommy dropped his head. "I know he's a low-class mutt like me."

"And don't you give me that sad-eyed *humble* stuff, Tommy Lucas!" To his horror, Carrie's eyes sparkled with angry tears as she leaned closer to rebuke him. "You've done nothing to try to train Skywalker to stay home. I think you like the fact that he chomps through his lead and freeloads off me every chance he gets!"

That, of course, was dangerously close to the truth. But the sudden delirium caused by his mouth being less than two inches from Carrie's pert little nose made Tommy blurt out the first thing that came into his head. "Well, I'd like to know who's the one that got him hooked on sugar in the first place!"

"Ooh!" Carrie stomped her foot. "So now it's *my* fault my entire career is about to slide into the Dumpster? Tommy, every person who comes to the reception will either go home raving or laughing about the food. Besides the fact that this is Matthew and Cheryl! I wanted this wedding to be perfect for them!" She folded her arms across her stomach and turned her back to him.

Tommy wondered what she would do if he took her by the shoulders, turned her around, and kissed her senseless like he wanted to. But Elvin Goff's interested gaze restrained him. He was sorry Carrie was mad at him, but it was way better than the awkward politeness of the past couple of months.

Suddenly the Lord put an idea into his head. "Uh, Carrie, you know those green things you made a couple months ago?"

Carrie gave a choke that might have been a laugh or a sob. "Tommy, *you* made them green, not me!"

He glanced at Elvin, who took off his glasses and stuck one of the earpieces in his mouth. His eyebrows looked like caterpillars climbing uphill. "Well, yeah." Tommy frowned at Elvin. "I guess I did. Anyway, I told Roxanne to put 'em in her freezer. You're welcome to 'em."

"I can't serve green mints at a wedding."

"Why not?"

"Well, because . . . because . . ." She turned slowly to look up at him, her eyes still narrowed with temper. "Yeah, why not? That would be faster than driving to Mobile."

Elated that he'd solved the problem so easily, Tommy grinned. "You'll make catering history!"

Carrie headed for the door. "Don't get cocky, buster," she tossed over her shoulder. "I'm still gonna feed that dog to my cat."

"What cat?" Startled, Tommy met Elvin's evil grin. "When did you get a cat?"

The Old Gautier Place in Gautier, Mississippi, was a lovely Creole cottage on a bayou off the Gulf of Mexico. Deep porches surrounded it on three sides; the roofline rose at intervals to intriguing pitches, and there was a charming widow's walk along the back that looked out on the water. The front lawn was landscaped with dogwood, crape myrtle, and azaleas, and a couple of towering magnolias brushed fingers with ancient knotty oaks and a pecan tree or two. It was a lovely and impressive place for a wedding.

The ceremony was to be in the back garden between the house and the bayou; Carrie had set up the buffet for the reception inside the cottage. Equipment for a jazz band waited under an enormous gauze-draped tent pitched on the side lawn, which Cheryl's parents had rented for dancing.

Carrie was ready. She had followed Tommy back to Granny's, marveling at Skywalker's complete recovery from remorse. He'd stuck his funnel head out the window of Tommy's truck, sniffing the crisp gulf breeze that chased away the humidity of the past week and ruffled the vegetation growing along the roadside.

Tommy had quickly and almost wordlessly carried the bags of candy from the freezer in the shed to her truck, understanding the need for haste. After all, he hadn't even started getting dressed, and, as best man, he was expected to arrive early for pictures. She'd given him a stiff good-bye and thanks, leaving him standing next to Granny's barbecue pit with his hands in his back pockets, Skywalker lurking in the background.

Walking around the reception room, twitching at tablecloths and giving last-minute instructions to the teenage waitresses she'd hired for the afternoon, Carrie breathed a prayer of gratitude for Tommy's talent for commonsense solutions to problems. Never mind the fact that he usually brought them on himself. Or on her.

She paused to admire the table holding the punch, mints, and nuts. The punch was an icy, clear, sparkling ginger ale concoction, with silk ivy twining underneath the crystal bowl. The greenery and opalescent glitter of confetti tied in nicely with the silver bowls of pink- and pistachio-colored candy scattered at intervals along the length of the table. She suspected that Cheryl would like the color better than bland white, anyway.

Since everything seemed in order, she put a piece of candy in her mouth and walked out onto the porch that faced the river. Leaning her hands on the rail, she lifted her face to the cool breeze off the water. The taste of mint and sugar on her tongue made her think of Tommy and the expression of open longing on his face when she'd left him at Granny's house.

But he hadn't called her back.

When she'd found Skywalker in her truck, she'd been secretly overjoyed, because surely a confrontation would force Tommy to say what he felt.

Why couldn't she say to him what she felt?

"Lord," she whispered, "it's just so hard. At one time I thought Brad was my helpmate, but I didn't listen to you until it was too late. Then I got so scared I couldn't trust my own judgment. And along comes Tommy, the exact opposite of everything I thought I ever wanted in a man. But, Lord, you've changed my desires in the last five months. I know in your eyes Tommy's a choice warrior."

Carrie felt sudden tears well up in her eyes as she followed the flight of a bird in the bright blue sky. "Maybe he's figured out that I'm not good enough for him. Help me let him go if I need to, Lord. Help me trust you."

She sniffed, smiled to herself, and watched the bird dive into the thick undergrowth along the bayou. " 'Those who wait on the Lord will find new strength,' " she quoted from Isaiah. " 'They will fly high on wings like eagles. They will run and not grow weary. They will walk and not faint.' Lord, thank you for giving me wings to fly."

Carrie almost didn't recognize Tommy when he escorted Janelle, sniffling into a hankie, down the aisle. He seated her in the front row and walked over to join Matthew, who impatiently waited for his bride in front of a splashing fountain.

Carrie stood at the window inside the cottage, ignoring the gathering of well-dressed family members and friends. She had eyes only for Tommy. He looked like a model on a billboard advertising formal wear. She'd been in such a tizzy over her candy that morning, she hadn't noticed his hair. Now she saw that it had grown into a short spike on top, with the back and sides neatly trimmed. He looked mature. Very mature.

The bridesmaids were going to drool over him.

You're drooling, too, you dope, she told herself. *Snap out of it.*

She had to, anyway, because the bride was coming down the aisle, beaming radiantly. Carrie watched Matthew's attention focus on his bride.

Father, please cover their marriage with your presence, Carrie prayed. *They're so young. They'll need you so much.*

Carrie turned her attention back to Tommy. *Lord, I've been self-centered,* she suddenly realized. *I've been thinking about myself and refusing to trust you. I will let go of Brad and both our sins and mistakes. Please give me courage to reach out to Tommy.*

With aching eyes, she watched his sober profile as he witnessed his cousin and his friend take their vows. She felt her heart being tugged by the joy and humor that always lurked behind his eyes. Then and there she made up her mind to risk putting herself in Tommy's capable and loving hands.

She couldn't wait to talk to him, but she had responsibilities to take care of now. The reception would start soon.

■ ■ ■ ■

As soon as Matthew and Cheryl were pronounced husband and wife, Tommy yanked at his bow tie and pulled the top two studs of his collar loose. He wondered if he could talk Carrie into eloping so he wouldn't have to wear one of these monkey suits again. He couldn't have said what made him know that she was open to him again, but as he'd watched her drive off this morning with all that green candy in her truck — he just knew. It was as if the Lord had finally given him a big green light. And he was going to drive full speed ahead.

He just hoped he wasn't getting red mixed up for green again.

He searched for her in the crowd, until he remembered she'd probably be inside the cottage, getting ready to serve punch and wedding cake and green chocolate. She was the caterer, a VIP at this shindig, so he'd probably have to wait awhile. Guests were already swarming into the cottage like a bunch of hungry bees headed for the hive.

Tommy wasn't big on crowds, but he decided it would be worth it to get a glimpse of Carrie in that chocolate dress again. He wiggled through the line by dint of determination and his most charming smile, and finally managed to carve out a spot for himself at a corner table. He gave the flower girl a quarter to scrounge up a cup of punch for him, which he tossed off in one gulp, then hungrily eyed the Ferrari-shaped chocolate cake on a nearby table. Nobody had touched it or the six-tiered white bride cake on the other side of the room. He supposed they were waiting for the bride and groom. Tradition was such a pain in the neck.

He must have drunk a gallon of punch before he finally spotted Carrie ducking behind a partition with a stack of clear glass dessert plates in her hands. So that was where she'd been hiding. He'd gotten up to follow her, when he felt a small, nervous hand grasp his elbow and heard a familiar thin soprano voice say, "I was hoping I'd run into you here, Tommy."

He looked down, his stomach clenching. "Mama."

She looked even thinner than she had the last time he'd been to her trailer to fix a leaky toilet. A stiff wind would blow her off those high, narrow heels. She was dressed in a tight, beaded dress that had seen better days, and she didn't have on any stockings. Her earrings were big enough to serve wedding cake on, and her graying hair was pulled up into a flirty twist.

"You getting enough to eat, Mama?" he asked gently, taking her hand. It felt like chicken bones in his big palm.

"Oh yeah, honey, I'm fine," she said, her dark-circled eyes smiling sadly. "You're lookin' fine. So handsome in that tux." She reached up to twitch at the dangling bow tie. "Never could stay in your clothes more than five minutes at a time, though. I swear if I had a nickel for every tetanus shot you got from goin' barefoot, I'd be a rich woman."

You'd be a rich woman if you wouldn't throw everything down the sinkhole at the casinos, he thought, but he'd told her that a million times already. Instead of voicing his irritation, he smiled. "Well, it's good to see you. If you need me, you can always —"

"As a matter of fact, Tommy, there is somethin' you can do for me." When she hesitated, that fist in his gut tightened again. "I need just a little extra to tide me over this month. The note on the trailer was due a few weeks ago, and I got this nasty letter. . . ." She looked up at him pleadingly. "Steve moved out last Friday, and I don't know what I'm gonna do."

Tommy absently stroked his mother's

hand, thinking. There was Carrie again, stopping to laugh at something her grandmother said to her. Roxanne had on a lemon yellow spring suit and a flower-bedecked straw hat that covered most of her red curls. Next to Carrie's elegance, she looked like a happy sunflower.

He looked down at his mother's anxious face. *Lord, what a responsibility you've given me. Please help me.*

"Do you have the letter with you?" he asked.

"No, I — can't you just give me the money? Two hundred dollars ought to —"

"Mama, you'd just take it down to the boats. Bring me the letter, and I'll take care of it for you."

Her hand clawed his elbow desperately. "No, I want to pay it myself!"

Tommy sighed, and somehow across the crowded room, Carrie's eyes met his. They stared at one another. He saw her gaze flick to the little woman clinging to his arm, then back to his face. Carrie bit her lip, her eyes softening with tears.

That look of pity nearly undid him. The doctor's daughter was not going to marry the grease monkey. But God had been his strength in all the other bad times he'd ever faced. And he loved his mother no matter what she did.

Tommy pulled his mother into a fierce hug. "Bring me the letter, Mama." He kissed her cheek, smiled at her, and walked outside into the bright May sunshine.

Carrie disposed of the stack of cups in her hands and left her mother and Granny in charge of directing the cleanup crew. She pushed her way through the crowd of young, old, and in-between women who were waiting in front of the porch to catch the bride's bouquet. Cheryl would surely forgive her for bypassing this tradition.

Carrie was going after Tommy.

Though Carrie had never seen her before, the little woman in the blue beaded dress had to be his mother. Her light brown eyes were faded and sad, but the straight, triangular shape of her face was the same as his.

He had hidden it well, but something the woman said had distressed him utterly, to make him leave Matthew and Cheryl's wedding celebration.

She found Tommy down by the water, sitting with his legs dangling off the end of the pier, his jacket draped over a piling and his white shirt gleaming in the warm afternoon sun. When she got closer, she saw that he'd rolled his pants legs up and taken off his shoes and socks.

He turned and squinted up at her as she sat down. "Well, hey," he said. "Is everybody gone already?"

"No. I came to talk to you. That was your mother, wasn't it?"

He gave a short laugh. "See the family resemblance?"

Oh, Lord, please help me help him, she begged. She put her hand on his wrist. A strong, bony wrist with a multitude of tiny cuts and scratches and scars from a multitude of services performed in Christ's name.

Oh, how she loved him.

"As a matter of fact, I did. Why didn't you introduce me?"

He picked up a rock from a pile near his thigh and pitched it into the water. It went skipping, skipping, and finally sank with a delicate ripple. He didn't look at her. "I will. If you really want me to."

"I do. Listen, I'm going to love whomever you love." *Ooh, Lord,* she thought, *that's skating close to the edge of presumption. Can he meet me a little here?*

Another rock went skidding across the river. "You say that, but you can't even trust me with whatever's been hurting you from your marriage." Tommy swallowed hard.

"Do you think I'm too young and too dumb to understand?"

"Of course not. I — oh, Tommy, I made so many mistakes, and it humiliates me to let you think less of me! But the Lord has used you in so many ways to heal my heart. Look at me, beloved."

He did, and a sheen of tears over his golden eyes twisted her heart. She continued. "Here's what I see. A man who loves people in deed and in truth, whether or not they love him back. A man who struggles with faith and always manages to give it over to Christ in the end. A man who encourages and forgives others at his own expense." She paused. "A man after God's own heart."

Tommy looked down and caught his lower lip in his teeth. He shook his head.

Carrie took the hand she held and placed it at the back of her head. "Hold me, Tommy. Kiss me like you did on Valentine's Day. I'm tired of being afraid to fail."

His hand clenched in her hair as they leaned together. He kissed her and kissed her, and Carrie had never felt so safe and cherished in her life.

"I love you, Carrie," he murmured, dragging his lips across her cheek and back to her nose. "Please tell me you're not doing this just to get custody of my dog."

She laughed and flung her arms around his neck. "No, and it's not for free auto service. It's not even for pest-control purposes." She looked right into his eyes and gave him her heart and soul. "I love you with a love that could only come from the Lord, Tommy. I can't imagine spending my life with anyone else."

"Me either." He kissed her again, then withdrew with a twinkle in his eyes. "But we gotta talk about that cat."

"What cat?" Carrie murmured dreamily, delighting in the solid thump of Tommy's heart under her ear.

"The one that —" He tipped her chin up and went nose to nose with her. "You were just yankin' my chain, weren't you?"

She patted his cheek. "Such an easy mark."

He punished her with another long kiss.

"So . . ." Tommy cupped Carrie's face in his big hands, stroking his thumbs along her cheekbones. "When we're married and I buy another Ferrari, you're gonna roll under it to work on it with me?"

"And you're going to learn how to make corn bread."

"And butter cake with chocolate icing!"

Carrie laughed and nodded.

"Yes!" He lifted an exultant fist. "There is a God!"

RECIPE

Chocolate Icing
This recipe was my grandmother's, passed down through my aunt Myrna (wife of coon-hunting Uncle JP).

1 stick oleo (1/2 cup)
1 cup sugar
1/2 cup evaporated milk
2 tbsp. cocoa
pinch of salt
2 1/4 cups powdered sugar
1 tsp. vanilla

Combine oleo, sugar, evaporated milk, cocoa, and salt in a medium saucepan. Heat to boiling; boil 3 minutes. Turn off heat and add powdered sugar and vanilla. Beat until consistency is right for frosting your cake. (This will take some practice, but it's worth the effort!)

ABOUT THE AUTHOR

Elizabeth White grew up in Southaven, Mississippi, where she dreamed of following in the footsteps of Louisa May Alcott, her all-time favorite writer — though she graduated from Mississippi State University with a music education degree. After five years in Texas studying church music at Southwestern Seminary and working in a bank, Beth and her minister husband moved to the beautiful Gulf Coast of Mobile, Alabama. After the birth of their two children, she took some English courses to renew her teaching certificate, and one fiction-writing course was all it took to get her hooked on writing for publication.

A love of romance, combined with a desire to tell stories illuminating the love of Jesus, draws Beth to writing inspirational romance. She has written four novellas for Tyndale House Publishers, a three-book miniseries for Steeple Hill's Love Inspired Suspense line, and four romances for Zondervan.

Besides her favorite roles of wife and mother, Beth also teaches second-grade Sunday school, plays flute and pennywhistle in the church orchestra, and paints portraits in chalk pastel. She loves to read, crochet, go on mission trips, and avoid housework. Beth and her husband are currently on staff at First Baptist Church of North Mobile in Saraland, Alabama.

■ ■ ■ ■

WHAT SHE'S BEEN MISSING

RANEE McCOLLUM

■ ■ ■ ■

GOD HAS GIVEN EACH OF US THE ABILITY TO DO CERTAIN THINGS WELL. SO IF GOD HAS GIVEN YOU THE ABILITY TO PROPHESY, SPEAK OUT WHEN YOU HAVE FAITH THAT GOD IS SPEAKING THROUGH YOU. IF YOUR GIFT IS THAT OF SERVING OTHERS, SERVE THEM WELL. IF YOU ARE A TEACHER, DO A GOOD JOB OF TEACHING. IF YOUR GIFT IS TO ENCOURAGE OTHERS, DO IT! IF YOU HAVE MONEY, SHARE IT GENEROUSLY. IF GOD HAS GIVEN YOU LEADERSHIP ABILITY, TAKE THE RESPONSIBILITY SERIOUSLY. AND IF YOU HAVE A GIFT FOR SHOWING KINDNESS TO OTHERS, DO IT GLADLY.

Romans 12:6–8

To Robert and Darlene McCollum
Hey! A story for you!

CHAPTER ONE

High on the list of things Anne Singletary thought were totally wrong with the world was the fact that no one went to bed early anymore. Even worse, when people discovered that she went to bed by nine o'clock every night, they looked at her as if getting a good night's sleep was downright weird. Old-fashioned and outmoded she might be, but Anne had to have nine hours' sleep or she would face the next day grouchy or unstable — or both.

Tonight she was late getting to bed, and that did not bode well for the Annual Men's Valentine's Day Sweetheart Dessert Contest and Silent Auction being held tomorrow at Anne's Kansas City church. This year was the thirty-ninth year for the Auction, and Anne was in charge for the first time. She had not, of course, made up the name.

Ruby Bougainville, who until last year had been the oldest member of the four-hundred-member church, had come up with both the idea for the fund-raising auction and its staggeringly long moniker. Ruby's mother, Charlotte Harris, had been a schoolteacher in Leavenworth, Kansas, in 1909 and had met her husband, cavalry officer Rhet Bougainville, at a box social at her school. The romance of it all had inspired Ruby, and although she herself had not married, she never gave up hope. She initiated the Annual Men's Valentine's Day Sweetheart Dessert Contest and Silent Auction as a way of memorializing her parents' romance. And, for a time, as a possible means of finding that sort of romance for herself.

Ruby had been in charge of the ordeal — er, the festivities — right up to her eighty-ninth year. Ruby had always made sure the auction's proceeds went to needy but overlooked causes, which was also one of Anne's personal crusades.

Anne did not particularly want to be in charge this year, but since she had volunteered for the job, she would take her duties seriously, which would be hard to do unless she got some sleep.

At a quarter to ten, Anne turned off her computer and looked down at the black Labrador curled up at her feet under her desk. He looked so comfortable with his large muzzle atop one of her slippers — not a fuzzy bunny slipper, mind you. Anne's slippers were functional, washable, and the kind you could actually curl up underneath yourself without having to deal with any uncomfortable rabbit ears.

"Herman," she whispered to the dog. The Lab rolled slightly and sighed, his floppy jowls leaving a streak of drool across the top of her left foot. The slippers, she reminded herself, were washable, and Herman *had* put in a long day in the pediatric wards of a couple of Kansas City hospitals. But it was time to play hardball.

"Herman!" she whispered more loudly. "Want a cookie?" A small explosion occurred under the desk. Herman's head came up so fast he bonked it against the bottom of the center drawer.

After producing the promised Milk-Bone, Anne tidied up her already neat kitchen. When Herman finished his treat, she let him out into her small backyard, let him back in a few minutes later, and headed for bed.

The phone rang. Anne retraced her steps and frowned at the clock.

"Hello?" she said in a firm, almost prim, voice. She always attempted to be polite to those people who didn't realize that nine o'clock was a perfectly acceptable bedtime, even for a woman of twenty-nine years. The time now, however, was ten fifteen.

"Anne Singletary?" A male voice spoke in her ear, sounding for all the world like it was early evening.

"Yes?" Anne could not place the voice. If this was a sales call for a vacation resort or a carpet cleaner, she was going to be very upset.

"Anne, it's Rhys Carter."

Anne blinked, reached for a convenient chair, and sat down with a thump. "Hello, Rhys," she managed, as if he weren't the very last person on earth she expected to hear from. And it was *what* time in New York? The man must be crazy!

Oh yes, that's right. He was.

A printout of a month-old e-mail message, pinned to the bulletin board by her phone, confirmed it.

Dear Anne,

I've decided to start a charitable organization. I would like you to be my spokesperson. Your name kept popping up in my mind as I contemplated this whole thing, and you know I've always gone with the voices in my head. I'd like you to pray about it and say yes.

Sincerely,
Rhys Carter

Anne had not seen the man in person — and had barely spoken to him — in the nearly twelve years since their high school graduation. But she knew enough about him to be only mildly . . . flabbergasted. Trust Rhys Carter to take a person's perfectly normal life and create total chaos. Enjoyable chaos, because it was nearly impossible not to like him, but chaos nonetheless. He was universally known for this.

Anne had not been at all surprised when her old friend Rhys — one of those infuriating people who had known exactly what he wanted to do in life since he was three years old, if not sooner — burst onto the national media scene about five years ago. This was the man, she remembered, who in high school was nearly voted senior class president while still a junior. This was the man who could debate for hours on whether blue was really a color; the arguments he could come up with on inane subjects like that could make you doubt it yourself. This was the man whose offbeat, out-of-the-box take on life had made him a wildly popular nationally syndicated columnist. Anne found it astounding that he could even remember her, let alone come up with an offer that struck right at her heart.

She had promptly replied to Rhys's e-mail,

asking if it would be possible to get a few more details about this charity. While she waited, Anne prayed about what God would have her do, shooting questions at him and waiting for an answer — from either God *or* Rhys. Although the questions varied, the answer was always the same. Silence.

Time and again, Anne had chastised herself for wasting so much time thinking about Rhys's cryptic message, which was so obscure as to be almost laughable. But her mind wouldn't leave it alone. It fit right in with her uncertain feeling that she wasn't doing anything important with her life.

"I got your e-mail," Rhys said into her shocked ear. "I'm sorry I never got a chance to respond. It's been hectic."

"I'm sure you've been busy." Anne did not deceive herself. Rhys's idea for a charity — as well as his idea for her as the spokesperson — was, at the most, half-baked and therefore far down the list of his priorities.

Rhys had the ear of zillions of people who loved the eccentricity of his column, where subjects ranged from serious political commentary to an ode to a particularly comfortable pair of socks. Even the people who objected to his frequent and unapologetic mention of his Christianity admitted that Rhys could write circles around virtually any other columnist you'd care to name. Judging by the success of the column, God had given his approval to Rhys's wish to have a Christian voice in the media and that, necessarily, must come first with him.

Anne believed strongly in the cultivation and preservation of God-given gifts. In this instance, she could not get upset with Rhys for maintaining his, even if it meant she had to wait a month to get some answers.

"I've been moving, actually," Rhys continued. "I just got into town tonight. I was wondering if we could get together for lunch tomorrow?"

Anne shifted the phone to her other ear to give her time to formulate a response. Herman gained her attention for a moment by flopping down at her feet and once again arranging his nose over her foot.

"You . . . you . . ." Generally Anne was not at a loss for words. She was not a chatterbox, but she could make small talk and adjust to awkward situations, something that came in handy in her life. She tried again. "You . . ."

"Moved to Kansas City. From New York. Today. Some, uh, things have come up in the last month that made the change advisable."

Moved to Kansas City! Anne's first

thought was that she was talking to the wrong Rhys Carter. He loved New York, or so he said on the morning talk shows where he made frequent appearances to promote his writing and entertain America. In Anne's opinion, all the female talk-show hosts fawned over him dreadfully. One of them had even said that his "witty, engaging writing style was simply an extension of the charm he displayed in person." Anne would have gagged on that bit of flattery — except that it was true.

That Rhys could impress New York so much and still keep his integrity and witness Anne considered one of God's amazing miracles. Rhys Carter's name attracted not a hint of scandal or hypocrisy. The man was a regular Billy Graham.

New York City had been Rhys's home for years. For him to move back to Kansas City was a significant act, even for someone as unpredictable as Rhys.

"You *moved* to Kansas City?"

Anne heard him sigh.

"Do you remember Jeff McGregor? He was the editor for the Kansas City *Sun.*" Anne racked her memory for the name. The *Sun* was now defunct; it had never been able to really compete with the *Star,* but —

"Oh! Jeff was the one who hired you as a

correspondent while we were still in high school."

"That's him. He had a stroke about two years ago and had to move into a retirement community."

"So sorry . . ." Anne wondered whether she had met the man.

"Yes, well, the upshot is Jeff owns — or owned — a forty-acre farm between Kansas City and Leavenworth. It's not a working farm. It's nice. Big house, excellent grounds. He used to hold writers' retreats up there every year. There were waiting lists, but I managed to get into a couple. When he had his stroke he had to give that up, and now to pay his bills he's had to give up the farm. Only he didn't want to sell it to just anyone. . . ." Rhys's voice trailed off and then he cleared his throat.

Anne's lightbulb clicked on, and she bolted upright in her chair. Herman adjusted the placement of his nose.

"You bought it," she said, amazed.

"Well . . . yes. I want to start having the retreats again. I'm going to continue on as Jeff would have, if he was able. Anyway, I'm in a hotel at present, but I'll be moving into my apartment — it's downtown — tomorrow. I have to eat, though, and I thought you might want to know more about the job I offered you. God has put a lot on my plate, but I think, with your help, I can make a go of both enterprises."

Anne blinked rapidly, her eyelids trying to clear the sudden downpour of information from the windshield of her mind. Anne did not run on New York time.

"We're holding the Auction tomorrow," she blurted, at a loss for anything else to say. "I'm in charge. I'm so sorry, but I can't possibly go to lunch." She hoped he didn't hear the desperate squeak at the end of that sentence. She glanced at the clock on the stove. Past ten thirty. Things were going to go downhill from here, she thought irritably. Her mind was obviously already going in that direction.

"The . . . Annual . . ." Rhys hesitated.

"The Annual Men's Valentine's Day Sweetheart —"

"Dessert Contest and Silent Auction," Rhys finished with her.

"Yes," she said, trying to sound proud rather than defensive. While attending the church, Rhys had never made a dessert for the Auction, excusing himself on the basis of having to write the article about it for the church newsletter.

"The AMVDSDCSA," Rhys repeated. She heard him turn away from the phone and pretend to cough in order to cover up a laugh. Anne knew Rhys didn't really disdain the Auction — or at least he hadn't used to. It was simply that the whole thing played hugely to his sense of the absurd.

"So how is it," Rhys controlled himself enough to ask, "that you are in charge of such a logistical nightmare?"

"Ruby died," she told Rhys simply. There was a slight pause and then Rhys spoke again, his voice deeper, slower, and softer than before.

"Anne, I'm sorry. I forgot about that." Anne could almost feel the compassion ooze through the phone. It was almost impossible, especially if a person had read his column for the past three years as had Anne, to miss what a truly compassionate heart this man had. Rhys, Anne remembered, was the one guy in the youth group who had never looked uncomfortable around tears and always had a hug for anyone who was hurting.

"I actually did read about it in the church newsletter. I appreciate your sending that to me for all these years, by the way. When exactly did she die?"

"It will be a year next month," Anne said. "You should have seen her, Rhys. I was at her house not long after last year's Auction, and she said — very cheerfully — that the good Lord had obviously decided he was going to be the only man for her. She died a couple of days later." Anne sniffed. "She went to her grave in a white dress, with roses all around her and a smile on her lips."

"And you cried buckets."

"Of course."

"And when no one else sprang at the chance to be the new commandant, you stepped in." It was a statement, not a question.

"Well," Anne said, "it was the least I could do for one of my favorite people."

"I understand," Rhys said. "You were always doing things like that, even years ago. So how is it going?"

Only her parents had bothered with that question. Everyone else at church seemed to assume she was handling the whole thing with her normal aplomb.

"It's going . . . well . . . ," she prevaricated.

"Out with it, Anne. I want to know the juicy details."

She chuckled and would have doodled her finger in the dust on her table, except there wasn't any. Anne hung her clothes on color-coded hangers and planned meals a month in advance; dust didn't stand a chance.

"I'd like to disagree with your unflattering

'logistical nightmare' comment, but . . ."

"But?"

"Well — this thing takes horrendous amounts of time, even though by now it should almost run itself. You know Ruby had the rule that not only could the wives or sisters or girlfriends not help make the dessert, but they couldn't help with anything else either."

"Yes, because — let me see, I got this lecture once — 'women in the church have so many things to do, mostly to do with either cooking or children, that they deserve at least one function where they don't have to do anything.' She wouldn't even let the women make the coffee on Auction day."

"Wow," Anne said. "You remember well."

"Certainly. So you're having trouble getting the men to pitch in? You always were a softie."

She chose to focus on his question. "No, that's just it. I've got no end of volunteers, but it's such a headache organizing them!"

"What are you having problems with?"

"Well . . . oh, Rhys, men are so helpful; they really are. I don't have any complaints."

"Really."

She made a sound of protest against the unbelieving note in his voice. "I don't!"

"Okay, maybe you don't have complaints,"

Rhys conceded, "but you've got stories. I like stories. Tell me a story, Anne, p-l-e-e-e-ease?" Anne's nine-year-old brother, Avery, could not have sounded any more pathetic. Anne giggled. She never giggled. Except when she stayed up too late. Oh, but what would it hurt?

"Hmm, I do have stories," she said.

"I'm listening."

"I had a couple of guys volunteer to buy supplies. I gave them a list — a very general list — because I didn't want to insult them. We ended up with gargantuan-size plates instead of dessert plates. Five hundred forks, but no spoons. And two thousand purple napkins instead of red for Valentine's Day as I requested, because they were on sale."

"So the problem would be . . . ?"

"Oh, hush. I put one man in charge of coffee and last night — last night! — twelve other men came up to tell me this guy couldn't make decent coffee if his life depended on it."

Rhys laughed, somehow making Anne feel he really understood her frustration.

"Oh, it's not that bad. The guys did a great job setting up the tables and chairs."

"I'm sure Ruby would be proud of you."

"I hope so. But it's still — not — what

—" a huge yawn escaped her — "I really like to do. Sorry."

"Past your bedtime?" Rhys asked dryly.

She yawned again. The youth group had always rolled their eyes at her inability to stay awake past ten at night, and she had taken an obscene amount of teasing for it. She glanced at the clock again. Past eleven.

"Do you still wake up at six without an alarm?" Rhys wanted to know. He groaned when she answered in the affirmative. "We all hated you, you know," he said. "If you'd had tires, we'd have slashed them. You were such a bore for lock-ins, going to sleep so early, running around in the morning so cheerful. Ick."

"Ick?" Anne repeated. She was truly sleepy but couldn't resist teasing him back. "Aren't you supposed to be some sort of hotshot journalist? And you're using a word like *ick?*"

There was a momentary silence on the other end of the line.

"Rhys?" Surely she hadn't hurt his feelings.

"Annie." There was a note in his voice she was unfamiliar with. And she hadn't been called Annie in years. She realized she had been chatting away, late at night, for nearly an hour, *with a man.* A man whom she had once liked a great deal.

She really shouldn't make too much of it.

"Yes?" she said.

"I think I'm going to enjoy getting to know you again."

His voice, a voice she had heard only rarely in the years since he'd left — in 1991, 1995, 1996, and 1999, to be exact — sounded as warm and fuzzy as Herman's muzzle still resting on her slipper. She swallowed.

"Thank you," she managed. Oh, she *liked* the way his voice sounded. Anne was too tired to rationalize away her response. Having all that famed charm directed at her was not a terribly unpleasant experience.

"What time is the Auction tomorrow?" Rhys asked.

"Two. I have to be there by noon." To her relief, her voice sounded normal, not all gushy. Rhys was very famous. He got enough gushy. She would not gush.

Rhys made a noise of acceptance. "There's no way you'll be able to make lunch then. I'd better let you get some sleep. Hey . . ." He paused.

"What?" Anne asked when the silence became too intense.

"I've got smoke coming out of my ears. Is there still time for me to enter the Annual

Men's Valentine's Day Sweetheart Dessert Contest and Silent Auction?"

Anne rubbed her forehead, doubtful she had heard him correctly.

"You haven't even moved into your apartment," she told him, as if he could have forgotten. "You can't have unpacked yet."

"Well, yeah, I'll have to go out and buy flour."

"And sugar."

"And a cookbook."

There was momentary silence.

"Well, I'll see you tomorrow then," Anne said. If the man wanted to bake, let him bake.

"Absolutely."

Anne went to bed wishing she could just hang out with her old friend Rhys Carter tomorrow instead of being in charge of the thirty-ninth AMVDSDCSA.

Rhys did not get to bed for another two hours, but that was normal for him. He stared around his posh hotel room, wondering what he could possibly make for the Auction. His lips curved in a grin as he remembered Anne's astonishment that he wanted to participate.

But that was why he moved to Kansas City in the first place. He wanted to be useful. Here he was — a successful, famous, prosperous, popular guy — and he felt . . . silly. Fruitless. Idle.

Yes, he'd written decent articles on corruption in the government; essays on China; a treatise on evolution; a thought-provoking debate with himself on how to fold socks; and odes to dandelions, antique cars, and hair mousse. He'd managed to be funny. He'd managed to become a household name.

Yet he'd managed to feel like he wasn't doing much of practical use in the world. Should he be writing articles, for instance, or teaching people to read his articles?

Then Jeff McGregor had called about his farm, and Rhys decided to help out by buying the farm and reinstating Jeff's retreats. Very helpful.

He'd read in the church newsletter that Anne Singletary brought light and life to local nursing homes, so he decided to start a charity and get her to head it. He'd contribute the money and the contacts and the celebrity appeal; she'd contribute her significant talents, which were being stifled by her lack of opportunity. Helpful *and* practical.

When Anne mentioned the AMVDS-DCSA, Rhys saw every reason to get involved and donate to the cause.

Never mind that he didn't have ingredients of any kind, or any experience, or any clue what to do next besides head to the nearest twenty-four-hour supermarket and spend some time in the baking aisle.

Rhys grabbed his coat and went out.

CHAPTER TWO

Rhys's dessert was the most extraordinary contribution Anne had ever seen at any Annual Men's Valentine's Day Sweetheart Dessert Contest and Silent Auction.

She gathered her courage, her wits, and the knowledge that she was good in a crisis — despite having gotten only three hours of sleep last night — and crossed the fellowship hall to help her old friend find a place for his rather . . . interesting confection.

Besides the trepidation caused by the sight of Rhys's dessert, she also had what she suspected were butterflies in her stomach caused by the sight of *him.* He wore a charcoal suit over a royal blue turtleneck, somehow managing to look both elegant and casual at the same time. His dark hair, cut short on the sides and back, had a hand-tousled look on top. Anne suspected he used more mousse than she did, but who cared? Rhys was more handsome in person than she remembered. And she had spent a ridiculous amount of time last night remembering. And wondering if he might . . . if they could ever . . .

Anne shook her head, the way a child shakes a jar of bugs trying to knock the critters down before opening the lid. It simply wasn't practical to think about a relationship with someone who had just moved to town in the past twenty-four hours. No one should move that fast.

"Rhys!" she said as she approached. "It's good to see you."

Rhys turned and leveled a smile on her that was guaranteed to charm the starch out of a librarian. Anne, no librarian, was not unaffected. He had always possessed a quality that could make an entire roomful of church ladies swoon as one — like large pastel dominoes pushed over by his charisma. Anne was wearing a nice, sensible black suit and she still felt wobbly.

As she stopped in front of him, Rhys leaned toward her. It was impossible to mistake his intent. She froze. Was he really going to kiss her? Not one of her irrational romantic scenarios last night involved him kissing her *today*.

Your cheek! her mind screamed at her. *He wants to kiss your cheek in greeting!*

Just barely before it was too late, Anne managed to present the proper part of her anatomy to save herself deep embarrassment. Irritated that she hadn't known immediately what he was doing, Anne reminded herself that he had spent the last few years hobnobbing with millionaires. She needed to get with the program. And cheek kissing meant nothing personal, no matter how many more butterflies showed up for the occasion. Nothing.

She forcefully turned her mind to practical matters and smiled up at her old friend. "I'm glad you made it. I wasn't really certain you would."

"What? And miss the opportunity to stun everyone with my cooking skills?" he asked.

Stun was certainly the right word. Anne fought to keep from gawking at the quivering mass on the platter Rhys held in his hands. Rhys had been stunning people all his life, but this was . . . was . . .

"Wow!" said a voice at her elbow. "That's cool!"

Anne raised her eyebrows at the medium-size boy who had appeared at her side. Anyone looking could tell they were related, despite the difference in their ages. And despite the difference in their opinions of Rhys's dessert.

"Rhys, this is my brother, Avery," Anne said. "Avery, this is Mr. Rhys Carter. Mr. Carter attended this church before you were born. We were in the youth group together." And had gone totally separate directions since then, obviously. Cheek kissing! She would be lucky if Rhys didn't think she was some sort of ignorant hick from the sticks.

Avery had ignored most of her introduction.

"Hello, Mr. Carter," he said and focused on the most important thing. "That's a really cool dessert!"

It might have been cool, Anne reflected. It was also nearly indescribable.

"Hello, Avery," Rhys said. He looked at Anne and shook his head slightly in amazement. Avery had been quite a surprise for Anne's parents; he was only nine years old and Rhys, of course, had never seen him.

"We're going to find a table so Mr. Carter can set his . . . dessert . . . down," Anne said.

"There's a spot over here." Avery pointed to one of the tables lining the walls of the fellowship hall.

"Lead the way then," Anne said.

"I knew you had acquired a brother," Rhys whispered as he moved past her, "but seeing him so grown-up already makes me feel antiquated. And being called Mr. Carter . . ." He shrugged and stood up straighter. "I feel really . . . mature."

Anne looked at the platter in his hands and then back at his straight face. "Don't," she whispered back.

She was happy to see him smile in response to her teasing. She may not know much about cheek kissing, but she knew how to make someone smile.

As they traversed the length of the fellowship hall, people openly stared. Anne, pleased that they gave Rhys and his platter a wide berth, wasn't sure if they stayed out of the way out of politeness because the tray looked heavy, or because they feared bodily harm if he dropped it. Either Rhys didn't notice the small smiles and soft chuckles that accompanied his dessert's progress across the room, or he was so used to being the object of attention that he was unaffected.

Anne suspected the latter.

Avery led them to a table with space enough to hold the gigantic tray, and Rhys set it down. Anne let herself look at his offering — really look at it — for the first time.

Rhys was lucky he'd been blessed with charm, charisma, and occupational success, because he sure couldn't cook. *Forgive me,*

Lord, for thinking such a thing. But you and I both know it's true.

The dessert appeared to contain — and Anne used the word loosely — chocolate pudding. *Lots* of it. Something vaguely white, possibly whipped cream, was also involved. Anne thought the concoction was intended to be tall and multilayered, judging by the edges of what might have been graham crackers peeping out from amidst the general snarl of ingredients. There were darker brown streaks and many suspicious lumps of an unidentifiable nature. A lonely maraschino cherry on top tried to lend an air of sophistication but failed dismally.

Anne would never say anything aloud, of course, but it looked as though the whole thing might have fallen to the floor at some point.

"Well," Rhys said brightly, "what do you think? Not bad for short notice, huh? I even had time to quadruple the recipe."

Her mind, having been poleaxed by a dessert that made up in sheer size for what it lacked in looks, was not working quite as quickly as it should have been. She couldn't tell whether Rhys was actually serious or making a joke.

"Gotta go tell Mom!" Avery exclaimed, giving her a few more seconds to think, and rushed off.

"It's quite, er . . . innovative," Anne managed. Tactfully, she thought. A science fiction movie could not have produced a more hideous-looking entity.

"It was a new recipe," Rhys said.

Now there's a big surprise!

"Where . . . ?" Anne began and then snapped her mouth shut and shook her head. She still couldn't tell if he was kidding, but just in case Rhys was actually enamored of his creation, she had better try to take it seriously. She wanted no humiliations of any kind here today!

Her lips were beginning to twitch. She produced a pen and pad of paper from a pocket in her "Life Is Short; Eat Dessert First" apron.

"Does the dessert have a name?" she asked.

"That," Rhys said with faultless composure, "is called the Rhys Carter Surprise." His vocal chords had to be bending over backwards to sound so sincere.

"The Rhys . . . Carter . . . Surprise," Anne said with a commendably straight face. She wrote the name at the top of the sheet, ripped the paper off, and placed it under a small fishbowl beside the platter.

"As you probably remember," she said to

Rhys without daring to look at him, "the desserts will first be judged for taste and beauty. *Um-hmmm.* Then anyone who wants to bid on it will write down her bid number and the price she is willing to pay, *hmm-HMM,* on a bidding paper, which she will place in the fishbowl."

Biting one's tongue really did work, she discovered. She would try to remember that the next time Mrs. Whitefield insisted on playing Pachelbel's entire "Canon" for the offertory. From memory. Mrs. Whitefield did not have an overly resourceful memory.

"And the highest bidder gets to share the dessert with its creator," Rhys prompted.

"Yes!" Anne said. "Just like in Ruby's mother's day. But we've had to make up a new rule — wives are not allowed to bid on their husband's desserts."

"Really?" Rhys asked. "Why is that?"

"Well, this is supposed to be a social event," Anne explained, much more in control now due to the pain in her tongue. "If wives keep taking pity on their husbands, buying their desserts and then sitting with them to eat, there will be no socializing done at all."

Rhys glanced at her with a scowl on his face, then indicated the Rhys Carter Surprise. "Well," he said, "no one needs to take pity on *me*."

This was so contrary to what Anne was thinking that the laughter burst forth before she could stop it.

The man simply exuded confidence. It was no wonder he had climbed so quickly to the top. Looking at him now, Anne had no problem believing that if Rhys truly wanted to start a charity, it would succeed. As long as it didn't involve cooking.

"I'm sorry," she wheezed, "but it's a dessert only a wife could love. I take it you didn't find a cookbook?"

"No. I remember having something like this at someone's house once, so I sort of made it up as I went along." Rhys plucked the handkerchief from his suit coat pocket and handed it to her to wipe her wet cheeks. "I didn't even have to use any flour or sugar or . . . eggs. . . ."

"No! Of *course* you didn't!"

Rhys sighed in patient amusement, smiling graciously at the small audience that had gathered in response to Anne's guffaws.

"Anne, are we about ready to start here?" The voice belonged to the pastor, who also happened to be Anne's father. She straightened and put Rhys's handkerchief to good use.

"Yes," she said. "Give me a few minutes,

Dad." Her father walked away after giving her a bemused glance.

"It's your fault, you know," Anne informed Rhys.

"My fault?" he sounded aghast. "I never make anyone do . . . whatever it is you were doing. I'm much more dignified than that."

"It is *so* your fault," Anne said. "You called too late last night."

"You're saying *sleep deprivation* is the reason you insulted my dessert by laughing at it?" Rhys asked.

"Exactly." Anne reached over to nudge the maraschino cherry back into the center of the concoction. "It really doesn't look that bad. Really."

"Hey, you'll never know what you've been missing until you try it."

"Oh, I can't —" Anne caught sight of her father beckoning to her and broke off. "I need to get this thing going," she told Rhys. "It's good to see you again. I hope you get a lot of bids."

Anne walked away without a backward glance and wondered who would end up with the Rhys Carter Surprise. For an instant — for several instants — she wished she could buy it.

His interest in you, she reminded herself, *is professional. And friendly. Nothing more . . .*

yet. She grinned, then sobered, then grinned again.

She could not bid on his dessert. No. The decision had already been made.

Her thoughts were interrupted by Avery, who all but skidded into her in his excitement. "I got you a bidding number!" he declared, holding up a slip of paper — folded and taped for privacy, of course. Avery procured a number for her every year, "to help Anne" as he put it, but he had other motives. Their mother habitually bid on fruit pies, oatmeal cookies with raisins, or items labeled "lite," all of which Avery disdained for being too healthy. Anne, remembering what it was like to be nine years old, normally took pity on him and used her number and money on whatever gooey dessert her brother pointed out.

"Oh, but Avery, don't you remember?" Anne asked, taking the number from him. She automatically slit the tape to see what number she had, then shook her head. It was irrelevant. "We discussed this. I'm not bidding this year."

This was a pragmatic judgment, made after she discovered that men unsupervised would bring her purple napkins instead of red. No way would she have time or energy to sit with the creator of whichever dessert

Avery picked, as she usually did, and it wouldn't be fair to saddle someone with her precocious little brother, just so he could scarf down a much-wanted treat. Besides, it was her contest this year, and she didn't want to look biased.

Ruby had always bid, of course. The man whose dessert Ruby bought was always subject to a bit of teasing, even if he was fifty years younger than she, because everyone knew that Ruby, at least in the early years, was looking for a husband. Although she had loved the woman dearly, Anne didn't want it to look like she was following in Ruby's man-hunting footsteps. She had never liked being the center of attention, and attention of that sort was the worst kind. Unfortunately, by heading up the contest, Anne had already sparked rumors. And she didn't know exactly how many people had seen Rhys kiss her on the cheek, but she figured about half the room. Therefore, she wasn't buying even the humblest plate of cookies. No way.

Avery's downcast expression upon being reminded of this, however, nearly did Anne in.

"Mom will never buy what I want," he said, his voice as despairing as only a nine-year-old's could be. "She'll say she will, but she won't. She never does."

Anne slipped the bid number into her apron pocket and pulled Avery close for a hug. Avery's arms went around her waist, and he hugged her back. Her brother could be a pain, she reflected, but he really was a sweet kid.

"Tell you what," she said. "After the bidding, if you see a dessert you like, you tell me, and I'll see if I can snag a piece for you. Would that be all right?" She hoped Rhys's dessert was edible, since she figured that was what Avery was going to want. Thank the good Lord she had made the rule about not bidding!

Avery shrugged. She had the feeling he wasn't listening.

"Maybe even two desserts," she coaxed.

"Maybe." Avery's voice sounded more hopeful. He released her, and Anne was relieved to see a huge smile on his face.

"Go now," she said. "I have to make an announcement."

She hated being on stage. Anne paused beside a chair that would serve as her dais from which to officially announce the commencement of the bidding. Standing up in front of people — all eyes on her — was one of her least favorite things to do. She caught Rhys's eye.

If she took Rhys's job offer, being on stage would become commonplace. For the past month, she had not bothered to think about that. It was only now, as she clambered up on the chair, that she let herself realize that a charity spokesperson was just that — a *spokes*person. *Speaking* to large groups of people. All eyes on her. Like now.

Why, oh, why did Rhys want her for this job? Why was she even considering it?

She was a virtual nobody. Her job as the secondary secretary at the church was a rather low-paying position, but the salary was adequate. She took care of calls and visitors so Mrs. Lattimore, the primary secretary, could tend to more important matters involved in assisting the pastoral staff. The unglamorous work gave Anne opportunities she would not otherwise have had, however, to do the things she wanted to do — things she thought God wanted her to do. She took James 1:27, the verse about visiting the widows and orphans, very seriously. If she had a "real" job, she would not be able to spend as much time as she did visiting nursing homes with Herman, taking supper to shut-ins, doing a bit of babysitting, or whatever else someone needed her to do.

Rhys needed someone who could handle

speeches before large crowds. He needed someone used to cheek kissing. Someone who could stay up late without acting like an imbecile the next day. Oh, for pity's sake. Right now, she needed to worry about the Auction. Not the Academy Awards.

She drew a big breath and hoped no one saw her knees knocking. "Ladies and gentlemen," she said in a steady voice from atop her chair. "Welcome to the thirty-ninth Annual Men's Valentine's Day Sweetheart Dessert Contest and Silent Auction."

She felt a smile grow on her lips as she remembered Rhys's laughter from the night before. Anne determinedly avoided his gaze, afraid that if she looked at him, she would burst out laughing again.

Be professional! This is what he wants from you! Show him — and yourself — that you are not a hick from the sticks!

"You all know how this works," she continued, pleased to hear her voice sounding civilized. "Bidding will end in half an hour. Let's remember this is for charity. Also, please stay in front of the tables to give the contest judges room to work behind them. Thank you. You may begin!"

Anne spent several minutes with the contest judges, all respected Christian ladies from other churches who had been judging the contest for years. There were three judges for taste and three for beauty. As she left them to their work, the beauty judges approached the Rhys Carter Surprise.

Every single dessert in the place looked more appetizing than the Rhys Carter Surprise, but the judges did a good job of looking impartial. At least they didn't hoot with laughter, unlike some other people she could mention.

Rhys, not paying any attention to his dessert, chatted with a group of ladies some distance from it. They were all giggling merrily. Anne wondered if he had kissed all their cheeks. She shook her head, debated for two seconds, then took advantage of his inattention to swing by the table and sneak a glance at the Rhys Carter Surprise fishbowl. To her relief, it had several bids in it. She didn't want Rhys embarrassed by having no one bid for his offering.

She listened to old Mr. Henry's story of how he had made three different cakes from scratch that morning, none of which had turned out right. He'd ended up using a mix and some tub frosting, and he was morose. Packaged mixes were quite acceptable, Anne assured him. Privately she thought that if Rhys had used a mix, she wouldn't be struggling to come up with words like *creative* and *original* and *inventive* to describe his dessert.

She checked in with the taste judges, barely managing to refrain from asking what they thought of Rhys's concoction.

Avery came by once to throw his arms around her for several seconds. He had always been a loving child.

Thirty minutes after the start of the Auction, Anne climbed back on her chair. "Bidding is now closed," she said with authority. "The estimable Pastor Singletary —" she threw an impish glance in her father's direction — "will read each winning bid. We will announce the results of the contest as soon as they are tabulated."

As she climbed down from the chair, Rhys smiled at her — an easy, friendly smile.

Anne did not blush — she never blushed — but the butterflies came back in full force.

Her father's voice brought her back to reality. "High bid on Mr. Hayden's chocolate chip cookies is seven dollars, going to bidder number seventy-six."

The winner of the cookies stepped forward amidst general applause. Rhys applauded too, Anne saw, but her mind caught on a remembered image. Just last week she had seen him clapping — in a picture on the society page of the Kansas City *Star*. With a gorgeous, doubtlessly well-bred and intelligent woman on his arm, Rhys had been in New York attending a charity dinner, for which tickets cost one thousand dollars per plate. A charity dinner of the type Anne would have to organize, attend, and possibly even speak at in order to make contacts and solicit funds.

Ick. Anne smiled in spite of herself, but her next thought was more sobering. Rhys attended charity dinners that cost a thousand dollars a plate. She ran a church charity auction that sold a plate of cookies for seven dollars.

The difference jarred her. If they raised a total of one thousand dollars tonight, she would be thrilled, but what would Rhys Carter think? Anne turned and went into the kitchen. Flopping down in a chair, she dropped her forehead into her hand. She had *not* had enough sleep last night. She did not normally have mood swings, and she seldom felt this desolate.

The AMVDSDCSA was a noble effort. The proceeds helped needy people. She wouldn't have agreed to head up the whole shebang if she didn't believe that. Of course she wished she could do more, but she was doing all she could . . . wasn't she?

Perhaps God required more from her than

simple tasks like fixing Mrs. Harrison's leaky toilet. Could Rhys's offer be her opportunity from God? To make more of a difference to more people?

"Eight dollars and fifty-five cents for Norman Clark's almond coffee cake!" her dad announced.

Anne stood and looked through the doorway of the kitchen at the spectacle of the Auction. *Eight dollars and fifty-five cents.* And the Auction was the most profitable event of the year.

Rhys's charity would be head and shoulders above this, she thought. Whatever could he be thinking, offering her the prestigious position of spokesperson? He was probably out there right now thinking what a pathetic effort the Auction was. She was a fool if she thought God would put her in charge of something like a national charity. Rhys's charity was way out of her league.

And Rhys himself was way out of her league.

He might still be the nice guy she knew in high school, the one who helped her organize youth outreach programs and once helped her weed Ruby's entire two-acre vegetable garden in July, without gloves, but she had to realize those days were gone.

"Get over it, Anne," she whispered. "He's moved on. He has places to go, people to see. He is much more important than you are."

She swallowed hard. She would never fit into Rhys's world, and she wasn't even sure she wanted to. She would tell Rhys no. She would not make a huge difference in the world the way he did, but so what? Right?

"Next up," her father's voice announced, "the Rhys Carter Surprise!"

Anne couldn't help it. She slipped through the kitchen doors to see who won the blob. And felt a twinge of envy toward whoever it turned out to be.

Rhys had called her *Annie* last night. She was probably reading too much into it, but possibly, just possibly, she should not make any hasty decisions about that job. She didn't want to say no and then be wrong. She ought to at least hear the details, assuming there *were* details. Yes. That was what she would do. She would act professionally and hear the details.

Rhys stood beside his dessert, grinning pleasantly.

Pleasantly. Oh yeah, that was the word she was thinking of. Try *unbelievably gorgeously.* Except that that wouldn't be very professional . . .

Her father went on and on about how famous Rhys was and how nice it was to have him home. Anne bit her lip. Why couldn't her father just get on with it! White-knuckled, she watched as he surveyed the bids on the papers. A look of wonder swept over his face, and Anne winced. What was wrong?

"Ladies and gentlemen!" her father said. "The winning bid for this . . . dessert . . . is the highest in years!" A rumble of astonishment emanated from the crowd. "Someone in this very room has bought this outstanding offering —" Anne heard her father struggle to control his voice — "for forty-three dollars!"

The crowd erupted in applause.

Forty-three dollars! Who in the world would pay forty-three dollars for *that?*

"And the winning bid number is . . ." Her dad drew the moment out agonizingly, and Anne truly thought she would do something drastic. "Bidder number . . . well, isn't this appropriate for Valentine's Day? Bidder . . . number . . . fourteen!"

The crowd erupted once again, but no one stepped forward. The crowd stopped applauding and started buzzing like a hive of confused bees. Rhys looked around, still grinning.

Anne was bewildered. Could the bidder have possibly forgotten her own number? She stepped forward into the crowd and craned her neck around. She was almost certain she had seen that number earlier. . . .

Dread ran up Anne's back, just like the mouse that Avery had once caught and lost in her bedroom.

"No," she gasped, "it can't be!" Digging in her apron pocket, she unearthed the numbered paper that Avery had brought her. She unfolded it and stared at the evidence that she had lost her mind.

Fourteen. *Fourteen!*

The lady standing next to Anne noticed. "Here she is!" the lady screeched. "Here's the winning bid!"

The crowd broke into thunderous applause, sweeping Anne forward on the wave of their enthusiasm and depositing her, dumbfounded, before the Rhys Carter Surprise.

Never had a dessert been more aptly named.

Her father beamed at her, probably proud of the way she stood up for the underdog. Rhys beamed too. Could no one tell she was utterly mortified?

She had somehow paid forty-three dollars for a dessert she couldn't eat.

And beyond that, Ruby Bougainville's legacy was alive and well.

"I don't blame her," Anne heard a woman's voice say. "If I wasn't dating Mark, I'd have paid twice that to get to share dessert with Rhys Carter."

Both her dad and Rhys had heard the comment, too, and she knew they wondered if it was true. *She* wondered if it was true.

Was it possible that her lack of sleep the night before somehow affected her so much that she had bid on a dessert she had no interest in, simply to be able to enjoy Rhys's company? All without knowing it? She didn't know that much about sleepwalking, but . . .

She, like Ruby, should now accept the dessert with great fanfare and go eat. *I can't possibly carry that hulk anywhere, let alone eat any of it!*

And what would she say to Rhys, who, judging from the sly looks of the people around him, was already dealing with insinuations about her motives?

Before Anne could run screaming from the room, Rhys elbowed his way through his tormentors, hefted the Surprise, and nodded at her. A matter-of-fact nod, as if he dealt with insane females every day. Anne followed as he made his way to one of the tables set up for eating in the center of the room. Mind churning, she collapsed in the chair Rhys held for her. All the possible scenarios for how this had happened sounded like plots for a bad movie. Mute, she stared at up at Rhys.

"I think it tastes better than it looks," he said.

"Oh," she said brilliantly.

"You know, I think I was supposed to make it in a trifle dish, but I thought it would look more impressive standing tall on its own. I borrowed a new neighbor's turkey platter." Rhys surveyed his dessert with a critical eye. "I didn't count on the pudding being quite so viscous."

He took a spoon, scooped up some of the goop at the bottom of the chocolaty pile, and heaped it on top. So that was where the "dropped" look came from, Anne noted.

"I guess I should thank you for buying it," Rhys continued. "I think a lot of people took pity on me, but you went above and beyond —"

"No!" Anne yelped. "I didn't take pity on you. I — I didn't bid on it at all."

CHAPTER THREE

Intrigued, Rhys sat down across the table from Anne. After talking to her last night and witnessing her mirth today, he felt they were already good friends again, despite the years that had passed.

He found it appealing that Anne was comfortable enough with him not to hide her thunderstruck expression now. Of course, Anne's emotions had always been easy to read. Not like most of the women he knew in New York. Not one of them would have been willing to show that they were this confused.

"You didn't bid?" he asked.

"I — I don't think so —" He watched as she pulled herself together to form a more coherent sentence. "Maybe I've been more stressed than I thought. Maybe I bid on it and just don't remember. They say lunatics are not aware of their condition themselves."

Rhys wanted to hug her and tell her she

was not as psychotic as she looked. But he decided against the hug. For now.

"You aren't out of your mind," he said and leaned back in the creaky folding chair. "Lack of sleep does not constitute insanity. I'm sure there's a reasonable explanation."

"Really?" She appeared to grasp that small hope like a writer holding on to a particularly clever metaphor.

"Really. Hello, Avery," he said to the new arrival at their table.

"Hello, Mr. Carter. I see my sister bought your dessert." Avery was a study in innocence, but something in his voice must have had an impact on Anne. Her eyes swerved to Avery's face, her overwhelmed expression replaced by a bunching of suddenly suspicious eyebrows.

"Why, yes, it looks as though she did," Rhys said, keeping one eye on Anne. This could get interesting.

"I thought it was the best one, Mr. Carter," Avery said. "I didn't think it was very polite for Mrs. Henderson to call it a whopping big disaster."

Anne, evidently thinking very hard, let this comment pass.

"Well, it's nice of you to say so." Rhys succeeded in repressing his chuckle. "Would you like to have a slice?"

"Oh, only if you want to share, Mr. Carter. I wouldn't want to be a bother."

Rhys saw the exact moment Anne's lightbulb clicked on. With sisterly outrage, she surged out of her chair. "Avery!"

Avery squeaked and edged closer to Rhys, who spared him a commiserating glance.

"I'm sorry, Rhys," Anne said with admirable courtesy and a tight smile, "but I believe there has been an illegal use of my funds!" Her scowl was guaranteed to put a scare into her devious little brother, but Rhys could see the smile lurking behind it.

"Avery," Anne said, "for reasons known only to you, you wanted that dessert from the moment you laid eyes on it. You knew I wouldn't buy it for you. You knew Mom wouldn't buy it for you. But something made you think *you* could buy it for you."

Rhys rolled his eyes. Anne had watched too many reruns of *Murder, She Wrote*.

"You knew I put my bidding number into my apron pocket. When I hugged you, you saw the perfect opportunity. Pilfering the paper, you waited until you knew I would be too busy to keep track of you, and then you used the number for your own ends."

Anne was not that good an actress, but she was sure fooling her young and impressionable brother. She stepped forward, looming over Avery as he pressed even closer to Rhys's chair. Rhys feigned a look of terror to make the ruse more effective.

"You knew that anyone who saw you place a bid would assume I had asked you to help me out," Anne said, shaking a finger under Avery's nose. Avery's eyes widened and crossed. He sucked in a deep breath — the last one he thought he would ever take, judging by the look on his face.

"There was just one problem with your little scheme!" Anne said. "You forgot that I . . . well, you assumed that . . . er, you did not think that . . ."

She was again at a loss, Rhys realized, watching her eyes take on the despairing glaze of a writer on a deadline, but before he could come up with anything suitable to help, Anne's facade dissolved in laughter. Sinking back down into her chair, she dropped her head into her arms resting on the table. Her shoulders shook.

"I give up," she gasped, and waved one hand in a sign of surrender.

Avery shot an iffy look at Rhys. "You think she's mad?" he asked.

Rhys bit back an affirmative answer. Instead he said in a low voice, "No. But I think you did embarrass her, and I think you do need to apologize for using her money without her permission."

"But every other year she lets me buy —"

Rhys held up a hand. "You didn't have her permission this year, did you?"

Avery's face fell. "No. And especially not for that." He indicated the Rhys Carter Surprise. Beside it, Anne hiccuped.

" 'S okay, Avery," she said. "You go on and have a slice of that. Or —" she glanced at the dessert, and two more tears ran down her cheeks. "Better have a scoop. I think a *slice* would be impossible. *Hee hee hee.*"

Rhys looked at Avery and shrugged. Avery looked at his sister, who was wiping her eyes.

"Well, I'm sorry, Anne," he said. "I didn't mean to embarrass you. But . . ." Avery seemed to be struggling with his thoughts. "But wasn't it smart of me to put the bid paper back after I looked at the number? 'Member when I hugged you that second time when you were talking to Mr. Conover? That's when I put it back!"

Anne's smile became drier every second.

"Very clever," she said to Avery and then turned to Rhys. She watched as he attempted to place a portion of the blob onto a plate.

"I'm glad you know the real explanation, Rhys," she said. "I was afraid you would think I bid on your dessert because I wanted your company or something." She rolled her eyes. "I have no wish to look like the famous journalist's groupie!"

Rhys handed the plate to Avery while counting out the seconds till Anne realized what she had said. He got to three.

"Rhys, I didn't mean that! I enjoy your company; I really do. And it's a fabulous dessert; it really is."

"Want some, then?" He was enchanted. Smart as a whip, practical, and as clear as water, Anne was just what his charity needed. No one in New York would fit the part, but Anne did. Who could possibly resist her?

"Oh no, I can't."

What? The least she could do was eat a piece of the creation she had spent forty-three dollars on. Maybe she wasn't as sincere as he'd thought. His disappointment must have shown on his face, because Anne reached across the table and touched his arm.

"It's not what you think, Rhys," she said, and her voice lost any vestige of teasing or laughter. "It's not the dessert. I'm just allergic to chocolate, remember?"

Rhys was diverted. "That's right," he said. "I had forgotten." He looked around at the vast display of desserts in the room, dismayed that out of everything he could have made, he'd brought something she couldn't eat. "Can I get you something else? Something non-chocolate?"

"No, but thank you," Anne said.

"She's not much on desserts," Avery piped up. Chocolate pudding ringed his lips. "Anne, can I go see what Mom bought?"

"Sure, Avery." Her brother dashed off through the crowd. Rhys was left sitting across the table, staring at Anne Singletary as though seeing her for the first time.

He had seen a couple of pictures of her in the church's newsletter over the years. She had always been pretty — blonde hair, blue eyes, freckles. But the pictures didn't catch Anne's vitality, her wide-eyed innocence, or — oh, he couldn't believe he was going to think it — her inner beauty. He hadn't expected those things to make her appealing to him in a purely feminine way. He liked her as a person; he was attracted to her as a woman. Uh-oh. He'd spent the last several years trying to stay out of relationships. It wasn't wise, especially with everything going on in his life, to contemplate one now.

"Well," Anne said, "we're supposed to socialize. So tell me something about yourself that I don't know."

He hated mushrooms?

Fall was his favorite season?

He was terrible at golf?

"I want to take you out to dinner," he said. The words were out too fast for him to choke on them, which he might have done had he known he was going to say them. For once in his life, he'd managed to astound himself.

"But I knew that," Anne said. "You already asked me to lunch to talk about the job. But dinner will probably work better with my schedule."

She didn't understand. The job had nothing to do with anything. He meant *I want to take you out to dinner.*

He had come looking for a spokesperson to run his charity for him, not a girlfriend. The word *girlfriend* usually caused his mind to lunge for his mental delete key, but this time it headed for the thesaurus. *Girlfriend. Sweetheart. Heartthrob. Sugarplum* — okay. That was enough.

"So . . . when do you want to go?" Anne asked. Rhys had the feeling that it wasn't the first time she had asked.

"Go?" His mind was still trying to figure out how a word like *sugarplum* had entered it. "Go where?"

"Out to dinner?" She looked so cute, with

her nose red from hysterics and her hair displaced and one eyebrow raised at his imbecility.

"Friday?" Rhys croaked. *Oh, to have her always look at him thusly . . .*

"Friday is no good," she said. "I have a date."

The lovely music that had begun to play in Rhys's mind — the birdsong, the angels singing — they all came crashing together in one discordant twang.

She already *had* a date?

For perhaps the space of three heartbeats, while the angels plucked feathers from their harps and his mind said *I told you so* and reached smugly for the Delete key, Rhys digested that news.

"Of course you do," he said, recovering as best he could. "But I'm a decent guy. You just spent forty-three dollars on your scheming little brother. I owe you dinner. The thought of a woman who is allergic to chocolate organizing a dessert auction fascinates me, that's all. That's all. I don't want to get in the way."

Apparently his detached demeanor was not convincing.

"Rhys . . . dinner is not a problem," Anne said, eyeing him warily. "It's just that Friday won't work. How about Tuesday? I really do need to know more about the job before I can consider your offer."

His offer. Right. He needed to convince her that she would be the perfect spokesperson for his new charity. *Sugarplum* was very similar to *spokesperson.* He had merely gotten them confused.

"Tuesday," he said bravely, "will be fine."

Rhys took Anne to the most exclusive restaurant he knew of in Kansas City. The *Ristorante Elegante* in Crown Center had only fifteen tables and reservations were nearly impossible to get, but he managed. He and Anne were seated at one of the more centrally located tables — not his first choice, but it would do. Anne, beautiful in a blue silk dress that complimented her pale skin and his gray dinner jacket, was uncomfortable and trying not to show it.

She smiled at him as he held her chair out; then she looked at the tremendous display of cutlery and glasses and candles and napkins on the table, and lifted her chin. Rhys hadn't considered this dinner a test for Anne, but if it had been, she'd already passed. It had taken him a little time, when he'd first hit New York City, to figure out all the protocols, but Anne could learn.

He had caught her unawares when he had

leaned down to kiss her cheek at the Auction, but she had recovered well. Tonight when he picked her up from her town house, she had not hesitated in the slightest to give him her cheek. He wondered if he ought to tell her he didn't normally kiss a lot of cheeks, and certainly not every single time he saw someone . . . hmmmm, no. He decided to keep that to himself.

He had to remember, however, that God had brought Anne to mind because she would be marvelous for the charity. Not for any other reason. Rhys had too many irons in the fire as it was without the addition of a . . . sugarplum. And anyway, that word had not bothered him in the past few days. Mostly because he had scribbled the words *she has a boyfriend* on a yellow sticky note and slapped it on his refrigerator door.

"I saw your interview the other day on the *Great Day in the Morning* show," Anne said as she looked over her menu. "Do you do that kind of thing often?"

"Well . . ." Rhys hesitated.

"Never mind. I know you do. I guess what I need to know exactly is what this position requires of me."

She put her menu down and looked him right in the eye, extremely somber. He could not make the mistake of thinking she was always as unbalanced as she had been at the Auction. A woman who commanded the respect of her whole church like Anne did could not be full of froth and bubbles.

More than one person at the Auction Saturday had called Anne a "sweet little thing" and then gone on to tell him how she had single-handedly remodeled their house or overhauled their car or saved their entire twenty-member family from starvation.

Rhys was discovering that Anne was like an onion, with each layer more potent than the last. Well, that image should keep any thoughts of romance from his brain.

"Anne, before I go into what your duties will entail," Rhys said, "let me tell you why I think you are the right person for this job." He leaned forward, his voice fervent.

"I remember way back in high school, how impressed I was with your commitment to the weak and the poor and the lonely. You had, and still have, a generous, giving spirit. You give unselfishly to whoever needs help. And you seem to do this because you believe it's what God wants, not because it brings you any glory."

"I'm flattered."

"No, it's not flattery. You see a need and you meet it. But what engages my attention is that you seem to have this unique ability to motivate people." Rhys tilted farther over the small table, brushing condiments out of his way.

"Do you remember the time you rounded up the youth group and convinced them to give up an entire Saturday to paint the preacher's house? You said — let me see — you said the house was shabby and you thought it was disgraceful that the pastor had to live like that."

"I had incentive," Anne said. "I was — I am — the pastor's daughter."

"Whatever!" Rhys smacked both hands on the table to emphasize his point. "You, on your own, motivated a bunch of lazy teen-agers to —"

Suddenly the space between him and Anne got a lot brighter. And a lot hotter.

Was it a sign from heaven? Rhys wondered. He had noticed earlier how the blue of Anne's eyes precisely matched one of the colors in his tie but had discounted it. Was God trying harder to get his attention now? Was this luminescence sparking some sort of connection between their two souls perhaps?

"Watch out!" a man yelled.

"Fire!" a lady squealed.

"Water!" someone else cried.

Rhys glanced down. "Aghhhh!" he said. His white linen napkin was on fire. Somehow he must have nudged it into one of the votive candles on the table. A small conflagration between the breadbasket and the saltshaker seemed likely to take over the whole table unless someone did something.

A waiter dashed up to the table and paused, probably trying to figure out how to pour his pitcher of water on the flame without dousing the blue-silk-clad lady sitting there.

But Anne did not hesitate. Reaching out, she grabbed a nonflaming part of the napkin, flipped it over the inferno, and then, to Rhys's astonishment, picked the whole thing up and rolled it quickly into a ball. The fire went out. Anne handed the charred napkin to the speechless waiter.

"That was disposable, right?" she said.

For four seconds — twice the amount of time it had taken Anne to see a need and meet it — there was dead silence at all fifteen tables, then a startled twitter swept across the room, followed by a bit of quiet applause. Anne smiled in acknowledgment before turning her attention back to Rhys. "You were saying?"

"Are you all right?" he asked.

"I'm pretty sure that's not what you were

saying, but, yes, I'm fine."

"Anne . . ." Rhys wanted to laugh. He wanted to cry. God had always blessed him, he thought, but God had outdone himself. "Anne . . ."

"I didn't enjoy it," she said.

"Well, of course you didn't. You could have singed your fingers right off."

"No, I mean I didn't enjoy organizing the youth group to paint our house. If I could have painted it by myself I would have. But convincing everyone to do it? No." She carefully relocated her napkin and leaned forward.

"That's why I'm a little concerned about my ability to do this job. I have no formal training and hardly any experience in fund raising. Even though you've been vague about it, I assume I'd have to attend charity dinners and stuff. I know it's all very high society, and I know I'll stick out like a sore thumb —" Anne laughed a little and held up the fork at the top of her plate. "I am mystified by the forks. I hate oysters. Can't even discuss caviar. And Rhys, I hate to tell you, but my knees knock whenever I have to speak in front of a group."

Rhys cleared his throat. There were, he supposed, a few things they would have to work on. "Well, yes, the job would be fairly high profile and require the kind of thing —" he indicated the fork — "that you mentioned. That's where the money is. That's the dessert fork, by the way."

Anne perused the fork like she was trying to commit it to memory, then set it down.

"But, Annie," Rhys continued, "you can learn those kinds of things. I think you have just the right combination of compassion and honesty to make people part with their money. Didn't this year's AMVDSDCSA make more money than it has in years?"

"That's because I spent forty-three dollars on the Rhys Carter Surprise."

"Whatever. You're good at this, Anne. You will be such a beautiful example of how a Christian ought to be. You're sincere and real, and people are going to know, because we'll tell them, that you have actually been down there in the trenches. They'll see how much good you do, and they'll be writing out checks left and right. And then we can do some real good in the world, Annie. We can make a real difference."

Anne was silent.

"You're intrigued. I can tell."

She smiled hesitantly. "Rhys, I enjoy my life. I do. But . . . I have started wondering . . ."

"What?"

"Well, if I'm being all I can be, I guess. If I should be doing more. Am I exercising all my gifts and talents . . . and . . . and . . ."

"Neurons?"

She laughed. "Neurons, synapses, whatever. You're starting a charity, an organization to help meet people's needs. I know all about people's needs. And I know I'm good at meeting those needs."

Rhys could detect no ugly sense of pride. She knew how to meet people's needs. She was good at it. Simple statements of fact. It was delightfully refreshing to meet someone who took her accomplishments at face value and didn't get all falsely humble.

He almost envied her. She had a right to be proud of herself, being right down there, getting her hands dirty with practical matters. He didn't have the foggiest notion about any of it. That was why he needed Anne.

"And although this job you are offering me seems to be the chance of a lifetime," Anne was saying, "I'm just not sure I'm capable of it."

They were both silent for a few moments.

"I'm certain you are capable," Rhys said, after realizing he had missed part of her speech. "And it would help me out if you could decide tonight that you are going to commit your life to this project."

Anne laughed again, and the sound was free from any cynicism. He was glad she had recognized the tongue-in-cheek nature of his pronouncement.

Rhys chuckled. "I don't mean to sound as if I'm making light of your decision."

"I don't think that." Anne met his eyes across the table. "I like that you can make me laugh, even with all these weighty thoughts running around in my head."

"I hope I can always make you laugh," Rhys said.

Whoa, boy! Where had that come from? He had a policy of never saying anything like that to anyone, teasing or not. He did not want to inadvertently send the wrong message.

Nevertheless, he kept eye contact with Anne, because for some reason he wanted her to know he was not teasing.

To his wonder, Anne didn't look away. She smiled very faintly.

"I'm glad you came home, Rhys," she said. "I missed you."

"So, are you ready to try out the skates?" Rhys asked.

Anne bit her lip. He had asked at church that morning what size shoe she wore and she had told him, and then waited in vain for an explanation. One that hadn't come until he'd showed up at her door with two pairs of in-line skates in one hand and *Emily Post's Etiquette* in the other. "This is to relieve you of fork confusion," he'd said, waving the book at her after kissing her cheek. Anne shook off the feeling that she was a hick from the sticks and accepted it graciously. The skates were another matter.

"I believe the last time I strapped wheels to my feet was back in junior high," she said now.

"So you need the practice. What if you're ever called upon to chaperone the youth group in-line–skating retreat?"

Anne shot him a disbelieving glance.

"I'm trying to give your practical nature an excuse to have some fun, Annie."

"Is this what you do for fun in New York City?"

"No, in New York I use these to outrun the taxis. Of *course* this is what I do for fun. Humor me."

"Last time I humored you, I ended up with a sprained ankle."

"What? When?"

She raised one eyebrow. "The youth group skiing trip to Colorado? The black-diamond slope?"

"Oh, that. That was different. Admit it. You were having fun until you hit that mogul wrong."

Anne rolled her eyes, then scowled at the skates. She'd seen many people in Kansas City using them. She did have a good sense of balance. It would give her another option for exercise. It did look like fun. She sighed. Rhys had always been able to talk her — or anyone else — into anything.

"Did you bring pads?" she asked.

"Elbow pads, knee pads, wrist guards, helmets — everything you need, my sensible sweetheart."

She tried to ignore the endearment, realizing the phrase was simply a neat piece of alliteration, the sort that could be used by countless other very handsome journalists if they happened to be sitting in her house waiting to teach her the art of in-line skating.

It really had nothing to do with her, and she ought to stop thinking about it.

"Well, my manipulative . . . uh, mercenarious . . . monarch . . . er —"

Rhys looked bemused. "How about, 'Well, my marvelous man'?" he suggested.

He looked way too pleased with himself, and Anne laughed. "I'm going to go back to the subject of the skates now, if you don't mind," she said and looked out the window. "Do you think it's too cold for this sort of thing?"

"No, it's lovely almost-March weather. No one else will be out, and you won't run over anyone."

"Such faith in my abilities!"

"Hey, just trying to be practical." Rhys spread his arms in defense.

"So show me how to put these on. I'm going to *practically* amaze you."

She had a blast, but the amazing part was that she and Rhys were still in one piece — or two pieces, she supposed — as they stumbled back into her house two hours later, laughing and exhausted. Herman eyed them from a distance, still upset that he hadn't been allowed to go. Anne hadn't wanted to endanger his life.

"I'd better go wash the gravel out of my hands and get some Band-Aids," she said as she took off her skates. "And a washcloth for your poor nose. Are you sure it isn't broken?"

"Oh, it doesn't hurt much anymore," Rhys said. She brought a wet cloth anyway and knelt beside him on her couch. Taking his chin in her hand, she gently dabbed at the blood welling from a small cut on the bridge of his nose where she had caught him with her skate during one of their more spectacular crashes.

"I'm so sorry," she said. "I really did try to step over you."

"It was my fault for falling in front of you that way."

"I tripped you, Rhys," she reminded him.

"Is that how it happened? I don't remember. I thought you were doing pretty well."

Belatedly realizing the intimacy of what she was doing, Anne managed to keep her hand steady. She shouldn't feel nervous about cleaning up Rhys's face for him. This sort of thing came naturally to her; she did it all the time. She didn't need to notice how handsome Rhys's face was, or how he sat perfectly still under her ministrations, with his eyes focused on her face. It wasn't like she was his girlfriend.

"I, uh, have to do more than 'pretty well' with your charity, you know," she said, pulling a subject from thin air. "I can't figuratively trip someone and then kick him in the nose and expect to be a success."

Rhys frowned at her over the washcloth, obviously wondering how they'd gone from roller blades to charities so fast and probably trying to decipher her strange metaphor.

Anne folded the washcloth and moved

413

back. "I'm sorry," she said. "I guess I've been worrying about it. I seem to be in a kind of fog." That was true enough. She waved her hand in front of her to indicate fogginess. If he only knew!

Rhys flung an arm over the back of her couch. He was not anywhere close to touching her, but Anne could feel his arm as if it were emitting some sort of force field. She concentrated harder on the problem at hand.

"It's just that you — that the charity — is something I have to think and pray about some more."

"You can do it, Anne. You're talented and caring and —"

She stopped him with a smile. "I know. I know you think those things. But Rhys . . . I really do need some details before I decide."

"Like?"

"Like . . . like why you want to start a charity in the first place. I mean, I think it's a great idea, but I guess . . . well, I guess you never seemed the type."

He bounced off the couch and ran a hand through his hair in what looked like frustration.

"Exactly," he said, turning to her. "Anne, when people find out that I am *the* Rhys

Carter, the one who writes all those articles, they're . . . well, they're impressed. Some of them are *really* impressed, like they've met a movie star."

"You *are* pretty famous."

"Yes, but, Annie, what am I *doing,* really? I have a friend in the city who is a doctor. We were at a reception a couple of months ago, and someone asked what she did. She told them; they nodded, then asked what I did. Then they spent the rest of the evening 'basking in my glory' as they called it." Rhys shook his head. "The night before, my friend had performed an emergency tracheotomy and saved a man's life, and these people didn't want to hear about it. They totally ignored her."

Anne was silent.

Rhys knelt at her feet. "I want to do something truly helpful, Anne. I can at least use my popularity to do some practical good. That's where the charity comes in. And I want you — no, I need you — to run it. Because I think you understand where I'm coming from."

She did. It was almost scary how well she understood. She didn't need to be naturally empathetic to feel Rhys's pain; they were two of a kind. They both felt they needed to be doing *more.*

CHAPTER FOUR

"He's in love with you," Avery announced several days later. Anne, invited to supper in her old home and helping by transferring uncooked spaghetti from a bag to her mother's pasta jar, promptly lost control of the process. Spaghetti went everywhere. Her mother came to help pick it up. Anne glared at her brother while snatching pieces of pasta off the floor.

"Who says?"

"Everybody. He always sits beside you in church. He's always talking to you. And you went out on a date. *Two* dates."

"That was *business,* and I'll thank you to mind your own."

"And you look at him all googly-eyed."

"I *do NOT.*"

"Anne," her mother said gently.

Anne breathed out firmly through her nose. "Sorry, Avery." Just what she needed: a lecture from her mother on the tone of her voice. Fortunately, Avery also had to shut up.

"I do not look at Rhys googly-eyed," Anne said calmly a few minutes later to her mother. "I'm going out with Charlie, for pity's sake. And I'm certainly not in love with him."

"With Charlie?" her mother asked.

"Yes, with Char— no, with Rhys. Or Charlie either! We're just going out. We're just friends. We're just . . . just . . ."

Her mother smiled. "Sweetie . . . just make sure your friendship with Rhys doesn't force you into a decision you may regret."

"What do you mean?"

"I mean you may not be able to hear God's voice if . . . well, if you aren't thinking straight. Rhys can be very persuasive. Don't let him talk — or charm — you into this job if it's not what you should be doing."

Anne would have liked to argue, but she couldn't. Her mother's wisdom was sound. Fine. She would keep Rhys's business proposition totally separate from the butterflies the mere mention of his name produced.

She just wished there weren't so many of them.

One thing helped: thinking about Jeff

McGregor. Anne had realized earlier that she was indeed slightly acquainted with Rhys's old boss, having visited his retirement home several times in the past. They had spoken briefly on those occasions, and she believed he would remember Herman. She had called and formally introduced herself, using her connection to Rhys (the thought made her strangely short of breath) as a way to break the ice. Some people had lots of friends and some didn't; it pained her to see elderly people with no visitors. Anne cultivated every relationship she could. When she asked Jeff about Rhys, she learned that although Rhys had been in Kansas City almost two weeks, Jeff had talked to him only once, and that was over the phone.

Rhys was busy, Anne kept telling herself. He had things to do. He still had a column to write. He had to unpack.

But Anne did not like the thought that as Rhys's charity spokesperson, she too might be too busy to visit an old friend.

Rhys saw Anne at the Wednesday evening prayer meeting, both Sunday services, and Wednesday prayer meeting again.

He had an imprecise idea in his mind that he had spent six hours and thirty-seven minutes in her presence since their in-line skating, and it simply wasn't enough. He had no time for a relationship, he told himself again, but this was business. He had to spend time with her if he was ever going to get this charity up and running.

Thursday morning, from his rented loft in downtown Kansas City, Rhys dialed Anne's phone number. To his surprise, she was home. He had called several other times and gotten the machine. She always seemed to be out doing something useful.

"Annie?"

"Yes?"

"It's Rhys. I've decided to write a cookbook." Just that morning, he had decided it.

"You — what?"

"Decided to write a cookbook. I'm going to call it the *Everything But Chocolate Dessert Cookbook,* and it will be the first fund-raising venture for the charity."

She did not immediately answer. Was that a child he heard crying in the background? What was she doing?

"Everything but chocolate?" Anne questioned at last.

"Because you're allergic to it. I'm going to try out all the desserts on you, because if you like them, everyone will like them. And because your input, as spokesperson, will be a hook for sales."

"If I decide to take the job."

"Well, yes."

Two eardrum-shattering shrieks resonated through the phone. He heard Anne sigh.

"Why don't you come over and we'll discuss it?" she asked.

"Ah . . . what are you doing?"

"I'm babysitting." A loud crash and then a wail bore that out.

"Oh, joy," he said.

"Just come over."

He went.

It was a madhouse. Rhys never had the chance to kiss Anne's cheek in greeting. Three small children of undetermined age and gender were flying through Anne's town house, trailed closely by a large black dog. The noise level prevented any conversation. Anne gave him a tight smile and pitched several articles of small clothing at him. Pressed into service, Rhys managed to subdue one of the kids long enough to stuff him into a coat, hat, and mittens. Anne took over at that point and herded the kids and the dog, like chickens, to the nearby park and playground, where she turned them loose.

She then sank back against a swing-set pole and rolled her shoulders beneath her red fleece jacket.

"I presume you have the little hellions here to teach them manners?" Rhys said pointedly.

"I have them here —" Anne's voice was frosty — "because their father is often out of town on business and their mother is quietly going crazy with them around all day."

It could have been the cold. The early March day was overcast, and it looked like it might snow later. But Rhys didn't think Anne had even had time to notice that. "I just insulted you, didn't I?" he said.

She turned, her expression contrite. "I'm sorry. I am probably going quietly crazy, too. But I have no ulterior motives for these kids. I'm doing a favor for a friend, simple as that."

"I apologize. I'm not used to small children."

Her black Lab ran up, tongue lolling. Rhys reached down to ruffle the dog's ears.

"What's his name again? Haggis?"

Anne laughed, her breath white in the air. "Herman. He is used to children and is having the time of his life."

Haggis — no, Herman — took off again to join the action on the playground.

"So tell me about this cookbook," Anne

said. Rhys covertly wiped his slimy hands on his jeans and leaned back against the other swing-set pole.

"Well, you know how well my first book is doing?"

"You mean *Quirky But Not Clueless*?"

"You've read it?"

"The church has it in the library. It's perpetually checked out, so no, I haven't."

"Well, it's just a compilation of some of my columns, so if you've been following those, you haven't missed much. Anyway, my publisher wants me to do another one."

His cell phone rang, and he excused himself to answer it, walking a few steps away. It was his agent. After checking to make sure it was nothing that couldn't wait, Rhys asked him to call back later.

"Rhys, a compilation of columns is a whole lot different than a cookbook," Anne said when he returned to the swing-set pole.

"Yes, but I haven't done anything really crazy lately."

"Unless you count moving from New York and making that flop of a dessert." She took her eyes off the screaming children long enough for him to see that she was only fooling with him.

"It's as good of an attention-getter as anything," he said of the new cookbook, when he had corralled his thoughts that had scattered like chickens at the sight of her teasing smile. "And if I have people's attention, I can focus that attention on the things that really matter."

"Well, you're good at it," Anne said. "Everybody thought you were weird for wearing that tornado costume to the Academy Awards last year, but the subsequent article you wrote on the devastation of tornadoes brought tears to my eyes."

"Annie, everything brings tears to your eyes." Hey, he could tease too.

"Whatever —"

Rhys's cell phone rang again, and again he stepped away to answer it. He kept an eye on Anne as he talked. She folded her arms against the cold and began excavating a trench in the playground sand with her booted foot. She kept her head down.

"Sorry about that," Rhys said when he was through. "I'd turn it off, but my leaving the city so quickly threw quite a few people into fits. Not that I don't get a lot of calls anyway. Where were we?"

Anne regarded him with a serene face. "The cookbook."

"Right, the cookbook. What do you think?"

"I have to admit that writing a cookbook

would be true to your strange form. Especially given that you can't cook."

"So you think it's a good idea?" He chose to ignore her last comment.

She was silent for a few moments. "Rhys, do you really think you are going to have time to do all this? What about Jeff McGregor's retreats?"

He shrugged. "Don't worry about it," he said. "The farm isn't going anywhere."

"Yes, but if Jeff is counting on you to resume —"

"Jeff's not going anywhere either," Rhys said. "What do you think about the cookbook?"

Anne looked like she wanted to argue with him but decided to smile instead. "I'll be your guinea pig on one condition," she said. "I may be taking my life into my own hands, judging by your last cooking effort, so I think there needs to be something in it for me."

Any more of her teasing and he was going to melt, no matter how cold it was. "And that would be?"

"I would like you to write a column — no, two or three, at least — about people who've been helped, not by money but by the giving of someone's time." She filled her sand trench back in, looking back and forth between it and the kids and dog.

"That's it?" He would have done a whole lot more. Climbed mountains. Swum rivers. He would have even done something really difficult, like washing dishes.

"I just think there are some problems you can't throw money at," Anne said. "I think people need to realize that. Maybe you don't see your writing as being very helpful, but I think you're selling yourself short. People listen to you." She glanced up from her filled-in trench to see what he thought.

"That's nice of you to say. And I'll write the articles. But I have a condition, too."

"What?"

"You have to let me hang out with you to do research. I know you have all these people you take care of, and I want to use that as a basis for the articles."

Please, please, please, please, please! He did not have time for a serious relationship; that was indisputable. And she had a boyfriend; he'd learned that her Fridays were filled for the next month. But he had admitted to himself the obvious: he was . . . strongly attracted to Anne Singletary. She was pretty, she was smart, she had talents he did not have. Rhys hated to use the word *crush,* but he thought that was the best definition of his feelings at this point. He was sure he had taken leave of his senses, searching as he was for any excuse to be around her. However, enough of his sense remained that he doubted he would fall down at her feet and beg her to reconsider if she said no. He would simply go home and pout like a man.

"All right," she said and began on another trench.

His sensible side did not allow him to screech "Yippee!" at the top of his lungs. "I must be making some kind of an impression on you," he said instead. "Writing a column on helping people with time not money while developing a cookbook to raise money is an idea I should have come up with. We work well together."

Anne's face turned grim. "If I take this job, I won't be home very much, will I?"

Rhys was too caught up in the idea of their working well together to think about the question much. He wondered if it would be too blatant to dig a trench of his own and have it meet hers in the middle.

"If it goes well, you'll be traveling quite a bit, I think," he said. "I know it sounds like I get out a lot, but most of the time I stay holed up in my office, writing, and don't do much traveling. But you'll be able to see a lot of the country. I know lots of —"

"I'd better get the kids back in," Anne interrupted, yanking her back off the swing-set pole. "It's getting pretty cold."

Rhys helped her round up the children, who were slightly less energetic after their play.

He wasn't usually dense, but it took him several minutes before he realized why Anne looked so pensive. Anne, as the spokesperson for his charity, would be on the road a good bit of the time. He hadn't thought to ask if she would mind.

Being . . . strongly attracted . . . to a beautiful, smart, funny woman was thrilling, but Rhys was not a total nitwit. Anne had feelings, hopes, dreams, fears. He had better stop being silly and start paying attention to the woman herself while he lived out every clichéd and hackneyed phrase ever applied to this type of infatuation.

Anne stared down at her blue silk dress, pressed into service for the second time in slightly over a month. Unless she wanted to wear one of her standard Sunday dresses to go to dinner with Charlie tonight, this would have to do. Charlie had just received a promotion; it was a special occasion.

What would Rhys think when he realized she had exactly one special-occasion dress?

And why did she care what he thought? She shook her head. If she agreed to be his spokesperson, she would buy more, but for now, the blue silk was serviceable and there was nothing more to be said.

It was the same with her car. The first time Rhys had seen it, he'd pointed with a shaking finger and an incredulous look. "You drive *that?*" he'd asked. Anne had shrugged. Her Escort ran; what else was needed?

She was beginning to realize, however, that her assessment of Rhys's being out of her league was more true than she had first anticipated. Rhys's sports car, his cell phone, his expensive suits, his lifestyle in the fast lane, the fact that he had probably not set foot in a Wal-Mart for years — it all added up to one thing. Rhys was high society. She was not.

She'd spent some time using the Internet to find out all sorts of interesting information about her possible future business partner. One of the things she found out was that although Rhys didn't seem to have a steady girlfriend, the women he was sometimes seen with were, without fail, society's finest: rich, intelligent, educated, and beautifully dressed.

Anne had a utilitarian hairdo and a secret horror of high heels. She sighed. She was wearing high heels tonight. For Charlie? She doubted it.

Rhys — and Charlie — would be here soon. Rhys had picked the worst day possible to attempt the first dessert for his cookbook. Hadn't she told him her Fridays were booked solid? But no, that was the only day he'd thought he could manage to cook anything, and of course, she had to taste the concoction while it was fresh. It wouldn't take long, he'd said. It wouldn't interrupt her date. Much.

The doorbell rang.

Two men stood on her doorstep, one holding flowers and looking a bit disgruntled, the other holding a foil-wrapped plate and looking not at all jealous.

Look at his choices! Anne growled at herself. *An important, sophisticated, professional man like Rhys does not need to be attracted to you!*

Rhys Carter was concerned with her taste buds and her spokesperson abilities (if she actually had any) and that was it. Right? Right. That was why he whistled at the sight of her. Charlie raised an eyebrow but said nothing.

Smiling nervously, Anne invited both men in. The plate Rhys was holding was nearly as large as the one that had held the Rhys

Carter Surprise. She noticed just in time that Rhys was leaning down for the obligatory cheek kissing and hoped she looked more composed than she felt. Wasn't it her date who should be doing that? What must Charlie think? She threw a smile in his direction and had the feeling it bounced off. Poor man.

"So, what have we got here?" she asked, indicating the plate Rhys was holding. She sounded, to her ears, chirpy and inane. She couldn't seem to make her eyes focus.

Then Rhys uncovered his dessert. It was hard not to focus on what looked like approximately ten dozen very large cookies.

"Here you go," he said. "Rhys Carter's special cookies."

Cookies. Despite the dizzying numbers and immense proportions, cookies still seemed pretty safe. Anne snagged one and inspected it. Flat and brown, the cookie was unimpressive except for its size. Small dark lumps were buried in the dough. Some kind of dates, maybe? She hesitated before biting into it.

The cookie, barely sweet with a spongy texture, tasted awful. Anne could not stop herself from making a face. "Rhys, did you taste this?" she sputtered.

"Well, no . . . I guess I wanted you to be

the first. Pretty bad?"

"Did you skip an ingredient by accident?" Anne choked down the bite she had taken and went to the refrigerator for milk. Charlie examined one of the cookies himself, sniffing in suspicion.

"I cut the sugar by two-thirds," Rhys said. "And skipped the butter altogether. And I put in only one egg. I was trying to make it more healthy."

Anne picked up the offensive cookie and broke it — or rather pulled it — in half. "And these dark little lumps would be . . . ?"

Rhys dipped his head. "Prunes," he said. "In place of chocolate chips."

Anne put the cookie down and turned to him. High society she might not be, but she knew what tasted good. And bad. She placed one of her hands on each side of his face to soften her words. It was a technique she often used with Avery and sometimes with her elderly friends at the nursing home.

"Rhys," she said, her face as stern as she could make it, "if you want to be healthy, there's always in-line skating, which would probably make for a less painful death than eating those cookies. They are unpalatable. You cannot change the recipe that much. It doesn't —"

His grin grew and grew until she was lost. His eyes sparkled, locked onto hers while she tried to figure out what she had been saying. Charlie cleared his throat sharply. Anne jumped and pulled her hands away from Rhys's face.

In a subtle yet pointed message, Charlie held out her coat. She took it and covered her embarrassment by pulling it on. Charlie helped, silently.

When she felt more in control, she turned around — and caught Rhys glancing from the platter of cookies to a drooling Herman.

"Definitely no cookies for the dog," she warned. Her voice came out more sharply than she intended.

"Perhaps you could send them over to the nursing home," Charlie suggested mildly. "They like prunes over there, don't they?"

Anne bit her tongue. "I think the ducks down by one of the ponds would enjoy the, er, cookies," she said at length. "Now we must be going." Charlie already stood by the door, his hand on the doorknob.

Rhys caught her arm as she passed him. "Sorry," he said, for her ears only. He looked sheepish. Anne gave him a small smile.

"For trying to feed the cookies to my dog? I forgive you."

Rhys's eyes flicked to Charlie, then back to her. "No, I mean I'm sorry for smiling at you like that in front of your boyfriend."

Her grin slipped. "Oh . . . er . . . ummm . . . that's okay." She stared at him.

"Go," he said and gave her a push.

She went.

She thought she had imagined that he had smiled at her in a particular way, but apparently he actually had. She could not get the thought out of her head.

Maybe it was the high heels. Maybe they made her look more uptown.

Of course by the end of the night, her feet were killing her.

Anne's car was worse than he had thought. Rhys was ensconced in the passenger seat, his knuckles white on the door handle. Anne had told him to let her know when he'd like to join her on her visits to do research for his column. He'd had to work up some courage, but it hadn't taken too long because . . . well, because he'd get to spend time with Anne.

But he hadn't counted on this. Anne's rattletrap vehicle should have been condemned. He could see pavement through a five-inch hole in the floorboard at his feet. She had to pump the brake pedal whenever she tried to stop. The door handle he was clenching was loose and might pull free at any moment. The hairs on the back of his neck, which he was sure were very shortly going to turn gray, stood straight up.

This was probably punishment for grinning at her the other night. But hey, ol' Charlie needed to know there was competition out there.

Rhys felt smug, knowing he was competition. Anne had to realize he'd been flirting with her. And he never flirted. He charmed, perhaps. He did not flirt.

Anne shifted gears in the ancient model Escort — which produced a horrifying clunk — checked the mirrors, and changed lanes.

He would have braved anything to see her, but this was terrifying. "Should have taken mine," he said for the fiftieth time.

"If your car was typical and had a backseat . . ."

"What? Haggis would have fit in the trunk; I know he would have."

"Herman. And he would not have fit in that tiny excuse for a trunk. Not that I would have put him in *any* trunk," she added.

In response to his name, Herman's head appeared between the seats, liberally dousing the shoulder of Rhys's suit coat with drool.

"Herman, get back!" Anne grabbed a tissue from the console and dabbed at the puddle. They were stopped at a red light, but Rhys took the sopping tissue from her to prevent any heroics. This car needed all her attention. He pointed to the steering wheel.

"Drive. Please. Where are we going first again?"

"To the nursing home."

Could he tell her he dreaded it? No. But a nursing home? It scared him, honestly. He was terribly uncomfortable with the whole idea. The sights, the sounds, the smells — these were the trenches. This was where angels feared to tread. His fear had even prevented him from going to see Jeff McGregor, even though Jeff was in a fairly ritzy assisted-living community, not technically a nursing home. Rhys sighed. He would be brave. He would be stoic. He would be —

Surprised.

"It doesn't smell," he whispered to Anne. He walked beside her down the hall, looking about at the amateur yet colorful paintings on the walls, the sturdy furniture, the drab but clean linoleum floor. They passed a couple of nursing assistants who gave Anne friendly greetings. "All the ones I've been in have been ugly and smell of bleach and — and —"

"When was the last time you were in a nursing home, Rhys?"

He had to stop and think. "Can't remember. A long time ago, I guess."

"Some, like this one, have come a long way. Some are still pretty bad, especially in the poorer parts of town." She paused and looked over at him. "I go to those, too."

Rhys swallowed. He felt like a whimpering snob. "Today?" he asked.

Anne looked at him carefully. "No," she said. "Not today."

They checked in at the nurses' station, then wandered down the halls, Haggis heeling properly on his leash. They stopped often to let the residents pet the dog.

"There's one man down this hall whom we must go see," Anne told Rhys. "He never came out of his room until I started bringing Herman by to see him. Now he keeps dog biscuits for our visits, and he'll be out for the rest of the day."

Somewhere along the way, a small, stooped old lady with thin white hair attached herself to Rhys's arm. She spoke to him in an unintelligible, childlike voice.

Rhys looked to Anne for help.

"That's Martha," Anne said. "Just smile at her and nod. That's about all you can do."

Rhys forced a smile and nodded. He even ventured so far as to pat Martha's arm where it lay on his sleeve. He jumped when she started singing nonsense at the top of her lungs. Anne turned, smiled at the woman, and placed a finger against her lips. Martha reduced her volume, and Rhys managed to control his urge to run for the nearest exit. He had thought running the gauntlet of eligible females in New York was bad. He had thought Anne's car was scary! The thought relaxed him. A little. He'd had training in other frightening situations. He could do this.

"Do you do this often?" he asked Anne between Martha's verses as they continued their trek down the halls.

"We try to get here about once a week," she replied. "Some of these people don't get any visitors at all."

A nursing assistant came then to pry Martha gently off his arm, and Rhys knew his relief showed on his face. He was ashamed, but Anne's eyes softened.

"It's not for everybody," she said, and he wondered if she'd perceived his thoughts.

"It's hard to handle sometimes, even for me."

She stopped to talk to an afghan-covered lady on a sofa, who seemed more lucid than many of the others. Rhys sat down in a chair and held the end of Haggis' leash while some of the other residents spoiled the dog rotten with attention and dog biscuits. Grateful for Herman's presence and free of any duties for the minute, he tuned in to Anne's conversation with Mrs. Thorogood. They were talking about venetian blinds.

They talked about venetian blinds for nearly twenty minutes. Rhys slowly came to understand that Mrs. Thorogood was not quite as all there as he had thought.

But Anne amazed him — thrilled him, dazzled him — with her tenderness. She actually looked like she cared whether the pull strings were on the left or the right. He saw it happen in conversation after conversation. Anne had the ability to talk to absolutely anyone and, without being patronizing, make each person feel understood and cared for.

Rhys watched in awed silence as she helped one of the residents with lunch, wiping the man's chin so deftly after each attempted bite that she lent a sense of dignity to what was at best an untidy proceeding.

"You are so good at this," he said.

For all of his genuine accomplishments, he felt like a wimp. He had never met a woman who impressed him like Anne did. His attraction to her aside, Anne was definitely *the one* for his charity.

On the way out, she turned to him and asked, "Would you like me to go with you to see Jeff McGregor?"

There was no condemnation in her voice, just sweet understanding.

Ah, yes. Anne was a wonderful woman.

CHAPTER FIVE

Herman had a shower every Monday. No one liked a dirty dog, and hospitals in particular didn't like them. Herman was welcome, but only if well groomed. Anne put on her oldest clothes, clipped her hair back, gathered all the paraphernalia, and began. Herman actually enjoyed being bathed and stood quietly while Anne lathered him. This, of course, gave her mind permission to drift. It drifted in pretty much one direction nowadays. Rhys Carter.

He had shown up for the nursing home visit dressed in a black Armani suit — or maybe it was Ralph Lauren — and the nursing assistants had been beside themselves. The man was unbelievably gorgeous in a suit. Anne had conflicting feelings; she felt a little like she was squiring royalty around. But in the nursing home, she felt comfortable. She was on her own turf, and Rhys had been the fish out of water. The word *snob* had even appeared in her mind before she could stop it.

"Herman, stay."

But then she had realized Rhys was scared spitless. Laughing at his fear never occurred to her. He was human, he was uncomfortable, and Anne sympathized. Her perceptions of class differences between them blurred a little.

Herman worked himself closer to the front of the shower stall, and Anne had trouble keeping the spray inside. She got covered with wet dog hair as she maneuvered the dog back into the proper position.

"Herman! Stay!" she said. "Stop wiggling!"

She had noticed that while Rhys sat waiting for her to finish her conversation with Mrs. Thorogood, his foot — which had been bouncing up and down with contained energy — ceased to move. He had smiled at her every time she turned around, and the expression she saw in his eyes made her giddy.

The thought of Charlie, however, sobered her. She had tried to convince him that Rhys did not mean anything untoward by showing up for another date, with another dessert (strawberries in sour cream and balsamic vinegar; again, inedible) but Charlie wasn't persuaded.

Anne wasn't persuaded either. She wasn't blind. She could tell Rhys was attracted to her. She was, quite honestly, attracted to him, too. Two days ago Rhys had brought a huge carrot cake to her house. She had eaten a small piece, suggested he grate the carrots next time instead of simply slicing them, and then they'd gone riding. Horses. Something else she had never done that he had talked her into — very easily, she admitted. Rhys was obviously at home on horseback, and she thought she could get used to it. They'd hacked around in the woods, talking and laughing. And now she felt — dare she say it? — connected.

But her mother's warning still rang in her ears. Contemplating a relationship with Rhys Carter would make it very difficult to think clearly about what God wanted.

"Herman, stay," she said, shoving the dog back again. "What is the problem this morning?"

Besides, she felt Rhys was moving too fast, not thinking enough — or was that her, doing the opposite? After all, Rhys was undeniably successful in everything else he did. Just because she felt that trying to start a charity without a real plan was absurd — Anne looked down at Herman and smirked.

"We don't know where this train is headed," she told him, "but let's go!"

Herman perked his ears up and took two steps. Anne pushed him back.

"Oh no, I said the wrong word, didn't I?" *Let's go.* Everyone was eager but her. "Not right now, fella," she said. "You're still all soapy. Behave."

Their visit to Jeff McGregor, however, had gone very well. Jeff's stroke had left him physically weak but mentally unimpaired. Once Rhys got past the initial awkwardness of seeing his old boss in a wheelchair, he and Jeff had a fine time reminiscing. Jeff thanked him profusely for buying the farm, and Rhys asked many questions about it. Anne listened to their conversation with marked interest, learning about Rhys and enjoying every minute. As they left, Jeff urged them to visit again soon.

"This place is nice," he had said, looking around him. "But it's not home."

Anne had every intention of —

The doorbell rang.

Eighty pounds of soapy, wet dog lunged past her. Anne tried to stop him and got smacked in the face with a bubbly tail. Herman skidded out of the bathroom and charged down the hall. Grabbing a towel, Anne went after him.

The doorbell rang again. Herman stood in front of the door, dripping water, dancing in his eagerness to get out. Anne tossed the towel over him, but he chose that moment to shake, casting off the towel and flinging droplets of soapy water at Anne from a distance. She shrieked.

There was no way she was opening that door.

"Annie?" Rhys's voice questioned. "What's happening in there?"

Just what she needed. Anne was fairly certain high-society, prospective charity spokespersons did not appear in front of their possible future bosses looking like — well, like this.

"Annie?"

She sighed and pulled open the door. Herman dashed out, making a beeline for the small patch of grass that was her front lawn. He flopped down and rolled, rubbing his head into the grass.

Rhys contemplated Anne silently.

"Don't ask," Anne said. "His baths don't normally go this badly."

"I see. I brought something for you to try."

"Come in then. Herman! Get in here!" The dog, grassy but bubble-free, loped happily up to the door and shook again.

"I'm wearing jeans," Rhys said. "Don't

worry about it."

Anne stopped grinding her teeth long enough to say, "Thank you. I'll get changed and then we can have dessert."

She felt she did a superb job of sounding confident about Rhys's latest culinary attempt, given the fact that it looked like a cheesecake and she knew from experience that cheesecakes could be tricky.

She changed quickly, then sat down at her table, where Rhys had already cut the cake. She had one bite and ran for the coffee-maker.

"Very rich," she said, her throat constricting. "But not bad."

Rhys cut a small sliver from his slice and tried it. "I believe I somehow became confused about the ingredients when I tripled the recipe. I think I may have quadrupled the sugar."

"You tripled the recipe?" Anne stared at him. "Rhys, you aren't trying to feed an army here."

He shrugged. "It's just so much work to cook one thing; I figure for not much more work you get three times the profit."

Anne silently went back to spooning coffee into the filter. She added a tablespoon more grounds than usual.

"At least it's better than the last one,"

Rhys offered. "The recipe said cheesecakes freeze well, so that's where the other two cakes are."

"Yes. Yes, they do freeze well. Perhaps next time we could reach a compromise on the sugar, however." Anne sat down at the table to wait for the coffee.

Herman nudged Rhys's arm to be petted. Rhys sniffed. "Is that lavender I smell?"

"What? Oh. It's the shampoo. It's new."

"You used lavender shampoo on *Herman?* Annie, this is a male dog. Males don't wear lavender. No wonder he made a break for it."

She saw his point.

Speaking of points . . . "Rhys, about those pesky details for the charity . . ."

He sighed. "Okay, here's the deal," he said, clasping his hands loosely between his knees. "I was sorta counting on you to figure out the details."

She was stunned and realized she seemed to be using that word a lot when it came to Rhys Carter. However, his revelation made things much more clear. She had been wondering why people would want to come and hear her say anything.

"Rhys, I don't think we've been singing from the same piece of music here," she said. "My part in this is not really the spokesperson position at all. That's *your* job. You'll give the speeches and go to the dinners, and I'll be more behind the scenes, hammering out the details of running the whole shebang."

"Well, yes," Rhys said. "That's what I've been thinking."

It hadn't been what she was thinking. But it relieved her immensely. And better yet, she thought she could probably actually handle —

"I guess I should have said 'director,' " Rhys continued. "But you'll still have to attend banquets, maybe make a speech here and there. People need to see you, need to be able to talk to you because you'll be the one who knows what's going on. I'll hook 'em, and you'll reel 'em in."

Ick. That meant she needed to learn fork etiquette after all. She'd read the Emily Post book from cover to cover, realizing she could probably go through the motions, but despairing that she could ever be truly "in" with the "in" crowd, no matter how many special-occasion dresses she owned. She wasn't even sure she wanted to be.

Besides, being the director of a charity might be more suited to her talents, but it was still a major decision. Was it worth giving up her whole life in Kansas City?

Because that's pretty much what it would come down to.

On the other hand, she was flattered because a director's job was important — and Rhys obviously thought she could handle it, even with all her shortcomings.

And he needed her to handle it. He *needed* her for this important endeavor.

"I . . . need more time to decide whether I'm going to do this," she said, stopping herself from making a snap decision. "I need to know exactly what you are going to take care of, and I think your first step is figuring out whom you are going to focus on. You need a cause. Do you have something in mind?"

Rhys glanced at Herman. "Saving dogs from baths in lavender shampoo?" He grinned at her look. "No, I didn't think so. I guess what I had in mind was sort of a Red Cross kind of deal, or Feed the Children, or Bible distribution or something. I know I want it to be specifically Christian."

Three ideas, all on tangents to one another. Anne reminded herself that Rhys was the sort of person who figured out how to rig a parachute on the way down.

He really *did* need her.

"Pray about a specific focus, Rhys, and I'll do the same. In the meantime, do you think you can get down on paper the division of duties, more or less, so that we don't have too much more confusion?"

"Ah, ever the practical woman," he said in a voice she didn't quite know how to respond to. "Your wish is my command."

"Really?" She grinned.

He ended up giving Herman another bath for her, with some baby shampoo she dug out from somewhere. And then he asked her out to dinner.

Coward that she was, she asked if Avery could come along.

And then she called Charlie and told him they needed to talk.

She and Avery met Rhys in the courtyard of the Cheesecake Factory, a restaurant in Kansas City's Country Club Plaza. The Plaza, fashioned after a Spanish open-air marketplace and well known for its fountains, horse-drawn carriages, and upscale shops, always made Anne think of romance . . . something she was really trying very hard *not* to think about, especially tonight. Avery was on his best behavior. Anne thought he was still recovering from their mother's lecture concerning the Rhys Carter Surprise.

The Rhys Carter Surprise. For Anne, the

phrase no longer brought to mind the giant dessert. No, now it was something much more dangerous. Even with her mother's warning ringing in her ears — repeated just last night — Anne had a very difficult time remembering that there was more at stake than her attraction to Rhys.

But maybe she was not giving herself enough credit. Yes, she was pleased that he was kind to the waitress in the restaurant, helpful to an elderly lady having trouble with her coat, patient with Avery, and attentive to her — but these were all things anyone would like in a boss, too, right? She could call this a business date.

That did not explain why she had felt it necessary to talk to Charlie. He took the news well. He said he had seen it coming. They were not dating exclusively, so the relationship had never been that serious. Although, Anne thought with a twinge of conscience, it might have gotten serious if Rhys hadn't shown up.

She had not informed Rhys of this development. She didn't want Rhys to think she was pursuing him, because she wasn't. She simply thought she owed Charlie the truth.

After supper, outside the restaurant, Rhys offered her his arm, and she took it as they meandered down Wyandotte toward the

Riverwalk. He asked if she would like to take a carriage ride, and she said she would prefer to walk. A ride in one of those glittering Cinderella carriages would be way too romantic — even with her little brother along. Rhys kept Avery supplied with pennies to toss into the fountains and began humming an old, romantic melody under his breath.

Anne's heart thumped hard against her chest before she realized that Rhys was only joining in with a song that had filtered out from one of the restaurants they passed as they headed back toward 47th Street.

She was obviously going to have to keep a firmer grip on her mind to stop it from jumping headlong to ludicrous conclusions.

Especially when Rhys looked down at her as he was doing now, his dark hair and handsome face so close to her own.

Especially when he reached to cover her hand with his, their fingers almost entwining.

Especially when the lights from the stores and the darkness of the night and the sound of the other people on the sidewalk all seemed to fade when Rhys looked down at her and said —

"Here's the toy store. Let's buy something really cool!"

Oh yes. A much firmer grip on her mind.

They bought Avery a super gigantic 3-D puzzle of the *Titanic* at FAO Schwarz and then walked to Rhys's loft apartment. Anne managed to be amused at herself for her earlier behavior. Acting lovestruck was a new experience for her, one not entirely repellent but certainly unusual.

Rhys might be able to conduct his life solely on the basis of whims and the grace of God, but she was more systematic. She would fall in love only after much deep thought and earnest prayer.

"Well, this is it," Rhys said, opening the door to his home.

He still hadn't unpacked, Anne saw. The brick walls of the one huge room were lined with stacks of boxes. In the kitchen area she could see several expensive pots and pans, giant-size sacks of flour and sugar, overflowing chrome trash cans, and a stack of recipe books, which gave her hope for his next attempt at a dessert. Near one curtainless window stood a contemporary wooden desk with a notebook computer on top and a printer on the floor beside it. Dry-cleaning bags obscured the brown leather sofa, over which hung a large, framed photograph of the Eiffel Tower, with someone's (probably famous, but she didn't know) signature on it. Behind one stack of boxes she could just see the brushed pewter footboard of Rhys's bed.

The whole place had a privileged, uptown, yet stark feel to it. She never had anything dry cleaned. Well, okay. One thing. Her silk dress. She didn't know anyone who owned leather furniture or chrome trash cans. She had never lived anywhere but on the outskirts of Kansas City. She had the feeling that if she looked in his refrigerator she would find strange lettuces, bottled water, and cheeses with unpronounceable names.

The dichotomy between the man she thought she was getting to know and the man who lived here struck her like a blow.

"Annie, are you all right?" Rhys peered at her uncertainly.

She looked up into his concerned face. "Do you have any caviar?" she croaked.

"No . . . hey, but I can order out for some, if you like —"

"No! No. I just . . . wondered. I'm fine! Fine." Order out for caviar! She didn't even know that was possible! Maybe Emily Post had a book on that . . .

"Okay, good," Rhys said. "I thought you were going to faint there for a minute, but it must have been a Fig Newton of my imagination. Here, put these on." He waved a pair of thick wool socks at her. "You gotta try this."

She took them without thinking and then asked, "Try what?"

"This!" Avery cried from across the room. "Watch, Anne!"

They spent the next hour running and sliding the length of the polished hardwood floor in Rhys's loft. The practical side of Anne assumed she was participating in such a ridiculous pastime for Avery's sake, but deep down, the other side knew she was doing it to see Rhys flash that delectable grin, to hear his laughter, and to forget about the caviar.

She liked having good, old-fashioned fun with him.

And they never said a word about the charity.

A couple of weeks later, Anne opened the door to find Rhys, bearing dessert, of course, on her doorstep. She had not expected him tonight. They had, after all, been together the day before. And the day before that. And . . . well . . . that had all been business. Rhys had gone with her and Herman to the pediatric wards of two hospitals and several nursing homes — including the not-so-good ones — to do research for his articles. Everywhere they went, Rhys praised her accomplishments, her compassion, her abilities — building up her confidence about being the director of his charity, which she was still unsure about. It was just business.

She lifted her cheek for Rhys's kiss, not quite able to meet his eyes.

"Aren't you going to introduce me, Anne?" the man behind her asked.

Rhys's gaze swerved to take in the other man, then moved back to Anne.

Anne made the introductions, feeling awkward. Alan McDaniel was an old friend, who was home on leave from the army. They were going to see a movie.

She did not know whether to explain the situation to Rhys or not. He knew she had broken up with Charlie, but she did not feel she and Rhys were dating each other exclusively — she wasn't even sure that they were dating at all. She didn't know if she had an obligation to account for Alan's presence, or if that was presuming too much about her relationship with Rhys.

Well, she couldn't just stand there wondering about it. She invited Rhys in and got out bowls and spoons to try his latest effort — rice pudding.

"Not bad," she told him after trying it.

No one had said much else till then, and the tension was distracting.

"But what is this unusual taste?" Alan asked, voicing the question that Anne had decided not to ask. "It's not the traditional cinnamon, is it?"

"That would be cardamom," Rhys said, his eyes challenging. "I heard once that some historians think manna may have been flavored a bit like cardamom, so I decided to give it a try."

"It's certainly different," Alan said and continued to eat. Anne put down her spoon and opened her mouth to inform Rhys of just how preposterous she thought those historians were — didn't the Bible say manna tasted like honey cakes? — but when her eyes met his, she realized his thoughts were on a completely different subject.

After a few seconds, she ducked her head away and discovered that subject — Alan — watching them with blunt curiosity.

"Alan," Rhys said, "what exactly do you do in the army?" His voice was cordial.

Alan transferred his attention to Rhys, and Anne sprang up from her seat to find a place in her refrigerator for the three quarts of leftover cardamom-flavored rice pudding.

That accomplished, she sat back down at the table with the guys. Rhys had just discovered a burning desire to write a column on some aspect of the military, and Alan was enthusiastically expounding on possible subjects. Anne half listened to their conversation while she held Herman's head on her lap — she was wearing jeans — and murmured to him softly while she ruffled his ears.

"Hey, Rhys, why don't you come to the movie with us?" Alan's voice penetrated Anne's state of suspended anxiety, and she jerked her head up. "You don't mind, do you, Anne?"

Very briefly, Anne met Rhys's gaze. "No," she said. "No, of course not."

"Good. It's not like this is a real *date* or anything."

He couldn't have made it more clear that he'd intercepted the vibes zinging around her kitchen.

She could have kissed him then, but she wanted to smack him later. He sat between her and Rhys at the theater and grinned while she fumed at his prank.

Later, as he walked out her door with a quart of rice pudding in a container, he winked. "You kids be good," he said.

Anne waved and then turned to Rhys. "I should take Herman for a walk," she said. "Would you like to go along?"

As they walked, they talked. About Kansas City. About New York. About God and parents and trees and church and dogs and politics and highway construction and kids and doughnuts. Five minutes into their walk, Rhys caught her hand and held it.

Anne decided that Herman had been cooped up too much lately and really needed a longer-than-normal walk tonight. When they eventually wandered back to Anne's house, Rhys took her key and unlocked the door for her.

"I should get going," he said. "Thank you for inviting me to walk with you." And then he leaned toward her.

Anne, who had been walking around in a happy fog, came abruptly alert. What did she do in this situation? Was he going to kiss her cheek? But he only did that in greeting! So was this a real kiss? *Was it?*

She turned her head at the last possible second.

Rhys hit the corner of her mouth with his lips. He drew back, and for a couple of seconds Anne thought he might try the maneuver again, but then he grinned at her. "Good night, Annie."

Anne went inside, leaned back against her door, closed her eyes, and prayed for strength. Although part of her had longed to kiss Rhys properly, Anne wanted her kisses to mean something. And she did not know at this point what she meant to Rhys. He had caught her off guard tonight, but Anne resolved that she would *not ever* kiss that man until she was sure they had more than a friendly, businesslike relationship.

Anne grinned. Her mother — and, she hoped, God — would be proud of her. She supposed that was adequate consolation.

CHAPTER SIX

"Where are we going today?" Rhys asked a few days later after greeting Anne at her door. She made absolutely certain she turned her cheek into his kiss, he noticed, and he fought to smother a grin. It was exactly what he had expected from the ever-practical Annie.

"We are going to see Mrs. Thorogood," Anne said. "She wants a tape of last Sunday's sermon."

Mrs. Thorogood was the lady at the nursing home who had an obsessive interest in venetian blinds. Venetian blinds, Rhys told himself as he sat through another of her dissertations, were mechanically fascinating.

"Now we need to take Mrs. Adams to her optometrist appointment."

Mrs. Adams, taking Rhys's place in the passenger seat of Anne's car, talked nonstop about canning jars and noisy neighbors and how cold it seemed this winter and how many grandchildren she had now and how her neighbor had bursitis *and* lumbago (she was really getting on in years) and how she hoped she herself didn't take a cold this year. Colds were so hard on her, she said, what with just the one lung and all.

Rhys, taking Herman's place in the back-seat, caught Anne's eye in her rearview mirror and made a face at her. *Mrs. Adams is a hoot,* he tried to tell her. *How are you keeping a straight face?*

She wouldn't dream of laughing, Anne's look said. *Shame* on him! And then she grinned.

She visited not out of obligation, Rhys realized, but because she liked to. She was a people person at the most basic level. She was a closet extrovert. And these people couldn't possibly love her any more than she did them. It was amazing how something Anne was so naturally gifted for coincided with what she saw as her Christian calling.

He was just as fortunate. Making a name for himself and being able to touch people's lives with his writing enabled him to spread the good news about God's plan and will for mankind, which he felt called to do. He and Anne, he felt sure, were smack dab in the middle of God's will for their respective lives.

Yet there was something about that thought that nagged at him, but he couldn't put his finger on it.

"Next is Admiral Maynard," Anne said after they had returned Mrs. Adams to her small house. "You'll like him."

The white-haired man had to be past eighty, but he wore a sharp navy blue suit and carried himself straight and tall with a dignity that had Rhys straightening and wishing he had polished his shoes.

"Well, now," the man said, giving Rhys the once-over. "What have we here?"

"Admiral, this is my friend Rhys Carter," Anne said. "Rhys, this is Admiral Reginald B. Maynard, retired, United States Navy."

Just the way she said the words made Rhys feel like coming to attention. "Pleased to meet you, sir."

The admiral waved his hand. "Call me Admiral if you have to, like Anne here. And come in, come in."

Rhys felt, despite the admiral's dismissive words, that Anne's attention to detail delighted the man. Rhys followed the two of them down the hall slowly, taking in the nautical decor, which he knew was not reproduction. No, this stuff was the real thing. He stopped to take in the black-and-white photographs on the walls.

"That's me," the admiral said and pointed. "On the way across the pond in January 1942, when I was just a brand-new ensign."

Rhys and Anne stayed for two hours. Anne got up quietly from her seat after the first hour and left the room, returning in time to bid the admiral farewell.

"Anne has heard all my stories, bless her heart," the admiral said to Rhys as they were leaving. He gazed down at Anne fondly. "She still comes back. I'd be a very lonely old man without her." He pierced Rhys with a steely-eyed look. "You take care of my girl, hear?"

Rhys wanted to try a salute, but he knew the admiral would either laugh or demand that Rhys drop and give him twenty. He grinned at Anne and settled for an earnest "Yes, sir," instead.

"Where did you disappear to?" he asked Anne as they drove home.

"I cleaned his kitchen," Anne said. "I haven't done that in a while. He likes to keep it shipshape —" she grinned at her little joke — "but he's nearly blind now. It's why he doesn't get out much."

"The admiral is *blind?* I didn't — how can — what?"

"Not totally blind, but his vision is fairly blurry. I don't want you to think he's sitting in that house feeling sorry for himself."

"No, I didn't think that. I just thought . . . I don't know."

"You made him very happy listening to him today, Rhys. You couldn't have given him any amount of money to replace your attention."

Rhys fell silent. So that was what Anne did, really. She made people the objects of her attention. She listened to them and she made them happy. She cleaned their kitchens.

He cleared his throat. "I wasn't very comfortable at the other two houses. Or at the nursing home," he admitted. "But I did enjoy the admiral."

He could feel Anne's gaze. Even he wasn't certain what he had been trying to say, so her long silence didn't daunt him.

"I rarely do things I'm uncomfortable with," Anne said at length, her voice sounding like she was ashamed. "I know what I'm good at, and that's what I do."

"You organized the Auction," Rhys pointed out. "And you weren't terribly comfortable with that." He cleared his throat again. "Would you be offended if I told you that the first time I touched Martha's arm, it reminded me of the stomach of a half-grown alligator I once held?"

She stared at him. "What?"

"Weird, isn't it? Her skin — all of the ladies' skin, in fact — is so soft, so delicate, but so was that alligator's belly." He shrugged. "I've always been a little sorry for that reaction."

"Well," said Anne after a moment, "I don't know. It sort of makes me feel more kindly to alligators."

Rhys sank down in his seat. "I was more afraid of Martha than I was of that alligator."

"But you aren't now, are you?"

"No. No, I've learned."

"So, that's personal growth," Anne offered. "God wants us to grow."

"Yes, but the question is," said Rhys, after pondering her statement, "how do you tell if you need to be replanted?"

"You mean, how do you know if you are root-bound?"

"Yes, or when you need pruning?"

"Or maybe more fertilizer?"

They both broke out laughing, then Rhys sobered. "Anne, about the admiral, and Jeff, and Mrs. Thorogood . . ."

"Yes?"

"I think I want the charity to focus on

people like that. Do you think you could work with that?"

Anne gave him a smile that probably had angels dropping left and right. "Since I'm going to be your director, I guess I'll have to, won't I?"

The doubts, of course, started immediately. Rhys had taken her to dinner to celebrate their mutual decisions, and then she had stayed up late, pondering the enormity of what she had agreed to.

This morning brought a whole new set of doubts, made worse, of course, by lack of sleep. Simply keeping track of the charity's paperwork would take up half her time. And what would she do with Herman while she was on the road? And why had her mother's smile been tight when she had informed her of her decision? Anne shied away from answering that question.

She was a director now. The pink sweat suit and white running shoes she had on were fine for what she did now, but she would have to go shopping soon. She would need a list. She glanced at her desk, neat and tidy with nothing more than a well-used calendar, a stack of flowered stationery, and several thank-you cards from people she had helped.

The flowered stationery would have to go. She would need something more professional. More . . . boring. Who would have thought that she would have to become even more practical than she was now?

She needed to read Emily Post again, too. And see if she could learn to like caviar.

Snatching the thank-you cards off the desk, Anne stacked them in order of size. Placing the cards in a storage box at one side of her desk, she noticed that the box was almost full. She would need to get another box —

Or maybe not. It wasn't likely she would get so many thank-you cards from people anymore. She would get letters of appreciation from organizations for coming to their functions and making speeches. Those would be better off in a file or forwarded to Rhys.

Instead of ongoing relationships with little old ladies she called friends, she would have business acquaintances with faceless voices and easily forgotten names. Instead of funny conversations with small children, she would engage in small talk with people who might mention their children in passing, all the while knowing she was after their money.

Anne plopped down in her chair at the desk and swallowed several times. It wouldn't be that bad. She was projecting worst-case scenarios. She would get used to this. It was a different ministry, that was all.

Anne knew Rhys didn't particularly enjoy the thousand-dollar-a-plate functions — the food was never that great. Or the television appearances — people tended to focus on his looks. Or the debutantes hanging on his arm — too much shrill laughter. "But he had to put up with cold, mushy asparagus for ten years for his ministry's sake," Anne mumbled. Surely she could handle boring stationery.

Together *(together!)* she and Rhys could help thousands of elderly people lead more fulfilling lives. Rhys would attract contributors, and she would determine the best ways to spend the money.

Rhys would know he was doing something of practical use in the world, and she would know she was doing something important for God.

Anne squeezed her eyes shut tight, but a memory intruded. During an earlier visit to that first nursing home, Martha had been hanging on Rhys's arm, singing her disharmonious song, and he had suddenly started singing along with her. Their tunes had not matched. Herman had whined. And Anne had wept from the sheer beauty of it.

Those were the kind of things she would miss by becoming the director of this charity.

But, she consoled herself, if it hadn't been for her, Rhys would never have set foot in that nursing home. Maybe she did have some weird ability to motivate people.

It had to be the lack of sleep that made her want to cry.

Two weeks later, Rhys stood alone in his loft, hands on his hips, glaring at the exposed heating pipes running across the ceiling, wondering if his prayers of the past few months had somehow become stuck in the ductwork. Snorting at the notion — while simultaneously filing the phrase away for use in a future column — he transferred his gaze to the floor, where the expanse of hardwood stretched away from him, cold and desolate.

Like his life.

He stalked to his window overlooking downtown Kansas City and wondered if he had ever done anything in his life quite as absurd as asking Anne to be the director of his charity. That idea was one of his rare clunkers.

Anne thought she had made a decision in line with God's will. Now he believed Anne was mistaken.

He cared for Anne. Admired her. Respected her. Desired her. Loved her. There, he'd said it. He loved her. And he feared he might have ruined her life.

He and his charity.

Smirking out at the night, Rhys leaned his head against the cold glass of the window. She could do the job; he had no doubts about that. The problem was she already had a job — no, a vocation — one that she loved and was good at, and that few other people in the world were either willing or able to do.

"So how is it," he asked himself, "that such a bright woman is *missing the point?*"

Didn't she realize how much good she was doing right here in Kansas City? Didn't she know how good she was at this one-on-one widows and orphans stuff? Didn't she know how few people really cared about people like she did? Anne could get so caught up in this new job — the one he had bullied her into! — that she would neglect the tender souls who needed her most.

It was a fine time for him to wise up.

Just that morning he had called her to ask her to go with him to visit the admiral and Jeff McGregor, and she had said she was too busy working out a plan for the charity.

She'd said, moreover, that she would be busy for the next three days.

Rhys felt like banging his head against the windowpane.

This was the woman who, when his cell phone had rung constantly one day while they were visiting a nursing home, took it from him, turned it off, and held it captive in her purse for the rest of the day. She'd given him a look that said clearly, *Get your priorities straight, buddy!*

What kind of monster had he turned her into?

What if, by his arrogant presumption that Anne would be better off as his charity director, he was depriving the world of the next Mother Teresa?

Rhys's forehead was going numb against the glass, but he kept it there as a punishment. He didn't think it would be kind of him to tell Anne he no longer wanted her for the job. She would automatically assume he didn't think she could handle the responsibility, and that notion, indirectly, was his fault, too.

Anne didn't think she was *capable* of much, because she thought she wasn't *doing* much, because people like him kept coming along and urging people like her to do "bigger" and "better" things!

And what did that make the admiral — chopped liver?

Rhys sank down in a chair and rubbed his chilly forehead. He was not used to being wrong. He would have to talk to Anne. Somehow, without bruising her feelings, he had to make her see that he had been mistaken. Yes. He could do that.

He sat for a time in his chair, composing in his mind what he would say, starting with the slaying of his pride and ending with "I was wrong."

Then something occurred to him. He didn't, in fact, know for sure that he *was* wrong. Perhaps God did want Anne for the charity. Perhaps he wanted her to grow a little.

And what if Anne's reasons for agreeing to the director position had little to do with God's will and everything to do with her feelings for him — which he suspected mirrored his feelings for her?

Rhys sat slumped in his chair for a much longer time than he had planned, rendered motionless by the enormity of the dilemma. He didn't know which was worse: ruining Anne's life by bullying her into becoming the director, or ruining her life by romancing her into becoming the director.

Rhys swallowed hard. His whole life had

been a series of unexplained but brilliant ideas, most of which had worked. Loving Anne Singletary was a brilliant idea, but right now it looked like a clunker. Anne was confused enough without his throwing words like *love* into the mix. It had not been wise of him to complicate matters with an emotional attachment.

He'd thought, over the past few weeks, that God had nudged him several times and said, "That's the one, Rhys," but maybe he had misunderstood. Maybe God had actually said, "Smack the gum, please" or "Track the numb leaf" or some other equally meaningless phrase, which meant something *totally different!*

His desserts were invariably dismal flops, but evidently he made a lovely hash.

Rhys jumped up and paced. He wished he could scream like his thoughts. He wished he were not such a calm, mature, and self-disciplined man, so he could ease his torment by ransacking his apartment.

Desperate for something to do, Rhys looked around his loft. He could type a really bad column really fast. He could engage in a frenzy of overdue unpacking.

At the sight of his cooking gear, his eyes lit.

Cooking. Yes. Cooking was supposed to

have a soothing effect. He would cook another dessert for Anne "Charity Director" Singletary's cookbook.

If she wanted to do business, fine. He would do business. He strapped on the apron that said overoptimistically, "Kiss the Cook" and went to work.

And since Anne was busy and couldn't be bothered for the next three days, he sent the completed confection by Federal Express.

Two days later Anne contemplated the squished layer cake with perfect comprehension.

Last time she had talked to Rhys, he'd acted like insulted royalty. This whole directorship thing was his idea; it was irrational of him to get upset because she was taking it seriously. He didn't need her to hold his hand while he went visiting anymore anyway.

It was probably his hormones acting up, and this was his peace offering.

She dialed the phone. "Rhys, it's Anne," she said when he answered. "I got the dessert. Thank you."

"Glad it made it." His voice was terse. He did not sound apologetic. He did not sound happy to hear from her. He did not even sound friendly.

What on earth was the matter with the man?

"I just thought I'd let you know that I think this is the best one yet," she said, forcing her voice into coolness. "Thanks — thank you — for sending it."

There was a short, dreadful silence.

"You are a terrible liar, Annie."

Of all the nerve! "I beg your pardon?"

"Sure, go ahead. It can't possibly be the best one yet. I reverted to type and forgot to put any sugar in it. You didn't even taste it, did you?"

"Ah . . . no."

A grunt was all the answer she got.

"Well, perhaps you can try the recipe again, without omitting the sugar," she said, trying to be pleasant and not feeling it. "What was it supposed to be, some sort of cake?"

Another short silence ensued, then: "I need to go. I'm going to visit Martha, who has apparently been asking for you."

Anne, torn between tears and fury, counted to five and then said, "Tell her I said hi."

"I will."

The line went dead. Anne stared at the phone for a minute, hung it up, then let her head drop to her desk. *Lord,* she prayed, *Lord, what am I doing wrong?*

Two minutes later, the phone rang again. Anne grabbed for it.

"Annie," Rhys said.

"Yes?" If she hadn't been so relieved he'd called back, she would have been embarrassed at how breathless she sounded.

"How much sleep have you been getting?"

Anne bit her lip to take her mind off the tingle of tears in her nose. "I think I got about four hours last night."

"Anne." Rhys's voice was both sympathetic and faintly reproving.

"I'm just so busy."

Rhys sighed. "Annie —"

"What kind of cake is this supposed to be?" she interrupted. "Please, Rhys," she said when he did not answer, "I need some normal, friendly conversation. I don't need a lecture." She was miserable enough.

"A white Rocky Road sponge cake," Rhys said after a minute. "You use white almond bark instead of chocolate for one of the layers."

"That sounds good."

"I got the idea from one of those cookbooks and altered it. You know, that's why I forgot the sugar. I wasn't working from a real recipe, just one in my head, and my brain forgot to write down *sugar.* Do you know, Anne, I was reading some stuff on the Internet and ran across an allergy page. It said that a lot of people grow out of their childhood allergies. Do you think it is possible that you have?"

"I don't know. I don't have any other allergies. And I haven't really worried about the chocolate one since I was four years old. It's really not a big deal."

"Maybe you should ask your doctor if he can give you some kind of test. What if you could have been eating chocolate all this time?"

"Well . . . I suppose I could. It would certainly mess up the cookbook idea, though. And what's the big deal about chocolate, anyway?"

Rhys snorted. "I'm sure you could live perfectly well for the rest of your life without eating chocolate, because you don't realize what you've been missing. But that aside, wouldn't it be better, medically, to know?"

Anne yawned.

Rhys chuckled. "Go take a nap, Annie."

"I will. And . . . thanks, Rhys."

CHAPTER SEVEN

"Well, Anne," Dr. Hamilton said a few days later, "I don't know what happened when you were four, but I don't see how you could ever have been allergic to chocolate."

Anne was shocked. She had decided to take Rhys's advice — both to take a nap and to make an appointment for allergy testing. Now she sat in Dr. Hamilton's office listening to the results of the test.

"But I nearly died," she sputtered. "I was sick to my stomach, and then my throat swelled up, and I couldn't breathe, and I nearly died. . . ."

The doctor shrugged. "It must have been something else. Probably your parents and the doctor looked for a cause for your illness, and the only thing they could come up with was that you had eaten chocolate and then had the classic symptoms of an allergy attack. Or what looked like an allergy attack. It may have been a spider bite.

Twenty-five years ago, we really didn't understand allergies that well anyway." He waved his hand at her bewilderment. "No harm done, Anne. You didn't know what you were missing."

Rhys had said the same thing, Anne thought as she walked out of the doctor's office. She didn't like the fact that she had believed something untrue for so long. What if there were other things — more important things — that she thought were true but weren't?

Like her decision about being the director of a charity?

No. Rhys needed her. God needed her. She was doing a good work. Producing much fruit.

She glanced at her watch as she passed the hospital, wavered, then drove on by. She did not have time to visit.

Two blocks later, she made a U-turn.

She would hire someone to do the charity's paperwork, she thought, feeling rebellious. Someone who liked that kind of thing.

As she walked near the emergency entrance on her way to the main doors, ambulance attendants were unloading a gurney onto the pavement. Anne said a small prayer for the patient, an elderly woman, as she waited to pass. The EMTs didn't look all that excited or rushed. Anne took another look at the gurney.

"Mrs. Thorogood?" Anne said in astonishment. She eased closer until she was sure, then fell in beside the gurney as two nurses wheeled it inside. "Mrs. Thorogood, what happened?"

The elderly lady brightened at the sound of Anne's voice. "Oh, Anne, what a surprise! Can you imagine? Of all the silly things, I went to clean the blinds today, and I fell off the chair and broke my hip." Her lower lip trembled in spite of her brave tone, and she grasped Anne's hand. "They say I have to have surgery today. Can you stay, Anne? Can you stay until I'm better?"

"I'll stay until you are out of recovery, Mrs. Thorogood. I'll be right here."

"I'm so glad," Mrs. Thorogood said. "You are a gift from God, Anne. I don't know what I would do without you."

Anne stayed. She called her father and informed him of the situation, then while Mrs. Thorogood was in surgery, she made her customary visits to other patients. Most of the children in the pediatric ward were severely disappointed that "the dog lady," as she was known, had not brought the dog, so she promised to return the next day with Herman in tow. Only later, as she sat and waited for Mrs. Thorogood to be awake enough to see her, did Anne realize what she was doing.

She was acting as though her life was normal. Like she would continue on as she always had. Like she had never heard of Rhys Carter's charity.

And she was totally at peace with that.

Suddenly Anne knew with a certainty she could not explain that the charity was going to have to get along without her because Mrs. Thorogood couldn't.

She left the hospital after assuring Mrs. Thorogood that she would be back the next day. She did not go home, however, but went to the church. She let herself in the back door and walked to the sanctuary, where she sat for a long time and prayed, listening for any indication that God was not pleased with her change of mind.

She heard no reprisals, but face after face appeared in her mind — Mrs. Thorogood, the admiral, Martha, the children in the hospital . . . and dozens and dozens of others. And in every mental picture, she was there with them. *With* them.

But I'm doing so little, Lord! Anne thought. *Shouldn't I be doing more?*

"I was hungry, and you fed me. I was thirsty, and you gave me a drink. I was a stranger,

and you invited me into your home. I was naked, and you gave me clothing. I was sick, and you cared for me. I was in prison, and you visited me."

God did not need *more* from her.

She didn't even cry. She just sat, relieved.

Eventually, the sanctuary doors opened, and she heard footsteps coming toward her.

"Your dad told me I might find you here," Rhys said.

Anne looked up at him in silence, wondering how in the world to tell him. And wondering if he would leave her when he realized she could not be part of his dream.

"Can you read my piece for next week's paper?" he asked. A printout appeared under her nose as Rhys sat down beside her in the pew.

He'd told her once, looking impossibly cute while he did so, that he valued her opinion of his writing. He looked now, Anne thought, a little dejected. Maybe he was having trouble getting rid of his adverbs. She took the paper. It would give her a little more time to avoid telling him —

She read the article's first sentence: "Anne Singletary has agreed to be the director for the charity."

Just barely, she managed not to crumple Rhys's work into a nice little ball suitable for tossing into the nearest trash can. "Rhys, I have to tell you something," she said.

"Read first." He pointed.

She held the paper out toward him. He didn't take it. She pressed it flat against his chest with her fingertips.

"No," she insisted. "I have to tell you this. I have always tried to do what God wanted me to do. But even my dad will tell you that discovering God's will is a tricky business. And I know you think you know what his will is, and I thought I did, but now I think differently. I think I now know — no, I *know* I now know — that I am not in God's will. Or rather, that I am now, but I wasn't a few minutes ago." She stopped because he looked baffled. Not surprising. She was even confusing herself. "Rhys, I'm sorry. I do know what I'm trying to say . . . maybe I should start at the beginning."

He looked alarmed.

She rushed on. "I mean, when you asked me to be the charity director, I thought I could, but —" She stopped again, this time because Rhys had taken hold of her hands, manipulating her fingers around the edges of the paper.

"Read," he commanded. "I think I say it better than you do."

"But I don't think you know what I'm trying to say." She stared at the printout, tears of frustration stinging her eyes.

She felt Rhys's hand cup her chin and tilt her head up to look at him.

"I know you spent three hours at the hospital today, holding the hand of a woman with alligator skin. I think you ought to read my article."

Anne took a deep breath, partly because the tender look in Rhys's eyes had rendered her incapable of inhaling for several seconds, and she needed the oxygen.

Then she bent her head over the paper and began to read.

Anne Singletary has agreed to be the director for the charity. What charity? you may ask. We'll get to that later. Right now, I need to tell you about Anne. She is eminently capable of this job. She brings a great deal of heart to whatever she does, and she has made a life out of meeting people's needs. She is dedicated, loving, self-sacrificing, merciful, understanding, and compassionate to those people whom many of us never think about. She spoons soup into toothless mouths. She babysits crazed kids for free because their exhausted mother cannot afford to pay her. She cleans the kitchens of retired admirals who can't see well enough to do it themselves. She gives — herself.

But she's going to give up this life because I asked her to become the director of a charity that I want to start in order to do some practical good with my life.

On another note, I have been doing some cooking lately. I've been making desserts — nonchocolate desserts — for Anne, because she is allergic to chocolate. I couldn't understand why my efforts flopped until I finally got it through my head (it took long enough, didn't it, Annie?) that I must simply stop fiddling with the recipes. You see, I had thought I could do better than the cooks who created the recipes. I also felt quite certain that none of the recipes made enough servings. So I fiddled. I messed with them. I experimented. I tripled the amounts. I deleted. And nothing came out quite right.

Which brings me back to Anne. Like the above recipes, I thought she could be "better." I convinced her she could do "more" than she was doing. I ignored the fact that Anne feels that "caring for the orphans and widows in their troubles" is her calling before God. I ignored the fact that she loves caring for them. I ignored the fact that God is the creator of the "recipe" called Anne.

I am not going to start a charity after all, at least not right now. I need some time to make sure I am doing what God wants me to do. As for Anne Singletary, I have something else in mind for her. . . .

Anne had not started crying until she read the part about God being the creator of her recipe. The words were so true, so right — and so ridiculously and totally Rhys — that she gave in to tears even as she smiled. Rhys handed her a tissue, which she put to good use.

"Thank you," she said a few seconds later when she had composed herself. "I needed that."

"I have another."

"Another article?" How was he going to top this one?

"No, another tissue."

"No, silly," Anne laughed. "I meant the article. You did say it better. That's exactly how I've been feeling. Thank you."

"Well . . . just glad I could . . . help." His voice broke on the last word, and he stared very hard at the pulpit. So hard that his eyes began to water.

Anne stared. "You thought you had really messed up my life," she said, her heart accepting with wonder the pain he felt on her account. "You were scared."

"Witless," he concurred in a whisper. He turned back to her, his eyes glistening. "I've made a living out of doing crazy things, but I never meant to make you so confused. I'm sorry."

"Sorry?" She slipped one hand around the back of his neck and drew his head close to hers, looking into his eyes at a distance of two inches. "For confirming for me that I'm in the right place right now? For helping me realize I don't have to be anything more than what I am?" Pulling back, she shook her head and grinned. "I don't want you to be sorry. But I'll let you make it up to me if it makes you feel better."

Rhys searched her face for several seconds before his laughter reverberated in the empty sanctuary. He lifted her hand to his lips. "Thank you, God," he murmured against her knuckles, his eyes closed. "Oh, thank you, God."

Anne turned her hand in his and tickled his chin with one finger. "What else did you have in mind for me?" she asked.

Rhys's eyes popped open so fast she thought she heard a click. "What?" His voice sounded strangled.

"In your article. You said you had something else in mind for me."

He relaxed. "Oh, that. That will have to wait. Say, until Friday, over dinner?"

"How about now, over lunch?"

"Umm, no. Friday." Rhys rose from the pew and Anne followed.

"I'll bake you cookies if you tell me," she offered.

"Tempting," Rhys said, walking out of the sanctuary. "But no."

"What if I wash your car?"

"Friday, Anne."

"Please?"

"No."

Anne teased him all the way out to the parking lot, but he refused to give in.

CHAPTER EIGHT

Friday he took her back to the elegant Restaurant of the Flaming Napkin, where the maitre d' smiled brightly and led them to a small table in an alcove that afforded them much more privacy than on their previous visit. Anne noticed that the one candle on their table was covered with a short glass chimney. Extremely prudent; Anne approved.

At some point after Rhys's invitation to dinner, she had remembered her allergy tests and informed him she could now eat chocolate with impunity. He had engulfed her in a hug and asked her if she would wait two days before she tried anything.

His mental wheels, she knew, were spinning at breakneck speed.

Her desire to taste chocolate again after all this time warred with her dread of what Rhys would attempt to feed her.

She was also very curious to know what

Rhys "had in mind" for her. It was too early for a marriage proposal — that eliminated the romantic possibilities — but Rhys wouldn't pursue the charity, either, and that removed business from the equation.

She didn't know what he would do now that she had bailed out on him. He had been so enthusiastic, so eager to make a difference. His idea had met its demise at her hands.

She didn't know quite what to do about it. Except apologize. "Rhys, I feel badly," she said after the salad was served.

He paused, his water glass in midair. "Trouble with the forks again?" he said and grinned.

"Hush. I've got all that figured out." Anne deliberately picked up the dessert fork and started eating her salad with it.

Rhys laughed and leaned his elbows on the table. "You're very cute," he said.

"Yes." Anne smiled. "I know."

"Why are you feeling badly then?"

"Because you are giving up your charity. I never thought it was a poor idea; I only questioned my role in it. I hate to see the whole thing come to nothing."

"I do have another idea," he said. "Care to hear it?"

"Tell me."

"Well, instead of holding writers' retreats at Jeff's farm, I'd like to turn it into a retirement home. Jeff and the admiral will be the first residents. I've already talked to them about it. They both told me to get your opinion."

She was astounded. "That's a wonderful idea!" she said.

"You think so?"

By the time Rhys had expounded on his new idea and the main course had been served, Anne *knew*. "I'll do it," she said.

Rhys paused with a bite of prime rib halfway to his mouth. "Do what?" he asked.

"Help you set this up. I can't be your director of nursing because I'm not qualified, but I can certainly help you with practical things like buying equipment and interviewing nursing assistants and stuff —"

"Anne, what are you talking about?"

"This *is* what you 'had in mind' for me, isn't it?" she asked, making quote marks in the air with her fingers.

For a moment Rhys's expression remained blank. Then he chuckled, shaking his head and muttering to himself. Anne scowled at him, but his subsequent grin was too beguiling for her to be truly annoyed.

"I'll admit I hoped you would help out with this, Annie," he said. "Your input will be invaluable. But no, it's not what I 'had in mind.' " Rhys made quote marks with his voice just as plainly as she had with her hands.

"I'm sorry," she said, wondering irrelevantly how she had ever managed to be seated across from such a beautiful man. "I don't mean to jump to conclusions. But . . . then what *did* you have in mind for me?"

Instead of answering, Rhys turned, caught the maitre d's attention, and nodded at him. Anne sat in bemused silence, then jumped as Rhys unexpectedly moved out of his seat . . . in order to get down on one knee in front of her.

She gaped.

"Annie," he said, taking her hand, "this is not exactly what it appears to be."

She gaped harder, if such a thing was possible.

"This is not a marriage proposal — yet," he said. "Because it has only been a few months since we've been reacquainted, and because we've just been through an emotional ordeal, and because I know that you are a sensible woman, I have no ring in my pocket. But I have, in the past three months, come to the conclusion that there is no one I admire . . . or desire . . . more than you."

Anne put her free hand up to her mouth,

feeling the familiar sting of tears in her nose.

Rhys was not finished. He cleared his throat. "I think perhaps God led me back here, not to find a charity director but to find the love of my life. Someone I believe I want to spend the rest of my life with. However, at this moment — at *this* moment — I am only asking your permission to court you . . . with that end in mind."

His voice had grown softer throughout his speech, but his eyes held hers with the intensity of Herman's at suppertime.

Rhys was giving her — giving them both — time. Because they had been wrong about the charity and because this was so much more important, Rhys was defying his impulsive nature and giving them time to know for sure.

"I would like that," Anne whispered.

"Would you?" Rhys whispered in return. Somehow his mouth was only millimeters from her own. Anne closed the small gap remaining.

Angels sang. Trumpets sounded.

A small cough rumbled discreetly behind them.

Rhys rose to his feet, still gripping Anne's hand. "Ah, superb timing," he said.

Anne could have argued that point, but she suspected Rhys was not thinking too clearly. She knew she wasn't.

A waiter holding a silver tray paused while Rhys slipped back into his seat, then set it down with a flourish. One red rose shared space with an oval-shaped crystal dish filled with —

"The Rhys Carter Surprise!" Anne exclaimed.

Rhys grinned. "You recognized it," he said.

"Oh, of course I did. I had a decent idea of what it was supposed to look like."

Anne turned the bowl to inspect it from all sides. If Rhys had made this, his skills had drastically improved. The smooth bottom layers of chocolate were covered with perky dollops of whipped cream and cute little chocolate curls. Two glistening cherries topped the beautiful creation, which was just the right amount for two people. The effect was like something out of a magazine.

Anne looked askance at Rhys. "Did you make this?"

"Ah no," Rhys confessed. "The master chef of this fine establishment agreed to fix it for me. He couldn't stand the thought of graham crackers and instant pudding, though, so he baked some sort of cookie instead and insisted on making the pudding from scratch."

"So he messed with your recipe?" Anne glanced up and let her eyes widen in mock horror.

"Yes! Yes, he did." Rhys looked smug.

"Well," said Anne, grinning, "I'm sure *he* knew what he was doing."

Rhys grinned back and managed to stun her yet again. *"Touché, ma belle petite omelette de fromage,"* he said.

Did a person have to speak French to understand that Rhys's unintelligible phrase was an endearment? Of course not. His eyes made the translation for her. Anne, for possibly the first time in her life, blushed.

Rhys chuckled and picked up one of the silver spoons on the tray. After scooping up a generous bite of the gourmet version of the Rhys Carter Surprise, he gestured to Anne to lean closer over the table. Moving the chimney-clad candle out of her way, she complied.

"This is it, Annie," Rhys said, gazing deeply into her eyes and holding out the chocolate-laden spoon. "Are you ready to see what you've been missing?"

RECIPE

The Rhys Carter Surprise

1 small box instant chocolate pudding mix

1 3/4 cup milk

Approx. 6 oz. nondairy whipped topping

10–15 graham crackers (regular or chocolate flavored)

Half a tub of ready-made chocolate frosting, optional

Assorted toppings, also optional

Get out some sort of straight-sided, flat-
bottomed pan — an 8-inch square cake pan
works very well. Place one layer of graham
crackers on the bottom, breaking them at
the seams to fit if you have to. Mix the
instant pudding with the milk and let it set
in the refrigerator for a few minutes. Fold
in the whipped topping. Pour about 1 1/3
cup of the mixture onto the graham crackers. Repeat the graham cracker and pudding layers, ending with pudding. You can

stop here and it will taste great. However, if you happen to have a container of ready-made frosting, you can heat it in the microwave on medium for about twenty seconds and drizzle half the tub over the pudding. Then if you want to, sprinkle nuts, mini-marshmallows, chocolate chips, mini-M&Ms, crushed Heath bars, or whatever on top of that. Put the whole concoction in the refrigerator for at least two hours to let the graham crackers soften. Cut into squares. (It won't come out of the pan very nicely. Just throw some more whipped topping on the individual servings — and don't forget the cherry!)

ABOUT THE AUTHOR

Growing up, **Ranee McCollum** wanted to be a veterinarian. After receiving a D in chemistry during her second year of college, however, she realized she was on the wrong track and became an English major instead. She promptly received a D in modern poetry. Her Prince Charming rescued her from the clutches of this wicked grading system and carried her off to become an air force wife, a nomadic life for which she's very well suited.

Ranee welcomes letters written to her in care of Tyndale House Author Relations, 351 Executive Drive, Carol Stream, IL 60188.